Coffee Stains SC/SA 1/26

THE AMISH MIDWIFE

**Center Point
Large Print**

Also by Mindy Starns Clark
and available from Center Point Large Print:

Shadows of Lancaster County
Under the Cajun Moon
Secrets of Harmony Grove

THE AMISH MIDWIFE

MINDY STARNS CLARK
LESLIE GOULD

CENTER POINT LARGE PRINT
THORNDIKE, MAINE

This Center Point Large Print edition
is published in the year 2011 by arrangement with
Harvest House Publishers.

The text of this Large Print edition is unabridged.
In other aspects, this book may vary
from the original edition.
Printed in the United States of America
on permanent paper.
Set in 16-point Times New Roman type.

ISBN: 978-1-61173-101-9

Library of Congress Cataloging-in-Publication Data

Clark, Mindy Starns.
 The Amish midwife : women of Lancaster County / Mindy Starns Clark and
Leslie Gould.
 p. cm.
 ISBN 978-1-61173-101-9 (library binding : alk. paper)
 1. Midwives—Fiction. 2. Adopted children—Family relationships—Fiction.
3. Family secrets—Fiction. 4. Amish—Fiction. 5. Lancaster County (Pa.)—
Fiction. 6. Large type books. I. Gould, Leslie, 1962– II. Title.
 PS3603.L366A83 2011b

 813´.6—dc22

                                                          2011004903

For Mindy's brother, Joseph Starns,
and Leslie's daughter, Lily Thao Gould.
When God wrote your stories, we are so
thankful that in His grace He included us.

All the days ordained for me
were written in your book
before one of them came to be.
PSALM 139:16

Center Point Publishing

600 Brooks Road ● PO Box 1
Thorndike ME 04986-0001 USA

(207) 568-3717

US & Canada:
1 800 929-9108
www.centerpointlargeprint.com

ACKNOWLEDGMENTS

Mindy thanks

John, Emily, and Lauren Clark, for input, inspiration, and never-ending teamwork. I am so blessed!

Vanessa Thompson and Al Cummings, for working so hard behind the scenes even when I'm on a deadline.

The members of my FVCN Small Group: the Akamines, Halls, Peases, and Smiths, for prayers, support, and patience.

Leslie thanks

Peter Gould for his endless encouragement and research assistance, Hana and Thao for joining in on the journey, and Kaleb and Taylor for their help along the way.

Melanie Dobson, Kim Felton, Kelly Chang, Emily King, Dori Clark, and Ellen Poole for their ideas and input early in the story; Mary Hake for sharing information about Conservative Mennonites; Libby Salter for her ongoing support as both a reader and a friend; and Laurie Snyder for sharing a new take on Psalm 139:16 with me.

Patty Deacon, RN, and Holly Frakes, RN, both who specialize in obstetrics, and Peter Gould, RN, for his input on both cardiac and general medical issues. (Any inaccuracies are mine.)

And all of the babies and children, both by birth and adoption, I have witnessed being welcomed into their families. I will always treasure the joy of those moments.

Mindy and Leslie thank

Chip MacGregor for bringing us together on this project, Kim Moore for making it all work, and the wonderful crew at Harvest House Publishers for their dedication to this book.

Dave Siegrist for his expertise; Jamie and Steve Shane of the Apple Bin Inn in Willow Street, Pennsylvania, for the perfect landing spot and appreciated insights; the Mennonite Information Center in Lancaster, Pennsylvania, for their invaluable resources; and Erik Wesner, author of http://amishamerica.com, for answering questions and providing clarification.

PROLOGUE

Baby number 244 was an easy one—three hours of labor, twenty minutes of pushing, and one healthy seven-pound-three-ounce baby boy. To put it in the vernacular of the parents, the infant slid into my hands like a football dropping into the palms of a wide receiver waiting in the end zone.

"It's a boy," I announced as I looked at the clock and noted the time: 5:33 p.m. "You did it, Brie."

"A boy," Stanley cried, turning to high-five his wife. The head football coach at Barlow High School, Stanley had guided Brie through the entire labor and delivery much as he must have ushered last year's team through to the playoffs. "Finally, our own little future Bruin."

"A Bruin," she echoed, meeting Stanley's palm with her own. Then she collapsed back against the pillows, laughter bubbling from her throat even as tears spilled freely across her cheeks. After three daughters, I knew they had both been hoping for a son.

I suctioned the baby, wiped off his tiny face, and then handed the scissors to Stanley, who didn't need much help cutting the cord for this, his fourth down at the one-yard line, so to speak. Grabbing a warm blanket, I wrapped it around the infant and placed him in his mother's arms, and then I added another warm blanket across them both. As soon as I returned to my chair at the foot of the bed, Stanley leaned toward Brie, touching his forehead to hers and wrapping his thick arms around wife and child.

"You did it, babe," he whispered, kissing her cheek.

"*We* did it," she replied, unable to tear her eyes from the infant she was clutching so tightly. "And you, Lexie," she added. "Thank you. For everything. You're the best."

I waved off the compliment, saying it was no sweat for a delivery this fast and free of complication.

Through the next fifteen minutes, as I finished things up, I kept glancing at the three of them—father, mother, child—searching as I always did for that moment, that origin of family, that flash of absolute belonging.

Though every birth was different, my search was always the same.

When I was done I headed for the door, telling them I would be back to check on things in just a bit.

"You guys know the drill," I added, pausing in the doorway to take one more look at the little family. "If you don't mind, be sure to send me—"

"A photo of the baby. We know," Brie said, laughing. "Don't worry, we will."

Out in the hall, as the door swung shut behind me, I couldn't help but smile. *Baby number 244. Good work, Lexie.*

When I reached the nurses' station, three message slips were waiting for me, all from the same person. As soon as I saw them, my legs grew weak. Sinking into the nearest chair, I was thankful no one was around at the moment to see my reaction. I had known this was coming, that this was going to happen sooner rather than later. Still, that didn't make it any easier.

Fingers trembling, I looked at the number as I dialed, even though I knew it by heart. My old friend and mentor, Sophie, answered on the first ring, blurting out the words I had expected to hear.

"It's your dad, honey," she said, her voice gentle but firm. "He needs you. It's time for you to come on home."

ONE

Three weeks later

For twenty-six years I thought I'd been told the truth. But I was wrong.

"Alexandra," my father rasped, his bony fingers fumbling for my hand.

"What is it?" I asked, leaning forward from my chair beside the bed, realizing that he was the only one who ever called me by my full name. Grasping my hand, he drew me closer, bringing my palm to his face.

"I'm sorry," he whispered.

"Sorry? Whatever for?" I asked, refusing to believe this dear man had a need to apologize to me for anything.

"For not telling you sooner. If your mother were still alive, she would have said something long before now."

"Said something about what?" I asked, trying to ignore an odd fluttering in my stomach.

For a long moment he didn't reply. Then he surprised me by saying it was about my adoption. It had been private, handled by an attorney, and though I had never been given many details about it beyond a few basic facts, my father seemed to have some sort of related, long-overdue information he wanted to share with me now.

"When your mother and I flew to Pennsylvania to get you, we met your birth grandmother," he began, telling me what I already knew, how she had handed me to them in the Philadelphia airport, wrapped in the baby quilt that was now tucked away in the linen closet in my apartment in Portland. "It was the only time your mother and I ever left the Northwest."

I knew that too. Before Mama became ill, we had taken day trips to Crater Lake and Mount St. Helens and the beach, but after she died he and I stuck pretty close to home, as they had before I came along in the first place.

"It pained your grandmother to give you up."

I nodded again, wondering where he was going with this, what he so desperately needed to tell me. But then he began to cough, deep, rattling spasms that seemed to draw the very life from his lungs. Once the coughing stopped, he laid his head back on the pillow and closed his eyes. Leaning forward, I whispered that he would have to save this conversation for later because right now he needed to stay quiet and get some rest.

The cancer that had started in his kidneys was in his lungs and probably working its way into his brain. Looking at his sad, sunken face now, I imagined the cells splitting, over and over. I willed them to stop, to rewind, but I knew it was too late.

● ● ●

After I washed the morning dishes, I bathed my father and turned him. The hospice nurse had asked me if she could order a hospital bed for the living room to make caring for him easier, but he wanted to die in his own room, the one he had slept in for the last fifty-two years, the one he'd shared with Mama.

At his request I played Bach's *Sei gegrüsset* on his old stereo, and then after he took a few spoonfuls of vegetable soup for lunch, he asked me to read to him, nodding to his old worn King James Bible on the bedside table. I opened it to Psalm 23, wanting something familiar, words I wouldn't stumble over. I read, "The Lord is my shepherd—" and then was interrupted by my cell phone trilling in my jeans' pocket.

"Go ahead," Dad said. "Maybe it's your sweetheart." His lips moved as if trying to smile.

I stood, digging out my phone. It was, indeed, James, his voice somber as he asked how we were doing.

"Getting by." I didn't want to give too many details with Dad listening. "How's your project coming along?" It was the week before midterms, and James had a big presentation due the next day for his master's in counseling program.

"Ah, I get it," he said, his voice softer, deeper. "You're there with your dad right now?"

"Uh-huh."

"I understand. Just tell me, are you all right? I mean, relatively speaking? You hanging in there?"

"Trying."

"That's my girl. I know this isn't easy. Losing a parent is hard enough, but your dad . . ." His voice faltered. "I mean, he's just such a special . . ." Again, he stopped, cleared his throat, and then finally gave up.

"I know," I whispered into the silence, aching for James as much as for myself. "I know." Taking a deep breath, I blinked my tears away and forced my voice to sound more upbeat. "So the project's going well?"

Clearing his throat again, James seemed glad for the change of subject. We chatted for a few minutes, and by the end of our conversation we both had our emotions back under control—until the moment we said goodbye and James added, "Give your dad my love, okay?"

"Will do," I managed to squeak out before quickly pressing the "End" button. Just because I was feeling weepy myself was no reason to get James going again too.

Wiping my eyes, I sat back down on the needlepoint cushion my mother made when she and Dad first married. They waited twenty-five years for a baby, for me. That was part of the story too—part of the miracle, they said.

"James says hello."

Dad nodded. He'd probably gathered that

from my side of the conversation.

"He has projects and then midterms," I added. "Otherwise he'd be here."

Dad nodded again, his eyes still closed. I thought that maybe it was too difficult for him to speak, but then he said, "You look nice today. You're so pretty with your hair pulled up like that." His eyelids fluttered as he spoke.

I pursed my lips. All my life, my father had told me how pretty I was, even when I was wearing jeans, a sweatshirt, and a simple ponytail. Even when I was thirteen and in braces, the tallest person in my class at five feet ten inches, including the boys and the teacher, and even when I was fourteen and couldn't wash my hair for a week because I had broken my arm.

"I think I'll rest a while," he said.

"I'll read to you later."

"Thank you," he whispered, his eyes still closed. "For everything."

He'd done a round of chemo, for me, but then he refused any more, saying seventy-six was a good age to die.

His snow-white hair grew back curly after the treatment. He'd always been handsome, but now he looked like a geriatric angel. I pulled a tissue from my pocket and dabbed at my eyes. He was wrong. Seventy-six was far too young for him to die.

As he slept, a new rattle developed in his breathing.

● ● ●

I carried a wicker basket of wet towels out the back door into the shade of the overgrown yard. Dad bought an automatic washer when I was in high school, but he never felt a dryer was necessary. The sun was warm for a February afternoon, and the towels would dry by nightfall, even in the shadows of towering evergreen, maple, and walnut trees. To my right was the windmill, completely still now due to the breezeless afternoon, and beyond the yard were the hazelnut trees Dad had lovingly tended all of his adult life, although he always called them filberts, the more old-fashioned term.

Regardless of what the trees were called, I had always loved the order of the orchard: the perfect symmetry of the trees planted row by row, the cleared ground, and the comfort of the green canopies in the heat of summer. I sighed. I'd have to sell the orchard—and hire someone in the meantime to prune and mulch and then spray the trees in the spring and harvest the hazelnuts in the fall if it hadn't sold by then. It was too much work for me to try to do on my own.

I reached into the cloth bag of pins at the end of the line and started hanging the towels.

Dad had stubbornly cared for himself as he battled cancer through the cold and dreary months of winter. I know there were days when he had still tried to care for the orchard too. When Sophie called me at the hospital a few weeks ago to say that Dad could no longer fix his own meals or keep up with the chores, I had taken an official family leave from the clinic where I worked and come right away, knowing I wouldn't be going home until he passed.

I had a wooden pin in my mouth and a towel in my hands when Sophie's Subaru turned into our driveway. I dropped both into the basket and started toward her. By the time we embraced, tears were streaming down my face.

"There, there," she said, patting my shoulder. "How is he?"

I sucked in a ragged breath and then exhaled.

"He's sleeping, but his breathing sounds different. The hospice nurse said she thinks he has a week left, but I'm not so sure. She increased his morphine yesterday."

Sophie's comfort enveloped me.

"Finish your laundry and then go back and sit with him. I have a birth to go to, but I'll stop back on my way home. I shouldn't be long."

I thanked her and waved. She was still slim and slight, but her hair was completely gray now, a silvery color under the Mennonite head covering— or cap, as I thought of it—that gave her an elegant look. At the base of her neck, her hair was twisted into a tidy bun.

Sophie had given me my very first job, hiring me as an assistant the summer I was sixteen to file papers, order supplies, and drive her to births when she was tired. I would also watch siblings, make tea, and wash dishes. She was a lay-midwife, initially trained by another lay-midwife, though she had never attended college or become a nurse. She did go to an occasional conference and took continuing education classes by correspondence, and she belonged to an association where she networked with other midwives. As a lay-midwife, Sophie had an Oregon license to do home deliveries, but that's all she could do. When one of her clients ended up at a hospital, she couldn't care for the mother or deliver the baby. A nurse-midwife or a doctor took over from there.

Some of my colleagues disapproved of lay-midwives, but I didn't, at least not when it came to a normal birth. Even though I'd had six years of college, Sophie still knew more than I did. She knew remedies to start labor and to stop it, methods to soothe and relax the mother, and natural ways to calm her. She knew when to take charge and when to step back. In high school I'd written an essay about the history of midwifery and came across a quote by a second-century Greek physician. He said a midwife needed to be of a "sympathetic disposition, although she need not have borne a child herself." That was Sophie. Never married. Never a mother. But always sympathetic.

It was because of her that I found the work I loved. Becoming a midwife was both my passion and my profession. Being a nurse-midwife meant I experienced all the joy of the delivery while being in the controlled environment of a hospital.

In the past few weeks, I had been so consumed with my father's care that I hadn't thought much about work. But I realized now that I missed it very much, missed the excitement and joy and even the heartbreak that were all part of the package.

Putting away those yearnings for now, I pinned the last towel in place, picked up the basket, and turned back toward the house.

Dad woke at six and asked for water. As he drank I offered him soup, but he declined. He was quiet for a moment, and then he said, "Your grandmother loved you very much."

I nodded. That was part of my story. And that my grandmother was tall, like me. She had told my parents then that my birth mother wasn't in a position to keep me, but I was loved very much. That was what my grandmother most wanted me to know: that I was loved.

I thought it was odd how Dad wanted to talk about my adoption now. We hadn't discussed it in years, not since I was a teenager. Back then, when I wrestled with matters of identity and religion, I asked my father if my birth grandmother had been concerned about his and Mama's faith.

"Why?" he had asked.

I probably rolled my eyes, and then I said, "Mama's head covering. Didn't the woman think it odd?" I had stopped wearing my own cap the year before, telling my father it had no meaning for me.

Back then I spent a lot of time thinking about my birth family, creating a story of my own to pick up where the few facts my parents knew left off. My Oregon birth certificate didn't have the names of my biological parents on it, but it did list my birthplace as Montgomery County, Pennsylvania, which I found on a map, a tilted rectangle not far from Philadelphia. The atlas described it as one of the wealthiest counties in the country, so after that I began to imagine my birth family living in their mansion in their fancy Philadelphia suburb and belonging to a country club. I could just see my grandparents playing golf during the summer and bridge during the winter.

I did a lot of research, scouring the library at my high school for information about Pennsylvania, trying to replace the fictions in my head with facts. I even studied the style of the quilt I had been wrapped in when I was first handed over to my parents. It was a simple block pattern of burgundy, green, and blue squares on a black background. One book said the design was often used by the Amish, whose quilts sold for hundreds and even thousands of dollars. I figured my grandmother had purchased it at an expensive handicraft boutique in the city. Either that, or she had gotten it straight from Amish country herself, which didn't look all that far from Philadelphia and was probably a common day trip for a woman of means and leisure.

I imagined my birth mother as eighteen or nineteen when I was born. Pregnant by accident. Old enough to love me but not to keep me. I imagined my grandmother to be between Mama and Dad in age—forty-four and fifty at the time—when she handed me to them, young enough to keep me but benevolent enough to give me to a childless couple. Though she might have been familiar with Plain people in general, because she lived in Pennsylvania and had purchased the quilt, I felt sure she had been a little alarmed by their age and dress. Already, Dad would have had white hair and must have had his black hat with him. And Mama would have worn her Mennonite cap, rubber-soled shoes, and a Plain caped dress.

Dad spoke slowly, something I found especially annoying back then in my teenage years. "Your birth grandmother didn't think there was anything odd about Mama's head covering," he said. He was shelling hazelnuts at the kitchen table. He looked at me with his kind blue eyes. "She knew we were Mennonite, Alexandra. We're whom she wanted for you—whom God wanted."

The tone in his voice hadn't been harsh, but it had been firm. And final. I was afraid I'd hurt his feelings.

Now Dad coughed. I offered him more water, but he shook his head, his eyes barely open. With each breath the rattle in his chest grew more pronounced, and after a while he closed his eyes and I thought he'd drifted off to sleep, but then he said, "Always remember how much Mama and I love you too."

"I will," I whispered.

"When your grandmother gave you to us, she handed over a box as well. A carved box."

A box had never been part of the story. I sat on the edge of the bed, and he relaxed his grip on my hand and turned his face toward me.

"Why didn't I know about this?"

"It wasn't something to give a small child, not like the quilt, so we put it away until you were older. Time passed, and then your mother . . ." His voice trailed off.

Then my mother died, and either he forgot or he chose not to tell me. I held my breath as I waited for him to continue.

"What can I say but forgive me? She would have told you about the box years ago."

"Where is it now?"

"In my closet."

I glanced toward the closed wooden doors.

"What's in it?" I asked.

"Some old papers." He coughed again. "That sort of thing. Nothing of too much importance, as far as we could ever tell."

He coughed some more, stirring the rattle from deep in his chest.

"I'll look at the box later." I squeezed my father's hand.

"The key is on the bureau." He placed his free hand flat over his chest, over the double wedding ring quilt my mother made their first year of marriage.

"The key?"

"To the box. It's in my coin dish."

I remembered coming across a key when I chose coins for my Sunday offerings as a child.

"Don't forget," he said.

"I won't." I let go of his hand and picked up his Bible again. Under any other circumstances, especially with Dad's blessing, I would have been tearing the closet apart as I searched for the box, but at the moment I couldn't bear to leave his side, not even for that.

I continued to read, even though he fell back to sleep by the time I finished Psalm 24. When Sophie let herself into the house, I was on Psalm 50.

"Go on," Sophie said, sitting on the edge of the bed, taking my father's hand.

I finished with, "Whoso offereth praise glorifieth me: and to him that ordereth his conversation aright will I show the salvation of God." I closed his old Bible with a thump.

"How did it go?" I asked.

"A boy. Five hours, two pushes, and six brothers thrilled with his arrival."

I smiled. I didn't see births like that very often in the maternity ward where I worked—that many siblings awaiting the baby's arrival, the whole family celebrating together.

"Have you decided what you'll do with the house?" Sophie asked.

I shrugged. I hadn't decided anything. I didn't want to sell it, rent it, or live in it. Nor did I want to sell the orchard. I wanted Dad in both the orchard and the house, alive. "I don't know," I said softly.

"How are things going with James?"

Sophie knew I had a habit of dumping men who became too serious. I thought I would feel differently with James because we'd known each other so many years, but now I wasn't so sure. We started going out right after Dad was diagnosed last year, which might have been a reaction on my part to my fear of losing my father. I'd always found James attractive, even when I'd pretended to hate him during high school, but there was a part of me that was afraid to trust him, to trust any man besides Dad.

James and I didn't talk much about our future. Sophie, the ladies at church, friends from work, and the people he went to school with all assumed we would get married. I knew James wouldn't ask me until he was done with graduate school and had a job, though. He'd become hopelessly old-fashioned in that way.

Two months ago I wanted nothing more than to marry him and start a family. But lately I had no idea what I wanted.

An uneven breath from Dad caught both Sophie's

and my attention. He inhaled again. We waited. Finally he exhaled.

"Sweetie," Sophie said as she stood. She reached for my hands and placed them on top of his, on top of his chest, on top of the quilt. "Sweetie," she said again. "I think it's time."

"No." I laced my hands in his, leaning over him. It was too soon. I wasn't ready.

He inhaled again. We waited.

"Come quickly, Lord Jesus," Sophie whispered.

"Breathe," I countered. But he didn't.

He had never been overly affectionate with me, nor I with him, but now I kissed his face, his cheek, his eyelids, his forehead.

"He's gone," Sophie said.

"I know." I squeezed his hands.

"Death is so holy, just like birth." Sophie smiled as tears spilled down her face.

I let go of his hands, hoping he was right and that he and Mama had just been reunited.

"God rest both your souls," I said, but the words rang hollow. I turned away and wept.

TWO

Dad's house was located just outside of Aurora, a small town in northern Oregon. Founded in 1856 as a Christian communal society, it consisted of period cabins, houses, and stately white meeting halls. The commune was made up of German and Swiss immigrants, but they disbanded when their leader died nearly thirty years later.

In comparison, the Mennonites were latecomers to Oregon, not arriving until 1889. What they did have in common with the Aurora Commune was that their roots, although a bit tangled, originated in Switzerland and Germany too.

That's what I thought about as I drove through tiny Aurora on my way to the funeral home in the larger nearby town of Canby. I was trying to distract myself from my grief, but it didn't work. As I passed by the barbershop where Dad got his hair cut, tears filled my eyes yet again, as they had all morning.

By the time I reached the funeral home, I had managed to compose myself. Almost on auto-pilot, I went inside and made the arrangements. Back out in the car when I was done, I sent a text to James, telling him that it was all finished and that I had scheduled the service for the day after next. He texted back to say he'd just completed his presentation and would head down in about an hour. I responded, asking him to wait until the next day. I needed time alone. I didn't tell him I felt as if I were moving under icy water, as if my thoughts were drowning, as if my words were bubbles floating upward to a cold and swirling surface.

I went home and put clean sheets on my parents' bed, carefully folding the hospital corners, and then smoothed the quilt back in place. Then I sat on the end, running my hand over the cherry footboard, nicked here and there by time but still smooth.

I grasped the post of the footboard, as if the action might pull me upward, out of my underwater world, and stood, opening Dad's top bureau drawer and running my hand over rows of cotton handkerchiefs. I closed the drawer. Dad's comforting scent filled the room. He always smelled fresh, as clean as a bar of soap. His shaving cup and brush were still on the bureau, left by me after the last time I shaved him, three days ago now.

Next to his cup was his china coin dish. I picked through it, sorting the quarters, dimes, nickels, and pennies, and stacked them on the linen runner the way I had when I was little, until all that was left in the bottom of the dish was the key. It was smaller than I remembered, and tarnished. I shoved it into the pocket of my jeans and hoped the box contained a photo of me as a newborn. Or a photo of my birth mother. Or my grandmother. Maybe even a simple letter, explaining everything.

I went to the closet and started on the lower shelf, sliding the clothes on hangers to the side to make sure there wasn't anything behind them. I saw nothing more than shoes and Dad's work hat and dress hat. I reached with my hand to the top shelf but didn't feel anything, so I pulled the straight-back chair from the corner of the room into the closet, wrestling it through the narrow door. I felt along the top shelf and flopped my hand around, trying to reach the far corner. Nothing. Then my fingertips hit against something. Bull's-eye. I scooted the object forward to the front of the shelf. I felt the carving before I could see the box, but a moment later I cradled it in my hands as I stepped down from the chair.

It was about a foot long by a foot wide and six inches in height. The wood was dark and intricately carved, as Dad had said. And it was dusty.

First I brushed the box off with a towel, examining the carving as I did. Trees and rugged mountains were carved around the sides, and on the top was a grand old building with turrets, balconies, and shuttered windows with a waterfall off to the right. The box was beautiful and unlike anything I'd ever seen. I sat down at the oak table in the dining room and turned the key in the lock, but nothing happened. I wiggled it, took it out, and inserted it again. Still nothing. I ran my hands along the lid, searching for some sort of trick to open the box. Again, nothing. I tried the key one last time and felt something give. I turned it as far as it would go. The lock clicked. I opened it quickly. Dad was right. There were papers in the box. Handwritten, in German. I'd taken a year in high school but could barely remember a thing.

The document was two pages long, yellowed, with the words *Die Schweiz* at the top. I willed there to be a photo—something personal. There wasn't, but from between the pages fell two locks of hair, each tied with a thin strip of black cloth. I carefully picked them up to study them. One lock was obviously the fine blond hair of a newborn. The other was thicker, longer, and darker. Mine and my mother's? Holding a lock in each hand, I couldn't take my eyes from the one I just knew was hers.

Finally, reluctantly, I put the locks back into the box and examined the document again. It appeared to be a letter to someone named *Elsbeth,* dated 1877. On the last page was a fancy signature that read *Abraham Sommers.* Elsbeth and Abraham. Were they husband and wife? Father and daughter? Something else? Maybe my great-great-grandparents were wealthy German timber barons in Pennsylvania during the nineteenth century. That fit in nicely with what I'd concocted years ago in my mind about my birth family. But why would my grandmother have wanted me to have the box and letter? Why had she included the locks of hair?

I stretched my back. Plenty of people in Dad's church spoke German. I would ask Sophie tomorrow. Both she and James were coming then to help me get ready for the funeral.

Scrubbing was something that brought me comfort, so I tackled the kitchen while James de-cluttered the living room and Sophie turned on the vacuum cleaner. I would go through Dad's clothes and books later by myself. James was such a packrat that if I let him help, I knew he would cart more things to his already overcrowded studio apartment in Portland than I would be able to take to Goodwill. This issue was a sore point between us, and I had no intention of contributing to the problem.

I cleared the kitchen counters and sprinkled cleanser over the worn Formica. Dad had always kept the house spotless when I was growing up and trained me well in that, but in the years after I left he began to let things pile up. A stack of newspapers here. A tower of books there. It wasn't as if he lived as a teenager—the dishes and laundry were always done—but it was as if he relaxed his standards a bit. As if he finally cleaned just for himself without having to worry about me. And that was a good thing.

"What's this?"

I turned toward James as I clenched the large gritty sponge. He stood in the kitchen doorway, the carved box in his hands. I'd left the box open on the table beside Dad's easy chair the day before.

"Oh, that." I tossed the sponge into the sink. "I found it yesterday." The vacuum cleaner stopped in the background, and Sophie appeared next to James.

"There's a letter." He held it up. "And two locks of hair."

I nodded.

Sophie's cap tilted a little to the left. "Who's it from?"

"From my birth grandmother. At least that's what Dad said."

"The letter's in German." James held the document in one hand and balanced the box in his other.

"I know." I rinsed my hands. "Do you know who could translate it for me?" I turned toward Sophie.

"Mr. Miller probably could. He used to teach German."

"That's right." I'd forgotten he'd taught for years at the community college in Salem. "I'll take it," I said to James as I finished drying my hands. He slipped the items back into the box, carefully closed the lid, and passed it to me with a reluctant smile.

Feeling oddly vulnerable and exposed, I stashed it back in Dad's closet, high on the shelf.

I finished the kitchen, scrubbing the decades-old appliances until they gleamed again. Dad was gone. Tears filled my eyes, and I stood up straight, brushing them away with my forearm. I'd never been one to cry easily, but now I was afraid if I started I might not stop. I slipped out the back door into the bright, cold day and stopped under the windmill next to the wooden bench that had been there as long as I could remember. It was weathered and gray. Behind me was the hazelnut orchard, all that remained of the original farm.

The back door slammed, and Sophie stepped out with the throw rug from the hallway. She shook it over the porch railing with vigor, snapping it back and forth. She was amazingly strong for such a small woman.

"Are you all right, Lexie?" she called out. I nodded and looked up at the metal blades of the windmill that were just beginning to stir in the slight breeze.

The door slammed again as Sophie went back inside.

I sat down on the bench. Sophie and her mother, Mrs. Chambers, had both been friends of Mama's. Though Sophie had been raised Presbyterian, she switched over to the Mennonite faith during the late 1960s at the height of the Vietnam War. Sophie's mother apparently respected her daughter's decision, but she chose to remain Presbyterian herself. As one of Mama's few non-Plain friends, Mrs. Chambers fascinated me. She drove a Mercedes and wore gold hoop earrings and used rouge on her cheeks. Sometimes we would visit her in her old Victorian house in Woodburn, and I would marvel at the intricate doilies and antiques and artwork that graced her fancy home.

Over the years I had the impression that my parents owed her a great debt, and when I was old enough I found out exactly what that debt was: Mrs. Chambers had been pivotal in my adoption. She had learned of me, of a babe in Pennsylvania in need of a new family, and had thought immediately of her friends the Jaegers, an Oregon couple who very much wanted a child but couldn't seem to have one of their own. Mama told me this startling fact herself before she died, insisting that although Mrs. Chambers had made the connection and even arranged for her lawyer to facilitate the private adoption, it was God Himself who had engineered the whole event and worked out every detail.

Sophie's mother died more than ten years ago, and I realized now that it was a shame that when I was a teenager yearning for answers I hadn't been resourceful enough—well, brave enough, actually—to speak to Mrs. Chambers myself and ask for details about my birth family. Because I hadn't, she'd carried that information with her to the grave. With my father now gone too, I could feel all chances of ever learning the truth slip through my fingers and begin to float away, like a lifeline from a frozen shore.

The breeze picked up suddenly, and so did the whir of the windmill. During my high school years, when I'd obsessed about finding my birth family, I found a Pennsylvania adoption search website and perused it for any information that might be about me. I found nothing. I also read that Pennsylvania is a hard state for a search. But maybe it was easier now than it had been ten years before.

Storm clouds gathered toward the west, and the metal blades of the windmill began to spin. Mama loved the windmill. She and I used to sit on the bench in the late afternoons when the wind picked up and watch it spin, me leaning against her side and her arm holding me tightly. Ever since I could remember, I'd prayed for a baby sister, but when Mama became ill I prayed multiple times a day for her to get well—and then for a baby sister. The day before she died, we sat on the bench. I was eight. Now I knew what an effort it must have been for her to struggle down the steps and sit with me one last time.

That night I had prayed, for what seemed the millionth time, that Mama would get well, and then I told God it was okay if I didn't get a baby sister after all, but that I really, really needed Mama to be okay. Early the next morning she died.

I turned my face toward the house. It had been half an empty shell these years since Mama's death. Now, with Dad gone, it was completely hollow.

Staying and packing up the house felt overwhelming. So did returning to my job. Suddenly, more than anything I wanted to get away—from here, from work, from everyone and everything that was familiar.

I asked myself what was stopping me from doing just that. My father no longer needed me. The clinic would probably give me a few more weeks of family leave. Why couldn't I simply take off for a while?

If I told James how I felt, he would say I was depressed. Maybe I was.

Or maybe I just knew that making a fast

escape might be the one thing that would keep me from drowning in the icy waters of my own overwhelming loss.

As quickly as the breeze had picked up it disappeared and the windmill stopped. I stood slowly and headed for the house. My grief for Dad had stirred my grief for Mama. The combination was nearly unbearable.

That evening James returned to Portland, where he would pick up my black dress and heels at my apartment and then spend the night at his studio on the east side of town. He would be back here the next morning in time for the funeral. As I rocked in Mama's chair, I heard a car in the driveway. I stood and headed for the back door, reaching the kitchen just as Sophie was letting herself in. She told me she had a new mother in labor.

"Hopefully the baby will come before morning," she added. "Lord willing, I'll be there for you tomorrow." Sophie stepped closer and focused her eyes on mine. "You looked so sad in the yard this afternoon."

I felt my face grow warm.

"Are you okay?" she asked.

"I've been thinking that maybe I should get away. That maybe a change of scenery would do me good."

"A vacation?"

I shrugged.

"A trip, yes, but . . ." I looked away. "More like a search."

She leaned back against the counter.

"This has to do with finding that box," she said.

"Sort of."

She studied my face for a moment, her eyes squinting.

"I remember when you wanted to find your birth family when you were in high school."

"Uh-huh," I whispered, thinking that Sophie and my school librarian were the only two people I had confided in back then.

"And now you want to look for them in earnest."

I met her eyes and then flushed with embarrassment, knowing this was all wrong. Dad had just died. He wasn't even buried yet.

"I think you should," she added with a confident, affirming nod.

I think you should. Rolling those words around in my head, I wanted to take her advice, but I couldn't get past the image of my father, still alive, taking my hand in his and struggling to tell me about the box. This stuff had always been so hard for him to talk about. I couldn't imagine what he would think about what I was considering now.

"I can't do that to him," I whispered. "Not so soon."

"It would be okay, Lexie. He wouldn't mind. Your mother wouldn't either."

If anyone would know, it would be Sophie.

37

"We'll see."

"All right. Let's discuss it later," she said, hugging me. "Gotta run for now."

She turned and opened the back door. It had begun to rain, a torrential Oregon downpour. The string of sunny winter days had come to an end. Sophie hurried to her car in the darkness. I was alone again.

I remembered when men and women sat on opposite sides of our country church when I was little, but that ended nearly two decades ago. We were quite modern now at Faith Mennonite, located a few miles west of Aurora, just minutes from Dad's filbert farm. Although the older women still wore head coverings, their dresses were made of floral patterns and store bought, unlike the dark-colored caped dresses of years ago. Changes in Mennonite fashion are what I thought of so I wouldn't think about Dad in the pine box.

James held my hand. I knew we made a handsome couple, both of us tall, he with his curly golden hair, green eyes, and kind face, me with my long blond hair, brown eyes, and thick eyelashes. He wore a suit and navy tie, and I was in a black dress and wool coat.

Just before the service began, Sophie bustled down the middle aisle of the church, sat beside me, and took my other hand. Obviously, her first-time mother had safely delivered. James and I were the youngest people at the service by far. Even Sophie, at age sixty-two, was young, relatively speaking; everyone else there was much older.

At the burial, I stood between Sophie and James so the oldest of the mourners could sit in the folding chairs provided by the funeral home. Old-growth Douglas firs towered above us, and the melody of the creek that ran along the far side of the cemetery played along with the notes of the breeze high in the treetops. The overcast morning grew darker as we gathered in a semicircle around the pastor. During the moment of finality, when he said "dust to dust," I slipped out of my denial long enough to register the coffin in front of me, my mother's grave to the side, and the gaping hole waiting for my father's body. The sky opened up just then, and the rain began, pummeling the canopy over our heads, running in rivers down the sides to the ground.

I sobbed, showing my lack of acceptance of the ways of God and displaying my lack of faith for all to see. Sophie and James stood close on each side. When the service was over, they kept me on my feet and supported me over the soft ground, out from under the shelter and into the rain, around the modest gravestones made of ancient lime and crumbling concrete, and toward James's old Malibu car. The whole way, the people around us huddled under umbrellas, men and women who had loved me since I was a baby, looked on with concern. I knew they had stashed casseroles, hams, salads, fresh rolls, pickled beets, and desserts in their cars before the funeral, and that they would all follow me back to Dad's house.

I willed myself to pull it together. I could have a good cry later, after everyone had gone on home.

"Hurry," I whispered to James, dabbing at the streaks of tears and rain that had soaked my face. "I need a couple of minutes before everyone arrives." A cold washcloth against my eyes might help.

It took James only a few minutes to get to the house, and Sophie was the next to arrive. When she entered the kitchen, he was setting up folding chairs in the living room, and I was running cold water over a cloth.

"How are you?" she asked, patting me gently on the back.

"Okay," I lied, turning off the faucet and wringing out the cloth over the sink.

"I know this is bad timing on my part," she said, dropping her hand and lowering her voice, "but I want to touch base with you before the others arrive. It's about last night's discussion."

I turned toward her, trying to recall which conversation she meant.

"About you getting away," she added.

Oh, that. I tilted my head back, closed my eyes, and laid the cloth across them.

"I was talking nonsense last night," I said, grateful for the coolness against my swollen eyelids. "I have to get back to work, not to mention I need to figure out what to do with the house and land. I'll be so busy—"

"Sounds pretty convenient to me," Sophie interrupted.

"What do you mean?"

"I know you, Lexie. You're the kind of person who makes things happen. You would figure out a way to do this if you really wanted to."

"Do what, exactly?"

"Why, go east and pursue the matter of your birth family, of course. Try and find them. That is what you want, isn't it?"

She was speaking so emphatically that I pulled off the cloth and looked at her.

"Sophie, you and I both know I wasn't thinking clearly when I brought that stuff up last night," I said, lowering my voice, not wanting James to overhear our conversation. "Even if I had vacation time left, which I don't, a search like that would take too long, certainly more than a couple of days."

She leaned back against the opposite counter, a sudden twinkle in her eyes.

"Extend your leave of absence. Then you could take as long as you needed without having to worry about your job."

"Yeah, right. And what do I live on in the meantime as I'm doing this big search? My good looks? That and a quarter won't even get me a cup of coffee."

41

"You could get a temporary position in Pennsylvania."

I titled my head, blinking.

"A temporary position? Like through an agency? One of those traveling nurse places?"

"Well, actually I was thinking of something a little less involved. I got a phone call this morning about a friend of a friend who is in trouble, a lay-midwife who might need help. Of course, thanks to our conversation last night, I thought of you immediately."

"Why me?"

"Because of where this woman just happens to live," she said. "Pennsylvania."

Not wanting her to see the sudden surge of hope in my eyes, I again tilted my head back and replaced the cool, damp cloth across my brow, asking what kind of trouble the woman was in and why she needed help.

"It's complicated and I don't have all the details," Sophie replied, "but if you're interested I'll make another phone call."

Was I interested? I wasn't sure. Certainly, I wouldn't rule it out—not yet, anyway. Sophie hurried on, adding, "I think it would be a good experience for you. She has an excellent reputation."

I valued Sophie's skills, and the home birth scene had taught me a lot, but I was strictly a hospital provider now. I reminded her of that.

"But you're so gifted," Sophie said. "Spending some time doing home births again might be just what you need as you work through your grief and pursue your past. *Pennsylvania,* Lexie. Think about it. Seems almost providential to me."

For a moment it did to me as well. But then I hesitated, wondering what part of the state this midwife lived in, if it were even anywhere near Philadelphia. Again taking the cloth from my eyes, I looked at Sophie and asked if she knew.

"She's in Lancaster County. That's near Philadelphia, isn't it?"

"Yes, sort of," I said, thinking of my story, of the quilt I had been wrapped in when I had been given to my parents at the airport. "Lancaster County is what's considered Amish country."

"Well, that makes sense then, because this woman is a midwife to the Old Order Amish."

"You're kidding," I said. I didn't know all that much about the Amish except that they were so conservative they made most Mennonites look positively liberal.

"Well?" Sophie prodded.

I pursed my lips, thinking. The thought of actually going to Pennsylvania was tempting, yes, but I was iffy on the arrangement Sophie was proposing. Better to go the more "involved" route, as she put it, and sign on with a traveling nurse agency instead.

Why hadn't I thought of that before?

"What about a license?" I asked, still playing

devil's advocate. "You know I'm not licensed to practice in any state but this one."

"Apply for one right away. It should only take a few weeks. That would give you time to finish here and take care of things at work. By then we should know what's going on with this midwife and what her needs are. She really does need help, Lexie."

A part of me wanted to laugh. It was so Mennonite to plan a getaway around doing some kind of service. I knew of families who spent all of their vacations in places like Bolivia and South Africa and East L.A. Even vacations had to have a purpose.

"And you think I could leave, just like that?" I asked, glancing toward the doorway to the dining room.

Following my gaze, she said, "If you talk it through with James, I think he'll understand." Moving closer, she put a warm hand on my shoulder and gave it a squeeze. "I know there's something inside of you, something incomplete. When you were a teenager—"

"I wanted my story," I blurted, tears filling my eyes again. "I still do."

She nodded. "Maybe God is whispering to you now."

"Oh yeah? What's He saying?" I asked, wiping my tears on my sleeve and thinking I hadn't heard from God—or He from me—in a very long time.

Sophie smiled, her eyes again twinkling.

"Maybe He's saying, 'It's time.'"

THREE

I leaned against the counter, wiping away my new tears with the cool cloth, and then pressed it against my face again. A car door slammed and then another.

"Would you at least pray about it?" Sophie asked as she started toward the back door.

"Pray about what?" James stopped in the doorway, holding the cup he'd left earlier on the coffee table.

"Nothing, really," I whispered as Sophie opened the door for the elderly crowd gathering in the driveway, carrying casserole dishes, pies, and baskets of rolls. As they flooded into the kitchen, Sophie took their food, James took their coats, and I took their hugs and the women's holy kisses. They were as eager to help as they were somber. In no time the table was spread with food, and they stood with their hands folded in front of them, waiting for someone to pray.

James cleared his throat. "I'll say grace."

I let out a sigh of relief.

His voice was a notch deeper than usual. We all bowed our heads as James thanked God for my father's life, asked God to comfort me, and then prayed He would fill the void left in all of us by

Dad's passing. Tears welled in my eyes again. James blessed the food and then said amen and motioned to Mrs. Glick, the oldest person in the room at ninety-three, to start the line. She pushed up the sleeves of her simple dress and snatched up a china plate. Her cap covered all but the front of her snow-white hair. Most of the women still wore head coverings, although at the other Mennonite church, the one on the other side of the interstate, no one did. By early high school, I wanted to belong to that church.

Mrs. Glick motioned to James to cut in behind her, but he shook his head, his eyes dancing. Widow that she was, she and nearly all of the other ladies had a crush on James. Through the years he would go to church with Dad now and then even while he was in college, driving down for the morning and staying for lunch. As it turned out, he made a much better Mennonite than I, although he hadn't joined the church. I had—but then I'd left.

Sophie and I filled coffee cups and punch glasses. Our group of seventeen seemed to be a little messy, so I hunted for and found more napkins in the top drawer of my mother's antique hutch. I paused for a moment, my hand flat against the cherrywood, wedged between two pies. Would I keep the hutch? It wouldn't fit in my apartment. Would I sell it? I couldn't imagine.

As James followed me around the table, heaping his plate with food, I tried to take a small spoonful of everything. I overheard Sophie tell Mr. Miller I'd found a document written in German. "Do you think you could translate it?" she asked him.

"Say what?" Mr. Miller shouted, leaning forward.

Mrs. Miller halfway cupped her hands around her mouth and yelled, "Lexie needs you to translate something." Sophie motioned my way. Every eye in the room landed on me.

"No need to do it now," I said, stepping toward him and making sure he could see my lips. "I can bring it by your house later." I marveled at Sophie's audacity, butting in about my letter and turning my wanting a little vacation into a search for my birth family and possible involvement with a midwife who was in trouble.

Mrs. Miller stood. "We're getting ready to go to Boise. To visit our son." She was always to the point.

"Let's take a look at it now." Mr. Miller smiled as he handed his empty plate to his wife and she headed to the kitchen. He was a happy man and always eager to help.

James settled onto the far end of the mauve sofa, beside Mrs. Glick. I stood for a moment, frozen, not sure I wanted all of these people to know what the letter said. Mrs. Miller returned to the room.

"Go on, Lexie," she said. "We don't have all day."

I put my plate on the coffee table and headed down the hall. Every eye in the room was no longer on me when I returned. They were all on the carved box in my hands.

"Oh, my," Mrs. Glick said.

"I've never seen anything like it." Mrs. Miller plunked back down into the chair beside her husband.

I pulled out the letter and handed it to Mr. Miller.

"Let me have a look at that box." Mrs. Glick abandoned her plate on the coffee table too and was inching her way to the edge of the sofa, her arms outstretched. I handed it to her.

"Isn't it amazing?" James asked.

Mr. Schmidt, who sat beside Mrs. Glick, ran his hand over the carved top. "Looks like sycamore wood."

I'd wondered what it might be.

"But it must have been carved when it was green." He squinted at the box. "Years and years ago. You don't see work like this anymore."

"Look at the turrets." Mrs. Glick spoke loudly. "And the waterfall." She pulled it away from Mr. Schmidt and held it so she could see the front. "And the flowers. They're edelweiss."

Mr. Miller kept his eyes on the document as he spoke. "Edelweiss? Are you sure?"

Mrs. Glick was too enthralled with the box to answer. I wanted to take it from her but turned my attention back to the letter. "Can you read it?" I asked.

"Most of it." Mr. Miller paused. "It's to an Elsbeth. From Abraham, her father." He squinted. "He says he's leaving her a place called Amielbach when

48

he dies in hopes she will return home someday."

A place called Amielbach. That must be the name of the house, the one carved into the lid of the box.

"Does he mention anything about Pennsylvania?" Surely that was where the house was.

"No. He doesn't say where the property is." Mr. Miller stretched his back. "The letter is written in high German, mostly. That's what I learned as a kid. But there are some odd phrases like . . ." He read words that sounded as if they were German to me —*wie* and *der*. Then something like *Esel am Berg*. He lifted his head. "It means being perplexed by an unexpected situation. But the phrase isn't high German. It's considered a Helvetism, a colloquial saying in Swiss German, which is technically an Alemannic dialect." I must have looked perplexed because he started to speak slowly. "It's a dialect similar to what's spoken by a group of Amish in Indiana. It originated in Switzerland, but it's evolved over the years. And the language the Swiss Amish use today is oral, not written." For a minute I thought he was going to dive into a full-fledged lecture about the development of German dialects, but then he stopped abruptly as if he remembered he wasn't teaching.

Sophie's head swung around, and she looked me straight in the eye. It was a knowing look, but I had no idea what it meant.

"It *is* from Switzerland." Mrs. Glick hugged the box. "I knew the flowers were edelweiss."

Mr. Miller extended the letter. "He goes on and on about being disappointed that Elsbeth is giving up her dream of being a teacher and her opportunity to work as a tutor. Sounds like it was for a wealthy French family. But that's pretty much it."

"Does it say *why* she gave up her dream?" I asked.

Mr. Miller again skimmed the pages. "No, just that he's sorry she did."

"Thank you." Disappointed, I took the pages from him. The analysis of the language was interesting, but I was hoping for more information. Next I reached for the box, but Mrs. Glick hugged it tighter.

I stretched out my arms and then clapped my hands together, as if I could command the box to come to me. "I didn't know there were Amish in Indiana," I said, hoping to distract her.

She stood, the box still in her arms. "They came with the last wave from Switzerland, more than a hundred years after the first group of Amish."

"You could stop by Indiana on your way to Pennsylvania," Sophie said softly as Mrs. Glick finally relinquished the box. "You might find some information there."

James half stood and then sank back onto the couch, his plate lurching backward with the movement, his roll tumbling to his lap. His eyes met mine. "Pennsylvania? Lex, what's going on?"

FOUR

I averted my eyes but knew my reddening face gave me away. "How about dessert?" I asked brightly. I turned toward the hutch and, speaking over my shoulder, said, "Mrs. Miller, your lemon meringue looks delicious." As my guests served themselves from the top of the hutch, James shot me a questioning look. I mouthed, "Later" and turned my head away.

After dessert Sophie said she had a mother to check on and she would talk to me soon. James assured the guests that he would clean up; we both knew most of them needed a nap by now. One by one they left, telling me I was in their prayers and whispering "God bless you" as they descended the back steps, gripping the rickety rail.

That left me and James staring at each other in a kitchen full of dirty dishes.

"What's going on?" he asked again.

I positioned the plastic plug over the drain. "I told Sophie I needed to get away, and she came up with a wild idea." I started the water.

He pulled the plug from the drain and clutched it against his side. "You want to go away?"

"Get away. I felt that way last night." I honestly didn't know how I felt today—except numb. I pointed at his hand and then back to

51

the drain. He tossed the plug into the sink.

I inserted it again and squirted out some detergent. "And then Sophie got a phone call about a midwife this morning." I told him the whole story as I trailed my hand through the water, stirring up the bubbles.

"Why do you feel like you need to get away?" His voice was hurt as he bent down and retrieved the wooden dish rack from under his side of the sink.

I eased a stack of china into the basin and without looking at him said, "Sophie thinks I need to find my birth family."

"Oh." His voice was gentle now. "Are you ready for that?" James was the one who had been studying abandonment and attachment issues. I was the one who had been trying, at all costs, to avoid talking with him about those things.

My chin began to quiver as I scrubbed a plate and lowered it into the rinse water.

"Did the box bring all this up for you?" He swished the plate around and placed it in the rack.

"I've wanted to search since high school."

"You never told me that." His voice sounded hurt.

"I feel more alone than ever."

"You have me." His voice was tender.

I nodded.

James and I had been partners in chemistry lab in high school. Back then, he was the bad boy, partying on the weekends, smart-mouthing our teachers at school, and teasing me about my cap and modest dresses whenever we were together. His parents divorced when he was a baby, and his dad remarried and started a new family. By high school James didn't have much of a relationship with his father at all. His poor mother was so busy making a living that James had enough freedom to get himself in trouble on a regular basis.

Though I found him intriguing—and smart, much to my relief, given that he was my lab partner—he made me nervous with his wide grin and reputation as a partyer. Then one day, several months into our junior year, he surprised me by asking if he could come over to study. I told him no. He showed up that night anyway and sweet-talked his way into the house. Dad helped us with our chemistry, something he'd been doing with me all semester, and when we were finished James brought up his English essay on conflict resolution. Dad was happy to help with that too, eventually explaining at length the Mennonite stand of nonresistance. Before James left, Dad asked him to go to church with us the next Sunday. Much to my horror, he accepted.

Slowly, as James insinuated himself into my home and my church, the two of us went from being enemies to being friends. For the sake of that friendship, we kept things platonic back then. Nine years later, we reconnected when he called me after he found out while at church about

Dad's diagnosis. Soon he asked me out to dinner, and in no time we were dating.

"We should finish the dishes so you can get back home and study," I said now.

Though I was using tomorrow's midterm test as an excuse, we both knew that I wanted to be alone, that I wanted this conversation to be over. How could I tell James he wasn't enough? That I needed something more to fill my empty soul?

He left soon after that, hurt clearly shining in his eyes. I hurried to pack my things. My plan was to go back to Portland for a week and then return here to Dad's place to go through his things before I decided whether to sell the house.

After Mama's death I prayed to God even more than I had before. I never told Him how I felt about her dying; instead, I told Him all the things I would have told her, a sort of cosmic joke on Him. Because He allowed her to die, He had to suffer my endless chatter. But gradually I stopped sharing. And sometime, by high school, I'd mostly stopped praying too. Not altogether. Communing with God was a hard habit to break, and from time to time I would catch myself blurting out—silently—a quick prayer. But even those brief petitions eventually stopped being regular. And they stopped being intentional.

It wasn't that I no longer believed, but I decided that God wanted us to take as much responsibility for ourselves as we possibly could. For me, that meant concentrating on academics. On the laws of physics and chemical equations and algebraic formulas. On absolutes that made sense. The idea of God didn't offend my rationality. What did was that there were no formulas and equations I could count on except for the laws of science. I decided I needed to take charge of me.

As I shoved my things into my suitcase, an empty eeriness settled over the house, and its creaks and groans startled me. I quickly finished packing and zipped my bag. Hurrying down the hall, I heard Dad's voice call my name. My heart raced as I turned and walked into his bedroom, but the sound I'd heard was only a branch from the maple tree scraping against his window.

By the time I had slung my bags in the back of my Honda CR-V, dusk had fallen. The windmill was statue still, and beyond the backyard the orchard darkened. Even so, the ordered trees offered comfort. I stepped toward them, longing to walk between the wide rows where I played as a child while Dad worked. But then that moment of twilight, where the world is neither light nor dark, lit upon the orchard and grief swept over me again, stealing my breath and leaving me weak. I turned and climbed into my car instead.

Fifteen minutes later, after having driven south on I-5, backtracking to the coffee shop by the Woodburn outlet mall, I powered up my laptop and googled "Amielbach"—unsuccessfully.

My search for "Abraham Sommers" produced several possibilities, including a couple with ties to Switzerland—although none to Pennsylvania or Indiana—but as I followed them, I couldn't determine which would be associated with the box or Amielbach or with me. It was quite the puzzle.

Giving up on that for now, I quickly skimmed my emails. There were a few work-related messages, including several condolences from colleagues and a photo of a baby I'd delivered the month before, sent by the new father with a sweet thank-you. I filed it with all the other pictures, and then I closed my computer, picked up my latte, and headed for the car, moving past the series of store windows with their shiny displays.

In all honesty, I wasn't a big shopper. It was hard to break my childhood frugality. I'd decorated my apartment nicely but inexpensively, and with the exception of a single pair of jeans, I didn't go for designer clothes. As I moved past the row of outlets now, however, I could feel my steps slowing. Finally I came to a stop, deciding that I could afford to treat myself to something nice for a change.

I'd never been inside the Coach purse store, even though women at work talked about the deals they had found there. I just couldn't bring myself to spend oodles of money on a bag when I could get one for a fraction of the cost somewhere else. I'd grown up with simple dresses, practical shoes, and inexpensive purses, but today I felt that spending some money on myself might make me feel better. Plus, it would be nice to have a designer bag if I did travel. Or if I met my birth mother. In an instant I picked back up on my fantasies from high school. As I walked through the doorway of the Coach store, I imagined meeting her. She'd be happily married by now, of course. Living in the suburbs of Philly. A professional woman. A lawyer or financial planner or something like that. It was hard for me to imagine that she'd had more children. Maybe she and her husband had decided not to. He wasn't my father, but out of respect for me . . .

"Good evening." A clerk greeted me.

I responded, thankful I still had on my dress clothes and heels. At least I looked the part of a savvy shopper.

Another clerk welcomed me a second later. As I browsed through the store, the fantasy began again. I would meet my biological mother at a nice restaurant in downtown Philadelphia—unless she'd moved to Manhattan. Then I'd go there. I'd wear slacks and a silk blouse and high heels to show I was proud of the height she—or maybe just my grandmother—had passed on to me. I'd look like her. Finally, I'd look like someone. She'd have blond hair and brown eyes and a wide smile, and she would hug me right away. Her husband wouldn't be with her because, selfishly, she'd decided to have me all to herself the first time we met.

I sighed. My fantasies hadn't changed much

since high school. I picked up a tote bag. Two hundred sixty-five dollars.

James would think it was ridiculous. He'd paid for college entirely on his own with a few scholarships and grants. He'd had to take off several semesters, working as hard as he could to save money to keep going. He would think it immoral to spend so much on something so trivial.

I looked at another wall of tote bags and then turned toward the back of the store. A sky blue shoulder bag caught my attention. Three hundred fifty-nine dollars. It had two outside pockets plus several inside.

"Here's a wallet that goes with it," the second clerk said. It was the same color as the tote and cost one hundred twenty-nine dollars. Mama had one that looked a lot like it when I was little, although she bought hers at a flea market.

I left the store with the Coach shoulder bag and the Coach wallet both secure in a Coach shopping bag. I felt a little better. At least for the moment.

Twenty-four hours later I was the provider on call for my clinic. I was the youngest practitioner in our center, even though I'd been practicing for almost three years. Two of our clients were in labor at Emanuel Hospital, babies 245 and 246 by morning, God willing.

This was a much different environment than what I'd witnessed assisting Sophie, but I learned a lot watching her, such as not to take up a lot of space at the birth, and that what was happening was never about me—it was about the baby, and then the mother, and then the father. I learned to simply tell a woman who said she couldn't go on that she could. I learned that some women scream through childbirth and some women don't. I learned that the ones who don't aren't in any less pain than the ones who do. From Sophie, I learned that giving birth was a natural, normal part of life. It was something I struggled to remember working at Emanuel with its fetal monitors, intrauterine pressure devices, ultrasounds, suction tubes, oxygen lines, IVs, blood transfusions, anesthesiologists, obstetricians, surgeons, and neonatologists.

I also learned that, even though a birth was never about me, each time I searched for something. A reaction from the mother when she held her baby for the first time. A look from the infant as she searched her mother's eyes. Acceptance from the father. Joy from the grandmother. After every birth I asked the mother to email me a photograph of her baby. Most of my patients did. I kept the photos on my laptop and sometimes clicked through them, one after another. I'd been a part of each one's incredible journey into this world.

When I arrived that Thursday night, a fifteen-year-old was laboring in suite four. I frowned. Another teenage birth. I hadn't seen her in our practice, which probably meant she hadn't received much prenatal care. Maybe she'd come to us late. I read the chart. The girl was considering adoption. The baby was three weeks early. I grimaced. A juvenile primigravida—meaning a first-time pregnancy—and early. She certainly wasn't the youngest I'd seen, but still my heartbeat quickened.

I pushed up the sleeves of my lab coat and headed down the hall, my blue clogs clicking against the shiny linoleum. The labor nurse stepped out of the doorway as I reached the suite.

"How are things going?" I asked.

"Good. She's a trooper. Already dilated to seven."

"Any support?"

The nurse nodded. "Her mom is with her. They make a good team."

My heart softened a little.

"I'll be back in a little bit." The nurse hurried across the hall.

I pushed through the door and introduced myself. The girl's name was Tonya, and she stood by the edge of the bed. Even at full term she looked small, except for her belly, which jutted straight out like a shelf. She wore her dark hair in a high ponytail with a pink ribbon, and her fingernails were painted fuchsia. Her mother, Tammy, shook my hand and met my eyes, assuring me that things were going well. They had taken a birthing class together and were prepared. Tonya rolled her eyes, but then a contraction gripped her. "This stinks," she muttered, grasping the headboard with one hand.

"You're doing great, honey," Tammy cooed. Taking note of the circles under her eyes and the rumpled state of her flowered blouse and brown slacks, I knew she had been at this for a while, helping her daughter through the pain.

Tonya moaned deeply as her contraction intensified.

The first delivery I ever saw had been atypically peaceful and serene, a mainstream mother who had chosen to use a midwife because of her nonmainstream ideas about birthing. When the woman's husband rubbed her back or stroked her hair, she told him thank you. Every time a contraction came, she leaned against him on their antique bed in their old farmhouse, endured it in silence, and smiled when it was over. When it was time to push, she closed her eyes, and after only two contractions out popped a baby girl, eyes wide, taking it all in. After the father cut the cord, Sophie wiped the baby off, wrapped her in a flannel blanket, and handed her over to the eager parents. They cuddled her together, and then mother and child melted back into the bed as one. Soon, the father brought their two-year-old son upstairs, where the boy snuggled with his mom and sister, patting both of their heads with his chubby hands. I recalled that I spent most of the afternoon standing in the bedroom doorway trying not to cry. Sophie remembers me helping the mother walk to the shower, stripping the bed, starting the laundry, and making toast with jam for the two-year-old.

That was the first. After that came many more, though of course their reasons for using a midwife varied. There were modest Mennonite mothers, Hispanic migrant moms, poor mamas without insurance, and a few like that first mother who simply wanted to give birth in their own home, on their own terms.

In my senior year of high school, I took anatomy and a medical career prep class, planning to be a labor and delivery nurse. But when I read in our textbook about the world of the nurse-midwife, I knew that was what I wanted.

Once Tonya's contraction came to an end, I told mother and daughter both that I would be back in a while to check on how things were progressing. Stepping into the hall, I moved toward the room of my second mother in labor, a patient of mine, Jane Hirsch. I had delivered Jane's first baby, a boy named Jackson, almost three years before. *Baby number 9.* Jackson now went to a co-op preschool, and Jane worked part time in a law practice that specialized in nonprofits. This time around I had really enjoyed doing her prenatal visits, watching the interactions between mother and son. Though dad often seemed a bit preoccupied with his work, Jane was a hip and fun and devoted mom, the kind I wanted to be someday.

"How are you?" she asked as I entered the room.

Jane's long hair was twisted up on her head, her face was much fuller than when I saw her last, more than a month ago, and her belly stuck straight up in the middle of the bed.

"Good," I answered. "How are you?"

She shook her head. "You have to tell me about you first. You were off work for three weeks. I was terrified I might have to go through this without you."

"My father passed." Unwanted tears sprang into my eyes.

"Oh, Lexie." She reached out her hand. "I'm sorry."

I was glad that her husband, an up-and-coming executive, wasn't there to witness my being so unprofessional. "It's okay," I said, giving her hand a quick squeeze and then withdrawing it. "It was expected."

"But still . . ."

I nodded and then forced myself to smile. "Have you had your epidural?"

"Just."

"And where's the hubby?"

"In the cafeteria." She laughed. "Lucky him."

Food was another one of the differences between a home birth and a hospital birth. At home the mom could eat yogurt and fruit and soup to keep up her strength. In the hospital, with one in three births ending in a C-section, food was withheld because a full stomach could be a sick stomach in surgery.

The monitor beeped, and Jane and I both looked at it. She was having a contraction—a good strong one. She held up her arms and waved her hands. "I hardly feel a thing," she said. "Just some pressure."

Some people have a memory for faces. I have one for births. Even though Jane's first baby was 235 births ago, I remembered his arrival perfectly. She had arrived at the hospital too late to have an epidural. That was her top priority this time.

"Who's with Jackson tonight?" I asked.

"Grandma. My mom. She'll bring him up in the morning."

Jane and I chatted a little longer, and then I headed back across the hall to check on Tonya.

She was on the bed now, sitting cross-legged.

"Do you want a drink of water?" Tammy asked.

The girl frowned and shook her head.

"How's it going?" My voice was subdued.

"Fine," Tonya growled, stretching out one leg and then the other. The monitor showed a contraction coming on. I waited to see what she would do. It didn't take her long to climb off the bed with her mom's help. Her face contorted, and she took a deep breath. Tammy stepped behind her and began rubbing her shoulders. I expected the girl to push her mother away, but she didn't. She groaned a little as the contraction ended.

"Let's check you." I helped her back onto the bed.

She was at ten centimeters, ready to push. She

was a trooper, not what I'd expected at all.

"I'm almost there?" she asked.

"We'll soon see. It's different for every—" I almost said *mom,* but because she might be relinquishing the baby, I said, "—one. Sometimes a woman pushes for quite some time." Up to three hours. "But other times the baby delivers after just a few pushes." I didn't add that was usually the case for second and third babies. I took off my gloves, dropped them into the garbage, and then decided to stay with Tonya for the next few contractions to see how quickly things went. It would be hours before Jane delivered.

Every once in a while I offered a word of encouragement while Tammy bustled around, dimming the lights, offering Tonya water, and timing each contraction. Even though she had the urge to push, it wasn't strong yet, not the way it would be soon. She leaned back against the pillows on the bed, her painted nails resting atop her belly, between contractions.

"Here comes another one," Tammy said, switching her gaze from the monitor to the clock. Tonya pressed her hands down on her knees and pulled forward. I stepped to the side of the bed and held one of her legs. She scrunched up her face and then started to grimace.

"Eighty-five seconds," her mother announced.

"You're doing great," I said.

"It hurts." She collapsed back against the pillows.

"It's supposed to," her mother said, matter-of-factly. I wondered if perhaps it was the mom who had decided Tonya shouldn't have an epidural. Maybe she wanted her to feel all the pain.

The OB nurse came in, and I slipped across the hall to Jane's room. She and her husband were watching the news. "How's it going in here?" I parked myself in front of the computer and read the nurse's notes. Thanks to the epidural, her contractions had slowed.

"Doing great," Jane answered.

Her husband and I chatted for a minute, and then just as I was getting ready to leave, a scream jolted the night.

"Be back soon." I walked quickly to the door and scurried across the hall. Tonya was pushing with all her might.

The OB nurse held one of her legs and her mom the other. I snapped on clean gloves as the nurse grinned and said, "I thought that holler would bring you running."

The baby's head crowned with the next contraction. "Tonya, you're amazing. Another push or two and—" I stopped myself from saying *your baby.* "And the baby will be here."

It took only one more push for an absolutely perfect little girl to slip into my hands. She looked up at me with wise old eyes and then hiccupped before I grabbed the suction. She hiccupped again and then began to whimper. She was tiny—

probably just more than six pounds—but good sized for being three weeks early.

"Time of birth is 11:57 p.m.," the nurse said.

I grabbed a warm receiving blanket and swaddled her. *Baby number 245.*

Tonya collapsed back against the pillows as tears raced down her face, pulling streams of black mascara after them. "I want to hold her," she said. Her arms reached out toward me.

FIVE

I searched Tammy's face and she nodded. I leaned forward with the baby, slipping her into the teenager's hands. Tonya pulled the little girl to her chest. "You're so beautiful," she said. How many new mothers had I seen say exactly that? Even at fifteen, even still a girl, she instinctually knew what to do. Tonya's mom hovered above the two, her hands clasped under her chin. "So beautiful," the girl said again and then she began to sob. The nurse and I moved toward the door to give them space.

I still needed to deliver the placenta. The nurse needed to weigh the baby. And there was the matter of what to do with the newborn. Probably put her in a warm isolette in the nursery after the nurse cleaned her up. That would leave Tonya and her mom alone to grieve.

"Are the adoptive parents here?" I whispered to the nurse.

She shook her head.

Thank goodness. I waited a few more minutes and then said, "Tonya, how about if you pass the baby to your mom? We have a little bit more work to do."

Their hands became entangled, and a second later the baby was in the new grandmother's arms. As I concentrated on caring for Tonya, I kept track of Tammy out of the corner of my eye. She was entranced with her new granddaughter, swaying gently, making eye contact, smiling, saying sweet nothings. She was in her own world, just the baby and her. It wasn't going to be easy for either one of them to let her go. I felt a pang for the hopeful adoptive parents. I thought of Mama and Dad, and for the first time wondered what the night I was born was like for them, if they were already in Pennsylvania or if they had waited to come. Why hadn't I ever asked Dad about those details? If I had, would he have told me?

The nurse directed Tammy over to the in-room isolette to weigh the baby. "Six pounds four ounces," she said. Tonya's mom held her hand on the baby's chest as the nurse cleaned her.

As I finished up, I thought of my own birth grandmother, wondering if she had been as enamored with me.

I covered Tonya with a warm blanket and

lowered the bed to a reclining position. In a second her mother stood beside her, holding the baby again. The resemblance between the three was incredible. All had the same delicate nose and heart-shaped face. Each had a little hill of a chin that jutted out.

Tonya began to sob again.

Her mother leaned over and kissed her forehead. "What's the matter?"

Tonya's body convulsed, and her face quivered.

Tammy perched on the bed, the baby still tucked in her arm like a football. Tonya reached out and stroked the infant's curled fist.

"It's hard," Tammy said. "I know."

"You *don't* know." Another sob racked her. "You got to keep me."

"I was older." Tammy wiggled closer to her daughter. "Done with school. I had a job. And insurance." Tammy's voice was low.

Tonya reached out for the baby.

"Sweetie," Tammy said.

"Please?"

Tammy's face contorted as she stood. The baby began to whimper.

"Mom," Tonya pled.

Now the baby was crying that traumatized newborn wail. "Shhh." Tammy bounced the baby, but the cry grew louder.

Tonya was sitting up now, reaching for her child, and then Tammy was sliding her into her mother's arms. "I can't go through with it," Tonya whispered, sinking back down onto the bed and pulling the baby to her chest.

Tammy nodded. "I'll call the lawyer in the morning." She didn't seem surprised as she collapsed on the bed beside her daughter and now silent granddaughter. They stayed that way for a while, and then Tammy said, "You should nurse though, if you're going to keep her."

Tonya nodded. I slipped out the door, dabbing at my eyes. I knew of other midwives and doctors who would have intervened. They would have at least asked Tammy if they had the resources and support they needed. I would flag Tonya's chart for a social worker to stop in and see her, but I wasn't going to get in the middle of it. Tammy seemed to know what she was doing. She knew what it took to raise a child. And she couldn't be more than forty herself. She was perfectly capable of raising another baby. No, I wouldn't get involved in this one. It hit too close to home.

I stepped into Jane's room, forcing myself not to think about the couple who was waiting, somewhere, hoping for that beautiful baby girl, having no idea of the heartbreaking phone call coming their way.

At 5:23 a.m. Jane delivered her eight-pound boy. By 7:15 she was tucked into bed, ready to sleep with baby Jefferson beside her and her husband hunched on the little window seat, already snoring.

70

The gray morning sun streamed through the leaves of the trees outside the window. I turned the blinds shut. "Give Jackson a kiss for me when he comes to meet his brother," I said as I patted Jane's foot.

She nodded and smiled. "Thank you," she whispered.

"My pleasure," I said. And it was. *Baby number 246.* It had been a perfect night.

As I slipped into the hall, I decided to peek in on Tonya one last time. A woman, obviously a maternal aunt by how much she looked like Tammy, held the baby. Tonya slept, her mouth slightly open, on the bed.

"Have you had any rest?" I asked Tammy.

She shook her head. "I will later." She turned toward me. "Does this happen very often? That a girl changes her mind about giving up her baby?"

"It happens."

"Do you think I should have discouraged her?"

I shrugged. "I don't think there's any right answer. I think it's entirely up to you." I touched the baby's cheek. I suddenly had the urge to tell Tammy that I was adopted, that I had a grandmother who had once loved me that I never knew. But I didn't. Instead, I handed her my card and asked that she email me a photo of the baby when she got the chance.

"You bet I will," she said.

Kin was the word that came to mind when I stepped out of the room. It was such an old-fashioned word. I remember Mama talking about her relatives who lived in Kansas and saying, "My kin . . ." I'd looked the word up in the dictionary a few months after she died and found "persons of common ancestry."

I was kinless.

The next day I applied for a Pennsylvania nursing license and emailed requests for information from three traveling nurse agencies. In the following weeks, on my days off, I sorted through Dad's things, trying not to drown in my grief. Memories of my parents and obsessions of my now-kinless state hovered like a thick fog on the Willamette River. Then came the mid-March morning, almost five weeks after my father had passed, when the fog began to clear.

I was riding my bike across the Broadway Bridge on my way home to Northwest Portland after a long labor and a difficult delivery of baby number 255. The weather was cold and the river was the color of steel. A tugboat pushed a barge toward the Saint Johns Bridge, and somewhere in the distance a whistle blew. Halfway across the bridge my cell phone began vibrating in the pocket of my bicycle jacket. I slowed and pulled it out. *Sophie.*

I stopped the bike, leaning against the railing as I said hello. A pigeon flew up from the underside of the bridge. Another bicycle went by me, the rider a flash of orange-and-yellow Lycra topped with a superhero helmet. Slapped across the back of the helmet was a bumper sticker, "Keep Portland Weird."

"Hi, Sophie," I said loudly, trying to be heard above the roar of the traffic on the metal plates of the bridge.

She told me she had more information about the midwife in Pennsylvania that she'd told me about the day of Dad's funeral. "It turns out she does need help," Sophie said. I could barely hear her and began to wheel my bike with one hand. She said the woman was in legal trouble. I guessed it was one of those messy lay-midwife licensing issues and was thankful I hadn't agreed to help the woman. I already had a lead on a traveling nurse job in Pennsylvania, and my nursing license had arrived yesterday.

"I don't know what the issue is, exactly," Sophie said. "I'll let you know when I find out more. But, and this is really why I'm calling, I'm pretty sure you and Marta—the woman's name is Marta Bayer—are related somehow. At least the mutual friend we have thinks so. I wish my mother were still alive to tell us how, exactly."

"My parents didn't have any relatives in Pennsylvania," I said, but even as the words came out of my mouth, I realized what she meant. She was talking about a blood relation.

A *birth* relation.

"Not adoptive relatives, Lexie," she said, confirming my thoughts.

I banged my knee as I struggled to keep my bike upright. "What did you say?"

"She's a blood relative. Maybe a cousin. Maybe closer."

"How close?" I whispered. When I realized she hadn't heard me, I cleared my throat and asked again, louder this time.

"She's young, mid-thirties, I think, so she couldn't be your birth mother. But still . . ."

"Why does the mutual friend think we're related?"

"Well, we're not positive about this," Sophie said, "but we think that her mother, my mother, and your biological grandmother were all childhood friends in Indiana. That's what we gathered when we met Marta at a conference a few years ago, anyway."

I strained to listen as Sophie talked through the connections that had generated their theory that this Pennsylvania midwife and I could be blood relatives. Soon my head began to throb inside my helmet. Finally, I asked Sophie if I could call her back.

Even as I tucked away my phone, got back on my bike, and continued across the bridge, I knew what I was going to do. In my mind, I had already rearranged my schedule. I would fly out right away, but before starting the traveling nurse position in Philadelphia, I would help Marta for a couple of weeks in Lancaster County. The timing was perfect.

Sailing downhill through the last wisps of fog, I knew that if this Marta person did indeed turn out to be a blood relative, she would be the first direct connection to my past I had ever had.

Because of privacy issues, I couldn't show James the photos of the two babies I received that day, one being Tonya's baby that she had, in fact, kept. Sitting in my room, I looked at the photos again as I waited for him, flipping back past them in iPhoto to the previous photos too. Baby after baby. Some asleep; some bright eyed. A few yawning; a few screaming. Some with a shock of dark hair; some with no hair. Some with curly hair; some with straight. Some with fine hair so light it was transparent; two with red hair so bright it looked like flames.

I didn't have any baby pictures of myself. Not one. In fact, I only had a couple of photos from my childhood. One of me as a distant two-year-old in the garden under the windmill. Another on my first day of school. Three with Mama the year before she died. One with Dad in the orchard when I was eight. It seemed to me that my parents only used one roll of film over a span of ten years. When I started working for Sophie, I saved up and bought a camera. It was my first big purchase.

The intercom buzzed, and I pressed the button to tell James I would be right down. As I closed my laptop and gathered my things, I thought about our relationship and my urgent need to get away.

Anyone else in my position, feeling this isolated

and alone, would probably be trying to reel James in about now. So why wasn't I? If one is feeling kinless, why not start a family? I knew other adopted girls who always had to have a boyfriend, who always wanted to be needed, who always needed to be wanted. That wasn't me. Once I finally got through my ugly duckling phase and started dating, I would break up when the guy became too serious.

James told me I did that because I was protecting myself. He said this happily at the time because we had been dating for six months, and he thought I'd made it past that phase with him. He wasn't as happy now. Now he said I was pushing him away because I was afraid he would leave me, because I'd been traumatized by Dad "leaving" me. He was correct that I was pushing him away, but regardless of the reason, I was tired of his constant analysis. More than once, as he patiently outlined my actions in light of my damaged psyche, I was tempted to return the favor, telling him that his compulsion to practice psychology without a license was likely a natural defense mechanism against his own latent abandonment issues. Take that, Dr. James Nolan!

I met him on the sidewalk under a flowering cherry tree that rained pink petals on his head. He smiled as he brushed them out of his curls, but it was a melancholy smile with a hint of fear.

We walked around my neighborhood, strolling along the sidewalks. I stopped to window-shop; James grew restless and shuffled his feet. I was hoping to eat at the Asian Bistro on Twenty-third Avenue, but we ended up at Pepinos for their five-dollar special. James refused to let me pay when we went out.

"Tell me about Pennsylvania," he said, unpeeling the foil from around his burrito. He knew I'd applied for the traveling nurse position; he knew I wanted to look for my birth family. In fact, I'd already posted my name, date of birth, and place of birth on the Pennsylvania adoption search site, hoping that someone from my family was looking for me too.

I told him about Sophie's phone call and my change of plans. "I'll work for a week or two in Lancaster County and then go to Philadelphia for four months." Chances were, even if I put the house and orchard on the market before I left, it wouldn't sell before harvest. I had to be back in case anything went wrong.

"Four months? Lexie, that's a long time."

I nodded.

"When were you going to tell me?"

"Nothing's certain yet. It's just looking like this might be how it all plays out."

As he tilted his head, a pained expression passed over his face.

I rushed on, telling him the midwife worked with the Amish.

"So you're going to be an Amish midwife?"

I smiled, thinking how odd that sounded. "Well,

technically I'll be a midwife *to* the Amish. But just for a week or two."

"Is Marta Amish?

"No."

"But she's related to you?"

"Yes."

"Okay, I think I've got it," he said, smiling. Then he turned serious and added, "Are you really ready to find your birth family?" He'd broached the subject in the last couple of weeks, but I had evaded discussing it.

"You're the one who's wanted me to deal with my abandonment and attachment issues for the last year," I said.

"But that's different than looking for your birth family."

"I just thought, you know, since Dad's passed on that it was a good time to look. I won't be hurting anyone's feelings."

"You were worried about that?"

"Or stirring up trouble."

"Trouble for whom?"

"It's not like I want a relationship with anyone, James. I just want to know . . .." my voice trailed off.

"Know what?"

I shrugged.

"What if it's not what you expected?"

"Well, I don't really expect anything in particular," I lied. "So I think I'm good."

He folded his hands on the table. "Wow."

We stared at each other for a moment.

Then he said, "What does this mean for us?"

"What do you mean?"

"Do you want to take a break while you're gone?"

I slumped against the bench seat. "Actually . . ." I'd been mulling this over and over. "I do. But just while I'm gone."

He drew in a deep breath. He let it out slowly and then said, "Is this a break as in 'so you can see other people'?"

I wanted to laugh. Who would I want to see? "No," I answered quickly. "Just a break so I can focus, think about my birth family, think about finding the information I deserve to know. I need to devote all of my energies to that, not to us." He looked at me intently, as if to say he hadn't realized that our relationship was such hard work. We both knew it wasn't. I dropped my gaze, adding, "But we can still talk. And text. Right? Occasionally?"

"Sure." His voice was chilly.

My heart constricted. He was my best friend. What was I doing? I took my camera from my bag and snapped a picture of him, trying to lighten the moment.

"Stop." He hated it when I did that. "You won't be able to use that with the Amish."

"Says who?" I put the camera on the table.

"The Amish."

"What? Besides dressing as though it's two

centuries ago, they don't believe in cameras?" I was especially sensitive to the dressing issue, even though my experience had been closer to dressing as if it were the 1930s. Still, I knew how humiliating it could be.

"I've been reading up on Pennsylvania." James stood and put our garbage on the tray. "Apparently, they put photos in the category of graven images."

"Oh." Exodus. The Ten Commandments. *Thou shalt not make unto thee any graven image.* Thank goodness I'd only be in Amish country for a week or two. What would I do without my camera?

Darkness had fallen as we left the restaurant. "What do you hope to find?" he asked, stepping around me so he was walking closest to the street. Dad used to always do the same thing. I was pretty sure James learned it from Dad.

"Didn't you already ask me that?"

"You didn't answer."

"My story," I said. "The truth."

James whistled. "That's a pretty tall order."

He didn't come up to my apartment. As always, he would only do so if there was someone else with us. I'm pretty sure he wasn't as chaste in high school.

I leaned in for a hug, but instead of embracing me, he grabbed my upper arms, pulled me toward him, and kissed me fiercely on the mouth. When the kiss was over, he straightened his arms, released his grip, and took a step back without a word.

My face burning with heat, my heart pounding so loudly I was sure he could hear it, I whispered my goodbye. Then I turned and unlocked the door of the building, stepped inside, and pulled it closed behind me. Climbing up the stairs, touching my lips as I went, I wondered what, exactly, I thought I was doing. When I reached my apartment, I switched on the living room lamp and stopped at the window. James stood on the sidewalk, just as he always did, waiting to make sure I was safe. Our eyes locked and held for a long moment, and then he walked away.

A coldness welled up inside of me. I turned on all the lights and my stereo. What was I hoping for? I shivered as I sank down onto my white couch. I wanted to *know* why they gave me up. And I hoped, once they got a good look at me, that they would be sorry they did. But I couldn't tell James that. I could barely tell myself. My cell phone rang. I fished it out of my pocket, hoping it wasn't work. I was shocked to register that I wanted it to be James. I hadn't felt this with other guys when I'd said I needed "a break."

It wasn't work or James. It was Sophie.

"I talked with Marta directly," she said, without saying as much as hello. "And it's worse than I was led to believe. She's being investigated for manslaughter."

"Yikes." I'd need to rethink going to help her. This was serious.

"Two counts. Mother and baby. And the partner in her practice retired to Kentucky right before this happened and can't come back because of health problems."

"Oh no."

"But it won't be any of your concern after all." Sophie paused.

I grabbed a couch pillow and held it against my chest, trying to follow what she was saying.

"She doesn't want you to come. She wouldn't tell me why. Just that some family matters are better left alone. She said to tell you thanks but no thanks. That was all."

SIX

After that conversation I left for Pennsylvania as soon as I could. I zipped down to Aurora and finished a few last-minute tasks at Dad's, and then I draped sheets over all his furniture. It seemed like the thing to do when closing up a house. I'd already hired a caretaker for the orchard, a man in the community who was working for another orchardist. He assured me he would spray for eastern filbert blight in a week or two and continue to prune the trees as he had time. Soon he would need to groom and level the ground, preparing it for harvest. He came highly recommended, and I trusted he would follow through with caring for the orchard.

I constantly thought about what I should do with the house and property and decided to at least gather information. A place with a thirty-acre orchard and another ninety acres in farmland had sold the year before at a good price, but I only had forty acres.

The Realtor, Darci, seemed to appreciate the house, which had been built in 1911. It was a simple structure with three bedrooms and one bath, but all of the old-growth woodwork was original and in good condition, as was the banister along the stairs. She said new window coverings and paint would help but weren't necessary. She didn't say anything about the kitchen, which needed to be redone, but the right buyers could do it themselves. She did notice where the foundation was crumbling and said that would probably be a costly and necessary fix.

I told her I was just gathering information, that I wanted to know how much the property was worth and then I would decide about putting it on the market.

She'd already run some comps and quoted me a price. It was less than what I had anticipated, but Dad's mortgage had long been paid off, and all I had to worry about were taxes. If all went well, the hazelnut crop was usually good, although there were certainly years when it hadn't been thanks to freak storms, droughts, blights, and the other everyday threats farmers have to deal with. The sale of the hazelnuts would more than cover the costs of maintaining the place, so I didn't have to be in a rush.

I told her I would think about it and maybe get back to her in a month or two, but probably not until I returned in the fall. She made sure she had my cell number, and I took her card.

I walked through the orchard then, one last time. The loamy scent of earth and rain rose up from the soft ground. The buds were just beginning to swell and the branches created the structure of a tunnel over my head. In another month it would be a canopy of shady leaves. A movement danced ahead at the end of the row, and for a minute I thought, *Dad!* The image in my mind was clear—his weathered face, white hair, straw hat, and rounded-toe boots. But when I reached the last row, I found the shadow of a poplar tree manipulated by the breeze. I turned and walked back to the house, seeing myself among the trunks of the trees. A toddler squatting on the ground, playing with a stick. A five-year-old with my doll. An eight-year-old mourning Mama. A ten-year-old climbing a tree. A teenager helping Dad with the pruning, fertilizing, and spraying. I'd grown up in this orchard. It was home as much as the house.

I stopped by the coffee shop to check the adoption site I'd registered on but found no response. I definitely needed more information to conduct a thorough search—such as the name of my birth mother. I'd tried a couple of weeks ago to get a copy of my original birth certificate with no success. I was told that without the consent of my birth mother, the certificate couldn't be released, but once I was in Pennsylvania I could go to the department of vital records in Harrisburg and make another request. Even if they blacked out the name of my birth mother, I still wanted a copy. Maybe they would leave my original name intact. I figured it couldn't hurt to ask again—and maybe someone would take pity on me if I did it in person.

Over the last two weeks I had called all seven of the hospitals I'd located on the Internet in Montgomery County, but every one of the records department clerks I spoke with said they couldn't help me. My biological mom could make a request, but I couldn't. I also came across a Pennsylvania law that allowed adoptees to write a letter to the court of the county they were born in, requesting information about one's biological parents. Although I couldn't request their identities, my letter would be put in a file and matched to them if they wrote in requesting information about me. It was a gamble, but I'd already sent off the letter, even though I only had my birth date, county of birth, and the fact that my grandmother was "tall." It was a pretty pitiful collection of information to start a search on. But now there was Marta . . .

As I left Aurora, driving through town for a last look at the old buildings and antique shops, I felt optimistic. I was going to Pennsylvania. I was much, much closer to learning my story than I had ever been.

My hope and optimism lasted until I reached my apartment and began packing, trying to decide what I should take on my adventure. I picked up the last photo I had of Dad from my dresser. As I focused on his angelic curls and faded blue eyes, grief descended again and I cried for him, for Mama, for my birth mother. For all my losses. Then I placed the photo in my suitcase and packed the wooden box and my baby quilt in a carry-on bag and felt a little better.

As cruel as it seems, I asked James to drive me to the airport. And, of course, he did, looking as if he hadn't slept all week.

I hadn't given him all the details about the reason for my sudden departure, but it seemed someone else had—someone named Sophie. "You're setting yourself up," he said.

"For?"

"Rejection." His voice was deep.

"I never expected acceptance. Just information." I knew I was lying. Of course they would accept me once they met me. They would love me and regret ever giving me up.

"I really have a bad feeling about this, Lex." For being so smart, James relied a lot on his feelings. That was probably why he was so comfortable with the world of psychobabble. He should have become a surgeon—a heart surgeon or a brain surgeon—

instead of tormenting me with his feelings.

"How about if I come with you?"

I reminded him that we were taking "a break."

He turned his twenty-year-old car with the duct-taped bumper onto Airport Way. "I don't care. I could come right now."

I shook my head. "You have school. And you don't have the money."

"I can withdraw this term," he said. "I'll use my tuition."

I looked straight ahead. "That would be ridiculous." He would be done after the coming fall term, and then he'd move back to Aurora or at least close by and open a practice and go on short-term mission trips to third world countries instead of ever taking a proper vacation. And he'd never have any money because he'd do half his work pro bono, and the money he did make would go toward his mission trips. I clutched my Coach purse tightly, which, after worrying about it, James hadn't even noticed. For all he knew, I'd bought it at a yard sale.

"Lex, you should wait. We could go together this summer. Or you could wait and go to Philadelphia in two weeks." He braked for a hotel shuttle that slowed ahead of us. "But don't go crashing in on someone who doesn't want you."

I didn't answer. *Someone who doesn't want you.* The words stung but not badly enough to stop me. I was going to go find this woman named Marta.

Sophie had given me the address of her office. I already had it programmed into my GPS. Obviously she was related to me. Why else would she have told me not to come?

I pulled my camera from my bag. He grimaced. I slipped it back inside.

"Thanks for giving me a ride," I said as he pulled up in front of the airline door.

"Are you flying into Harrisburg?"

"Philly," I said, liking the way it sounded. *Philly. Philly. Philly.*

He put the car in park and beat me to the trunk. "Call when you get there," he said.

I nodded.

"And come home if it's too weird."

Home. I wanted to cry.

He hugged me quickly.

Surprised that I wished he'd kissed me, I said, "I'll be back," trying to sound upbeat.

His eyes darkened and then he smiled just a little. His lips moved but I couldn't hear his words.

"Pardon?"

"We'll see," he said.

He left me and walked around the car to the driver's side. I rolled my bag toward the revolving door and stepped through, my Coach tote over one shoulder and the cloth bag with the carved box and my baby quilt over the other. When I turned my head, his old beater was easing its way into the stream of traffic.

Eight hours later I rolled the same bag through the Philly airport, imagining Mama and Dad there twenty-six years before with me in their arms. For the first time I wondered why they met my birth grandmother at the airport and not a lawyer's office or her home or their hotel. Where did they stay when they were in Philly? Downtown? Out by the airport? How long were they here? Did they see the Liberty Bell? Independence Hall? Who held me on the plane?

An hour later I was sailing past the Philly suburbs, heading west on the Expressway in my Ford Taurus rental car. Patches of snow, with blooming crocuses poking out, hid in the shadows at the side of the road. The river to my right ran high and muddy. The bare trees along the hillsides hung heavy with vines.

"I'm in Pennsylvania," I said out loud, and then I wondered if Dad would have come with me if I had asked him to a couple of years ago. I turned up the radio to drown out my sorrow.

I'd decided to get off of the Turnpike at Valley Forge and take the back roads the rest of the way to Lancaster County because one of the guidebooks I'd skimmed had recommended it for a better view of the countryside. At first that made for slower going, with far more lights and traffic than countryside, but eventually the congestion lessened and the scenery improved.

I nearly slammed on my brakes at the sight of my first Amish farm. A man drove a team of four mules pulling a plow through a field. He wore a straw hat, cobalt blue shirt, black trousers, and suspenders. A woman and a girl, both wearing dresses out of the same blue material, black aprons, and white bonnets, bent low in a garden plot. Two barefoot toddlers played in the grass. As the scene went by, a line full of clothes flapped in the breeze, the white house and barn both backdrops to the colorful display. Soon I was driving forty miles an hour with a line of cars behind me. The farms were immaculate. Tidy fields. Trimmed lawns that looked robust even in the early spring. Gardens newly planted or being planted. White houses and barns. Clothesline after clothesline, usually strung by sturdy pulleys from the back porch to the barn, of solid-color shirts and dresses in maroon, forest green, and blue. And black pants, aprons, and white bonnets. It dawned on me it was Monday. Wash day. Tuesday was ironing and gardening. Wednesday was sewing and Thursday market day. Friday was cleaning, Saturday baking, and Sunday the day of rest. It was all spelled out in the song "Here We Go Around the Mulberry Bush," which I use to chant. I was seven before I realized Mama ran our house on the same schedule.

The matching clothes, immaculate farms, and whitewashed houses and barns had a stylized appeal. I liked things uniform. It appealed to, as

James would say, my sterile sense of decor. But none of it was sterile. It was all very much alive. The people. The scents wafting through my open window. The vibrant colors snapping on the lines. It was orderly and patterned and obviously it all had a purpose.

Ahead, along the busy road, a group of children walked, swinging black lunch pails that looked like what Dad used to take out to the orchard when he was too busy to come in for lunch. Two girls skipped. A boy kicked a rock. The car behind me honked. My speed had dropped to thirty. I accelerated before a corner, and then this time I did slam on my brakes. Ahead, in the middle of the lane, was a black buggy with a gray roof and an orange caution triangle on the back. Now I had an excuse to go slow.

I passed a one-room school where a young woman swept the porch. Walking ahead was a mother holding a young child's hand with a baby on her hip. As I passed them, I saw a boy on a bicycle-like scooter weaving along the shoulder of the road. The car behind me passed my rental and the carriage, which, surprisingly, clipped along at twenty-five miles an hour. Ahead was a straight stretch, so I passed the carriage too, glancing over my shoulder. A woman drove it, the strings of her heart-shaped bonnet blowing away from her face. I looked in my rearview mirror. The horse was beyond beautiful. It moved like a racehorse, its lean muscles rippling with graceful determination.

A few minutes later I was in the town of Strasburg—that or I'd time-warped to 1776. I half expected to see George Washington walk out of one of the brick houses. The entire town looked like a Federalist colony with building after building of red brick with white trim and black shutters. At the crossroads in the middle of town, an Amish carriage waited for the traffic signal to change. Ahead a gaggle of Amish girls stood on the sidewalk. It was hard for me to tell, but they looked as if they were fifteen or so. They had gathered around a boy with a tray in his hand. The sign on the shop above the teenagers read "Pretzels." There were several other shops in the little downtown district. The village was obviously a tourist draw.

A few miles out of town, the GPS instructed me to turn left onto a one-lane country road. Green pastures rolled up the sloping hillside. A flock of sheep dotted one side. A McMansion topped the hill to the left. I sighed. Obviously not everyone in these parts was Amish. But next was an Amish farm. A woman stood on the back porch, working the pulley to bring in the line of clothes.

I maneuvered a turn in the road and immediately faced a covered bridge. I eased the car over it, holding my breath as I hoped it would hold, hoped the GPS wasn't sending me on a road meant only for carriages. The wooden planks groaned as the car bumped back onto the asphalt. At the top of the hill, the GPS instructed me to turn left onto a highway.

"Arriving at your destination," the digitized voice immediately declared. To the right was a brick cottage and to the side of it an outbuilding. My heart began to pound. I turned the car into the driveway and parked, my hands frozen on the steering wheel.

At the least I hoped to be able to meet Marta, to see if she looked anything like me. But honestly, I also hoped she would change her mind and tell me everything she knew about my story. By tomorrow I'd be in Harrisburg searching for my original birth certificate. Or meeting my birth parents.

I forced my right hand to put the car in park and turn off the ignition. Then I slowly opened the door, patting the pocket of my jacket to make sure my camera was where it belonged. Maybe I could sneak a photo of her—especially if she did look like me. As I stepped from the car, the front door to the cottage opened and a young woman stepped out. She wore a cap over auburn hair, and for a second I thought she was Amish. Obviously the GPS hadn't done its job. But then I noted her dress—a yellow print. The cap had a round shape to the back, not heart-shaped like the Amish woman's in the buggy. Maybe this young woman was Mennonite. Whatever she was, she was far too young to be Marta. She was younger than I.

"Since when have you been driving?" she said,

breaking out into a smile as she came down the steps.

I turned my head, half expecting to see someone behind me. I turned back toward the girl just in time to watch her freeze at the bottom step, her smile disappearing just as quickly as it had come. "Oh, sorry. I thought you were someone else."

She moved backward and up one step.

"Who? Who did you think I was?" I asked, moving forward, trying to sound far more matter of fact than I felt. She thought I was someone else, someone who looked like me.

"Uh . . . no one. Never mind. Can I help you?"

I hesitated. A boy, maybe twelve or thirteen, clad in navy blue slacks and a short-sleeved checked shirt, banged through the door. As he gaped at me for a moment, I thought I could see the flash of recognition in his eyes as well, but then it passed. Standing a head shorter than the girl, who wasn't that tall herself, he simply acknowledged me with a nod, flicking impatiently at blond bangs that fell across his forehead.

"Hi," I said. "Did you think I was someone else too?"

He shrugged but didn't reply.

My head spun. These kids could be relatives of mine. Had they seen in me the familiar features of someone else in the family? An aunt or a cousin? Did they recognize the unique tilt of my nose or the shape of my face from other relatives? I wanted to ask, to press it further, but at the moment they both seemed very unsure and nearly ready to bolt back inside.

I cleared my throat, trying to rein in my emotions and focus. "I'm looking for Marta. I heard she needed an assistant." I felt bad, just a little, about my white lie.

The girl turned to the boy. "Did Mom say anything to you about needing help?"

He shrugged again. "No, but it makes sense, considering—"

The girl gave him a "Be quiet *now*" look. Then she turned back to me. "She's not here."

"Could I wait?"

The untied ribbons of her cap danced along her collarbone as the girl shook her head. She looked to be about fifteen, but her confident demeanor made her seem older.

"I'd wait in the car." I spoke quickly. "Or I could come back in a little while."

"How about if you leave your number? She can call if she chooses." The girl squared her shoulders.

I tried not to let my disappointment show. There was no way Marta would call me. I decided to stall. "Sure. Do you have a piece of paper and a pen?"

The girl nudged the boy and he disappeared inside, leaving the two of us to stare at each other. He reappeared with the paper and pen, and I jotted down my cell number, writing beside it, *Pennsylvania Certified Nurse-Midwife.* I handed the girl the pen and paper. "Maybe you could put in a good word for me." I hoped my voice sounded light but she frowned. "Thank you," I said, wishing I were better at small talk.

They both said goodbye, grimly, as I climbed into the car. I waved as I started the engine. Slowly I shifted into reverse and then looked behind me. A black Toyota Camry pulled in to my right. A woman popped out of the car. She wore a cap and black cape and completely ignored me.

The girl said something to her and pointed toward my rental. The woman shook her head. I turned off the engine and climbed from the car. "Marta," I said, stepping toward her. "I'm Lexie."

Her eyes met mine, and in the space of a single moment I thought I could detect an entire parade of emotions rippling across her features: shock, joy, sorrow, fear. Blinking, she seemed to struggle for control. Then, slowly, all signs of emotion disappeared from her face, her eyes turning cold and hard. Watching her, I realized it was almost as if somewhere inside she had slammed shut a solid steel door.

Taking a deep breath, Marta crossed her arms at her chest and spoke, her voice betraying nothing. "I told Sophie to tell you not to come."

"But I need to talk with you. I have a few questions—"

"I can't answer them." She dropped her hands to the sides of her body. There, in the late afternoon light, I couldn't help but search for some sign of a physical resemblance between us. I was tall and slender and blond, and she was short and round, the hair under the cap on her head a sandy gray.

"Sophie said—" I began, but she cut me off with a wave of her hand.

"I'm sorry. You have to go. Now."

Turning around, she began moving toward a small outbuilding. As she went I heard a buzzing, and then she reached under her cape, pulled out a cell phone, and answered it.

"Yes?" she snapped, pressing the phone to her ear.

I remained where I was, completely still and totally stunned. The boy and girl stared. The sunny afternoon took on a chill, and it was then I realized I was standing in the shadow of a row of fir trees. The shadow extended to the cottage as well, though not as far as the nearby chicken coop or the small outbuilding that Marta was marching toward now. Taking a step forward, I focused on that outbuilding and read the sign on its door: *Marta Bayer, Midwife.* That must be her office.

Oddly, she didn't go inside but instead paused at the doorway, still speaking into the phone. Her tone sounded shrill, but I couldn't make out the words. Was she talking about me? Telling some long-lost relative of mine to sound the warning that I had come to town despite having been told to stay away?

"You should leave," the girl whispered.

"I really need to talk to your mom." I kept my eyes and ears focused on Marta.

"I've never seen her like this." The girl's voice was confidential now, and that caught me by surprise. A door banged to my left, and I looked over my shoulder to see that the boy had gone back into the cottage.

Still outside by the other building, Marta began pacing back and forth as she talked. I took another step forward, listening intently.

"That's ridiculous," she said. "I've done nothing wrong." She stopped and turned her head upward, toward the treetops. "But I have a mother in labor."

Ah. So she wasn't talking about me, but about her suspension.

"Maybe I can help out," I said softly to the girl.

"I doubt it."

I looked again at the short, plump figure in the distance, her face still tilted upward. Was she praying? Cursing? Hoping? "How long will the suspension last?" She closed her eyes. "I see. Well, keep me posted." At that, she took the phone from her ear, pressed a button, and continued the rest of the way into the building without so much as a backward glance.

"Please leave," the girl pleaded again once the door had fallen shut behind her mother.

I shook my head. Moving slowly to give Marta time to cool off, I started toward the little building myself. When I reached the door, I gave it a single rap, twisted the knob, and opened it. As I stepped inside, I half expected to find Marta in the midst of some sort of tantrum, maybe tossing around some files, or upending a chair. Instead, she was sitting at a plain wooden desk, talking into the phone again, her eyes on a chart that was open in front of her. From her much gentler tones, I decided that this conversation was with someone different than the last.

"How far apart?" she asked. Whatever answer she got, it wasn't one she wanted. "All right. Hold on a moment, please." Grimly, Marta put a hand on the receiver, lowered the phone from her mouth, and looked up at me. I thought she was going to speak, but instead our eyes simply held for a long moment. Finally she raised the phone to her mouth again and spoke. "I'll be right there," she said. Then, still maintaining our gaze, she added, "Oh, and I'll be bringing an assistant with me."

SEVEN

Marta drove. I didn't speak. I barely breathed. I was ecstatic that she'd asked me to help her and still afraid she'd change her mind. It was the foot-in-the-door that I needed. She sped over the covered bridge and up the lane. At the main highway she turned left, away from Strasburg. I took my camera from my pocket. The highway dipped and ahead, in a valley that looked as if it had been scooped out of the landscape, were lush fields and an occasional stand of trees. White houses and barns and outbuildings peppered the scene. I snapped a couple of photos and then kept my nose to the window. Finally, I asked the status of the mother in labor.

"Thirty-six years old and it's her seventh child," Marta said. "Barbara's been in labor for a couple of hours."

Five minutes later, Marta pulled into the drive-way of a farmhouse and stopped behind a carriage parked in front of a garage.

"*Mamm*'s in the kitchen," an Amish girl called out to Marta, swinging a basket of eggs. She wore a black apron over a magenta dress. A younger boy, maybe eight, ran past her, toward the barn. "Go help *Daed*. The milking can't wait!" she called after him. The boy made a face and zigzagged on his way.

Marta grabbed a black bag from her trunk and strode toward the back door after the girl. I followed, suddenly feeling as if it were my first birth, not baby number 256.

A refrigerator stood just inside the kitchen door. I did a double take. So much for what I'd heard about the Amish not having electricity. The mother, who didn't look much older than I, stood at the counter next to a stove. "I was just hoping to get dinner in the oven," she said. She had on a white nightgown and a cap and smiled as Marta introduced me, but then she held up her hand and leaned against the counter. Marta stepped behind her and rubbed her back. I decided now wasn't the time to ask about the kitchen appliances.

"That," Barbara said after a minute, "was a hard one." She turned toward her daughter. "Start the potatoes. But first go tell your *daed* it's time." A toddler, a little boy with a bowl-shaped haircut, slid into the kitchen in his stocking feet and wrapped his arms around his mother's legs. She said something to him that I couldn't understand, in Pennsylvania Dutch I assumed. One of the words sounded like *wunderbar*, which was on the very short list of the German words I remembered. It meant "wonderful," "fantastic." Maybe she was telling the toddler he was wonderful or that the baby would be. Then she turned to the girl. "Take Samuel with you out to the barn."

"*Ya, Mamm.*" The girl exhaled—the sigh of exasperated big sisters heard round the world—and then took her little brother's hand.

"*Danke.*"

I followed Marta and Barbara down the hall until Marta pointed toward the bathroom and I stepped in, taking off my jacket and pushing up the sleeves of my shirt. The bathroom had granite countertops. Add that to the stove and refrigerator in the kitchen. There were no outlets or switches and no light fixture above my head. I scrubbed at the sink, using handmade soap.

By the time I reached the bedroom, my hands held high, ready for a pair of gloves, Marta was praying silently with Barbara, who was on the bed. I stopped in the doorway until Marta whispered, "Amen." Then she told Barbara I would actually catch the baby.

"Oh, Marta, what is going on?"

"It's just a requirement for a short time. That's all."

Barbara would have done fine with neither Marta nor me there. In fact, baby number 256, or baby number one in Pennsylvania, came so quickly that Barbara's husband didn't arrive in time for the birth, only to cut the cord. "Well, Barbie," he sighed, bending to kiss her after he was done. "That's what happens when the baby decides to come at milking time." He was a big man with a scraggly beard and square fingernails.

Two hours later we had completely cleaned up, including starting a cold soak of sheets, towels, and baby blankets in the utility sink. Marta and I left just as two of Barbara's sisters arrived. They said they would start the laundry in the pneumatic washing machine and hang it out to dry before they went home. I didn't ask anyone to email me a photo, nor did I ask if I could take one. I took one last, long look at the baby, committing the image of his perfectly round face and dark hair to my memory.

Sleep deprivation and culture shock—including

an Amish woman with the nickname Barbie, a bathroom nicer than mine, and appliances— caught up with me, and I dozed on the way back to Marta's cottage. When she pulled into the driveway I opened my eyes, feeling woozy.

"You can stay here tonight," she said. "We'll talk in the morning."

I pulled my suitcase from my trunk as she marched to her office, her black cape flapping behind her.

I knocked softly on the cottage door and then louder. No one answered. Maybe the kids had gone somewhere or were already in bed. I grasped the knob just as the door flew open, yanking me inside. The girl stood in front of me, a wooden spoon in one hand. She had an apron on now, and her head covering had come unpinned on one side and was a little askew.

"Your mom said I could spend the night," I said.

She stepped aside and motioned me in, but instead of saying anything to me she yelled, "Zed, get off the computer and tidy up your room."

I stood in a small living room with a woodstove, a sofa, and a single wingback chair.

A groan came from off to my right—the dining area. "Can't she sleep in your room?" Zed sat at a desk, his eyes fixed on a screen.

"No!"

"How about the alcove?" Clearly Zed was trying to come up with a workable solution that didn't involve him having to get up from the computer.

The girl looked me up and down. "How tired are you?"

"Exhausted," I answered.

"Follow me."

She led the way up a narrow open staircase, and I followed, lugging my suitcase, which housed my small travel collection of worldly possessions, up each step. My Coach bag kept falling off my shoulder and down my arm, banging against my knee. When the girl reached the top of the landing, she pointed to the right. "That's Mom's room." The door was closed. "Here's the bathroom." She pointed across the hall and then to the left. "And my room." Her door was closed too. "You can sleep here." She turned and behind her was a little alcove with a single bed.

"Thank you." I stepped around her and wedged my suitcase into the little space next to the wall, wondering if it would be better if I found a hotel. Or a bed-and-breakfast in Strasburg. But then I'd have even fewer opportunities to get information out of Marta.

"Do you have anything else in your car that you need?" the girl asked.

I started to shake my head but stopped. "Well, there is a carry-on bag in the trunk. Maybe I shouldn't leave it out there." I doubted if crime was much of a problem in the area, but I didn't want to risk it.

The girl held out her hand. "I'll go get it for you."

I handed her my keys and collapsed on the bed. When she returned she cleared her throat, and I forced my eyes open.

"I'm Ella." She stood over me, the box in her hand.

I smiled. She looked like an Ella. "I'm Lexie," I answered.

"I know. You said that when you first got here."

"You're right," I answered, propping myself up on my elbow.

"It fell out of the bag." She held the wooden box out to me. "I've seen this house before."

"Where?" I asked, sitting up all the way and taking the box.

She placed the bag on the end of the bed and tilted her head. "I'm trying to remember." She wrinkled her cute little nose. "It's not coming to me, but it will." She turned to go and then said over her shoulder, "We'll eat in fifteen minutes."

"Wait. I have a question."

She stopped.

"At the Amish birth tonight, the family had a stove and a fridge."

"So?"

"I thought the Amish didn't use electricity."

"They use other kinds of power," she said. "Those were probably propane."

"Oh." I vaguely recalled that the Mennonites in Kansas related to Mama didn't use electricity. I'd been thankful growing up that we weren't part of that group. But I didn't remember that they used other sources of power. I reclined back on the bed, my arm draped over the box.

When I awoke the next morning, I still had my jacket on and my baby quilt was tucked under my chin. The box was gone.

EIGHT

According to my nearly dead cell phone, it was eight thirty. I'd had a text from James late last night asking if I had arrived, but I hadn't heard the message alert, let alone replied. I answered now with a quick *Yep*, realizing as I hit "send" that it was only five thirty in Oregon, and it would be a while before he got it.

I slipped out of bed, noting that the house was completely quiet, and searched the little alcove for the box and then retreated to the first floor. It was immaculate. Not a dirty dish in the sink. Not a book or a pair of shoes or a stack of papers anywhere. There was a note in block letters on the table. *Oatmeal in the cupboard, milk in the fridge. Have a good day! Love, Ella.* And at the bottom of the note, in different handwriting: *Prenatal @ 10 a.m. Be ready by 9:15.* It wasn't signed, but I was sure it was from Marta. For a woman who didn't want to talk with me when I arrived, she certainly seemed to be taking me for granted now. Fortunately for her I was desperate enough for answers to put up with her brusqueness.

I searched the kitchen for coffee but couldn't find a drop or bag or bean. I did find tea bags and made the strongest cup of tea I could manage. I drank it as I walked through the cottage, searching for my box. Zed's room was off the kitchen, but I didn't go in. Back upstairs, Ella's door was open a crack and I pushed it gently. She had a twin bed with a solid blue cover, a straight-back chair, a small desk, and a dresser. The walls were bare. At the far end was a row of pegs with dresses and a coat hanging on them. The box wasn't anywhere visible. Maybe Marta had taken it.

I eased open her door. The sunlight came in through the window over the bed, which was covered with a plump comforter and a simple quilt folded at the end. A kerosene lamp sat on the table beside the bed. The walls were completely bare, and there were no knickknacks or photos on the dresser, but there was a photo by her bed of what appeared to be a much younger Marta and a handsome early twenties–age man with blond hair.

"What do you need?"

I spun around.

Marta faced me. She wore the same dress as yesterday and the same head covering.

My face reddened and I stuttered. "I had a box with me last night." I took a deep breath. "It's gone."

"No. It's under your bed. I put there for safekeeping." She reached around me and pulled the door to her room shut.

"Oh." I stepped toward the alcove. "Thank you."

"We'll leave in fifteen minutes," she said.

"I'll get a quick shower and be ready."

As she descended the stairs, I knelt down and with my hand searched the area under the bed. The box was there. Perfectly safe.

"Sally Gundy is a new mom," Marta said. We were in her car again, making our way along a country road. "Her family is in Ohio, but she and her husband live here with his kin on their property."

Kin. I shivered from my still damp hair. "How far along is she?" I held my camera in my hand.

"Six months."

"Any complications?"

Marta shook her head.

We rode in silence past a one-room schoolhouse. A group of children played baseball in the yard, including girls in their dresses. "Is that an elementary school?" I asked, snapping a photo of the children's backs as we passed by.

"It goes through the eighth grade," Marta answered.

"Are there Mennonite schools?"

"Yes."

"Do Ella and Zed go to one?"

Marta glanced at me quickly and then back at

the road. "No. They attend public schools."

"How old are they?"

"Almost sixteen and thirteen." These terse answers weren't going to get me anywhere close to the information I really wanted.

"Ella seems quite capable," I said.

"She's had to be."

I'd already noted Marta didn't wear a wedding ring, though that didn't necessarily mean much. Most Mennonites back home didn't wear wedding rings, so maybe the ones around here didn't either. Regardless, I could see no reason to believe she had a husband, not even one who was away on business or something. Other than the photo in the bedroom, there were no signs of a man having been around at all, and there had been no mention by the kids of a father, past or present. It was pretty clear Marta was a single mother.

She turned onto a narrow lane. A moment later a compound of buildings appeared in front of us. Two of them were houses, and then there was a large warehouse behind them and some other outbuildings, including a barn. At least ten carriages were parked along the side of the warehouse in a row, and in the adjacent pasture a large group of horses grazed. Lined along the warehouse were sections of picket fences and planters shaped like wheelbarrows, and one even had a wooden windmill attached to it.

I slipped my camera into my bag and followed

Marta across the lawn toward the smaller house. An older woman on the porch of the larger house called out, and Marta waved and said, "How are you this morning, Alice?"

"Gut," the woman answered. Her hair had the blondish-white look of an aging redhead, and she wore a freshly starched cap. Two little girls, likely twins, slipped out the screen door onto the porch. They both wore miniature caps with thin brown braids poking out from underneath.

"Mammi," one of them cried happily. The older woman turned and scooped up the child into her arms, and then she faced us again and smiled.

In the distance the sound of a saw hummed. A sliding door to the warehouse was open, and a cloud of sawdust billowed out.

Marta picked up her pace as she marched across the lawn. "Sally and her husband, John, live out here in the smaller house," she explained, "though it's going to get a bit tight once the baby comes."

"Is that John's mother?" I asked, nodding my head back toward the big house.

"No. His *grossmammi.*" Marta exhaled. "Grandmother, I mean."

I glanced back to see the older woman now sitting on the steps, an apple-cheeked twin on each side of her. Another woman appeared at the back door and called out toward the warehouse. "Ezra Gundy!"

The sawing stopped, and the cloud of sawdust began to dissipate.

"Ezra!" the woman yelled again, louder this time. "You didn't finish your chores!"

"That's Nancy," Marta whispered.

Nancy was noticeably shorter than Alice, her hair reddish with streaks of gray. A second later, when a young man strode through the open door of the warehouse, she put her hands on her hips and scowled.

The teen wasn't wearing a hat, and his bright red hair seemed to be trimmed into stylish layers, not cut in a bowl shape like the other Amish males I'd seen, both young and old. At least his outfit of black trousers, a forest green shirt, and suspenders seemed Amish enough.

As I watched, Nancy marched down the back steps and strode briskly across the yard, her dress flapping in the breeze behind her as she went. When she reached the boy, she spoke in hushed, stern tones. Though I didn't know either of them, I had to stifle a smile. My father had been slow to anger, but I always knew I was in for it when he summoned me using both first and last name.

"Come on." Marta grabbed my arm, and we hurried up the steps of the little house.

Inside, two young women with dark hair and pale blue eyes, both in full Amish garb, greeted us. The older one was about nineteen, and Marta introduced her as Sally, the patient we had come to see, though the bulge at her belly barely showed in her loose-fitting dress. Sally offered to make tea, which we declined, and the younger one offered to take our coats. She looked a lot like Sally, so I wasn't surprised when she was introduced as the younger sister, Ruth.

As Ruth hung our coats on pegs near the door, Sally gestured toward the living room, where sunshine poured down through skylights, illuminating the small sitting area. Marta and I sat side by side on a couch that had been covered with a bedspread and tucked in at the cushions. Sally and Ruth joined us on nearby chairs. Looking again at the younger one, who seemed to be about the age of a high school freshman, I asked if she had the day off.

"Off?"

"From school."

She covered her mouth with her hand and giggled.

"Ruth is fifteen," Sally explained. "She's been out of school for nearly two years now."

My surprise must have shown on my face, because beside me Marta clicked her tongue scornfully and said, "You don't know much about the Amish, do you?"

Sally smiled. "We only go through the eighth grade."

I couldn't help but bristle. "No need for girls to be educated?"

"Not just the girls," Marta said. "The boys too."

"But why?"

"It's about pride, mostly, which they feel often

tends to go hand in hand with being overeducated," Marta explained.

"Ya," Sally agreed, nodding. "The eighth grade is sufficient."

"But there's still so much to learn!"

Sally shrugged. "The learning doesn't end, just the schooling. We're always learning. From our parents, the community, maybe even as an apprentice or through a correspondence course. In many different ways. Even from siblings." She looked over at her sister and winked. "Right, Ruth?"

The girl giggled again, nodding. She was just so young!

"Are you studying a trade?" I asked her.

Ruth smiled behind her hand and glanced at her older sister.

"Ruth is spending the spring and summer working with me." Sally sat straight.

"Like a mother's helper?"

Ruth nodded.

A shout from the yard caught her attention, and she stood and drifted toward the window.

"What is going on?" Sally asked, also standing.

"Ezra is in trouble again," the girl said, moving to the side of the window, a twinkle in her eye.

Sally sat back down. "I am afraid that Ezra's behavior has been quite amusing for my sister."

"I imagine so," Marta said, and then she turned the conversation away from Ezra and onto Sally's pregnancy, asking first about her diet. I couldn't fathom diet was a problem for most Amish women.

Sally was six months along and planned to give birth here in the *Daadi Haus*. Her mother would come from Ohio after the baby was born and stay a few days, but she had seven children who were still at home and could only spare a short time. That was one of the reasons Ruth had come to stay.

"Will you be delivering my baby?" Sally asked Marta.

"Of course."

"But I heard you weren't able to deliver Barbara's last night—"

"Oh, that was a minor complication. And Lexie was able to help me with that."

Sally stood. "Well, God provided, didn't He?" She called Ruth away from the window and asked her to go tell John that Marta had arrived. Then to Marta she said, "He wants to listen to the baby's heart too." We followed her down the hall as the front door banged shut. "I already ordered the birth kit you recommended. It arrived last week." Sally was so small that from behind she looked about the same age as Ruth.

It seemed as if the little house had recently been remodeled, and the scent of fresh paint lingered. The simple molding was all new and unmarred, but as we turned into the bedroom it was obvious that all the furniture was hand-me-downs. An antique bed, barely a double, nearly filled the small room. On the nightstand was a cardboard box, most likely the birthing kit. It would contain a plastic sheet, bed pads, a delivery towel, and other items. Some of Sophie's clients ordered kits for each of their births, while others gathered the items themselves. I was sure it was the same with the Amish.

As I took Sally's blood pressure, a young man bounded into the room, his hat in his hand. His hair wasn't as bright as Ezra's, but it was definitely red, as was his sparsely grown beard. His brown eyes were cast down, and he nodded shyly to Marta and barely met my eyes as I was introduced. He sat on the edge of the bed beside Sally as she stretched out on the bed. I recorded her blood pressure in her chart. It was 110/80. *Perfect.*

"Did Ruth come back with you?" Sally asked her husband.

His voice had a lilt to it and was barely audible. "She's sitting on the porch with *Mammi.*"

"Most likely spying on Ezra."

John blushed.

Marta handed me the fetoscope, and I found the baby's galloping heartbeat. I let John listen first and he grinned. Sally patiently waited her turn and then squeezed her husband's hand as she listened. Next I measured Sally's fundal height and recorded it in her chart too. Twenty-five centimeters. For looking so small she was right on target for twenty-four weeks.

John excused himself and said he needed to return to work. Sally sat up, refastened the pins at her waist, and then walked with us out to the porch. "Ruth," she called. "It's time to bake our bread."

The girl waved goodbye to Alice and the twins and skipped across the grass. She smiled at me as she passed.

Alice stood, lifting one of the little girls onto her hip. She had a black cape over her dress now. The sun passed behind a cloud and the air grew chilly.

"Marta," she said. "Did Will reach you?" The woman's voice was soft and calm, but something about her tone gave me pause, especially when I noticed Marta's subtle but distinct reaction, her face paling at the mere mention of the man's name. "He had a question for you."

Marta shook her head, her eyes giving away nothing. She opened her mouth to speak, and then she hesitated, handing me her bag and motioning toward her car. Apparently, I was being dismissed just as things were getting interesting.

"I'm seeing Hannah tomorrow," Marta said to Alice, turning her back to me as I moved away. "Will he be working at the greenhouses?"

"Yes, he should be."

"Good. I will speak to him then." Though her words sounded matter-of-fact, the tone of her voice was anything but. "How is Christy doing?"

I walked slowly, listening.

"She's here today and resting inside," I thought I heard Alice reply.

Their voices fading out of my hearing range, I

gave up and climbed into Marta's car. I set her bag at my feet, wondering what all of that was about, and stared at the large white house in front of me. The windows were new and energy efficient. Four Adirondack chairs graced the wide front porch. A flat of germaniums sat on the front steps, ready to be planted. One of the twins ran to the edge of the porch and smiled at me. I waved and then made a silly face. She made one back, and we both laughed. A moment later Marta appeared.

She started the car in silence. As she pulled out of the lane, we passed Ezra, who was standing off to the right with a shovel in his hand. Beside him was a small tree ready to be planted. He was still hatless, and the sleeves of his shirt were pushed haphazardly up to his elbows. He caught my eye and grinned, exuding an instant charm. Though I was at least six years older than he, I had the distinct feeling that he was trying to flirt with me. I smiled back and then turned away, suppressing a laugh. He was trouble, that one.

"Who is Will?" I asked Marta, not surprised when she didn't answer. Instead, she focused on her driving as she headed toward the highway. Her face was still so pale, I decided not to press the issue for now.

Glancing back toward the busy farm we had just left, I thought about all of the various people I had met there. Amish families were so large I wondered how anyone could keep track of their names, much less their various connections. "So tell me again how everyone here is related," I said.

Settling back in her seat and relaxing her grip on the wheel, Marta explained that Alice was the mother of Nancy, who was married to Benjamin. "Alice and her husband didn't have any sons, so their son-in-law runs the family business." She went on to say that Nancy and Benjamin had one daughter and three sons. The youngest, Ezra, was the red-headed boy we had watched getting scolded. The middle boy, John, was married to Sally, the patient we had come to see.

"Their daughter, Hannah, is also a patient of mine. She's due in May. I have an appointment with her in just a couple of days."

"What about their oldest son? What's his name?"

Marta hesitated a moment before answering. "Their oldest son is Will. He runs a large nursery," she said evenly, and then she pursed her lips tightly, as if she had said too much.

"So who is Christy?" I asked, changing tactics.

Marta grunted at my persistence. "The twins' older sister. She's eleven."

"And they are the children of . . . ?"

"Will. They are the children of Will. But they stay with their Aunty Hannah—or sometimes Nancy and Alice—during the day."

"Why? Where's their mother?"

Marta simply shook her head, and I could tell by the set of her chin and the grip of her hands on the steering wheel that this line of conversation was closed. She put on her blinker, slowed, and turned onto a wider road. Frustrated, I stared out of my window and counted to ten, knowing I should hold my tongue.

"So you grew up Mennonite?" Marta asked finally, breaking the silence.

"I did."

"General Conference, then? Certainly not Old Order."

"There aren't any Old Order left in Oregon," I said, explaining that the Old Order Mennonites came in the late 1880s but over time joined less conservative groups. "The little church I grew up in is now independent." Though that church was by no means liberal, I'm sure *I* appeared to be, especially to Marta. Especially because I no longer even identified myself as Mennonite.

"How is it you know nothing about the Amish?" she asked.

I bristled. "Why should I? There hasn't been an Amish settlement in our region for more than a hundred years." I didn't add that in Pennsylvania, the Amish and Mennonites may have been closely linked, but in Oregon they weren't. In fact, no one there ever gave the Amish much thought unless something was in the media.

"You really didn't know that in the Amish culture children stop school at the eighth grade?"

I shook my head, certain I would have remembered that. "So the school we passed is it? A one-room, eighth-grade education?"

Marta nodded. Despite Sally's earlier assurance that the learning continued beyond school, I couldn't help but think that the Mennonites were looking better all the time.

My own experience with the Mennonite religion started out well. How could it have not? I was one of the few children at my parents' church, and I was adored. I also got the faith part early in life. Jesus loved me. God had a plan for my life. I wanted to be baptized as soon as I could. I even wanted to wear the head covering at first, although my motivation was—back then—that I wanted to wear what Mama had worn.

But the older I grew and the more I read, the more confused I became. Congregations had split over whether or not to have Sunday school and whether baptism should be by immersion or pouring water over the head. Head coverings varied from group to group. In middle school wearing a head covering set me apart, but by high school I felt like an outcast. How could wearing pants instead of a skirt seem immodest? Did it really matter whether a woman's head covering was heart shaped or round? Had God stopped listening to my prayers once I put mine away all together?

The Anabaptist movement, of which the Amish, Mennonites, Brethren, Dunkers, Hutterites, Apostolics, and more all belonged, had begun in Switzerland in the 1500s during the Protestant Reformation. The word Anabaptist meant, literally, "second baptism" and had risen out of the belief that God intended baptism to be not for infants but instead for adults, ones who made a conscious decision to follow Christ. This position put them in direct violation of State dictates, but they stood firm on their belief, which resulted in imprisonment, martyrdom, and finally a movement that grew strong and spread and splintered and spread some more.

I sighed. If Marta expected me to learn all the ins and outs of the Amish—which I surmised probably made the Mennonites look simple by comparison—she was crazy.

"The Amish really are a separate culture, one you need to be willing to understand," she said.

"Yeah, well . . ." I turned my head toward Marta and caught her looking at me.

She turned her eyes back to the road. "I'm serious, Lexie, when you work with the Amish you need—"

"Whoa!" Work with the Amish? Where did she get off assuming I was sticking around? "Listen, Marta, it's been fun helping you out and all, but what I really need is some information. Sophie thinks you know about my biological family. She thinks . . . she believes you and I might even be related." I didn't add that judging by hers and Ella's reaction when they met me yesterday, I was feeling pretty sure of that myself.

"How long can you stay?" she asked.

"I have a job waiting for me in Philly—"

"That's not what I asked," Marta interrupted, turning onto the highway. "How long can you stay?"

"I have a job waiting for me in Philly," I repeated, my jaw clenched, "and it starts in two weeks. But there are other things I need to do first, Marta. Like find a place to live. Map out my route to the hospital." Get to the department of vital records in Harrisburg and convince someone to let me see my birth certificate.

"I don't think I'll need you after a day or two. You'll be free to go then."

News flash, Miss Marta: *I'm free to go right now.* What gave her the right to be so presumptuous? I leaned my head back against the seat, wondering how this woman could be so sweet and tender with her patients and so sour with me.

"How's this?" I said finally. "I'll give you the two days *if* you'll talk to me."

Marta missed the turn to her house. "About?" I'd never known a midwife to play dumb before.

"My birth family."

She didn't respond, so after a moment, I decided to throw out a question or two to show her what I meant. Holding back on the big guns for now, I decided that my first one should be relatively benign. "Tell me what you know about the house on my box. Ella said she's seen it before."

Marta's knuckles tightened on the steering

wheel. "Ella's a fanciful girl. She probably saw something like it in a picture book from the library."

So much for holding back. I decided to go with the big guns after all.

"Who was my mother?" I demanded.

Nothing.

"Who was my father?" I persisted.

No answer.

"Are you and I related? If so, how? Are you my cousin? My aunt? My sister?"

She began shaking her head from side to side. "This is exactly why I didn't want you here," she hissed.

"But this is exactly why I came. I'll stay and help, but only if you'll answer my questions."

She sighed loudly and then grew silent. That silence hung heavily in the air between us.

"Lexie," she whispered finally, "it's not my place."

I looked away, surprised by the hot, sudden tears that sprung into my eyes. Not *Lexie, I don't know anything,* or *Lexie, it's none of your business,* but *Lexie, it's not my place.*

I didn't know how to reply to that. If not her place, then whose?

More tears came, and as I wiped them away in frustration, I turned toward her, ready to let her have it. Instead, I was shocked to see a single tear sliding down her check. She quickly swiped it away, composed herself, and offered no explanation. I could see she was feeling ambivalent. I was asking for information, and though she may have said no with her words, something in her wanted to say yes—or at least maybe.

Maybe, if she got to know me better first. *Maybe*, if I helped her out with her patients. *Maybe*, if we started on safer ground.

Marta turned onto a four-lane highway and accelerated. The green sign that whizzed by read "Willow Street Pike," and it seemed as if she were driving with intention, that she had a destination in mind.

So did I. In that moment, looking out at the beautiful countryside as we flew past, resolve solidified in my chest like a fist. I had come to this place to find my story. One way or another, I'd get there, no matter what it would take.

For the moment, I just wanted to know where Marta was bringing me. "Where are we?"

"Lancaster. I have another prenatal visit."

"I thought we were in Lancaster—"

"County. Now we're going to the city."

I tried to imagine the two Amish families I'd met living in a city. The road descended into a gully, and as we came out of it, parklike lawns appeared to the right with large brick houses, one after the other, at the crest of the hill. They were Federalist-style buildings, and again I felt as though I'd arrived on a living history set.

The brick houses soon gave way to row houses,

one after the other, divided by alleyways and punctuated by occasional graffiti. Every couple of blocks there was a small market with a group of people gathered in front of it. A few old people sat on the stoops or in cheap plastic chairs on small porches. It was all very urban looking. I couldn't fathom an Amish family living here.

Marta turned down an alley. "Our next visit is with Esther, who is twenty-seven. Second pregnancy. She's at thirty-seven weeks. Her husband is a student at Lancaster Seminary."

I raised my eyebrows. That certainly didn't fit in with an eighth-grade education.

Marta parked at the end of the alley, and I followed her up the cracked cement steps to a row house. After rapping sharply on the weathered door, she glanced my way, the hint of a smile beginning to show on her face.

NINE

"Come in!"

I could hear the woman's accented voice before I saw her. The door swung open wider and a little boy pushed against it. His skin was dark and his hair curly. In two chubby hands he held an orange that he dropped onto the stoop when he saw Marta. He raised his arms and she lifted him up in a swoop of motion, her cape flapping a little as she did. I bent down and retrieved the orange, and as I handed it over I couldn't help but notice that Marta was smiling broadly for the first time since I met her.

"Hello, Simon!" she gushed to the boy.

The woman greeted Marta with a kiss, and then she took my hand that wasn't lugging Marta's medical kit and kissed my cheek as well, her belly bumping against me. "Welcome," she said.

Marta introduced me to mother and child both, bouncing the little boy in her arms. I took his hand and shook it, and he smiled but then turned his face away, rubbing it against Marta's shoulder.

"We go to the same church as Marta and her family," Esther said. "Simon is quite fond of Ella and Zed too." Except for her bulging midsection, Esther was thin, wearing sweatpants, a long-sleeve cotton T-shirt, and slippers. She was tall, her hair cropped close to her head.

Simon began to squirm and Marta lowered him to the floor. He scurried across the floor to a desk, the orange tucked under one arm, and reached up to a keyboard with his other hand. Esther hurried behind him and gently pulled him away and pushed the desk chair into place, scooting back the keyboard as she did. "He likes to help me with my work," she said, laughing. "I edit research papers, that sort of thing." She shrugged, as if to say at least it pays the bills.

I placed the medical bag beside the couch.

"How long have you lived in Lancaster?"

"Two years now. We go home in May."

"And home is?"

"Ethiopia," Esther answered. "That's where we first met Marta and Ella and Zed."

I glanced at Marta, who explained, "We were on a mission trip with our church. I helped at a clinic, and Ella and Zed cared for children in an orphanage."

I knew my eyes grew wide. I couldn't imagine Marta in Africa, her children in tow.

"The church has been sponsoring us here," Esther added. "It's just a few blocks away."

Marta directed the conversation to the pregnancy, and she pulled her tape measure out of the bag and gave it to Simon. He began to measure his mother's belly, crosswise. "Let me help," I said with a laugh.

Esther asked me where I was from and was fascinated to hear about Oregon. She was pleased to find out that I'd grown up in a Christian home and said how blessed I was. She hadn't come to know the Lord until she was eighteen.

As we were getting ready to leave, Esther asked Marta to pray for the baby and the labor. All of us, including Simon, bowed our heads and Marta said a sweet prayer, asking the Lord to strengthen Esther for her delivery and to protect her and the baby. After she finished Esther hugged her, clearly touched.

Next she hugged me. "Will I see you again?" she asked as we started down the steps.

"No," Marta said, answering for me. "Lexie is

going to Philadelphia to work at a hospital."

I wished Esther well.

"I thought you were a midwife to the Amish," I said once we had settled back in the car.

"I am."

"But not exclusively?"

"Of course not. Amish. Mennonite. I had a Pakistani mom last year. And a few *Englisch* too."

"Englisch?" I asked, trying not to mock her accent on the word.

"That's what the Amish call the non-Amish. People use my services for lots of reasons. Maybe they don't have insurance and can't afford hospitals. Maybe they just want a home birth. It varies."

Just like Sophie's practice back home.

"How about your church? Is it Old Order or General Conference?"

Marta sighed. "It's somewhere in between." Then she said, "I need to make a stop on my way home. I hope you don't mind."

I shrugged, surprised she had bothered to ask.

A few minutes later, we were in the heart of downtown Lancaster. Marta parked in front of the courthouse, which was a relatively new big brick building with daffodils blooming in planters along the entrance. We got out of the car, and I followed her across the street to an old brick building that had a sign by the door that read "Attorneys at Law." I expected Marta to send me back to the car, but she didn't, so I followed her into the building and through a foyer with a marble floor and then up a staircase. I was thinking that the lawyer was probably more than Marta could afford, but by the time we reached her office on the third floor next to the janitor's closet, I'd changed my mind. Marta knocked on the door that had *Connie Stanton, Attorney* etched into the glass. After a long couple of minutes, the door swung open and an older woman stood in front of us. She had salt-and-pepper hair swept into a messy French roll and was wearing a wrinkled navy suit.

"Oh, Marta," she said as if coming out of a daze. "It's you." She gestured for us to come into her office. There was no waiting room, just her desk and four folding chairs. Marta and I sat while the woman stood behind her desk. "What can I help you with?" she asked.

"The order. You were going to see about having it waived," Marta said.

"Well." Connie pawed through a stack of papers on her cluttered desk as she spoke. "I made a few phone calls." She picked up a document. "The judge won't lift it. I'm going to file a formal appeal, but don't hold your breath."

"But I've done nothing wrong," Marta said.

"Yes, yes. And that's what the grand jury will realize next week." Connie slipped on a pair of reading glasses and looked at the paper in her hand. She hadn't made eye contact with Marta since we'd arrived. "In the meantime, you absolutely cannot practice. If you do, you'll be in contempt of court."

"What exactly does not practicing mean?" I asked, glancing at Marta.

The attorney took off her reading glasses and looked at me and then at Marta. "Whom did you say this is?"

"A colleague."

"Oh. Well, not practicing means not practicing. No exams. No deliveries. No postpartum care. Nada."

I glanced at Marta. She was rubbing her forehead with her fingertips.

"I will call if I can get the judge to lift the order," Connie said. "In the meantime, no practicing. Have your colleague do all of the care—and I mean all of it. This is a small community, and you know how people talk."

Marta slumped against her chair.

"We should meet again soon. The DA is waiting for the autopsy report before the grand jury meets. By the way, you have the right to testify when they do."

"What would be the point?" Marta asked.

Connie put on her reading glasses again and pulled out a notebook.

"Exactly. I don't think it would do any good. I think the testimony from Lydia's husband will be far more convincing. Especially if the grand jury started asking you a lot of questions." She opened a notebook. "Let's see . . . Friday afternoon is open. Four o'clock. Come see me then."

Marta nodded and stood. I joined her. I said, "Nice to meet you," to the attorney as I followed Marta out the door. She was silent as we descended the staircase. When we reached the sidewalk, I asked her how she found Connie Stanton. The woman hadn't impressed me at all.

"One of the men in my congregation arranged it. She's representing me for free."

"Oh," was all I could manage. Things didn't look good for Marta. Not at all.

As she pulled onto the street and then made a quick turn, I silently rehearsed ways to use this situation to my advantage, to force her to tell me what she knew about my birth family. I could threaten to tell the judge that, technically, she'd practiced both last night and this morning. I could go to the local newspaper about her case. I could report her to the state of Pennsylvania.

When we stopped at a red light, I was distracted from such thoughts when, much to my surprise, a man on the street pointed at us and laughed. The woman with him lifted her camera to her face.

"What's up with them?" I asked.

"They think I'm Amish and find it funny that I'm driving a car."

"Does this happen a lot?"

"Often enough. Some tourists eventually figure out that there's a difference between the ways

Amish and Mennonites dress—like the shape of the head covering, the fabric of the dresses—but obviously not these two."

Soon we were passing the row houses again in downtown Lancaster, the clusters of men gathered in front of convenient stores, the old women sitting and smoking on their stoops.

"Thank you for helping me this afternoon. I appreciate it." Marta's words hung in the air between us. When she glanced my way, I thought I could detect a small crack in her armor, a little hint of vulnerability in her expression. "Obviously, though," she added, "I still need your help."

"Obviously."

"I know your job in Philadelphia will be starting soon." When I didn't reply, she added, "I'd like you to stay. If you won't, can you at least do the prenatal appointments this afternoon while I make some phone calls to try to find someone else?"

Avoiding her question for the moment, I asked why some of her prenatal visits were in homes and some in her office.

"It all depends. I'll go to the home if it's a hardship for the mother to come to me. Or if it's a family I've worked with for years. Otherwise, I encourage the women to come to the office." She drove in silence for a few more minutes and then said, "I can't pay much—not what you're worth. And I can't give you the information you think you want. You'll understand someday—probably when you're older—that some things in life are really better left alone."

"The people who say that are usually the ones who already have the information they need."

"Be that as it may . . ." she replied, her voice trailing off.

And with that, we had reached an impasse. Though I was no longer concocting schemes in my head for forcing her hand, there was no way I would do this without the promise of something tangible in return.

"How about an exchange? I'll give you one day of help if you'll answer one question, a new one," I said. And before she could object, I added, "One that it *is* your place to say."

She waited, unwilling to make that deal until the question itself had been thrown out on the table. Fine. Turning in my seat, I studied her face for a long moment and then spoke.

"Marta, have you ever seen me before? In person?"

"What? Of course. Just yesterday—"

"I'm talking about *before*. When I was a baby, a newborn. Before I was sent away from my birth family, clear to the other side of the country. Did you ever see me? Did you ever touch my curls or let me wrap my tiny fingers around one of yours or look deep into my eyes and wonder who I might grow up to be?"

She didn't answer at first, but the agony that

began to contort her features told me what I wanted to know. I had already guessed her age and done the math, realizing that she had been a preteen when I was born—old enough to fall in love with the infant of a sibling or a cousin or a neighbor. Old enough to remember, all these years later, when that infant had been whisked away, never to return.

"Right now I'm not asking you the name of my mother or father," I persisted. "I'm not asking you to spill someone else's deep, dark secrets. All I'm asking is for you to tell me about *you*. When you were a little girl. Did you ever see me in person?"

Though we were nearly back to the house by that point, Marta surprised me by putting on her blinker and pulling over to the side of the road. After the car bumped to a halt she put it in park, buried her face in her hands, and quietly wept. Between her problems with work and my persistence in my quest, I realized the poor thing was practically at the breaking point. As tough as she seemed, I had to wonder if she was in danger of being pushed too far, if in fact my presence here had already put more on her than she was capable of handling right now.

A part of me wanted to reach out to her, to pat her on the shoulder, to tell her never mind, that it was okay, that I would stay and help regardless. But instead I sat perfectly still and waited to see what would happen next. Finally, she dug a tissue from her pocket, wiped her eyes, and blew her nose. When she had managed to pull herself together, she sat back against the seat and looked off into the distance, sorrow radiating from her red, swollen eyes.

"The first time I held you, I counted your toes," she whispered, which brought on a fresh round of sobs.

The first time I held you, I counted your toes.

As she sat next to me and cried, I blinked away tears of my own and tried to let her words sink in. She had known me. She remembered. It wasn't much, but it was a piece of my story.

Heart suddenly surging with joy, I waited for more, but after she pulled herself together again, she put the car in drive and eased back onto the road. Obviously, that was all she was going to give me for now. I decided that was okay. If nothing else was forthcoming from her right away, I could always try more deliberately later with Ella.

"Thank you for telling me that," I said, reaching out to give her arm a squeeze. "In exchange, I believe you just earned yourself one day's worth of midwifery."

The next afternoon, after I finished the last prenatal appointment of the day, I filed the folder into the metal cabinet and then turned my attention to Marta's desk. There were a couple of handouts on nutrition and exercise that clients hadn't taken with them. I filed those too and then locked the cabinet, slipping the key into the pocket of my jeans.

It had rained all afternoon, but as I closed the door to the little office the drops stopped, and a few rays of sunshine streamed down through the pine trees. Marta had instructed me to tell all of her clients that she was taking the day off; that was all I was to say—nothing more and nothing less. It was clear, both yesterday afternoon and today, from the responses of the women, that Marta had never taken a day off before.

I turned the knob to the front door of the cottage, eased the door open slowly, and stepped inside.

"Loser." Ella stood in the archway to the dining room, her left hand making an "L" with her thumb and index finger, scowling at Zed, who sat at the desk, his hands on the keyboard of the computer. "You can't do this to me. I have homework to do!"

"What do you think I'm doing?" Zed didn't look at her as he spoke but kept his gaze ahead on the screen and his hands on the keyboard.

"I think you're instant messaging."

He turned toward her, his face red. "Yeah, I am, about *homework.*" He flicked his bangs away from his forehead.

"I wish mom had never brought you here!" Ella planted hands on her hips.

I cleared my throat.

She didn't budge. "She should have left you in the middle of the road or wherever it was she found you."

"Young lady! We do *not* talk that way in this

house!" The voice was Marta's, shouting from the top of the staircase.

"I was just kidding." Ella sounded as though she were eight.

"Come up here *right now*."

Zed watched Ella retreat and then his gaze fell on me. "I was adopted," he said matter-of-factly.

"Really?" I never would have guessed. He and Ella looked as much alike as any siblings. She had auburn hair and his was blond, but they both had a slight build and wiry limbs.

"Really."

"Me too," I told him, nearly tripping over the words. "I was adopted too."

His eyes glued to the screen, he merely nodded in reply.

"Does Ella talk like that often?"

He shook his head. "She didn't mean anything."

I stepped into the dining room. He *was* instant messaging. "I have a laptop," I said. "Any chance I could get online here?"

"We don't have wireless. Sorry."

I shrugged. "Just thought I'd ask." I'd be gone before long anyway.

Ella clomped down the stairs and spun around into the archway, her forefinger and thumb at her forehead again. "I'm grounded from the computer, so now I can't do my homework at all." Zed ignored her, and she took a few steps back and grabbed her coat. "I'm going for a walk."

The front door banged and she was gone.

I stepped back into the archway and looked toward the stairs. "What has your mom been doing all afternoon?" I should give her a report about the women.

Zed still didn't look up from the screen as he said, "Making phone calls in her room. She said not to disturb her."

"Oh." I turned toward the window. Ella stood under the stand of pine trees. "I think I'll go for a walk too," I said, grabbing my jacket. I'd give Marta an update in a little while.

As the front door closed behind me, Ella turned and scowled. She had a cell phone in her hand and was texting. "Mind if I join you?" I asked.

She shrugged, flipping the phone shut and putting it in her apron pocket.

"Are you really going on a walk?" I asked.

She shrugged again.

"I'd love a closer look at the covered bridge."

She took off, the ties of her bonnet blowing over her shoulder, and her open wool coat flapping with each step. I hurried to catch up with her, trying to come up with a couple of questions to get her talking.

I wasn't successful with a conversation starter and defaulted to asking her about school. "What grade are you in?"

"Tenth."

"Is the school close by?"

She shook her head. I was matching her stride for stride now, thanks to my long legs, along the shoulder of the roadway.

"It's about a fifteen-minute bus ride."

"And it's public, right?" I asked as we dashed across the highway.

She nodded.

"Are there other Mennonites there?"

"Some," she answered.

I wondered if she felt as conspicuous in her Mennonite garb as I had when I was her age. Today she wore a blue print dress with a pointy collar and cuffs at the end of the sleeves. It was modest and obviously homemade.

"Do you like to sew?" I asked.

She shrugged again. "It's not my favorite thing."

"Your clothes—your mom and Zed's too. Are they hand sewn?" I couldn't tell if Marta's dresses were manufactured or not. They had buttons, and her cape was definitely store bought or else made by a good tailor.

Ella laughed. "No. We buy ready-made when we can. I sewed this for my 4-H class." She tugged on the skirt of her dress. "Some of the women in our church sew, but we don't have time. Not with Mom's work and school and keeping up the place. It's not like there are a lot of rules or anything. Not at the church we go to."

An Amish buggy passed by on the other side of the road. The man driving it gave a little wave and

Ella acknowledged him, but I couldn't tell whether she actually knew him or not. We walked in silence for a few minutes, and then I asked, softly, "How old was Zed when he was adopted?"

"I shouldn't have said that." Ella pursed her lips together. She was practically marching now.

I kept my mouth shut. The road dipped down a little, and I could see the covered bridge in the distance. I took my camera from my pocket and zoomed in, snapping a photo.

"He was a baby. I was almost three. I remember when Mom brought him home. He was so tiny. I used to hold his bottle for him." She paused. "That's all I know. Everything's hush-hush around here. You wouldn't believe what my mom won't talk about."

Yes, Ella, actually I would.

"Such as?"

Ella grimaced. "Well, that's the thing when someone won't talk. You really have no idea what they're keeping from you." She continued. "Everyone thought Mom was crazy for adopting Zed, her being a single mom and all. I think maybe that made her hesitate to talk about things."

A sheepish look flashed across her features.

"What?"

She laughed. "I guess the less I knew, the less everyone else knew. I was kind of a gabby little girl."

I smiled. That wasn't hard to imagine. "When

did your mom become a single mother?" I hoped it was okay for me to ask that.

"My dad left sometime after she brought Zed home."

My heart fell a little. "Oh, Ella. I'm sorry."

"It was a long time ago."

For a fifteen-year-old it was a long time ago. But not for Marta.

"My mother died when I was eight. I still think about her every day."

"That's just it," Ella said. "I don't even remember my dad. For some reason I can remember Zed as a baby, but I have no memories of my father."

I inhaled. That would be so hard. "So he was Mennonite?" I ventured, assuming Marta had married into the faith.

"Originally, he was Lutheran—something like that. Protestant, anyway. Both Mom and he became Mennonite when they married."

"Do you know why he left?" I knew I was pushing, that I probably shouldn't be asking a teenager such a personal question.

She rolled her eyes. "Of course not. Oh, you know, Mom said, 'Life just got to be too much for him.' Things like that, but I really have no idea."

We reached the bridge and walked to the middle over the creaking weathered boards and stopped. The rafters of the bridge were bare too, unlike the whitewashed sides.

The creek was high and the water flowed around

the rocks. Downstream at the bend, on a rise, was an Amish farmhouse.

Ella kept talking. "I don't even know my dad's parents. I'm guessing they're dead."

"How about your mom's family?" I hoped my voice was steady.

"I have an aunt and uncle. And a cousin." She stole a glance at me. "And there's *Mammi*."

"Mammi?"

"My grandma. She's Amish, so we use their word for it."

"She's Amish?" I repeated dumbly. "Your grandmother is Amish?" Was it possible that I had been born into an Amish family?

"Yeah, Mom grew up Amish too, though she never joined the church. Why? What's the big deal?"

"Nothing," I said, trying not to look so stunned. "It's just funny that your mom didn't tell me when we were at the Amish houses."

"Well, now you know how little Mom actually says to anyone. She lives in baby land. Nothing else matters."

"Did your mom tell you I'm adopted?"

"Of course not." Ella held her hands up as if she'd just proved her point.

"I'm from Oregon, but I was born in Pennsylvania."

"And you've come to find your birth family?" Ella's eyes brightened.

"Partly," I said, trying not to sound desperate.

"That's what I would do. I'm always telling Zed I'll help him find his birth family, but he's not interested." Ella tugged on the ribbons of her bonnet. "I could help you."

My heart lifted. "We'll see." I didn't want to sound too enthusiastic about what I'd been fishing for all along.

"Where would we start?"

"The house on the carved box. Do you remember where you saw it before?"

She clasped her hands together. "It was a long time ago."

"And?" I prompted her.

"I'm not sure now. It may have been a picture that I saw."

"Oh." I'd been thinking she'd seen the actual house. Maybe Marta was right about Ella being fanciful.

She nodded. A pigeon flew down from the rafters of the bridge and I startled. Ella laughed.

"Tell me more about your aunt and uncle," I said, trying to keep her talking, hoping she would be more forthcoming than her mother had been.

"Klara and Alexander?"

My head jerked to attention. "Alexander?" I whispered.

She nodded.

His name was Alexander. My name was Alexandra. Could there be a connection between our names, between us?

"I'd like to go see them," I said, my voice sounding strange to my own ears. Suddenly, I felt cold inside.

Ella shook her head. "My cousin and *Mammi* have been sick. Besides, if you think Mom is closed mouth, you should see my Aunt Klara. She hardly opens her lips to say hello, let alone talk about anything important."

"What about your Uncle Alexander. What is he like?"

"Nice, but he pretty much defers to Aunt Klara. Everyone's afraid of her." Ella paused. "Except Mom's not. And I guess I'm not really either." She poked her head farther over the rail and then said, "We should head back. I still need to make dinner."

As we stepped off the bridge and back onto the pavement, Ella asked, "What do you know about your birth family?"

"Nothing," I answered. "The box is all I have. And a letter written in German."

"No birth certificate?"

"Just my Oregon one."

"Your adoptive parents never gave you any more information?"

I shook my head. "There's just one more thing I've been told." I paused. Did I have any right to bring Ella into this further?

"Which is?"

We were on the shoulder of the lane and a big

pickup truck rounded the corner toward us. We both leaped to the side.

"Lexie?" Ella looked straight at me.

"A friend in Oregon thinks your mom knows my biological family." I exhaled slowly. "In fact, this friend Sophie thinks your mom might even be related to me."

Ella grabbed my hand and squeezed it as we stepped back onto the lane. "Really?"

I nodded.

She put her hand to her mouth.

"What?" I asked.

She shook her head. "Nothing. It's just that—" She dropped my hand. "I think I know where to start." She started running, her black shoes slapping against the asphalt.

"Ella!" I called out, following her. "Wait!" I didn't want her confronting her mother. I wanted to be the one to do that. But though I was in good shape, I was no match for this fifteen-year-old wearing a dress and bonnet, flying up the hill.

TEN

I muttered "Alexandra and Alexander" as I came through the door. Was Ella's uncle my father? If so, and if he had sired me out of wedlock, that could explain Marta's determination not to answer any of my questions.

Not my place to talk about it indeed.

I heard voices upstairs but couldn't make out the words. Zed was still on the computer. "How's it going?" I asked.

"Fine." He met my gaze for half a second and then turned away.

I sat down on the sofa in the living room, feeling that I should go pack my things—surely Marta had found someone else to help her—but I didn't want to go upstairs. A few minutes later Marta called down the stairs. "Zed, go feed the chickens."

He bounded right up and hurried out the back door.

Marta started down the stairs, followed by Ella. "You had no right," she said, her hazel eyes piercing through me, "to share your desires to find your birth family with my daughter."

I stood and held up both hands, wishing she would calm down and wondering how to make her understand that I was willing to do whatever it would take to get to the truth.

"Ella says she has an uncle named Alexander," I explained evenly. "My name is Alexandra."

Marta took the last step. "And you think the similarity between your name and his are more than coincidental?"

I nodded.

"You're being *fanciful* and you are setting a bad example for my children." She stood a foot from me now.

146

Ella stepped out from behind her mother and said, "But Lexie has a right—"

"Right?" Marta turned toward her daughter. "Is this what they teach you in public school? Rights instead of respect? Questioning instead of trusting?" Her intensity landed on me again. "Lexie, please tell me, did you have parents who loved you?"

I nodded.

"And cared for you?"

I nodded again.

"And raised you to know the Lord?"

I nodded a third time.

"And it seems as if they recognized your gifts and encouraged your education and dreams."

"Yes," I said.

"Then why are you here?" she asked.

"B-because," I stammered, "I want my story."

Her eyes drilled me as she exhaled. Then she stepped past me, brushing my arm as she did.

I stood in the middle of the living room, feeling both guilty and frustrated. Ella collapsed onto the bottom stair.

Marta was in the kitchen now. I heard a pot bang against the stove and the water run. Then the phone rang once.

I sank down onto the sofa and listened to the snippets of conversation I could make out.

"How far apart are the contractions?" Then, "Oh, dear." A minute later, she said, "I'm sending my assistant."

I groaned.

In no time Marta was standing over me. "I have a mother in labor. And she's a month early."

"And?"

"And Ella will go with you to show you the way." She turned toward her daughter, who was still sitting on the bottom step. "Sleep if the labor goes on, though, so you'll be ready for school tomorrow."

Ella nodded.

"They'll feed you there," Marta said to both of us. "I'll get my bag for you out of the office." I followed her out the door, heart pounding in sudden anger, wondering if the woman had always been a bully or if that was something she had grown into. Between working the rest of yesterday afternoon and all of today, we both knew that I had already given her the time she'd earned and then some.

Zed stepped out of the chicken coop and watched as Ella, with her algebra book and notebook in her hand, opened the door of my rental and climbed into the car. Marta rushed out from the office and tried to hand me her bag. Instead of taking it, however, I simply folded my arms across my chest and leaned against the car.

"Lexie?"

"Sorry, Marta, but you know very well that the time you earned is up. The good news is that another answer will gain you another day."

The woman looked at me aghast, as if I had

sprung a second head. I felt a brief flush of shame, disliking myself in this moment almost as much as I disliked her. Behind her, Zed seemed thrilled, as though he might start snickering.

"Here, I'll make it easier for you," I said. "You choose the question this time. Whatever you want—a name, an address, a memory. Your choice."

Our eyes met and held, a game of chicken I would not lose. Finally, slowly, Marta broke our gaze and looked downward, color flushing her cheeks.

"I can't," she whispered.

Suddenly I felt guilt well up within me, and I faltered. A mother had gone into labor. I had no right to make her suffer because of my problems. I was just about to give in and take the bag, get in the car, and head out on the call without another word when suddenly Marta again met my eyes and uttered a single word that sounded like "Amielbach."

She cleared her throat and tried again. "Fine. When you get back, I will tell you what I know about Amielbach."

I wanted to drive my victory home, to say something sharp, such as "See? That wasn't so hard now, was it?" But I could see from the expression on her face that it was, indeed, quite hard.

"Thank you," I said softly instead, reaching for the bag and taking it from her, feeling humbled.

Moments later Ella and I were crossing the covered bridge on our way to the Stoltz farm.

• • •

Not only was Sharon Stoltz early, but she was also spotting. I was afraid she had placenta previa, which meant there was no way she should deliver at home. I called 911, and once the ambulance arrived I took a disappointed Ella back to her house and then plugged Lancaster General into my GPS and headed off to meet Sharon and her husband, Levi, at the hospital.

They were still in the ER when I arrived, and a young doctor was with them. I introduced myself, emphasizing that I was a nurse-midwife, not a lay-midwife as he had probably assumed.

"And you practice around here?" he asked. He had dark hair, striking blue eyes, and a square chin. He was also tall, much taller than I was.

I explained I was from Oregon and had been helping Marta Bayer out yesterday and today.

"Marta Bayer. Isn't she—"

"Yes," I answered before he could finish.

He reached out his hand and shook mine. "I'm Sean Benson, baby doc," he said. "It's my pleasure to meet you, Lexie Jaeger, nurse-midwife from Oregon." His eyes twinkled, and then he turned his attention back to Sharon but still spoke to me. "The EMTs said you thought she had placenta previa, and you were right," he said. "We'll transfer her up to maternity. You're welcome to stay, though in an unofficial capacity, of course. It's up to you."

I searched Sharon's face. She was twenty-nine

and this was her fourth baby, but her first in a hospital. "I'm happy to stay," I offered.

"Thank you," she whispered. "I'd like that."

Ten minutes later, all of us, including Sharon in a wheelchair, were in an elevator making its way up to the fourth floor.

"What brought you to Lancaster County?" Sean asked.

I explained about the traveling nurse position in Philadelphia, and then I added that Marta and I had a mutual friend who encouraged me to come out and help.

"So you don't usually do home births?"

"No. I work in a level-one trauma hospital in Portland. Emanuel Hospital." I was actually aware of wanting to impress him. "We get a lot of high-risk deliveries."

"Sounds like what we do here." Sean's eyes were kind. "Lots of complicated pregnancies and births—but good old-fashioned births too." He looked at Sharon. "Which is exactly what we're hoping for you."

I knew it wasn't unheard of for someone with placenta previa to deliver naturally, but I also knew it was unlikely. I helped Sharon get settled, with the help of her nurse, and then started snooping around. The delivery rooms hadn't been redecorated as recently as Emanuel's, but they were more than adequate. There were two surgery rooms at the end of the hall, and the nurses' station was located in the middle. I asked Sharon's nurse about their stats, and she said that more than thirty-five hundred babies a year were usually delivered at the hospital. She added that the population of the city of Lancaster was fifty thousand. That surprised me. I had thought it was bigger—probably because of the urban feel downtown. Though there were several hospitals in the area, she said that Lancaster General was the biggest.

"Do many Amish deliver here?" I asked.

She shook her head. "Mostly just emergency cases, like this one."

"And what do you think of cases like this—ones that start at home and then end up in the hospital?"

She looked uncomfortable.

I smiled. "It's okay. I really want to know."

"Well, I've seen too much of what can go wrong to ever have a home birth, I can tell you that."

I nodded. I had too. But I'd only seen one home birth client come into Emanuel in all the time I had been working there. The midwife, who was new in her practice, had brought in the mother while she was still in early labor because the baby was breech. I knew that Sophie had delivered plenty of breech babies at home before, but I told the young and far less experienced midwife that she had done the right thing by coming in. A couple of the doctors who were working that night made snide comments about lay-midwives and home births, and I wished I could have protected her from the criticism by handling the patient's care myself. But unfortunately the mother needed a C-section, and that was the one thing on the OB floor I couldn't do, although I sometimes assisted.

Now, I told the nurse I would hang out with Sharon and for her to go ahead and attend to her other patients. I would let her know if we needed her.

Levi must have just told a joke because as I entered, Sharon was laughing.

"Where can we get a bed like this?" Levi asked, pushing the switch to make it go up.

"Not too high," Sharon commanded.

He lowered it quickly, grinning from ear to ear.

Sharon was already hooked up to an IV. She also had a fetal monitor connected by bands to her belly.

"Will you deliver the baby?" she asked.

"No, Dr. Benson will. I'm not a provider here. I'm just lending support."

The ultrasound technician arrived, and in no time he was waving his magic wand over Sharon's belly. I peered at the screen. The placenta previa was partial, not full. It would be a close call as to whether she could deliver naturally. I'd probably opt for the C-section.

Sean stepped into the room just as the technician was finishing. "What do we have?" he asked.

"Partial," I answered.

He looked at the screen. "I think we can proceed," he said.

I kept my mouth shut.

"I'll be back." Sean hurried out of the room.

Sharon had a long contraction after the ultrasound technician wheeled his cart from the room. "It's hard to be on the bed," she said when it was over.

"You can get down. Just stay close to the IV pole and the monitor."

After a few more contractions, Levi said he thought he'd go take a "look see" around the hospital if that was all right with Sharon. She nodded her approval. Clearly, neither one of them understood the dire situation. After he left she smiled. "He's always so curious about how things work. How a building is built. How others do things differently."

"Is Levi a farmer?" I sat on the end of the bed and Sharon stood beside it.

"*Ya*, he farms and also has a horse shoeing business."

"And you?"

She blushed. "The usual. After all, I'm a wife and a *mamm*."

"Do you sew? Quilt? Can?"

"Oh, *ya*," she said. "I do all of that. And help the children with their schoolwork. And Levi with the branding and shots, and I keep the books for the farm and business." Another contraction came over her, and she quieted.

Levi came back a half hour later and then Sean checked on Sharon soon after that. He said that all was going well, and he seemed to be right. The spotting had stopped. She was still several hours away from delivering. I dozed for a while in the recliner and then after I awoke, Levi took a turn. Sharon had been back on the bed for a couple of hours and was able to doze between contractions.

At four a.m. she was ten centimeters dilated and had the urge to push. Sean came in right away.

"It's your fourth baby, right?" he asked as he scrubbed down.

"Yes." Sharon grimaced.

"Well, chances are you're almost done." He scooted the rolling stool to the end of the bed. "Go ahead and push with the next contraction."

I didn't count the baby as number 257 because I didn't catch him—Sean did. And, again, I didn't ask to take his photo because I didn't want to offend Sharon and Levi. But I felt all the emotions of having delivered him as I stood by Sharon's side and Sean held up the little boy.

"He's perfect," he cooed. His eyes glistened as he suctioned the newborn and then put him on Sharon's chest as he showed Levi where to cut the cord.

I covered Sharon and the baby with a warm blanket. Sharon didn't need any instruction to get the baby nursing as Sean finished up. I wondered if Marta would have called 911. It didn't matter. I was thankful I hadn't taken a chance.

Levi asked if he could use the phone in the room. His younger brother had a cell and could let the extended family, including his parents who were staying with his and Sharon's older children, know about the new baby.

An hour and half later, before I left, Sharon said she'd prefer being at home but was going to enjoy every minute of the peace and quiet that she could. Levi said he would have preferred the bill of being home but would concentrate on the healthy baby. He bent down and kissed the little one, who was tucked into the crook of his mother's arm.

"How does the hospital bill work for you?" I asked.

"Oh, it won't be too bad. We pay into a co-op that will cover most of it—after we pay the first five thousand or so."

I wanted to whistle. Five thousand dollars was a lot of money. But without the co-op the cost could ruin a family financially. No wonder the Amish preferred home births. Thankfully, Sharon hadn't had to have a C-section, which would have been even more expensive. Before I left I took a mental photo of the image of Sharon, Levi, and their baby boy curled up on the bed together. I took in the love between them. Sharon's trust. Levi's contentment. The baby's sweet lips and nearly translucent eye-lids. They were almost asleep, which was exactly what I wanted to be doing—until I just about knocked Sean over in the hall.

He jumped back a step as I barreled out of the room, asking, "Where are you off to in such a hurry?"

I came to a halt and apologized. "Nowhere, really, except maybe a few hours of sleep." Marta hadn't said anything about prenatal appointments. And besides, she'd probably lassoed another midwife in to help her by now. I was anxious to get back so she could honor her part of our bargain.

"Do they allow sleeping in Oregon?" he asked with a laugh. "Cuz they really don't here." He walked beside me as I headed down the hall.

"Just the minimum," I responded. "Whatever that is." It wasn't a witty comeback, not at all, but I was trying.

"How about some breakfast?"

"Hmm. Food. Do they allow that here in Pennsylvania?"

He laughed. "Just the minimum." Then he whispered, "And it's not that good."

The food turned out to be fine. Scrambled eggs and sausage. A croissant. And a cup of black coffee to get me back to Marta's safe and sound.

"So, you're an Amish midwife," he said as he spread blackberry jam on a slice of whole wheat toast.

"No—well, tonight I was." I rolled my eyes. "Or wasn't." I started to smile. "Actually, you were the midwife tonight."

"Touché," he said. "My mother would be so proud."

"Oh?"

"She and my dad live in the backwoods of

Vermont. That's one of the things she's tried to lure me home with—that I could open a birth clinic and do home deliveries." He laughed. "She doesn't get it."

We chatted more about the hospital and births. He had done his undergrad work at Columbia, his medical training at Chicago Medical School, and his residency at George Washington University. He'd been at Lancaster General for two years and had just applied to Johns Hopkins. I tried to do the math to figure out how old he was; four plus four plus two plus two equaled at least thirty.

When I told him I'd gone to Oregon Health Sciences University, he said he'd applied there for medical school. "It's a good place," he said.

I nodded. It was. I'd been well trained.

"So, how did you end up helping an Amish midwife who's in trouble with the law?"

"She's actually a Mennonite midwife. I mean, she mostly works with the Amish, but she's Mennonite herself."

"Same difference," he said, dismissing the whole lot of them with a simple wave of his hand.

"Not exactly," I replied, feeling strangely offended, though I wasn't sure why.

We ate in silence for a few moments as I wondered if Sean was a man of faith. As much as I'd distanced myself from God through the years, I still wanted—someday—a guy who believed. *Like James*. I winced. I couldn't get around the fact that it was important to me.

"My parents might as well have been Amish," Sean said, gently shaking his head as he spoke. "Bless them, but they were—are—off their rockers. I mean, I believe in God and all of that, don't get me wrong, but they totally ingested the Sermon on the Mount, which meant we never had any money. Every time they saved up a few bucks they would give it to 'someone in need.'" He did the quotation gesture with his fingers. "They have been taken so many times I couldn't begin to keep track. Someone would be skipping off with their life savings of seven hundred bucks while we kids would wonder where dinner was coming from."

"How many kids?"

"Six," he replied. "I'm the oldest. I always helped with the younger ones. Mom home-schooled all of us. She still does the last two."

"Looks like it worked."

He hooted. "I basically educated myself. It was a miracle I made it into college, let alone med school."

My phone beeped as he finished talking, and I checked my text message.

It was from Marta. "Looks like I have a prenatal visit at eight." The time on the text read 7:30. I exhaled. "I'd better get going." I stood. "Thank you for breakfast."

Sean took my tray. "I guess I won't be seeing you around."

"Not if all goes well."

"How long are you here?"

"I'm not sure. I need to go to Harrisburg briefly, and then I start my position in Philadelphia . . ." My voice trailed off. Was he going to ask for my number?

"So," he said, beaming at me, "we could see each other again."

"Um, maybe." I was caught off guard by his full-face smile. "I really have no idea what my schedule is going to look like for the next couple of days, though." I tried to push all thoughts of James from my mind.

He held up his iPhone. "Give me your number, and I'll give you a call." His voice was playful.

Without really thinking it through, on impulse I recited my number, which he quickly keyed into his phone.

"I'll call day after tomorrow," he said. "After I've had a chance to catch a nap." He winked as we said goodbye.

The thing was, I didn't think I'd still be in Lancaster County the day after tomorrow. But then again, maybe I would. If I wasn't, would Sean come to Philadelphia to see me?

More importantly, would I be glad if he did?

ELEVEN

I had three prenatal appointments in Marta's office that morning and finished up at eleven. When I entered the cottage, Marta sat at the dining room table with a cordless phone in her hand and an open file in front of her. Without saying hello she said, "We need to check on Barbie and her baby on our way to a four o'clock appointment at the Kemp home."

"First I want the information that's coming to me, and then I'm going to sleep for a couple of hours," I answered and then clenched my teeth. The woman was a slave driver, and I was complicit.

"How about some food?" Was that a glimpse of humanity Marta just displayed?

"Thanks, but I'm not hungry," I muttered, rubbing my eyes and wondering if our conversation should wait until later, when I wasn't too exhausted to take in whatever she had decided to tell me about Amielbach.

"My word is good, Lexie," she said evenly, as if reading my mind. "Take your nap now. We'll talk later."

Trusting her on that one, I used the last speck of energy I possessed to get myself up the stairs and into bed.

Later that afternoon Marta insisted on driving me to the appointments. I reminded her of what her attorney said, and she answered, "That's ridiculous. My being on the property doesn't constitute practicing." She added that if she didn't go with me, I'd never find the Kemps' farm.

The visit to Barbie's was quick and uneventful. Everything was going well. Her sisters were back for the day, the baby was nursing, and Barbie was resting as much as she could. The entire appointment took all of fifteen minutes, and then we were on our way to the next visit. Marta sped along the country roads, deftly navigating the twists and turns, slowing for buggies and scooters, and accelerating on the straight stretches when she could.

Finally she turned onto a narrow lane. The house was back from the road past a row of nine greenhouses. I counted each one. Outside of the last one, Amish men were loading flats of plants onto trucks.

"Who drives the trucks?" I asked.

"Englisch," Marta answered. "The Gundys hire them."

"Gundys? I thought we were going to the Kemps'."

"Hannah Kemp used to be a Gundy."

"Is she related to Sally Gundy?"

"They're sisters-in-law."

"So she's Ezra's sister?"

Marta nodded. I knew the whole county had

to be related, and I also knew it was probably a hopeless cause to even keep the relationships between the few ladies I'd cared for so far straight.

Mennonites love to know whom you're related to. At large gatherings, people will ask who your grandparents were—mine had lived in Kansas and were all deceased—what your mother's maiden name was, all of that. I hated those questions. Sometimes I would hear people whisper, "She's Paul and Clarissa Jaeger's *adopted* daughter." Adopted. It always sounded like a dirty word.

In high school I noticed that if an adopted person committed a crime, the article in the paper would often identify them as adopted, but I never saw people who did something good identified so. I began to wonder if maybe adoptees never did anything good until I came across an article on adoption that included famous people, such as Aristotle, Edgar Allen Poe, and Faith Hill.

"Do the Amish adopt much?" I asked Marta.

"Not particularly," she answered, her eyes on the lane ahead of us. We were nearing two houses.

"How about the Mennonites?"

"It happens," she answered. "But it's not common."

"Is Zed curious about his birth family?"

Her mouth twisted to the side. "Ella never should have revealed to you that Zed is adopted. That's our family's private matter." She parked beside a carriage and opened her door quickly.

We walked past the newer house, which was quite large, toward the smaller house that looked as if it were a century or two old. A pink Big Wheel was parked on the sidewalk by the back door of the smaller house, and a purple ball had been abandoned in the flower bed. Marta knocked, but no one answered. A door to the house across the driveway banged and a woman appeared.

"Marta!" she called out. It was Alice from two days before. "Hannah's over here." Three little girls slipped past; the twins who had been with Alice before and a girl with auburn hair. She appeared to be about five years old. All three were dressed in maroon frocks with white aprons. None of them wore a cap, though their hair was neatly twisted into buns at the back. Their chubby feet were bare.

I followed Marta to the big house, climbing the stairs to the wraparound porch after her. The slats had been freshly painted and baskets of red geraniums hung from hooks spaced evenly along the ceiling. Flats of impatiens were spread on the lawn along the flower bed, waiting to be planted.

Alice held open the door and herded the little girls back into the house. "They just got up from their naps," she said. "I was getting them a snack." I followed Marta into a big kitchen with a large, rustic table in the middle. The three girls climbed side by side onto the far bench. Each had a cookie in her hand. All three looked past Marta and at me with their big eyes.

"We always wear dresses," the oldest one stated, pointing at my jeans.

Alice said, "Shhh."

"Sometimes I wear a dress." I stopped in front of the girls. "To church and things like that."

"I know," the older girl said. "You are *Englisch*. That is what you all do."

"Never mind Rachael. She likes to practice her English."

I must have looked puzzled.

Alice responded, "The children learn Pennsylvania Dutch at home. It isn't until school, usually, that they learn English."

"Ezra teaches me," the little girl said and then laughed. She was obviously quite precocious. "Yesterday I learned that the word for *kind* is 'child.' And *kinder* means 'children.'"

My heart swooned at the words, two that I remembered from my year of German. But they meant more to me now. They held the English words "kin" and "kind," yet they meant "child" and "children."

"That Ezra." Alice shook her head. "He's going to be the death of us all."

A pregnant young woman with hair the same bright shade as Ezra's, whom I presumed to be Hannah, stepped into the archway between the dining room and living room. She wore a maroon dress and stockings but no shoes. "Hello," she said to Marta. "I'm glad you found me over here."

Marta nodded. "How are you, Hannah?"

"*Gut*. It's best for Rachael and me to spend most of our time here with the twins, Christy, and *Mammi*. For all of us."

Marta nodded again and then introduced me. "Lexie will be working with you today while I stay in the kitchen with Alice and the girls."

Hannah had a questioning look on her face but didn't say anything. "I was resting in the spare bedroom," she said. "Follow me."

I went through the relationships of the Gundy/Kemp family, at least what I knew so far, as I followed Hannah down the hall. Alice was Nancy's mother. Nancy's husband was Benjamin. Their children were Will, Hannah, John, and Ezra. John was married to Sally. Hannah was married to—

"What's your husband's name?" I asked as she stopped and motioned me through a door.

"Jonas."

I stepped into a bedroom. "And he works with your dad too?"

"More for my brother Will. In the greenhouses."

The room had a single bed in it and a bureau, with no pictures on the wall. "Do you plan to deliver your baby in here?" I asked.

"Oh no," Hannah said. "This is Will's house. Our home is next door."

I continued with the family tree as I pulled the measuring tape and blood pressure cuff from the bag. Rachael belonged to Hannah and Jonas.

Christy and the twins to Will and . . . whom?

The little girls bumped against the door and then entered the room, giggling as they climbed up onto the bed.

"This is Melanie and Matty," Hannah said.

"Mel and Mat," Rachael interjected.

I explained to the children that I was going to measure Hannah to see how big the baby was, though I realized about halfway through that the twins couldn't understand a word I was saying.

"Mel and Mat's *mamm* had a *boppli* inside her," Rachael said matter-of-factly. "But he died. *Ya, Mamm?*"

Hannah nodded solemnly.

"And so did their *mamm*." Rachael's eyes were downcast.

I looked at Hannah, hoping she would explain what the child was talking about, but her face was stone still.

Mulling that over, I ran the tape measure up her belly and recorded the number in her chart. Next I wrapped the blood pressure cuff around her arm. The little girls watched closely as I squeezed the bulb.

"What's *boppli* in English?" I asked Rachael.

She sat back on her heels. "Doll?" she asked her mother.

"Baby," Hannah answered. Rachael nodded and smiled.

Baby. I took Hannah's blood pressure and recorded it also in her chart. The twins' mother had died and so had her baby. At first, I thought Rachael meant the baby was stillborn and then the mother died later. But maybe not.

Maybe . . . I looked at Hannah, an icy coldness washing over me as comprehension crept into my brain.

"Rachael, you three run along now," Hannah said, sitting up. "We'll be in shortly."

The child whispered to Mel and Mat in Pennsylvania Dutch, and they left the room.

"Was the woman Rachael was just talking about Marta's patient?" I whispered as soon as they were out of hearing range.

She nodded. "You didn't know?"

"The patient who died recently?"

She nodded again. Afraid my knees would give out, I lowered myself to the edge of the bed, wanting to put my hands to my face.

The woman Rachael was talking about was the patient Marta was charged with killing. I never would have guessed by how all of them acted. What other secrets could these people keep?

"Are you okay?" Hannah's voice was full of compassion.

I held up my head. "I'm fine. Just caught off guard, that's all." I gathered up my things and followed Hannah into the kitchen.

"How about a cookie?" Alice asked.

I sat down beside Rachael at the table. Soon a plate with a cookie on it for me and glasses of milk for the girls appeared. The three little girls all exclaimed, *"Danke, Grossmammi!"* in unison.

My thoughts returned to the Gundy family. Even as they were all still mourning the death of a mother and infant son, there would be two new babies in the family soon: first Hannah's and then Sally's. I imagined upcoming holiday dinners around the very table where I sat. The laughter. The teasing. The good food. The devotion to one another. The extended family all together, from the great-grandmother to the smallest little one. In a word, I was jealous.

Marta, Hannah, and Alice moved away from the table. "How is Will?" Marta asked quietly.

I couldn't hear Hannah and Alice's response because Rachael chattered away, mostly in words I couldn't understand, and the twins responded over and over with, *"Ya, ya."*

But then the girls quieted for a moment.

"He wants to see you," Hannah said. That I heard quite clearly. "But the district attorney told him not to. It's forbidden."

Marta nodded. "So I've heard." She walked to the back door and lifted her coat off a peg. "Well, Hannah, you'll have another appointment in two weeks and then after that every week until the baby arrives."

She smiled. "I will be ready. So will Rachael."

The girl turned toward her mother and smiled at the sound of her name.

I told the little ones goodbye and thanked Alice for the cookie. Rachael climbed down from the bench and scurried across the tile floor, taking my hand. "Come again?" she asked.

"Perhaps," I said.

Hannah stood beside her grandmother, looking the picture of perfect contentment. Yet I knew she must still be full of grief. Her sister-in-law had died just before Dad did, less than two months before. But her grief was unexpected, doubly so. I envied her contentment, her acceptance. And envied her *grossmammi* standing so stoically beside her, helping her with her daughter and nieces.

I imagined all of them planting the impatiens after we left. I had the urge to ask if I could stay and help, but it was interrupted by the back door flying open. A tall man with the Gundy red hair and a full beard stood in front of Marta. He looked more like Ezra than John, but he was much larger than both of the younger men.

He took off his straw hat and looked down on Marta. "I hoped I'd see you."

"Will," Marta said. "How are you?"

"My soul is well. My heart . . . well, you know."

She nodded and reached for his hand. "I know the DA told you not to talk with me—"

"And I won't. Not about the case." He clucked his tongue. "Although I do not understand this. I asked the detective to leave well enough alone, including burying her in peace without an autopsy, but he said it's the state that is bringing charges, not me. I told him you told us to go to the hospital and that I listened to Lydia when she refused. It was my fault as much as hers, but certainly not yours."

"Don't talk that way," Marta said. "Just tell the grand jury what happened."

"That's just it," Will answered. "Some things in life happen, they can't be changed."

I couldn't help but question Will's philosophy. If people acted in responsible ways, most tragedies could be averted. Not all, of course, but most.

Rachael stood to the side watching her uncle, while the twins had turned around on the bench and were balancing on their knees.

When Will exclaimed, "Where are my girls?" all three came running as if they had been waiting for his cue, giggling as they did. He swept them into his arms and then asked, "Where's Christy?"

"Resting," Rachael answered. "*Grossmammi* said for us not to bother her."

He peered over the three blond heads at his grandmother.

Alice shrugged. "She's having another hard day, that's all."

He nodded and then squeezed the girls until they squealed. "I still have my joy," he said to Marta. "God is still *gut*."

"*Ya,*" she answered, but I thought I detected a hint of bitterness in her voice.

"Speaking of, how is Klara and Alexander's only joy? I heard she was ill again."

"I hadn't heard," Marta said. "I'll have to ask Klara." Marta started toward the back door, but Will kept talking.

"Who is this?" He was looking at me now.

"My assistant," Marta answered, her hand on the doorknob.

I stepped forward and extended my hand. "Lexie Jaeger."

"I'm pleased to meet you." His shake was firm. "So you're a relative of Marta's?"

My eyes popped wide. Why would he assume that?

Marta answered quickly. "She's from Oregon."

"W-why do you say that?" I stammered at the same time.

He shifted the girls higher in his arms and they squealed again. "Well, for being *Englisch* you look like—"

Marta interrupted him. "We need to go."

"Like who?" My voice was loud.

Will glanced at Marta and then at me. He opened his mouth, but then Alice swooped into our half circle and placed a hand on his shoulder. "Marta needs to get home," she said. The next moment we were out the door.

In the car, I tried to get Marta to talk. "Whom do I look like?" I asked.

"Will was just making conversation."

"I don't think so," I said. "Ella mistook me for someone else the first time she saw me."

"Well, I've said this before. She's a fanciful girl." She backed the car around and started toward the highway.

"What is Klara and Alexander's child's name?" I asked.

She didn't answer me.

"Marta?"

"Ada," she finally said. "Her name is Ada."

I asked why Will referred to her as Klara and Alexander's only joy.

"She's their only child," Marta said.

"Klara couldn't have any more?"

"Something like that," she answered. She turned onto the highway in the opposite direction of her home and said she needed to stop by the store. She seemed distracted, more than usual. I had my nose to the window, taking in the countryside. We passed a farmhouse that was just a few feet from the road and then a stucco schoolhouse with a bell in the tower. The children had all gone home. "Did you see Christy?" I asked, still looking out the window.

Marta shook her head. "Alice said she's having a hard time, but she needs to accept that her mother is gone and move on."

My back stiffened. What did Marta know about losing a mother? Hers was still alive and well, while Christy's and mine had been taken from us far too soon. In many ways, I knew the child would never get over such a fundamental loss. Certainly, I hadn't.

"What's wrong with Ada?" I asked, trying to keep the anger from my voice.

"She has hereditary spherocytosis."

"Pardon?"

"Abnormally shaped blood cells. It causes hemolytic anemia."

That I had heard of. Not great, but at least it wasn't life threatening. "So she has transfusions? For treatment, right? And she has to be careful not to rupture her spleen?"

Marta nodded.

"Did they catch it when she was little?"

"Not until she was twenty. She'd always been sickly, but it took them a while to figure out what it was."

"Does anyone else in the family have it?" I asked.

"Not that we know of."

We rode in silence for a few minutes, me thinking about what all might be in my genes that I had no idea about and then about the past that I had no idea about, either. I wanted Marta to bring up Amielbach without being asked, but I knew the chances of that were thin. Finally I said, "It's time to pay the piper."

"Later, when we are home."

"Might be better to talk here in the car, where the kids can't eavesdrop."

She didn't respond to that as she slowed for a

174

carriage just ahead. Two little boys, preschool age, peeked over the back end of it. Both wore black hats, and one held a baseball in his hand. I turned my attention to the fields. A lane appeared, then a silo, and then a barn. For some reason, my pulse quickened. Then I saw the house, off to the side in a stand of pine trees.

"Stop," I said, rolling down the window and reaching for my camera in the pocket of my jacket.

The house wasn't anything spectacular. It certainly wasn't Amielbach. It was white, like so many other Old Order Amish houses, but it had a balcony on the second floor. A balcony that somehow seemed familiar.

Marta appeared not to have heard me.

"Please stop!" I said, this time louder.

Instead she pulled around the horse and carriage and sped away.

TWELVE

It was no surprise that Marta marched in the direction of her office as soon as she parked her car, leaving the gallon of milk and the bag of apples on the backseat.

I got out and slammed the passenger door like a teenager. I'd been ranting ever since she refused to stop at the house with the balcony. She'd been ignoring me, as she would a teenager, even as I had stormed along beside her through the grocery store.

Now I stood next to the car and yelled again. "You promised you'd give me the information!"

"I will," she called over her shoulder. "In a minute."

I stomped up the three steps to the cottage. I didn't need James's help to figure out that Marta was heavily into avoidance. I could come up with that on my own.

Once I reached my alcove, I dialed his number and then let it ring until it went into voice mail. I hit "end." It was mid afternoon back home. He probably had a class. I sent him a text and asked him to give me a call when he had a chance.

A minute later he replied: *With study group. Will call later.*

I spread out on my tiny bed.

If Marta were related to me, did I really want to know anything more about this family? What if everyone was as coldhearted as she?

I closed my eyes for a couple of minutes and was close to dozing off when I heard Ella's bedroom door open and footsteps in the hall. When she said "Oops" my eyes flew open. Ella was darting away from the alcove with Zed behind her.

"Come back!" I ordered, stumbling off the bed to the floor.

"I'll be right there." I could hear Ella's steps in the hall.

I looked to my right. Her doorway was about

ready to swallow her with Zed next in line.

"Ella!"

She stopped. Maybe my voice reminded her of her mother's.

"Come back here."

Zed turned first. As Ella swiveled around, I saw the carved box in her hands.

"We just wanted to get a better look." Her voice was as meek as her expression.

"That's fine, but there's no reason to be so secretive about it." I reached for the box and opened it. The locks of hair and letter were still inside.

Zed stood with his arms crossed over his checked shirt, his head downcast.

"How about you?" I asked. "Have you seen the house before?"

He shook his head.

"I remember where I saw a picture of that house," Ella said. "It's in the family Bible."

"Here?" I glanced toward Marta's room. Is that where she would keep it? Had a clue been that close to me all this time?

Ella shook her head. "I was snooping. It was a couple of years ago at Aunt Klara's, and I was looking for a puzzle to do with *Mammi*. The Bible was behind a stack of games."

I titled my head, imagining Amish children sitting around playing games and doing puzzles with their grandparents, touched by the sweet image.

"I started to thumb through it—the pages were

really thin—and found a loose piece of paper with a picture of the house." Her eyes grew wide with the memory.

"Was there anything else in the Bible? A list of births and deaths?"

Ella wrinkled her nose. "I don't know, but that was what I was wondering the other day when I told you I would help you find your birth family. The day I found the drawing of the house, Aunt Klara came into the room, so I had to put away the Bible and pick out a puzzle, pronto."

I sat back down on the bed. "Tell me about Ada."

Ella's face reddened as she glanced at Zed. He shrugged.

"Your mom said she's your cousin. Klara's daughter," I said.

Ella nodded.

"And she looks like me."

"Mom told you that?" Ella sounded dumbfounded.

I frowned. "No. Will Gundy did."

"Oh," Ella said.

"Is it true?"

"Kind of. Maybe. A little, anyway." She shrugged. "I'd need to see the two of you together . . ." Her voice trailed off.

I leaned forward. "Please take me to your aunt's house."

Now it was Zed's turn to look unnerved.

Ella made a face and then said slowly, "Well, I

don't think I should. But maybe I could go . . ." Her brows tightened. "Maybe you could drop me off, and I could say I'm doing a family history project for school and need to ask *Mammi* some questions." She turned toward her brother. "Remember those projects? In the fourth grade? But Mom wouldn't give me any information so I made it all up, and you just copied mine when it was your turn?"

He nodded solemnly. I remembered those sorts of projects. They were the kind that made an adopted kid feel like a freak. I'd always get a stomachache on the days I presented. I'd felt like a poser.

"What do you think?" Ella asked. "It might be a way to see if there's more info in the Bible."

"Sounds good," I said, even though I really wanted a look at Ada myself. Patience had never been a virtue for me—except when it came to labor and delivery. "What about your mom?"

"She has a meeting tomorrow afternoon with her lawyer. At least that's what she said this morning."

I agreed to the plan, although I did feel bad that I was encouraging both children—Zed by association—to go behind their mother's back. Then again, I didn't feel bad enough to give up hope of finally getting some information—especially if Marta was going to keep blowing me off.

I slipped the box under my bed and closed my eyes as Ella and Zed scurried down the stairs. I dozed and then woke to Marta standing over me. It was dark outside and I could barely make out her form.

"Amielbach is a property in Switzerland," she said. "It was in my mother's family until a number of years ago." She spoke as if she were reading from a script or had rehearsed, over and over, what to say. "I have no other information about it."

I sat upright, coming out of my fog. "Was the property sold?"

"Yes." Her voice still sounded robotic.

"By?"

"My mother, I presume."

"When?"

She stepped backward. "I don't know, exactly."

"How about approximately?"

"More than twenty years ago."

I was sitting on the end of the bed now. "Why?"

She stepped back again. "That's all the information I have." She turned. In a couple of steps she was descending the stairs.

"Marta!" I was scrambling after her. "Please." By the time I reached the staircase she had disappeared. In a minute I was in the living room and then the dining room. Marta sat at the table next to Zed, his algebra book between them.

"Yes?" she said, without looking up.

I stopped. I didn't want to risk my plan with Ella and Zed for the next day by pushing Marta further. And she had upheld her end of the bargain. "I was wondering if there's anything leftover from dinner," I said. "I must have slept through."

···

James didn't phone me back, but when I awoke the next morning I had a text from him, apologizing for not calling. I texted him, saying I'd delivered one baby already and was present for another birth at the hospital. I included that I'd had breakfast with an OB doc and it was fun to hear about the baby business in Pennsylvania. Then I asked him to call late that afternoon his time, and I would update him about my adoption search. I was hoping to have more information after Ella visited Klara's house.

I spent the day seeing patients in Marta's office. When the last one left, I finished my charting and anticipated taking Ella out to Klara's. As I closed the cabinet, the front door opened and Marta stepped inside, her cape around her shoulders and what looked like a homeopathic bottle in her hand. "Could you take this to Esther?" she asked. "I'm late for a meeting."

I twirled a strand of hair. Esther's wasn't that far from her lawyer's office. Had she gotten wind of what Ella and I planned to do?

"And could you take Zed and Ella with you? It would do them good to see Simon."

I took the bottle. It was tincture of valerian, a sleeping herb. It wouldn't take that much longer to go by Esther's, at least I didn't think it would. My geography of Lancaster County still wasn't very good. And it gave us an excuse to be out. I agreed, not that Marta had any doubt I would. She was almost out the door without so much as a "thank you" when she stopped and turned around.

"What else?" I asked, waiting for yet another demand from this difficult woman.

Instead, I was surprised when she took a step toward me, her cheeks flushing a bright pink, and spoke. "Nothing. I just wanted . . . I . . . Thank you. Not only for bringing that to Esther, but for everything. I know I haven't said it much since you got here, but thank you."

Could it be that under the hard Marta shell beat the heart of a real live person?

"I hope you understand that you have come here at the single most difficult point in my life," she continued. "I know I tend to be short with people and dismissive and brusque, but this homicide charge is just so very scary and stressful . . . I've been far worse with all of that than usual . . ." As she struggled for the right words, I couldn't believe the effect of what she'd already said had on me. Like a warm, soothing balm washing over a wound, her words of thanks and apology had been needed by me more than I realized.

"You're welcome, and you're forgiven," I told her, holding up one hand as if to assure her that she'd said enough and didn't need to go on. "Thanks for telling me."

She nodded, but before she turned to go, she gave me a slight smile. "I wish you could know me when I wasn't in the midst of absolute disaster. I'm really not a bad person."

I chuckled. "I wish you could know me when I'm not in the midst of a desperate search. I'm not so bad either."

We shared a smile, and then she gave a single nod and turned to go. As the door slowly closed behind her, my own smile lingered for a bit. But as it faded, I began to feel guilty, as though I were the one who owed *her* an apology now. Here I was about to involve her children in my own schemes, behind her back, just as the woman had decided to offer me an olive branch.

Timing never had been my strong suit.

A half hour later, Esther greeted us and ushered us into her row house. Tantalizing spices greeted us. "I'm making stew," she said. "Can you stay for dinner?"

I politely declined, and Ella added that we had another errand to run.

Simon was on the couch, covered with a crocheted afghan, and was just waking. He smiled at Zed and then rubbed his eyes with his chubby hands.

"Hi, bud," Zed said, kneeling down beside him.

Simon scrambled to his knees and held up his arms. Zed lifted him and then held him, a little awkwardly.

"Ah," Ella said. "Why do you want Zed to hold you? What about me?"

Simon giggled and dove toward Ella. She caught him and settled him on her hip like a pro.

I gave Esther the valerian and asked how she was doing. We chatted a little about her insomnia. In my practice, we recommended that women exercise during the day and drink chamomile tea at night. Rarely did we prescribe sleep aids, although every once in a while we did. A few times I had suggested that a woman look into valerian—something I knew from working with Sophie—but I always left it entirely up to the patient. I'd never think to give one of them a bottle of the stuff—it just wasn't done in the professional world of nurse-midwifery.

"We should get going," Ella said, tugging on my sleeve like a little kid. Simon was pulling on the strings of her cap, yanking it from side to side, but the straight pins held it in place.

Simon and Esther gave everyone a hug, including me.

"Where's David?" Zed asked.

"Downtown," Esther answered, her eyes a little downcast. Zed left it at that.

In the car, though, Ella said, "I know where David is."

I wasn't really interested, but Zed asked where as I started the engine.

"The courthouse."

Now I was interested.

"He and a bunch of other people from church are there in support of Mom."

"Can we drive by?" Zed asked from the backseat.

"But not get out?" I didn't think Marta would want her children involved in any protests, and I certainly didn't want to be.

Ella nodded. "No one will recognize your car if we just pass by."

"Duck if you see your mom. If she's at her lawyer's office, it's just across the street."

I eased out of the alleyway and turned onto Queen Street. A few minutes later I cut over to Duke. Ahead a group of people stood perfectly still on the sidewalk. There were no signs. No one was marching. I drove by slowly. There were people in regular clothes, women in Mennonite dresses and caps, and a group of Amish women and men. There were a handful of African women wearing colorful skirts and blouses and one African man, whom I assumed was David. There was a woman in a sari, and I wondered if she was Marta's patient from Pakistan. We didn't have to worry about anyone seeing us. Every head was bowed.

I shivered. They weren't protesting. They were praying.

Zed's voice was nearly a whisper in the back seat. "Cool."

I glanced at him in the rearview mirror.

He was looking out the back window. But then he ducked. "There's Mom!" His voice was louder now.

"What's she doing?" Ella spun around.

"Getting in her car. On the other side of the street."

"She's not going over to the group?"

"Nope." Zed turned back around and slumped down.

"She's such a case." Ella turned back around.

"Maybe she did earlier," I said, surprised I was defending Marta.

Ella shook her head. "We just learned about social misfits in school." She groaned. "I think Mom's one."

"No, she's not," I countered. "She's great with her clients."

"That's it," Ella said. "That's the only time she's normal. And now that's all messed up too."

I tapped the steering wheel with my thumbs. I remember being embarrassed by Dad in high school. Not only of his old-fashioned clothes, but of what he said, even if it was perfectly normal, even if it was pithy and insightful. Being embarrassed by parents was part of growing up.

I changed lanes and turned onto Walnut Street to head back out to the country. But Ella was right. Marta was a misfit. If I were James, I would be sympathetic and wonder what had made her that way. But I wasn't James.

My cell, which rested in the cup holder of my rental, began to vibrate. Ella picked it up. "Ooh," she said. "A text from—" she grinned at me. "Sean."

"Don't open it." I smiled back and held out my

hand for the phone. I would read it while Zed and I waited.

Fifteen minutes later I realized we were close to the Kemp and Gundy farm. "Are we almost there?"

Ella nodded.

"Is it down a lane?"

"How did you know?"

Most of the houses were within a few yards of the road. Very few were down a lane.

"Does it have a balcony?"

She nodded again and turned toward me.

"I saw a house after your mom and I visited Hannah Kemp that—" That what? "Creeped me out," I said.

"It's not creepy," Ella said. "Not at all. I've always really liked it."

She was right. The house hadn't been creepy. That was how I'd felt. "Won't your Aunt Klara think it odd if you just show up?" I asked. "Won't she ask how you got here?"

Ella shook her head. "She'll think Mom dropped me off. She used to do that sometimes so I could see *Mammi* while Mom visited a patient."

We drove in silence for a minute except for Zed tapping the window. Then Ella said, "Turn at the next right and then stop."

She didn't give me enough warning, and I had to turn sharply into the lane. I slammed on the brakes when I saw the house again. A door, flanked by windows, in the middle of the second floor led to the balcony that spanned the front of the house. A wrought iron railing, covered with vines, surrounded the balcony. Some people claim to have infant memories, but I thought them ridiculous. Besides, I'd been born in Montgomery County. I'd most likely never been to Lancaster County before in my life until I arrived four days ago. Even if I had, no newborn would remember a house. Maybe a scent or being frightened, but a house was too big for an infant to even see.

"You should drive down the road a little. I'll text you and then you can meet back here."

I nodded. I wasn't used to being bossed around by a fifteen-year-old, but I wasn't going to argue with anything she said. As I stared at the house, I felt isolated, rejected, damaged—and cold. I wanted to speed back to Marta's, pack my things, and flee.

I gripped the steering wheel as I watched Ella hurry up the lane in the late afternoon light. She wore a green print dress and a black sweater. She practically skipped along. She had a confidence I envied. Ahead, I noticed a smaller house, a *daadi haus*, behind the main one. Clothes were on the line. I was learning that Monday wasn't the only wash day for the Amish. Just like for the rest of us, it could be a daily chore.

In my long moment of angst I forgot Zed was with me, but then he scrambled out of the back and into the coveted shotgun seat. "There's a turnout up the road a ways, by some willows."

I was happy to back out of the lane, away from the house. For now.

In no time I parked under the trees, digging my camera out of my bag. I liked the way the light wafted through the budding branches, the switches all wispy with the tender shoots. "I'm going to take some pictures," I said to Zed.

In a moment he was out of the car too, and as I pointed the camera up into the golden-green heart of the tree, he settled in the crook of the trunk where it had split in two.

"What kind of camera is it?" he asked.

When I told him the make and model, he said he had seen some great reviews for it online.

"What kind do you have?"

When he didn't answer, I lowered the camera and turned toward him. I asked again.

He shrugged. "I don't. But if I did, I think I'd go with an EVF rather than a pentaprism. No offense."

I stifled a smile, thinking it was hard to be offended when I didn't even know what he was talking about.

"Does your mom have a camera?"

He shook his head.

"I don't get it. Mennonites take pictures."

"*We* don't."

I snapped his photo. He smiled, his brown eyes barely showing under his bangs. He was a natural, putting his hands in his pockets and turning his head toward me with a slight hint of a smile. I took another photo.

"Can I try it?" He hopped down.

"Sure." I handed it to him and looped the strap over his neck. He took a couple of shots of the underside of the tree canopy and then a couple of me. I hammed it up, leaning against the trunk as if posing for a portrait.

"How do I look at what I've taken?" he asked, and I realized that for all of his big words, he possessed mere knowledge, not practical experience.

I clicked the view button and showed him how to flip through the photos. He kept going past his and on to the ones I'd taken of Lancaster County. "Wow."

I looked over his shoulder. He'd landed on a photo of the back of an Amish man plowing his field, the hooves and backs of his four mules partially blurred with the movement. I'd taken it with my zoom a good hundred yards away.

I couldn't fathom living life without a camera. "How about when you went to Ethiopia? Didn't you have a camera then?"

He shook his head. "But I remember everything and I wrote it all down. All about the people, the little kids, the food, the cities, the countryside, the colors, the textures. I won't ever forget it."

Was that why I took photos? Because I didn't want to forget? Did I feel forgotten because there weren't any photos of me as a baby?

"What do you want to do when you grow up?"

He shrugged and handed the camera back to me.

"Come on, Zed." I draped the strap around my neck. "I bet you're the kind of kid who knows."

He smiled.

"Out with it," I teased.

He looked down at his shoes. "Well, I kind of want to make movies."

"Movies?" I tried not to sound surprised, cer- tain if cameras were on Marta's list of "the forbidden" that movies would be too. "Have you ever seen a movie?"

He blushed. "I've seen clips online. And I saw *Shrek* at a friend's house when I was little."

I kept myself from smiling. "What kind of movies do you want to make?"

"Movies about people. I have an idea for one set in Ethiopia, about a kid in a camp—"

My cell began to vibrate in my pocket. I remembered I hadn't read the one from Sean. I dug out my phone. The immediate one was from Ella: *Come get me!*

"Let's go." I clicked to the text I'd missed from Sean as I hurried to the car. *Dinner tonight?* My heart jumped. I'd have to deal with that one later.

I thanked Zed for coming along as we waited for Ella. He smiled but didn't say anything. She was coming up the lane, practically running. Behind her a woman operated the pulley that the wash line was attached to. Dresses and pants lurched forward and then back, like puppets in a show. I wondered if the woman could see us because we could see her, but she appeared to be focused exclusively on the laundry in front of her and didn't turn her face in our direction.

Ella did run the last hundred feet to the car, glancing over her shoulder one last time as she opened the door.

She was barely out of breath. I backed out of the lane.

"It's the same mansion as the one on the box," she said. "It's an illustration with the date 1873 in the corner."

"What about the Bible?" I asked, turning onto the highway.

"I found it in the same place, behind the puzzles. Aunt Klara went out to check on *Mammi* to see if I could visit." She paused.

"And?" I didn't mean to sound impatient.

"In front were all sorts of names and the dates for births and deaths." She turned toward the backseat. "Our names are in there, Zed, and our births." She giggled. "And Ada's."

"And?" Now I did mean to sound impatient.

"A girl named Alexandra."

"When was she born?" I felt as if I were underwater again and my voice was garbled, the words coming out as bubbles, bobbing to the surface.

I could barely hear Ella as she gave the birth date, the very same as mine.

THIRTEEN

We rode in silence. I slowed for a buggy. A car behind me honked. I ignored them. After a while Ella said, "I think you can pass."

I realized the car behind me was long gone and we were on a straight stretch. I sped around the buggy.

"Are there parents listed for Alexandra?" I was practically whispering. "In the Bible?"

"No father, just a mother." Ella looked straight ahead. "Giselle."

"Do you know who she is?" I tried to concentrate on my driving.

"I've never heard of her before, but—" she stopped.

"Ella?" I tried to catch her eye.

"She's listed as a sister to Klara and Mom. Their maiden name is Lantz."

"We have another aunt?" Zed asked from the backseat.

Ella ignored him. By his lack of protest, I gathered he was used to it.

I locked my eyes on the road. *Giselle.* My birth mother's name was Giselle. She was a sister to Marta and to Klara. A fifteen-year-old had accomplished in a few minutes what I wouldn't have been able to do in weeks or months—maybe even years. "Was there a birth date for her?" I was choking on my heart.

Ella exhaled and then spoke quietly. "Klara was coming in through the back door, so I had to stuff the Bible back behind the puzzles."

"Did you see *Mammi*?" Zed leaned forward.

She shook her head. "Klara said she was sleeping. She said I should ask Mom anyway about the family history—she knows as much as anyone. She says *Mammi* isn't very talkative now."

I shivered. Was she dying?

Even without seeing her grandmother, Ella had done great. "Thank you," I said, patting her leg. "Have you thought of a career as a detective? Because you're amazing."

Ella smiled, clearly pleased with my praise.

The sun was setting now, streaking the fading blue sky with lemon yellow, pale lavender, and creamsicle orange. Ahead, a windmill was silhouetted against the scene. My heart lurched. This information challenged everything I'd ever fantasized about my birth family. I glanced down at the Coach purse on the console. My birth mother wasn't a professional woman living in Philadelphia or Manhattan. She was, most likely, a shunned Amish woman living who knew where. It was as if both she and I, together, had been scrubbed clean from her family. *Our family.* I shivered.

I had a friend in middle school who used to

say, "God gives us our relatives; we choose our friends." She came from a big Irish Catholic family and was related to half the county.

I thought of her saying that now. Never, in my wildest dreams, would I have chosen an Amish family from Lancaster County. But why would an Amish family in Lancaster County not choose me? If my mother couldn't keep me, why wouldn't my grandmother? I'd seen how much the Amish loved their children. I couldn't imagine Alice, and she was a great-grandmother, ever giving up Rachael, Melanie, or Matty when they were babies. I think she would die first.

"Are you sure you've never heard of Giselle?" My voice broke the silence.

"Never," she said. "And I've never heard of a cousin Alexandra—of you, right?"

"I think so," I whispered.

"How old is your mom?" I asked.

"Thirty-eight," Zed answered from the backseat.

"And your Aunt Klara?" I glanced into the rearview mirror.

Ella shrugged. "I don't know. But older, that's for sure." She sat up straighter. "I'll go back and look at the Bible again." She reached over and touched my hand on the steering wheel. "I'll do whatever I can."

"Thanks," I said, choking.

"So we're cousins then, right?" Zed's head was between the seats.

"Somebody's slow." Ella took her hand away from mine, reaching behind her to tousle her brother's hair.

"But Mom doesn't know?" Zed's voice was full of confusion.

Neither Ella nor I answered him. Of course Marta knew, but I didn't want to be the one to confirm Zed's suspicion about his mother.

By the time we reached the covered bridge, dusk was falling. I eased onto the wooden slats carefully, releasing my anxiety with a sigh when the car rolled back onto the pavement on the other side. By the time we reached the cottage, though, my angst was gathering steam again, but Marta was nowhere to be found. I marched out to her office, ready to confront the woman whom I now knew was my aunt.

"You're right," she said, calmly, after my rant. "I am your biological aunt. We share some of the same DNA. That's all." She sat at her desk. "I am very sorry that you came out here to find this out. I did my best to stop you once I suspected who you were." She looked up at me. "I was told, all those years ago, that your adoptive parents had renamed you. Clearly they didn't, and that caught me off guard."

"Please tell me what you know," I begged.

"There's nothing to tell. I haven't seen Giselle in over two decades. I haven't had a letter. Not even a postcard."

"And no one else has heard from her?"

She shrugged. "That's not really my business to tell."

I stared at her.

"Alexandra," she said. I shivered. It was the first time she'd called me by my full name, and the way she said it sounded as if she'd said it before. "Some things are better left alone," she added.

I crossed my arms. "I would like to meet my—" I stopped, about to say "grandmother," but instead I used the more familiar term, mostly to see how it would feel on my tongue, but perhaps also to get a rise out of Marta. "*Mammi*. I want to meet *Mammi*."

Marta winced. *Bull's-eye.*

"And Klara," I said, feeling emboldened. "And Ada. And even Alexander."

She looked as if I were throwing darts at her, aiming at her narrow eyes. "That's not a good idea," she finally said. She stood. "We were raised to forgive and forget. It's offensive to us for you to come rushing in here, asking questions and stirring up the past."

I felt as if I'd been slapped.

She continued. "I don't know how they do things in Oregon, but this isn't how we do things here." Her hands were flat on her desk, and she leaned forward. "I appreciate your help with my practice, but I do not appreciate you involving my children in your schemes."

My phone beeped.

"As far as tomorrow," Marta said, sinking back down into her chair, "you have four prenatal appointments here in the office in the afternoon. You'll have the morning off."

I didn't respond. How could she expect me to keep helping her?

"I have more work to do now," she said. "Please go." She folded her arms atop her bare desk.

As I left, she lowered her head to her arms on the desk. I closed the door and stood for a moment in the darkness. The evening breeze whispered through the pine trees. A car whizzed by on the road. I thought I could hear the sound of the creek down the hill where it rushed under the bridge. Was the last sound, the one I couldn't quite identify, Marta's muffled crying behind the door?

The new text was from Sean, asking about dinner again. I walked over to the pine trees and stopped at the base of the largest in the small grove. I couldn't handle Sean and dinner, not tonight.

Light from the dining room window illuminated the side yard as I sank down to the damp ground. They had rejected me as a loveable newborn. What had made me think they would accept me now?

Years ago when I was teenager, after I'd decided to wait to search for my birth family, I came across a book about adoption on Sophie's desk. The title was *The Primal Wound.* I skimmed the book. It scared me. Put me on edge. I'd never imagined that adoption was so complicated. The premise was, being abandoned by one's birth mother left the worst wound possible, one that would really never heal. Later, as an adult, I came across the book. I'd remembered it from before as being four or five hundred pages at least, but it wasn't. It was actually a small volume just over two hundred pages. When I saw the book as an adult, I wondered if Sophie had been reading it all those years before or if she had left it for me to find. My gut feeling was that she had been reading it, but with me in mind. She was never one to meddle—until now.

My phone began to ring. It was James. I tripped over my words as I spilled out what had happened.

"Wow. How are you feeling?"

How did I feel? Anger swept over me. He'd known all along they would reject me. "Why did you let me come?" I demanded.

"Lex. What's going on?" His voice was annoyingly patient.

"What's going on?" My voice was shrill now. "Marta is my aunt. Her sister Giselle is my birth mom. That's what's going on. But she won't tell me any more than that."

"Who won't tell you any more?"

My anger surged. "Marta."

"Maybe she will if you give her some time."

I sat up straighter against the tree, the jigsaw bark of the trunk against my back. More time?

Maybe James was dating someone else. Maybe he didn't want me to come home. "I don't want to find my birth mom only to be rejected by her too."

"There are worse things than being rejected."

"Like?"

"Not being loved." His voice was low and deep.

"Aren't they the same?"

He was silent for a moment, and then he said, "No."

I thought about that. I didn't agree. "I've got to go."

A minute later I texted Sean: *Are you still available for dinner? Let me know when and where.*

Where was a Thai place in downtown Lancaster not far from the hospital. *When* was eight thirty, but before I met Sean I cut across to the Lincoln Highway and stopped at a coffee shop whose sign advertised free wireless Internet, a place called the Morning Mug. I had ten minutes of Internet time before they closed. I turned on my laptop and ordered a cup of herbal tea. Immediately I logged onto the adoption site where I'd registered before I left Portland. I was supposed to get an email if anyone responded to my post, and so far I'd had nothing. First I clicked on to "Lantz," now that I had a name, to see if there were any postings concerning me, but still there was nothing.

"We close in five minutes," the barista called out to me. I was the only customer in the shop.

I ignored him and clicked into my account. A second later a posting box was in front of me. I'd skimmed my previous posting with my birth date and location. Now I wrote: "Birth mother's name is Giselle Lantz." I hesitated. Should I add that Giselle was Amish?

"We're closing," the barista said, standing at the counter with a bar towel in his hand.

I added, *Birth mother's family is Amish and from Lancaster County, PA,* hit "publish," backtracked to the Google home page, and then typed in *whitepages.com.* I quickly typed in *Lantz, Giselle, PA.* There was one match, located in the town of Emmaus. No address was listed, but I jotted down the phone number.

"We're officially closed."

"Thanks." I slipped my computer into my case and grabbed my tea.

Downtown Lancaster wasn't exactly hopping on a Friday night, and I found a parking place without any trouble. Sean met me at my car and gallantly opened the door for me. He must have showered at the hospital because his short hair was still damp and he smelled of cologne. He wore a blue dress shirt that complemented his eyes, a tailored jacket, nice jeans, and leather shoes. I slung my Coach bag over my shoulder, and as I stepped from the car, he placed his hand on my elbow and kept it there as we walked. I liked that.

Over spring rolls, red curry, pad Thai, and hot tea, I told him about my day. He listened attentively, nodding in sympathy. I ended by saying I had no idea what I should do, if I should flee to Philadelphia or go back home.

"I hope you don't go back to Oregon. Not when we're just getting to know each other."

"You probably say that to all the midwives who stumble into your hospital."

"Probably." His eyes danced playfully.

He asked me about Marta, and I said as far as I knew the autopsy report hadn't come back yet, and that it seemed to be what was holding up the grand jury.

His eyes brightened even more. "Ooh, an autopsy."

I understood his interest. It would sound absolutely morbid to the average person, but just as James obsessed about the motivations of the mind and psyche, we medical people couldn't get enough about why a body would do what it did.

"Have you ever seen an autopsy?" Sean leaned back in his chair, his blue eyes sparkling.

I shook my head.

"They're fascinating. I remember the first one I ever saw, back in med school." He went on to say that the corpse was a twenty-eight-year-old male whom his buddies had found dead after a weekend of partying. "So it was assumed he'd overdosed."

The autopsy itself had taken more than four

hours, and preparing all of the samples took another few days, but the toxicology testing of the blood and urine didn't come back for weeks.

"That's probably what's holding things up now," Sean said. He took a drink of tea and then went back to his story. "Because the coroner suspected an overdose, he took specimens of the liver and brain too." He paused. "I wonder if they would do that with an Amish mother."

I had no idea, unless they thought Marta had given her some sort of drug, illegally.

"The really cool thing was when he opened up the body. He made this big Y-shaped incision."

I was beginning to wonder if Sean should have been a surgeon.

"And then pulled all the organs out."

I smiled.

"It was obvious as soon as he was opened up that he'd had a massive bleed. It was his heart. A ruptured aorta."

"What did the toxicology show?" I asked.

"Nothing. He'd had a few beers. That was it."

I shivered. "What happened next?"

"The coroner put everything back in. The family had an open casket. No one could tell the difference. But at least they had their answer."

Obviously Lydia hadn't had a ruptured aorta or the investigation would be complete. I hadn't thought of her funeral. Would they have had an open casket? I thought of Melanie and Matty and their sister, Christy. Would the children have gone to the funeral? I thought of Will telling his wife goodbye.

"What do you know about the case?" Sean asked.

"Not much. Sounds as though Lydia had high blood pressure. And at some time during labor Marta said they should go to the hospital, but Lydia refused. I know Marta called 911, but it was too late."

"Did she do CPR?"

"I'm assuming so." I couldn't explain to Sean how hard it was to talk to Marta.

"And how about the baby?"

"It sounds as if it asphyxiated. They did a C-section at the hospital . . ." I looked into his eyes.

"I was off that night."

I nodded. I assumed he was. "But the baby was already dead."

He leaned back in his chair. "What a nightmare. It's these rare cases that really make me balk at home births." He smiled. "No offense."

"None taken," I said. I had malpractice insurance, but the risk of losing a baby weighed heavily on me no matter what. It did in a hospital setting too. I was always aware of the possibility. But it was worse at a home birth without suction devices and a C-section suite down the hall. During a home birth, it all seemed so natural, so right, but before and after and in the middle of a sleepless night, I scared myself with thoughts of dead mothers and babies.

We chatted a little bit more about Lancaster County. Sean agreed that the Amish horses that pulled the buggies were beautiful. I told him they reminded me of racehorses.

"Some of them are," he said. "Retired race horses." He told me about his neighbors in Vermont who had horses and how he grew up riding and doing a little bit of jumping. "I would love to have a horse someday," he said. "Maybe when I settle down." His eyes danced again. He asked me about growing up in Oregon, and I told him about the hazelnut orchard and the creek along our property and the view of Mount Hood from the top of the hill. I didn't tell him about Mama dying or Dad's recent passing. Those details would have to wait until we were closer—something that, as we sat across from each other, seemed imminent.

He ordered dessert—mango custard that tasted as if it'd come straight from heaven. Later, I sat back as he signed the bill, thinking how nice it was to go on a date with a man who didn't have to worry about money.

He walked me to my car and took my hand as he said, "Could we do this again sometime soon?"

I hesitated, fighting back a twinge of guilt even as I reminded myself that James and I were officially on a break. I was allowed to see Sean, given my current status.

"Yes," I answered as he opened the door to my Taurus. "I'd like that." As I pulled away from the curb, I whispered, "Tomorrow couldn't be soon enough." For at least half of the dinner, I hadn't given my birth mother—or James—a thought.

But on my way home, I parked my car directly in front of the now dark and closed coffee shop, located their wireless signal, and logged on again to do a quick check of my email. It could happen, right? She could have responded already. Maybe she felt my angst, felt my need. But there was nothing.

I could call the number in Emmaus, but it was late, already past ten thirty. I would call first thing in the morning.

FOURTEEN

After a restless night's sleep, I sat in my car and dialed the phone number of Lantz, Giselle. A man with a shaky voice answered. I asked to speak to Giselle.

"Oh, I'm sorry, honey," he said. "You didn't hear? She passed on a few months ago."

"Passed on?" I gasped.

"That's right, sweetie."

The man sounded ancient. Thinking about that for a moment, hope fluttered in my chest, and I asked how old she had been when she died, if he didn't mind me asking.

"She was ninety-two. Why?"

Ninety-two. It wasn't her! Though I felt bad for this poor old man, I was deeply relieved for my own sake. I told him I had the wrong Giselle Lantz, offered him my condolences, and then hung up, crumpling the piece of paper in my hand.

I pulled out of Marta's driveway a minute later and drove through Lancaster County, wishing someone else was at the wheel, wishing I could snap photos indiscriminately of the farms I passed. Maybe Sean would join me sometime soon for a day in the country.

I'd asked Ella and Zed to come with me, but Marta said they had chores and then homework. It turned out the family was doing spring cleaning—scrubbing the little cottage from top to bottom. I had offered to help, but Marta said I would just be in the way and should have a day to myself.

There were a few other tourists' cars parked at the quilt shop where I stopped, across the road from a country school. I was hoping the place sold maps. I had my GPS, but I couldn't get a handle on the geography, where the city was in regards to the farms I'd been visited, where Klara's place was in regards to where the quilt shop was. The young woman standing behind the counter directed me to a rack of maps. I chose one and then headed to the back room where the quilts were on display. They were gorgeous. I recognized many of the patterns from my childhood when Mama used to be part of the quilting circle at church: spinning star, country love, log cabin, autumn splendor. The poetry of the shapes and stitching matched the names. If Dad were still alive, I'd buy him one, even at over a thousand dollars. There was a baby quilt with Noah's Ark on it, and in the far corner was a quilt that resembled mine with large blocks of mauve, blue, green, and black. It was priced at three hundred dollars.

If Dad were still alive, I'd ask him why they kept the name Alexandra. If he were still alive, I'd ask him to fly out here and talk some sense into Marta.

I headed back to the main room and looked at the trinkets. For living a simple lifestyle, the Amish sold a lot of knickknacks—refrigerator magnets, Christmas ornaments, and other souvenirs. I moved on to a table of handmade soap. The goat's milk smelled the best. I picked up a couple of bars.

As I paid for the soap and map, I realized the young woman was pregnant. I asked when she was due. "Three months," she answered, quietly. She didn't seem shy—just hesitant.

"Who is your midwife?"

She said she hadn't chosen one yet.

I told her I was working with Marta.

"Ya," she said. "My cousin told me about you. Marta is her midwife."

It turned out I'd seen her cousin the day before for a prenatal visit.

"How many midwives are there for the Amish?" I asked.

She said she had no idea.

"But more than two?" I was half joking.

She laughed. "There are more than fifty thousand Amish in Pennsylvania," she said.

I had no idea. That was as many people as in the city of Lancaster.

"And," she said, giggling a little, "we keep multiplying."

I nodded. I'd read somewhere that the Amish population had doubled in the last sixteen years. As other groups of people had fewer and fewer children, the Amish kept their average of seven per family steady. That was a lot of babies. I'd also read that fewer Amish kids today than ever before in their history left the church. I thought of Ezra Gundy and wondered if he was on track to join the Amish church as well. If so, judging by his non-Amish haircut and flirtatious behavior, I had a feeling it wouldn't happen anytime soon, that he was more concerned with sowing some wild oats right now.

The young woman handed me my bag, and I thanked her.

"Best wishes," I said as I headed to the door.

"Ya," she answered. "And to you."

From there I turned onto the highway toward Strasburg, thinking I would take the route I was most familiar with back to Marta's, but when I realized I'd missed my turn, I kept on driving, heading toward Klara's. I stopped alongside the road, hoping the blackberry bushes along the fence line would hide my car, even though they were just brambles at this time of year. I scooted over to the passenger seat and aimed my camera out the window and through a hole in the vines. I snapped a series of the house, first wide-angle shots, and then close-ups of the balcony, the molding along the roofline, and the porch. I took photos of the section of the *daadi haus* that I could see, and then I zoomed in on the rounded shape of the bare branches of an oak tree in the front yard.

Off to the side were a few fruit trees, probably apple. As I photographed those, I was startled when a man appeared in my viewfinder. He was middle aged, most likely Alexander.

If he wasn't my father, why else would Giselle have named me after him? Maybe he had been helpful to her before I was born. Maybe he and Klara had even taken her in and that was why she'd named me Alexandra, as a thanks to them, and then it was *Mammi* who insisted on giving me up. I shivered.

If he was my father, I realized that with this recent information he would also be my uncle. I nearly laughed at the absurdity of it. My speculations sounded like a country western song. Clearly Giselle had become pregnant outside of marriage, and that was no doubt frowned upon by the Amish, but there was no indication of any scandal.

She'd probably had a wild *rumschpringe*, that period of life when Amish teens were given more freedom and allowed to explore the outside world prior to joining the church. Though pregnancy wasn't the norm during *rumschpringe*, it certainly couldn't be unheard of, either.

The man turned his face toward me as I snapped another photo. I hadn't meant to get his front but I had. He was still in my viewfinder and looking straight at me. Maybe he could see the car, but there was no way he could see my face. I clicked the view button, enlarged the image, and looked at the photo I'd just taken. He had a dark, full beard with streaks of gray. I couldn't tell the color of his eyes. He wore a straw hat, black pants with suspenders, and a blue shirt. He looked similar to every other Amish man I'd seen. I raised the camera again, gasping when I realized he was walking across the field toward me.

I panicked. Suddenly, I felt like a little kid in trouble. Shamed, I climbed back to the driver's side, started the car, and pulled onto the highway, glancing behind me a moment later. The man was jogging toward the fence line, watching me go with a questioning look on his face.

I spent the rest of the morning in downtown Lancaster, taking photos of old buildings.

Sunday morning, Ella asked if I would give her and Zed a ride to church. I rolled toward her in my little bed. "What about your mom?" I asked sleepily.

"She's fasting and praying today in her office."

I yawned. "Are you sure you want to go?"

Ella's voice sounded hurt. "Yes."

"Zed too?" I focused on her. She was already dressed.

"Yes." She stepped back onto the landing. "We need to leave in half an hour."

I propped my head up on my elbow. "Can I wear jeans?"

"Wear whatever you want." For a split second she sounded like Marta.

Their church was in Lancaster, a few blocks from Esther and David's house. The parking lot was full, so I drove around the block and squeezed into a space in front of a row house.

"Hurry," Ella said, scrambling out of the car. "We're going to be late." I followed her and Zed followed me, lagging behind. The church was made of bricks with a white steeple and was fairly small. We entered through a basement side door into a fellowship hall, where a few people lingered, drinking coffee and chatting.

"This way." Ella hurried up a staircase that came out into a foyer. Esther was across the way, and Simon rode on her hip. When he saw Ella, he reached for her. Music was playing in the sanctuary, and soon we were inside. It took me a moment to realize that the men sat on one side and the women on the other. I settled into a pew in the middle of the room with Esther, Ella, and Simon. Zed found a seat closer to the front with some friends.

"David leads the singing," Ella whispered. Sure enough, the man we had seen in front of the courthouse two days before stood up front. There was a screen behind him with an image of a waterfall.

Many of the women wore head coverings, but not all. Several other Africans were in the congregation, plus quite a few Hispanics. A group of teenage girls sat in the row in front of us wearing short skirts. A few, even in the cool spring weather, wore tank tops. One of the girls turned and said hello to Ella.

David's voice was deep and loud. I didn't recognize most of the songs until a few hymns at the end, including "How Great Thou Art." Simon couldn't settle on sitting with his mom or Ella. Finally he scurried across Ella's lap to me, and I gave him my cell phone to play with. He liked that and leaned against me, his compact little body melting against mine.

A woman who worked for six months in an orphanage in Honduras spoke about her work, using a PowerPoint presentation of the facility and the children. Many had lived on the streets and were tough and wily, but their hearts softened when shown care and kindness. She also had photos of a merry-go-round and swing set the church had paid for. She said the children had to be taught how to play and use their imaginations. They hadn't been encouraged to do that before.

The next image was of a group of little boys playing soccer.

"Futball!" Simon said, dropping my phone and clapping his hands together.

Ella giggled as she retrieved my cell from under the pew in front of us. By the time the presentation was over, Simon was fussy and Esther took him back, holding him securely against her big belly. He rested his head on her shoulder. After a few minutes his eyes grew drowsy and he slept. It wasn't until the pastor started his sermon and Ella nudged me that I realized I'd had my attention fixed on Simon.

I tried to listen to the teaching, which was on forgiving seventy times seventy, but my mind kept wandering. Could I forgive Marta for being so cold and stingy? She was spending the day fasting and praying, but she was totally without empathy for me. The best thing I could do was get out of her home and her life. I had no business letting myself be mistreated by her. She had the ability to give me all the information I needed in ten minutes, information I was sure she had. The fact that she didn't was just more evidence that I needed to take care of myself, that I couldn't trust anyone else to take care of me.

"We forgive because God forgave us," the pastor said.

I wanted to raise my hand to say that in order to accept God's forgiveness, we had to admit that we had done something wrong. He didn't just give forgiveness freely. I wasn't so sure God expected us to forgive people who didn't admit they had done anything wrong—people who went on their merry ways, living in denial and oblivious to what had been done to us. People like Marta and who-ever else was keeping secrets from me.

At the end of the service, David led the benediction and then dismissed the congregants. Simon stirred on Esther's shoulder, and Ella tried to take him so his mother could stand, but the little boy began to cry.

" 'Tis fine," Esther said. "David will get him in a minute."

Soon Zed and David were beside us, and Esther introduced her husband to me.

"Will you deliver our child?" he asked as he took his son into his arms.

I shook my head. "Not unless Esther has the baby in the next couple of days, which we don't want." I smiled. "I'm headed to Harrisburg on Tuesday and then on to Philadelphia." That was my new plan.

Ella crossed her arms. "Who's going to help Mom?"

"I'm sure she has some ideas," I answered.

David shook my hand. "Well, it's a pleasure

to meet you. I hope our paths will cross again someday."

I nodded, but I knew they wouldn't be in the States much longer and I didn't foresee myself ever going to Ethiopia. I hugged Esther and patted Simon's back. He gave me a half smile and then hid his face against his father's neck.

As I drove home, Ella asked me what I thought of the sermon.

Zed groaned. "You sound like Mom."

Ella ignored him.

I told her I'd heard many variations of that same sermon and not one of the preachers addressed what we should do when the person we needed to forgive wouldn't acknowledge they had done anything wrong.

"Forgive." Ella spoke with force. "Matthew 6:14 and 15 says, 'If you forgive men when they sin against you, your heavenly Father will also forgive you. But if you do not forgive men their sins, your Father will not forgive your sins.' It doesn't say anything about the offender acknowledging their sins."

I blew air up my forehead.

Ella didn't seem to notice. "That's what *demut* is all about."

"De . . . what?"

"*Demut*. It means to let things be, to not try to control everything and everyone." She had that know-it-all way of a teenager. Or maybe of a firstborn who was so used to being right that she could make anything sound like fact. "It means, with humility, to trust God and leave justice to Him." Ella sighed. "I'm really trying to do that with this case against Mom right now."

I didn't answer.

"I mean, I wish I could control this, but I can't. I know she's innocent. She would never do anything to harm a mother or a baby, but I don't have any control over what happens with the court system. I have to let it be. To trust God. To forgive those who are trying to bring harm to us."

We rode in silence for a few minutes as we left the city limits. I mulled over the concept of Marta as a victim. I was so used to thinking of her as someone who was harming me.

"I don't get *demut*," Zed finally said. "I mean, I know the Amish are really into it, right? That's where Mom got it. But how about that one Amish family that lives on the other side of the bridge? Remember when they had a whole bunch of tools stolen and they knew who did it, but they never pressed charges?"

Ella looked at me. "It was their *Englisch* neighbor's nephew who did it."

"And then he broke into some other houses and hurt an old lady," Zed continued. "If the Amish would have pressed charges in the first place, it would have been a whole lot better for everyone involved. Even the criminal."

I nodded in agreement. "That's how justice works," I said. "It brings closure for the victim and protects others."

Ella stared straight ahead, not speaking. I decided not to push it and asked Zed if I could get on his computer for a few minutes when we got home.

"Sure," he said, but he didn't sound very convincing.

"How are you at Internet searches?" I asked.

He perked up a little. "I'm good."

"I'm trying to locate information on an Abraham Sommers who lived in Switzerland in the 1870s that would link him to Amielbach. And I tried to get information on Giselle, but none of the leads panned out."

"I'll see what I can do," he said. "My German is pretty good. Maybe that will help me with the Switzerland connection."

"Cool," I said and meant it.

Ella was still staring out the window. I liked how loyal she was to her mother, even though the woman didn't deserve it. I liked both of my cousins. A lot.

FIFTEEN

The Monday appointments passed quickly. Between patients I thought about the man in the field I'd seen Saturday morning and the questioning look on his face. Surely word was out about a midwife from Oregon helping Marta. Would Klara and Alexander have known that's where I ended up? Or did *Mammi* keep that to herself? Would Giselle have known?

I had to go back to Klara's. I would pack my things tonight, go by the house in the morning, and then head to Harrisburg. By tomorrow I'd be back in Philly.

Giselle. The mystery mother. There hadn't been anything posted on the registry when I checked the day before.

My thoughts bounced around as I listened to the heartbeats of the babies and took the blood pressures of their mothers, recording each detail in their charts. Most of the women asked about Marta. I told them she needed to take some time off. That was all. Now that I had examined close to fifteen clients, I began to try to figure out the connections between the women, guessing at who might be sisters or sisters-in-law. But the women would lower their eyes and not respond. Finally the last patient of the afternoon, a woman in her late thirties named Peggy, told me, gently, that Amish women didn't talk much about pregnancy.

I was dumbfounded.

"Why not?"

She shrugged. "It might be a little bit superstition. Also, we don't draw attention to ourselves."

"But how can women who live so close to each other not talk about the most important thing in their lives?" I draped my stethoscope over my shoulder.

"Well, we have our husbands and our other children and our work to keep us busy. We have plenty to talk about."

That was true.

She checked the position of her bonnet with her hands. "It's just the way we Plain folk do things," she said. "That's all."

I nodded, even though I could barely comprehend what she was saying.

I glanced at the clock on the desk. It was four thirty. "Will you still have to fix dinner when you get home?"

"Oh, no," she answered. "My oldest daughters are doing that." She slung her black cape over her shoulders. She'd just told me her oldest child was twenty and her youngest was four. She had seven in between. "I'm going to stop by the big box store."

"The what?" My voice cracked as I tried to imagine the woman at a Costco or Sam's or BJ's.

"*Ya*, it's not too far out of the way." She spoke in a lighthearted, carefree manner.

She was eight and a half months pregnant. I imagined her lifting cases of cans into her buggy. But cans of what? Wouldn't she put up fruits and vegetables herself? Maybe she bought toilet paper and laundry detergent.

Or maybe she just browsed. Soon she would have baby number ten, and it might be a while until she got out of the house by herself.

"We're having services at our house come Sunday," she explained. "And I'm also stocking up for when the baby comes." She fastened the top hook and eye of her cape.

I couldn't help myself. "What do you buy there?"

"Everything. Frozen pizzas. Lasagna. Canned goods. Soups." She smiled. "Paper products. Socks. Towels. Whatever it is I need. The prices are good."

She tied her black bonnet under her chin as I walked with her to the door. Dark clouds had blown in during the afternoon. "Drive safely," I said as she climbed into her buggy, trying to shake off another misconception I had of the Amish.

"Ya," she said. "I always drive carefully."

Ella had told me several buggy crashes occurred every year. Collisions with cars. Nighttime wrecks. Even an accident involving a snowmobile last winter.

I waved and watched the woman pull onto the highway, her horse practically prancing as he gathered momentum on the blacktop. Peggy smiled and waved. In a second she was gone.

The front door slammed and Zed appeared, a hoodie in his hands. He glanced at me but didn't speak. He shoved his arms through the sleeves of the sweatshirt as he made his way around the side of the house. The air had grown damp and chilly. As I walked back to the office, the sound of an ax rang out from the backyard. The front door slammed again, and Ella came out with the scrap bucket for the chickens.

"Hello," I called out to her.

She waved and then veered away from the path to the coop and toward me.

"What's up?" I asked.

She wasn't wearing her bonnet, and strands of hair had come undone from her bun. "Mom wanted some peace and quiet. She had a phone call and now she's upset."

"Oh."

"She said she needed time on the computer and we needed to go outside."

I'd been hoping to check if there was a registry message on Zed's computer, but it looked as though I was headed to the coffee shop again.

"We're having leftovers for dinner," Ella said. She made a face. "It's clean-out-the-fridge night. Mom's freaking out about money."

"I'm so sorry, Ella. Leftovers are fine," I said, pivoting away from her toward the office. After I finished the filing and cleaned the office, I found Zed and Ella sitting on the steps of the front porch. A stack of wood was by the door.

"Mom says she can think better if we stay out here." Zed zipped up his sweatshirt and Ella put her arm around him. She wore a too-big coat that looked as if it had been her father's.

"I need to go into town and check my email. Want to come along?" I asked.

Ella frowned.

"I'll run it by your mom." I pointed toward the front door. "I need to go get my laptop."

They parted and I slipped up the stairs between them.

Marta was at the computer, scrolling down the screen, a pen in her hand and a piece of paper on the desk with a list of names and phone numbers written down.

I cleared my throat. Her head turned toward me, slowly. "I'm going to head into town," I said. "Is it okay if I take Ella and Zed with me? I'll get them some dinner."

She nodded and then her eyes drifted back to the computer screen.

A minute later, with my laptop in hand and my tote bag over my shoulder, I hurried out onto the porch. Ella and Zed were standing under the eaves of the cottage, away from the rain that had just started.

"Let's go," I said. "We'll get dinner while we're out."

Zed reached the car first and scrambled into the backseat. I held my computer bag close to my chest, not wanting any water to seep through the zipper.

As I started the car, the rain began coming down in sheets, and I thought of Peggy in the downpour. Did buggies hydroplane? Did the horses spook if there was lightning?

Inhaling deeply and blowing it out, I pushed those thoughts from my mind. I had enough going on without fretting about Peggy too.

"Where do you want to eat?" We could have dinner and then stop by the coffee shop.

Neither kid responded at first.

"Burgers?" Zed offered.

"Or pizza." Ella shrugged.

"Do you like Japanese food?" I asked.

"Have we had that?" Zed poked Ella's shoulder over the seat.

"I have, but I don't think you have."

"When did you have it?"

Ella blushed.

A minute later I pulled into the strip mall. I'd noticed the restaurant the day before.

"Can I check out your computer?" Zed asked. "Once we're inside?"

I nodded. "Go ahead and carry it in."

In no time we were settled at a table and admiring the decor: dark teakwood tables and chairs, Japanese screens, black stoneware, and ivory carvings. We opened the menus. Ella said she liked sushi. Zed asked where she'd had it.

"A place downtown."

"With?" He clutched my computer to his chest.

"None of your beeswax." She glared at him. Obviously she wanted to impress me but keep him in the dark at the same time.

"What would you like?" I asked Zed.

"Whatever you order is fine." He looked around. Voice softening, he added, "But not too expensive. I don't want to break your bank."

I decided on a noodle dish and a chicken dish. Ella chose an order of sushi. By the time we had closed our menus, Zed had my computer out of the bag and on the table in front of him, across from me. I was pretty sure a laptop at dinner was on Marta's forbidden list too.

Zed clicked around for a minute and then smiled. "I found an open network," he said, flicking his bangs away from his forehead.

"Really?" I leaned forward. "Let me check my messages."

He turned the computer around, and I clicked onto my email. The waiter approached our table, and Ella ordered for all of us.

I didn't have any messages from the registry. Ella looked over my shoulder. "Don't you think she probably married?" She'd figured out pretty quickly what I was up to. "If so, she would have a different last name."

"Maybe," I said. "But I need to start somewhere."

"Do you think she lives around here?"

I shrugged.

"If she did, don't you think she'd come see us sometime?"

"You would hope, but maybe something happened that made her feel like she couldn't come back." What sort of things tore a family apart? Misunderstandings. Betrayals. Shunnings. But even people who were shunned came back to visit or at least stayed in contact. What would make Giselle leave and never return?

Zed leaned back in his chair, his big brown eyes shaded by his bangs.

"Do you ever think about your birth family?" I asked.

"Nope." He crossed his arms. "Never." His voice was firm.

I slid the computer back to him and he smiled.

The rain continued as we left the restaurant. Surely Peggy was home by now. She was probably finishing the dinner dishes and urging her four-year-old toward bed. Her older sons had probably carried in the groceries and unhitched the horse. Her husband was probably checking the livestock one last time and thinking about which field to plow in the morning, as long as the rain stopped.

When we reached the cottage, Ella and Zed were in a good mood as we clattered up the steps to the porch. The lights were off on the first floor, and Ella felt around for the switch. The computer was turned off too. The clear opening of the woodstove showed that a fire was burning, hot and bright.

"Mom?" Ella called up the stairs.

There wasn't an answer.

"She's probably out in her office," I said.

"I'll check." Ella stepped out the door as Zed sat down at the computer. I stopped in front of the stove, warming my hands.

Ella returned a few moments later. "She's out there making phone calls. She wants to see you," she said to me.

When I got there, Marta was sitting at her desk with only a small reading lamp on. She wore her cape and didn't have the heat on in the room. There were shadows under her eyes, and she wore her black bonnet. She looked like a woman who was ready to flee.

"Sit down," she said, motioning to the chair by the door and then returning to the paper in front of her. She made a mark and then looked up again. "The grand jury convened today." Her voice was monotone. "I'm to be arraigned Wednesday."

I wasn't surprised. "What are the charges?"

"Negligent homicide." She squinted as she talked. "The autopsy came back Friday and was presented to the jury. There were no signs of a heart defect. No indication of cardiac arrest. So they assume it was my negligence because I didn't call 911 sooner, based on Lydia's blood pressure."

"Are they surmising it was preeclampsia-induced shock?" It was the third leading cause of death in late-term and postpartum women.

"I'm guessing that's it."

"What do you think?" I shot Marta a quick look. Her face was expressionless.

"She didn't have any of the other signs. No swelling. The baby was full term. No abdominal pain."

"What about fatigue?"

Marta inhaled and then exhaled slowly. "Most women who are nine months pregnant suffer from fatigue." She had a point. Still, preeclampsia sounded plausible to me.

"The autopsy should have shown if it was preeclampsia, though. Elevated liver enzymes. Low platelets."

"Those results were inconclusive," Marta said. "A little high for the liver enzymes. Borderline for the platelets."

"How high was her blood pressure?"

"It spiked at 160/110. That's when I told her she needed to go to the hospital."

"Not that it's any of my business, but do you have some savings set aside? Some way to cover the bills until this whole mess is taken care of and you can practice again?"

"Not really," she said vaguely.

"How about your bail? Any idea how much that will be?"

She tilted her head. "Excuse me?"

"Your bail. How high will it be?" I didn't even ask whether or not she'd be able to pay me the small amount we'd agreed on that she owed me. I already knew the answer to that. Thankfully I had some money set aside.

She spread her palms flat on the desktop. "I don't know," she answered. "My lawyer didn't say."

I couldn't imagine her bail would be all

that high. She wasn't exactly a flight risk, even though she looked like it right now. "When is my replacement arriving?"

She tapped her finger on the list. "I've called close to thirty different midwives from Pennsylvania and nearby states. I'm expecting a return call —maybe a couple—tomorrow. Then I'll know."

I was sure she was stalling. I would bet good money that she didn't have a couple of prospects, or even one, ready to call. What would happen to the mothers who were expecting her care? And what would happen to Ella and Zed? Would they be eating oatmeal for dinner? What if Marta couldn't post bail and ended up in jail? Surely someone from their church would come through and help. It wasn't my responsibility.

But they were my cousins . . .

Birth cousins. Not legal cousins, I reminded myself. I had no obligation. Except that I liked them more and more every day.

"I'm sorry for all of this, Marta, but I was planning on leaving in the morning," I said.

"So be it," she answered.

I backed out of her office and crossed the sodden lawn. The wind and rain were blowing through the stand of evergreens. I stepped into the side yard. Zed had left the ax in the chopping block. I remembered doing that when I was about his age and then the lecture from Dad, reminding me that we needed to take good care of what we had, that it was a way of honoring God. I yanked the ax from the wood and slipped it under the tarp over the woodpile.

Later, as I settled into bed, I heard Marta knock on Ella's bedroom door and go in. I tried to stay awake to hear any words they might exchange, but I fell asleep to the sound of the rain against the alcove window. It wasn't until the morning when Ella came out of the bathroom, her eyes puffy and red, that I realized how upset she was about the news of her mother's arraignment. Her whole world had just shifted.

I slipped from the bed and pulled out the carved box. I wrapped it in my baby quilt and then slid it back in the cloth bag. Next, I packed my bag. I would stop by Klara's house and demand to see *Mammi*. Then I would head to the hospital to see if Sean was free for a farewell lunch. If not, I hoped he would come to Philly to see me sometime soon.

I'd had enough of Lancaster County.

SIXTEEN

Ella and Zed had already left for school by the time I finished my shower. I'd wanted to tell them goodbye, but maybe it was better this way. I'd never been very good at farewells. I lugged my suitcase down the stairs and through the living room, ignoring Marta, who sat at the dining room table with her phone to her ear and the same list from the day before in front of her. Next I gathered my computer and the bag with the box and quilt, my coat and my tote bag, and deposited them in my car. All that was left was to tell Marta goodbye.

I stood in the living room, warming my hands by the woodstove while she spoke on the phone. I purposefully tuned her out. Maybe she was still trying to recruit another midwife to help her. Maybe she'd found one, after all, and was working out the details. Maybe she hadn't found one and was trying to cancel her appointments for the day—which would be quite a feat, considering that most Amish seemed to check their message machines in the barn only once every few days. Oh, well. It wasn't my problem.

"Lexie?"

I stepped into the archway between the two rooms.

"I wanted to say goodbye." The ribbons on her head covering hung loose and the rings under her eyes were more pronounced than the day before. She wore the same mauve print dress she'd had on for the last few days, but now it was wrinkled and limp. "Thank you for your help," she said, extending her hand. I took it and she squeezed mine, and then she quickly let go. "Blessings to you and your work in Philadelphia. I'm afraid I'll have to mail a check to you rather than pay you now. Though it might be a few weeks."

"Of course. Take your time."

On impulse, I gave her a hug, one she stiffly endured, though she didn't hug me back. A minute later I was hurrying down the front steps, but something made me stop. I turned around. Through the window I could see Marta sitting back down at the table and then burying her head in her arms. In a moment her shoulders began to convulse. I took another step down the stairs and stopped again. Slowly, I turned and forced myself back into the house.

She was sobbing.

"Marta," I said.

The sobbing stopped. "I thought you'd gone."

"I heard you—"

"I'm fine." Her voice was muffled. "Please go."

"Is there something I can do? Before I leave?"

"No."

I stepped back out the door and a few minutes later, after texting Sean about lunch, I was on my way. It was a perfect late March morning: clear, cool, and crisp, yet promising to bloom warm and bright. On the highway I slowed behind a buggy and then navigated a hairpin turn, coming upon a cemetery in the corner of a field with every tombstone exactly alike in both size and shape.

I passed the buggy and realized I was avoiding thinking about the task at hand. Thanks to the information Ella found in the family Bible, I knew where my grandmother was. The woman I had imagined all these years wasn't whom I'd thought, but at least I had located her. And I had another cousin to meet and an aunt and an uncle. I passed the turn off to the Kemp and Gundy farm and came up behind another buggy. Maybe it was Nancy or Hannah or Alice. Maybe it was Ezra or Will. I sighed. If only my birth family were like that. I went around the buggy on the next straight stretch, giving the driver a wave and watching him nod in return. It was an old man, hunched over, his long gray beard hanging down against his chest, the collar of his jacket turned up on his neck. He held the reins loosely and seemed to be enjoying the ride.

My heart began to race again as I neared the lane down to Klara's. I turned and then stopped at the entrance to the lane, peering down the dirt road and then scanning the fields. I saw no one and began to ease my foot off the brake. There was nothing to do but get it over with.

Just as I began to accelerate, my cell phone rang. I pulled it from the pocket of my jacket. It was Marta. I answered it cautiously.

"I wouldn't be calling if I had another choice," she said. "Believe me."

I stopped the car again, in the middle of the lane. Believe her? She was unbelievable. That's all there was to it.

"But Peggy is in labor and her contractions are two minutes apart."

I thought of her trip to the big box store. Maybe it had been too much.

"She lives close to where you are at—or where I think you are."

"I don't have any equipment with me."

"I'll meet you there with the bag." She gave me the address and I jotted it down, hoping the GPS would be able to find it.

"Thank you," she said.

I stared down the lane again. I could chance taking the time to try to meet my grandmother or I could go take care of Peggy. Contractions two minutes apart for a woman who'd already birthed nine babies probably meant she was breezing through the transition phase and was close to delivering. I didn't actually know because I'd never delivered a mother with anywhere close to that many births. Right now my obligation was to Peggy, no doubt about it.

I backed out of the narrow lane, keyed the address into my GPS, and turned right onto the highway, leaving the house behind. My heart rate slowed, even though I was hurrying to a birth. I passed the weeping willow trees where Zed and I had waited together just five days before. It seemed like a month ago already. A mile later I turned into a farmyard right on the highway.

A girl older than Ella stood at the back door. "Hurry!" she called out. I raced toward the house. "She's in her room."

A younger girl stood at the kitchen sink, washing dishes.

I dropped my jacket on a chair. "Is your *daed* here?"

"No," the older girl said as I followed her down the hall. "He works construction. He's on a job."

Peggy was wearing a dress, with no apron, that hung loose around her and she knelt beside her bed, her hands clasped as if she were praying. "I think it's time," she said.

I asked the older girl where the bathroom was, and she pointed across the hall. I told Peggy I would be right back after I scrubbed. I pushed my sleeves to my elbows and began washing my fingers, hands, and forearms. If Marta didn't arrive soon, I wouldn't even have latex gloves.

By the time I was scrubbed and back in the room, Peggy was on the bed. A minute later, the baby came out with one push and I caught him easily. *Baby number 257.* He howled right away, a good sign considering I didn't have a bulb to clear his airway. I ran my finger through his mouth, and it came out clean.

I cut the cord with a pair of sewing scissors, sterilized by the oldest girl under my instruction, cleaned up, and had Peggy in a fresh white nightgown and the little boy nursing in no time. The older sisters came in and out of the room, bringing food to their mother and blankets for the baby. I didn't have scales to weigh the little one, but I guessed he was close to seven pounds. The four-year-old, also a boy, wasn't much interested in the baby, but he came in to say hello and then returned to the yard to play with his toy trucks.

It was nearly an hour later that Marta arrived with the medical bag. I was surprised to find Ella with her. They waited as I finished up. When I weighed the baby, I wasn't surprised to see that I had been right; he was seven pounds three ounces. After recording the details in Peggy's chart, I filled out the certificate of live birth and then added a worksheet detailing how to apply for the Pennsylvania birth certificate—not that Peggy would need it. Having been through this nine times before, she'd already had plenty of experience.

When I was finished, Marta pulled me aside and handed me another chart. It was Esther's.

"She's in labor," Marta said. "That's why I took Ella out of school—to go with you to help with Simon."

I nodded.

"Will you go?"

"Of course," I answered. Did Marta think me heartless?

I gave Peggy's daughters instructions to walk with their mother when she got up to go to the bathroom, to make sure they gave her plenty to eat and drink, and to call my cell phone if anything seemed amiss with their mother or the baby. The girls nodded as if they didn't need my instructions, even though it had been four years since there had been a birth in the family. I took a final look at the baby boy, etching him into my memory, thinking "Peggy's baby." She said she wouldn't name him until her husband arrived. Her oldest daughter had tried to call the cell phone of one of the men he worked with, but the call had gone into voice mail, so her husband didn't even know that he was now the father of a tenth child.

As I walked to my car, I checked my phone. Sean was available for lunch, but I texted him back to say I was involved with an unexpected delivery and would have to touch base with him later.

By the time Ella and I followed Marta out of the driveway, it was eleven fifteen. "There was a full moon last night, right?" I was joking. I'd recently read a study that debunked the lunar effect theory as an old wives' tale.

"Mom always says women are more likely to deliver during full moons."

"People have thought for years that it was the pull of gravity because our bodies are eighty percent water," I said. "But the full moon theory has been proved wrong."

Ella scowled and said whatever the reason for it, it was true.

I changed the subject. "Peggy's daughters sure seemed to know what they were doing."

Ella gave me a funny look. "It's not like they haven't done all of this before."

"It's been a few years."

"You expect too little out of people," Ella said. We rode in silence for a moment and then she spoke, a little hesitantly. "Peggy already had her oldest daughter when she got married."

"Really?" I wasn't sure if I was encouraging Ella to gossip, but she definitely had my attention.

"Yeah. Peggy got pregnant by her boyfriend. She thought they were going to get married. But then he didn't want to join the church and she did. So she had her baby and joined the church. Later she got married to someone else and started having all those other kids."

My instincts had been right. Not all Amish would give up a baby for adoption. My situation could have been handled differently . . .

Oops. Here I was again. Back to speculating.

We passed back by the willow trees and then the lane to Klara's house. As we neared the road to the Kemp and Gundy place, I noticed Ella's nose was against the window. A roar filled the car. I slowed. Sure enough, coming up the road was Ezra on his motorcycle, his red hair sticking out from under his black helmet. Ella smiled. He must have spotted her because he pulled out behind us and followed closely. I slowed, allowing more distance between us and Marta, who was still ahead. On the straight stretch Ezra passed, waving and smiling. A truck came over the crest of the hill opposite him, and he darted back into his lane just in front of us. A half mile later he pulled over to the side of the road, and we passed by as he waved again.

I accelerated. "How long have you known Ezra?"

"Since we were kids. Mom would visit his grandma." She paused. "They used to all be friends."

"Aren't they still?"

"Sort of. I guess. Not like they used to be."

"They seemed friendly enough last week when we were there for Hannah's appointment."

Ella nodded. "We just don't see them much anymore, but I used to play with Ezra when we were little. He's two years older."

Marta turned off toward her cottage, and Ella and I continued on to Lancaster. I asked if her mother pulled her out of school very often to help with a birth, and she said no. Esther had asked if she could come to take care of Simon though, because she didn't have any family to help.

When we arrived at Esther's, she called out that the door was unlocked. We entered and found her stooping at her desk, her hands on her keyboard. David was in the kitchen, and Simon was sitting on the floor of the living room, wailing. When he saw Ella he stopped for a minute, gulped a breath of air, and then started again.

"He's been this way all day," Esther said, straightening up. She nodded toward her computer screen. "I have a paper I need to finish editing. It's due tomorrow."

I wondered if we'd come too early; if Marta had overreacted out of her devotion to Esther and her family. The woman didn't look as though she was in labor, let alone ready to give birth.

David strolled into the living room, stepping over the screaming Simon. He shook my hand and said, "So you will end up delivering our baby after all." He smiled widely.

"It looks that way," I said, glancing at Esther. "How far apart are the contractions?" Marta had said three minutes.

Esther held up a hand. Was she having one now? A minute later she said, "I quit keeping track." She turned back toward her computer. "I just have a few more minutes on this, and then I can send it off."

Ella was down on the floor trying to talk to Simon. He crawled away from her and then plopped down on the far side of the room, next to the bathroom door.

"He's been out of sorts since last evening," David said. "Since Esther's labor started."

"Last evening?" I stole a glance at her again. She was most likely standing because she couldn't sit.

"Around eight," David said. "And she only got a few hours of sleep. She worked on that paper most of the night."

Esther was statue still again, and I wondered if she were having another contraction. She'd already been in labor for fifteen hours. "Show me the bedroom," I said to David. Esther wasn't going to have the baby until she sent the paper off, so she might as well get it done. I would set up my supplies. I hoped that once she was ready, the birth would go quickly.

By the time she joined us in the bedroom, she was nine centimeters dilated and fully effaced. David rubbed her back while Ella fed Simon lunch and then put him down for a nap. But he didn't sleep. He stood in his crib, screaming for his mother. He knew something was up, knew in some instinctual way that his life was about to change. Finally, Esther asked Ella to fetch him and rock him in the living room, which she did until he fell asleep, and then she slipped him back into his crib.

Esther and David's little girl arrived at 1:47 p.m. They named her Caroline—a perfect name for a perfect baby. *Baby number 258.* She had her mother's chin, her father's nose, and her brother's forehead. When Simon awoke, Ella carried him in and he patted his little sister's head and then clung to his mother, his chubby hands entangled in her clean pink nightgown.

Caroline took it all in. *Simon. Esther. David.* The woman—*me*—hovering nearby. And the girl—*Ella*—whose face was filled with awe. I asked Esther if I could take a photo of her family. She agreed, asking Ella to squeeze in too. After I'd captured the image, she asked if I would email her the photo. She would send it home to her mother and sisters.

When we left three hours later, I was thinking

about my own birth again and my upcoming search in Montgomery County. Why Giselle would have left Lancaster County to have me was a mystery, and even though I was anxious to be on my way and get some more answers, I knew I was in no shape to drive to Harrisburg this evening. I couldn't search for the birth certificate until tomorrow anyway, so that left me getting a hotel or staying at Marta's for another night. I sighed. I sent Sean a text, asking if we could do lunch the next day.

Before going home we headed for Peggy's. I felt we had left too soon, in too much of a rush. I wanted to make sure she and her little baby boy were fine. For once Ella didn't speak as we drove. She perked up when we drove by Ezra's place, but he was nowhere in sight. I glanced down the lane when we passed Klara's. *Tomorrow.* If all went well, I would stop at Klara's, have lunch with Sean, and then leave for Harrisburg.

My life was beginning to feel like the movie *Groundhog Day*, where everything is exactly the same, over and over and over again.

Everything was fine at Peggy's. In fact, she was surprised to see me. The family was eating an early dinner of enchiladas, taco salad, and cornbread—all cooked by the older daughters. Peggy declared it the most delicious meal she'd ever eaten. The baby was sleeping in a bassinet next to the table. Her husband, Eli, stood, introduced himself, and shyly thanked me. Then he sat back down, and a daughter on his right passed him more cornbread.

"I'll bring the baby in for a checkup in a week," Peggy said.

I didn't know what to tell her. Marta wouldn't be seeing patients in a week, and I would be gone. I told her to call Marta to set up an appointment. I stopped myself from imagining a newborn riding in a buggy without a car seat, or even with a car seat, but I told her the midwife would come to her.

"Oh, no," she said. "I'll be more than ready to get out of the house by then."

I held the little boy—Peggy whispered that his name was Thomas—and untucked his blanket and T-shirt. The area around his belly button looked good. He wasn't feverish. He looked up at me with a wrinkled forehead and inky eyes. I buttoned him back together, and as I did he reached for my finger and squeezed. If only I knew what he was thinking. Did he recognize me? Had I left some mark on him? I handed him back to Peggy and told the family goodbye.

Who had left a mark on me?

As we drove by the weeping willow trees, I knew I wouldn't wait until tomorrow.

SEVENTEEN

Ella asked me what I was doing as I turned down the lane.

"Stopping at Klara's," I answered.

"This late?"

I nodded.

"Can I wait in the car?" she muttered. "I'm not nearly as brave as you."

"It's cold out," I said. "And getting dark."

"I have my coat. And I'll hide in the backseat. But could you stop the car now? Before you get any closer to the house?" She slouched down, staring straight ahead.

I wasn't crazy about leaving Ella alone way out here, but the look on her face convinced me to allow it. I pulled over to the edge of the lane and climbed out. As I walked the last fifty yards, Holstein cows gathered around the white fence. The large white barn was most likely outfitted as a dairy. Beyond it was a weathered outbuilding and behind that, in the waning light, I could make out twin, parallel lines of trees. Most likely a creek ran through the property there, something I had missed the other day when I'd been spying from the road through my camera.

Walking along the field, I thought of baby Caroline and little Thomas, of how warmly they were welcomed into their families. I thought of the trust in their eyes.

I gave James the impression I hadn't done any reading on adoption, but that wasn't true. I'd read enough to know about an infant's ability to grieve.

I often wondered if a relinquished newborn had the same feelings of loss as a newborn whose parents were killed in a tragic accident or moved away or otherwise disappeared from their lives. None of the babies would be able to comprehend what happened, but still the emotions of losing everything familiar would be there.

I'd definitely studied what birth was like for a newborn. I knew I would have recognized Giselle's smell and her voice. And I knew, whether I was taken from her at birth or a few days after, that I had mourned her. I knew that without her colostrum and then breast milk that I was at a greater risk for allergies, infections, and disease. I knew buried within me, subconsciously, was the primitive terror of being separated from her. I knew she was my first tragic loss and that, no matter the protection I'd been given since, that loss impacted my lifelong sense of trust.

I kept my eyes on the house as I thought about her, and I thought about her because it was easier than thinking about the people inside the house as I walked up the brick path.

The porch steps were just a few feet away. The curtain in the upstairs window on the left side of the balcony fluttered. I stopped, willing myself to breath, willing my heart to not thump right out of my chest.

The only other time I'd been close to this scared was when Dad took me to college my freshman year. It wasn't college that scared me—not the academics, not making new friends, not living away from home. It wasn't what I thought my new classmates would think of Dad's hat and clothes that scared me, either. I was over all of that by then.

At first, as I sat and cried in his car and he put his arm around me, I knew what didn't scare me—but I couldn't pinpoint what did. I just knew I was terrified.

He told me to give it a week. He said if I still felt sad he would come get me, and I would still have time to enroll in Chemeketa Community College. I called him after a week and told him I was fine. Three weeks later he called to ask when I was coming home for a visit. He said he'd been missing me and hoped he would see me soon. After I told him goodbye and hung up the phone, I sat on my bed and cried. He was still my father. He still wanted me. I realized then that I'd been afraid he was done parenting me. Even though he'd said I could move back home, I'd been afraid he didn't want me anymore.

He came and got me the next weekend for a visit.

The upstairs curtain of Klara's house fluttered again, and I climbed the steps. Here I was, my beloved father dead, forcing myself on people who hadn't wanted me twenty-six years ago and most likely didn't want me now. I crossed the porch, knocked on the heavy front door, and waited. For the first time it occurred to me that they might not answer the door. In that case I'd go around to the *daadi haus* and find *Mammi* myself. I knocked again. And waited. I knocked a third time and then turned on my heels. I barely heard the door creak open a crack. I turned back.

"Yes?" A man stood at the door, probably the same one I'd seen in the field the week before.

"My name is Lexie Jaeger. I'm looking for Klara."

The door opened all the way. His face was worn and weathered, and up close I could see that his eyes were gray.

"She's out back. Could I tell her what you want?"

"I can wait," I said. I thought of Ella. She'd have to bear with me.

The man squinted. Finally he said, "Come on in then. I'll go see how long she's going to be."

He led me into a living room and motioned me over to a brown couch with a green crocheted afghan draped over the back. I sat and looked around the room. There were the bookcases Ella mentioned and the stack of puzzles. Behind them would be the Bible. I wondered if I had enough time to look, but it was as if I were glued to the couch. Though I already knew my name was in it, I was still the unwanted child. I didn't have the right to look.

There was an old, old clock on the mantel that ticked off each second, and above it was a framed cross-stitch that said "Bless this house and all who enter." I scoffed and turned toward the kitchen. A long plank table with benches on either side filled one end. It could seat twelve at least. The kitchen was open with white cabinets and gray Formica counters. Plants filled a window box above the sink. Jars of peaches, pears, and tomatoes filled an open floor-to-ceiling pantry cupboard off to the side.

I heard the back door open and what sounded like two people coming inside. A woman's voice was speaking in Pennsylvania Dutch. She didn't sound angry and she wasn't loud, just firm. The man didn't answer.

The woman was in the kitchen now, coming toward me around the table. She was tall and had the same austere appearance of many of the middle-aged Amish women I'd seen. Her sandy hair, just a strip of which was visible at the hairline, was balding at the center part and covered with a black bonnet. Her dress was the same pale blue as her eyes.

According to the family Bible, if this was Klara, she was my aunt.

She froze when she saw me, and I studied her face, expecting to see the same wild range of emotions I had observed the first time Marta laid eyes on me. Though Klara's reaction was just as extreme as her sister's had been, it wasn't nearly so ambiguous. Where Marta had shown at least a flash of something akin to joy, this woman's face exhibited nothing but a tightly controlled rage. Suddenly, her eyes began darting around the room, searching, I presumed, for someone who might have come with me.

"Lexie," I said, stumbling to my feet. "I'm Lexie Jaeger. From Oregon." I stepped around the couch. "Are you Klara?"

She simply nodded and put her hands behind her back.

"Then you must be Alexander," I said to the man.

"I am," he answered, meeting my eyes for a split second and then looking at the floor.

"I have questions—"

"You need to go," Klara said.

"I want to see *Mammi*."

"Mammi?" The tone of her voice jolted me.

"And Ada." I squared my shoulders.

"No. You need to go." She stepped toward the front door. *"Now!"*

I didn't move but instead looked to Alexander. His head was turned, his attention directed toward something at the far end of the large room. Following his gaze, I spotted an open wooden staircase along the back wall. From somewhere above us, a female voice called out, "Who's here?"

Dashing to the base of the stairs, Klara answered quickly in Pennsylvania Dutch. Then she turned back toward me, her features twisted in fury.

"You have no idea what you're doing," she hissed.

Again, I looked to Alexander, who was nodding. He, too, seemed to want me to go, though in his eyes I saw not anger but something more like pleading. Desperation. Whatever their individual reasons were, neither one wanted me here.

"I need to see *Mammi*," I said softly to them both. Though this man in front of me may very well have been my own father, at the moment my grandmother would have to be my priority.

Klara's eyebrows raised, two pale brown arches in a ruddy forehead. "No!"

"I have a right to see her. You know I do."

While Alexander stood quietly by, Klara bustled forward and grabbed my hand. Her skin was rough and cold, and I tried to pull away but her grip was firm. Suddenly, she lunged for the front door, dragging me along.

"I want to know everything! I want to know about Giselle!" I exclaimed as I struggled against her, shocked that this older woman was much stronger than I.

"*Mamm?*"

As the steps of the staircase began to creak, Klara let out a deep growl and gave one last, powerful thrust, jerking open the front door and trying to push me through onto the porch. I managed to stop her by gripping each side of the door frame and holding on as tightly as I could.

"*Mamm*! What are you doing?"

Klara froze, and over her shoulder I could see a young Amish woman hurrying down the stairs. Her feet were bare. She wore a traditional dress but no apron, and her blond hair was pulled back in a bun, but no cap. Instantly, Klara released me. I seized the opportunity to move fully inside again, just beyond reach of her icy fingers, and plant my feet firmly, like a tree with roots shooting into the earth.

The woman was on the bottom step now. She was shorter than I, and thin, too thin. As she came closer, I saw that her eyes were brown, like mine, and we shared the same upturned nose.

"What's going on?" Her voice was full of concern.

Klara smoothed her skirt and apron, and tucked a loose strand of hair under her cap. "She's from Oregon," she said, her face becoming an emotionless mask. "Visiting Amish country." She clasped her hands behind her back again and looked at me. "Isn't that right?"

For a surreal moment life stopped and I took it all in. Alexander, watching and waiting, as if defeated, to see how it would all play out. Klara, trying with all her might to pretend as if nothing of importance was taking place right here, in this moment. And a lovely young woman, who I assumed was my cousin, gazing at me with such intensity that I felt as if I were splitting in two.

Then she reached for my hand and gave it a shake. "I'm Ada." Her smile was warm and

251

genuine. She looked the way I wanted to feel. *Trusting. Protected. Hopeful.*

"Ada! *Deine kapp*!" Klara snapped.

One delicate hand fluttered to the back of the woman's head, and she blushed. "I was getting ready for bed when I heard voices."

"She needs her rest. This is too much for her," Klara said to me. "She's ill."

"I heard," I answered.

"You did?" Ada asked. "From who?"

"The Gundys."

She looked at me straight away, her mouth solemn but her eyes smiling. "How are they?"

Klara stepped between us, forcing our hands apart, and spoke to Ada again in Pennsylvania Dutch. Ada sighed and whispered, *"Ya."* Then she turned to me. "You will come again?"

"Ya." I winced, hoping I didn't sound as if I were mocking her. The word had slipped out. "Yes. I would love to see you again."

"Come along, then." Klara opened the front door and stepped out. I followed her, turning to wave at Ada, but she was already heading back up the stairs, the skirt of her dress swaying a little with each labored step.

I followed Klara out the door and then veered to my right, heading toward the *daadi haus*.

"Where are you going?" Klara's face was still stony.

"To see *Mammi*."

"I'm afraid that's not possible right now."

I kept walking.

"The door to her house is locked." Klara had her hand over the pocket of her apron.

I turned then and looked straight at her. My face wasn't placid. Nor was it still. I could feel it growing redder by the moment. "Unlock it then, or I will march right back into your house and up those stairs and tell Ada I'm her cousin."

She stared me down for a few moments. I held her gaze. A cow mooed in the distance. A cat leaped from the porch down to the ground and then darted toward the field. I caught the scent of fresh-tilled soil in the breeze.

I followed a few feet behind her. By the light of the moon I could make out bare trellises lining the side of the house. We reached the backyard and skirted the perimeter of a garden plot. At the *daadi haus* a modern, battery-operated lantern sat on a table on the porch, and next to that was a lone rocking chair. The little house was painted the same sparkling white as the other buildings on the farm, with no embellishments. At the base of the front steps was a pot of daffodils in full bloom.

"She's asleep," Klara said as we reached the door and she quietly unlocked it. "But you may look at her."

She stepped inside and I followed, my heart pounding furiously at the thought of seeing my own birth grandmother for the very first time—

well, actually, for the very first time since she carried me into an airport twenty-six years ago and handed me over to a pair of strangers.

Blinking, I stood there inside the stuffy room and took in the sight of the old woman. She was sleeping in a recliner, tufts of white hair like cotton balls poking out from under her cap. Her head was tilted back and her mouth was open just a little. My eyes fell on her chest, which seemed so still, and I held my breath until I saw it rise and fall.

"What's wrong with her?" I whispered.

"She's getting older." Klara shrugged.

There was a quilt spread across *Mammi*'s lap, and with a small gasp I realized that it looked exactly like the one she had sent with me when she gave me over to Mama and Dad. For some reason, just seeing it there softened my heart toward this woman and made me feel connected to her in a unique way. Maybe she *had* surrendered me to strangers in an airport, but it wasn't as though she just walked in there and gave me over randomly.

We're whom she wanted for you, my dad had said. *Whom God wanted.*

"Did she make that quilt?" I asked Klara now.

"Decades ago."

"How old is she?"

"Seventy-eight."

She was only two years older than Dad had been, but compared to him she seemed ancient. "I have questions for her," I said.

Klara exhaled loudly. "I don't want to wake her up."

"What does her doctor say?"

"Not much." Her voice softened a little. She glanced out the window into the darkness.

"I wanted to ask her about Giselle."

Klara stiffened.

"And about *Mammi* meeting my parents in the Philadelphia Airport—"

"You need to go," Klara said. Her voice was harsh.

"Please. Won't you help me?"

Klara stepped back out onto the porch, and again I followed her. As she locked the door she said, "Did Marta put you up to this?"

I almost laughed. "No."

"What has she told you?"

I shrugged, thinking if I said "nothing" it would give her even more reason not to give me any information either. "I just want to know my story," I said. "Why I was given up." I couldn't make out the expression on Klara's face as she marched away from me. "I don't think it's too much to ask," I called out, my voice rising.

Shadows leaped around the yard as we reached the front, and Klara suddenly stopped and spun around to face me. "What do you want from me? Ada is sick. I can't afford to live in the past. What's happened has happened."

"So, it's pretty much forgive and forget in

your opinion too?" My heart raced again.

"Is that what Marta told you?"

I didn't answer as I walked around her to the brick path.

"Don't come back," she said. "You've done enough damage as it is."

Oh, I'd be back all right. I kept walking until I heard the front door slam. Then I turned around. The curtain in the upstairs window fluttered again. I waved. Seething inside and rehearsing what I would say to Ella, I marched up the lane.

But when I reached the car, she wasn't there. I called out her name, but she didn't answer. I phoned her cell, but she didn't pick up. My anger began to turn to panic. Maybe I'd been too trusting to leave her. Maybe someone had taken her.

I started the car. As I reached the highway, a motorcycle roared by. On the back was Ella.

EIGHTEEN

I turned right and followed. Of course it was Ezra on the front of the bike. I kept my distance, not wanting to cause him to wreck, but I blinked my bright lights to get his attention.

Ella wore a helmet and a leather jacket. I presumed both were Ezra's because his head was bare and he wore only a T-shirt. Ella's dress fluttered free around her legs, and she leaned against Ezra's back, her cheek on his shoulder. "Please don't wreck," I whispered. I'd seen far too many motorcycle accidents during my ER rotation.

I honked as we neared the willow trees and flashed my lights again. Finally, Ezra pulled over. By the time I stopped, both were laughing. Ella climbed from the motorcycle, smoothing her dress down, and then whipped the helmet off her head, her long auburn hair falling loose. She retrieved a handful of bobby pins and her cap from her apron pocket.

Ezra gave me a sheepish grin as I climbed out of my car. "We're old friends," he said.

"So I heard." I hoped I looked like the gruff older cousin, ready to bust the kid. I turned to Ella. "We need to get going. Give Ezra his jacket."

She obliged and then gave him a flirty wave as well.

"See you Sat—"

"Thanks!" she called out, obviously trying to drown out his words.

He winked.

I knew then they thought I was ancient, unable to interpret their not so subtle communication. I decided not to drill her about going on the motorcycle ride. It wasn't my place. When we passed Klara's she asked me how it went. I answered her vaguely, not giving many details.

"I was so nervous waiting for you," she said. "When I heard Ezra's motorcycle, I ran out to the road."

Likely story. I was sure she would have ran toward the sound of Ezra's motorcycle no matter what else was going on. "So," I said, "that first day when I met you and you thought I was someone else—"

She squirmed a little.

"Who did you think I was?"

By the light of the full moon, I saw her roll her eyes. I stayed quiet.

Finally she said, "Ada."

"Why didn't you tell me?"

She shrugged. "Zed thought so too."

"Ella—"

"I didn't know you then, Lexie." She paused. "And I thought Mom would be mad."

"Why?"

"I grew up with her telling me I talked too much, that I didn't have any boundaries. All of that. She expected me to be this nice little girl. But I'm not nice. And I'm not Amish."

I wanted to laugh. She was one of the nicest people I'd ever met. And her life didn't seem that different from the Amish.

"I'm sorry," she said, turning toward me. "So you and Ada are cousins. You already knew that, right?"

"Yes," I said.

"But you two look more alike than most cousins —for example, more alike than you and I do."

"Genetics," I said. "It could happen." But I wasn't sure. Maybe we were just cousins who happened to share a number of dominant genes, but I suspected that we were even more, that we were half sisters instead.

"Are you going to stay?" Ella turned up the heat in the car.

"I probably should . . . at least until Saturday," I answered, giving her a sideways glance.

"Don't tell Mom."

"What do you have planned?"

"Volleyball and a sing."

I raised my eyebrows.

"Honest," Ella said. "That's what Amish kids do."

"Even ones on their *rumschpringe*?"

"Ya," she answered. "Even those. Besides," she said. "Saturday is my sixteenth birthday."

Marta stood at the kitchen sink, washing dishes when we arrived. She'd made a broccoli-and-rice casserole for dinner that Ella and I ate as we told her about Esther's delivery. Next I told her about checking on Peggy and little Thomas.

Ella shot me a look but she didn't need to. I had no desire to tell Marta about my stop at Klara's. I still felt as though I'd been gutted alive. Besides, what if Marta and Klara formed an alliance and ganged up on me? I couldn't handle them one-on-one, let alone two-on-one.

Worse, I was still feeling guilty about my own behavior from earlier, when I had so stubbornly forced Marta's hand once I knew we had a patient in labor. Though I deserved to get all of the information she had given me thus far—and plenty more, for that matter—I still didn't like the way I had gone about it, and something in me wanted to make amends.

"Would it help if I stayed another week?" I asked Marta. "I can call the agency tomorrow. If I use the extended-stay hotel, I don't need to find a place to live." I had to go back and see Ada and soon. Once I left Lancaster County, I didn't know how long it would be before I could return.

She did that funny little lip purse I'd seen so many times. Finally she said, "I don't want to put you out."

I stood and picked up my plate, carrying it to the sink. "Think about it."

"Maybe just until I find someone else. It should only take a few days."

"Just until then," I said, suddenly exhausted. I quietly washed my dishes and put them in the rack, hoping Sean would be free for lunch the next day.

NINETEEN

"Please let me go." Zed's voice carried up the staircase the next morning.

I couldn't make out Marta's answer, but as I started down the steps, I heard, "Ella isn't going either. You'll both be at school."

"But it would be a good civics lesson." Zed was as close to whining as I'd heard him. I stopped on the last step.

"The answer is no." Marta handed him his backpack. "Ella," she called into the kitchen. "You need to get moving."

She came out in a moment, her coat already on. She kissed her mother on the cheek but didn't say a word. A second later she led the way out of the house with Zed tagging along behind.

"I'd like to go," I said. There were no prenatal appointments scheduled for the morning.

She shook her head without looking at me.

"You need someone with you, Marta. I'll take notes in case you forget what was said."

She frowned. "Believe me, I think I'll remember." The arraignment was scheduled for ten, but Marta was required to turn herself in by nine.

I left the house an hour after she did. The morning was the warmest yet since I'd been in Pennsylvania, and the trees along the road were beginning to bud, making me wonder if the leaves on the hazelnut trees back home were unfolding. It would be time to spray soon.

A crowd was gathered outside the courthouse again—both Amish and Mennonite, both men and women and several babies and young children. I didn't see any buggies and assumed the Amish had hired drivers to bring them into town. I found a parking place a couple of blocks away and hurried to the courthouse. The crowd must have gone inside because the sidewalk was clear. I stepped through the double doors and passed through the security checkpoint, and then I ascended the stairs to the courtroom. The wooden benches on both sides were filled with Marta's supporters.

"Lexie!" David sat in the middle of the room and motioned to me. I joined him, asking about Esther, Caroline, and Simon, a little surprised that he would leave them all alone so soon. He assured me that Esther had insisted he come to support Marta.

Speaking of support, I began scanning the crowd, wondering if Klara would show up for her little sister, but none of the faces under the caps belonged to her. One, in the back row, belonged to Alice, though. She nodded at me and smiled. Will Gundy wasn't in the room.

A few minutes later Marta and Connie Stanton entered and sat on the front right side of the room. Moments later a man, whom I assumed was the DA, entered. And then we all rose as the bailiff announced the judge, an old man with a full head of snow-white hair that contrasted dramatically with his black robe.

I had told Marta I would take notes, but I was so mesmerized by the proceedings that I hardly wrote anything down on the pad of paper I'd brought. The DA read the charges of two counts of involuntary manslaughter and one count of practicing without a license. He said that Marta Bayer had played God that night with the life of Lydia Gundy and her unborn son, and that if Marta had acted responsibly both would be alive today. Then the judge asked for the plea and Marta responded, clearly, "Not guilty." The judge addressed her, saying that the charges were serious and reminding her that both a mother and baby were dead under her watch. "Three children are without a mother and little brother, and a husband is without his wife and son," he said. "This is a lifelong sentence for them."

Marta's head, from the back, did not budge. Nor did her shoulders. Tears filled my eyes. Would two more children—teenagers with no father—end up without their mother too?

The judge said that a pretrial hearing would be scheduled for two weeks. "In the meantime, you will be held in the Lancaster County jail," he said to Marta. "Bail is posted at five hundred thousand dollars." Even though I hardly watched TV, I'd seen enough crime shows to know that meant Marta would have to come up with fifty thousand to get out. I also knew she didn't have that kind of money. I looked around the room. Chances were that no one in the courtroom did, either. I was sure there were plenty of Amish and Mennonites who were land rich, but they probably didn't have fifty thousand dollars in cash available to cough up at a moment's notice. A murmur rose through the courtroom, and the judge hit his gavel on the desk.

After the judge dismissed the court, Marta turned around, searching the crowd. I stepped out into the aisle and she motioned to me with just a nod of her head. Connie Stanton stood beside her, gathering her files and papers. I stepped around people filling the aisle and made my way against the stream to the divider.

"Tell Ella and Zed what happened." Marta's voice was calm.

"I will."

"I don't know when I'll be home . . ." She blinked quickly. "I never thought this would happen, but just in case I had made arrangements a few days ago for the children to go to Esther and David's. Though now that the baby's come . . ."

"No, they can't be there. I'll stay. The kids can remain at home, and I'll stay with them."

"It's too much to ask of you—"

"I can keep up with your appointments and deliveries as well."

"What about Philadelphia?"

I shrugged. "I'll tell the agency I've been delayed."

"Are you sure?"

"It's a family emergency," I added, stressing the word "family" and wanting her to hear me.

"Thank you," she whispered, and from the look in her eyes, I knew she had.

The bailiff came toward her, and then it was time for her to go.

I followed the crowd to the back of the room, turning before I exited. The bailiff led Marta past the judge's bench to a door, where he punched in a code. A second later he opened the door and she slipped through.

On the sidewalk in front of the courthouse groups of Amish and Mennonites mingled. I stood for a moment, feeling awkward and alone. I searched for David, but he must have already left.

"Lexie." It was Alice, motioning for me to join her. I did and she introduced me to a couple of other Amish women as Marta's helper. I asked how Hannah was, and Alice said, "Tired. She's been resting. In fact, I should get going to help her with the girls. But first I'll tell Will what happened." She took a deep breath. "Something must be done about this." Alice gave me a half hug and slipped away into the crowd and then down the sidewalk. A moment later she climbed into the front seat of a van.

My steps were heavy as I walked around the corner toward my car. I needed to take a look at the schedule and sort through who was due when. Delivering babies was such a juggle between prenatal appointments, deliveries, and follow-up care. With Marta doing the scheduling and canceling of appointments, I'd been spared the stress of all of that. Now I would need Ella's help. I hoped she would know whom to call if a mother didn't have a phone or didn't check her messages very often.

While I was still in town, I went to Esther's

house to check on her and Caroline. I also wanted to let her know I would be staying with Ella and Zed at the cottage, so they wouldn't have to move in here temporarily after all. I gave Esther the bare bones of the hearing, knowing David would fill her in more fully when he got home later.

As I examined little Caroline, Esther talked about how the baby wanted to sleep all the time. I suggested that she unwrap her when it was feeding time—that perhaps being so warm and cozy made it hard for her to stay awake. Simon was still out of sorts and wouldn't let me come near him. When I left, Esther was sitting on the couch with both the baby and Simon on her lap.

As I reached my car, my phone beeped with a text from Sean. He was available for lunch. We ate at a Vietnamese restaurant in downtown Lancaster. The family who owned the place was friendly, and in conversation we learned that they had fled from New Orleans during Hurricane Katrina. Sean and I each had a bowl of beef noodle soup, the perfect lunch for a drizzly day.

He was concerned about Marta, and I gave him a play-by-play of the arraignment. When I told him how high the bail was, he whistled in response but said he wouldn't be surprised if someone posted it. "There are many Amish who are much wealthier than they appear."

When everyone looked pretty much the same, it was hard to tell.

"The DA must think Marta was negligent in not calling 911 sooner." I twirled noodles around my chopsticks.

"What was Lydia's blood pressure?"

I told him and he agreed it was high. I also explained the preeclampsia angle.

He leaned back in his chair. "Does Marta carry oxygen with her?"

"Yes. Two tanks." I now carried one of them in my car. "And I'm sure she used it. Why wouldn't she have?"

I thought about how Lydia might have died as I put down my chopsticks and picked up the plastic spoon. I'd heard of people dying in their sleep before, even young people, and the autopsy not turning up a cause. "Do you think her attorney can get the charges reduced to practicing without a license?" That was a really weird thing about Pennsylvania. The state didn't issue licenses for lay-midwives— most were licensed through national organizations. But if things went wrong the state had no qualms in prosecuting midwives for practicing without a state license, even though they couldn't get one.

"Probably not." He paused for a moment and then speculated. "There must be evidence in the chart that she should have called 911 sooner or referred Lydia to a physician."

I nodded. Surely the DA had subpoenaed the chart at the beginning of the case. Though I had just recently met my aunt, I knew in my heart there was no way Marta would have altered her charting afterward.

As I drove away from the restaurant, I thought of all the other things I would need to do. Ella cooked, but I would have to do the grocery shopping. Maybe pay the bills, which meant I should take a look at Marta's books to see if they were balanced. I would visit Marta in jail by tomorrow or the next day to get the information to help me keep her home and practice afloat.

When I reached Marta's, I pored over the schedule. The next two weeks were filled with both office visits and home visits. I would fit in postpartum and well-baby checkups as needed. As a nurse-midwife working in a hospital, I didn't do well-baby checkups. Pediatricians did. With home births, after the one-week checkup, the baby went to a pediatrician and then later all of the vaccinations, which it seemed the majority of the Amish opted to do, were started.

I had five mothers due in the next two weeks. I would commit to staying in Lancaster County that long, until I could talk to Ada and until the change of plea, unless one of the other midwives Marta had asked to help her came through.

I figured Marta had a ninety percent chance, maybe a ninety-nine percent chance, of not keeping her business. If she plea-bargained and pled guilty to practicing without a license, I assumed that if she kept practicing, she'd be arrested again.

If she didn't plea-bargain and the matter went to trial, she would probably end up serving a sentence or at least being on probation. She wouldn't be able to practice then, either.

Helping out a little longer wasn't going to make a difference in the long run, but maybe it would help Ella and Zed in the short run. I also thought it important not to abandon those five mothers here at the very end of their pregnancies.

My last appointment for that afternoon was, thankfully, at two. I would be finished before Ella and Zed arrived home from school and able to talk with them about their mother. I closed the appointment book and stood. It shouldn't be me, someone they hardly knew, doing the telling. It should be family. It should be Klara.

The afternoon went by quickly, too quickly. In no time at all the last mother left and I had the office cleaned and ready for the next round of appointments.

I waited in the cottage for the kids. I was afraid if I met them at the bus they would think something tragic had happened. With ten minutes to kill, I decided to call Sophie. She picked up on the second ring. I told her what had happened with Marta. She didn't seem surprised. She thanked me for being willing to stay longer for the sake of Ella and Zed.

Then she told me all the church members said to tell me hello. They'd had their weekly Bible study the night before and had prayed for me.

Sophie also said Mrs. Glick inquired about when I would be back.

I smiled, wondering who would have told me if my dad had landed in jail. It wouldn't have been some stranger. It would have been Sophie. Or Mrs. Glick.

"Have you talked to James?" Sophie asked.

"A little." I sat down on the sofa beside the cold woodstove.

"He said you've made a doctor friend."

I sat up straight. "He did? He called you?"

"Just to check in," Sophie said.

Right.

"Was he upset?" I'd mentioned to James that I'd met Sean at the hospital and had breakfast with him, but I hadn't told him about the other meals we'd shared.

"No." Sophie paused. "Just matter of fact."

"Oh." Had I wanted him to be upset? "Sean's not really a friend. More like an acquaintance. He's an OB doc at Lancaster General." My face grew warm, and I admitted to myself that I was lying. I quickly changed the subject to well-baby check-ups, going over the details to make sure I was covering all the bases. They weren't complex, but I wanted to make sure I was doing what I needed. Then I asked her if the hazelnut trees had leafed out.

"You should ask James. He was working in the orchard last Sunday evening."

That caught me off guard, and I started to ask

about the caretaker I'd hired, but then I heard the kids coming up the steps, and I told Sophie I needed to go. We hung up quickly.

Zed was the first one through the door. "Where's Mom?" he asked, searching the living room and then stepping toward the dining room. Her car wasn't parked outside, so he knew she wasn't home. I hadn't thought about retrieving it.

"She's not here," I called out to Zed as he hurried toward the kitchen.

Ella came through the door and the screen slammed behind her. "What happened today?"

"Both of you sit down," I said. They both stared at me, not moving. I stood. "Your mom's been charged with negligent homicide," I said. "Bail was set."

"Where is she?" Zed's voice had a frantic edge to it.

"In jail."

Ella stepped around to the sofa and sat down, hard, her head falling into her hands. "How much is the bail?"

"Fifty thousand dollars needs to be posted to get her out."

Neither Ella nor Zed spoke.

"I'll go see her tomorrow." I needed to call to find out when visiting hours were. "I'll see if you two can go too."

Still both were silent, and after a moment Zed stepped into the dining room. The whir of the computer started a moment later.

"You'd better talk to Mom before you take us to see her. She might not like it," Ella said through her fingers.

"Okay." I hadn't thought of that. I sat down on the other end of the sofa. "Things will work out."

Ella took her hands away from her face. "How can you know that?" Tears filled her eyes. "You have no idea if they'll work out or not. And if they don't, what will Zed and I do? Become wards of the state?"

"Ella—"

She jumped to her feet, flinging a couch pillow against the sofa.

"Ella." I stood, stepping toward her, but she flew to the staircase, her coat still on, and disappeared up the steps. I waited for the slam of her door but it didn't come.

TWENTY

Feeling lost, I decided to focus on dinner. Zed didn't look up from the computer screen when I passed through the dining room. I wondered about him tying up the landline, but then I decided Marta would call my cell if she needed to talk. I searched through the little pantry cupboard. There was a box of saltine crackers. Chicken stock. A can of black beans. A box of whole wheat pasta.

A jar of what looked like homemade spaghetti sauce—at least, I hoped it was. And a couple of jars of canned pears. I check the freezer above the refrigerator. There were several plastic containers of jam and a couple bags of green beans. It looked as though we would be having spaghetti for dinner and I would be going shopping tomorrow. I started water for the pasta and then put the sauce on to heat. There was a little bit of cheddar cheese in the fridge. I would grate that to go on top of the sauce. I wondered what the kids took for lunches. Maybe I would need to go to the store tonight.

"Hey, Zed." I stood in the doorway to the dining room. "Do you take sandwiches for lunches?"

He shook his head without looking up. "Hot lunch."

"Do you have money for that?"

"Yeah . . ." His voice trailed off.

It was only five fifteen by the time dinner was ready, but I decided we might as well eat. As I set the table, there was a knock on the door. I knew Zed wouldn't answer it, so I hurried into the living room. Alice was at the door with a casserole dish covered in foil. "I brought you a little something for dinner," she said.

I thanked her and asked her in. She declined, saying, "Just hug the children for me. Tell them I'm praying for their mother."

A minute later, as I turned off the burner under the sauce, there was another knock at the door.

It was Peggy's husband, Eli, with a store-bought frozen lasagna in his hands. "Peggy sent me over with this." He thrust the lasagna toward me. His face reddened and he turned to leave quickly.

"Thank you," I said, wanting to ask about Peggy and the baby, but he'd already reached his carriage.

Three more people dropped food off before I had dinner on the table, two Mennonite women and another Amish man. As I headed to the staircase to call Ella to come eat, she came bounding down, her cell phone in her hand. "It's Mom," she said. "She wants to talk to you."

I took the phone. Marta said, "My car's in the parking garage two blocks from the courthouse. Could you get it back to the house for me? There's an extra key hanging by the front door."

"Sure," I said. Maybe Sean could help me.

"And speaking of cars, a couple from our church have a car you can borrow. I don't think you should keep paying for that rental. It's a waste of money."

I agreed. She told me they would drop the car off in the morning.

Without as much as a transition, she said, "And please encourage the children to be hopeful. There's no reason for them to be alarmed. Ella was pretty upset, but I think I talked her out of it."

I asked her about visiting the next day with the kids, but she said that wouldn't be necessary. She sounded touched when I described all of the people who had shown up with food. We chatted about clients for a minute, and then she asked to talk to Zed. I sent Sean a quick text about the car as Zed took the phone.

He said "Okay" several times and then, "I love you too. Bye." That was all. Then we sat down to eat.

We bowed our heads and prayed silently and much longer than usual. When Ella said, "Amen" out loud, I marveled at the change in her outlook, not sure if the swing was due to her age or personality or prayer, or if her mother still had that much control over her. There was another knock on the door before we even started to pass the pasta. I stood. I was pretty sure I wouldn't have to go to the grocery store in the morning after all.

Sean was free to help, and he came in to meet Ella and Zed before taking me to get Marta's car. He spoke warmly, shaking their hands and telling them how sorry he was about the events of the day. He encouraged them to be hopeful that things would work out. He then followed me to the car rental agency on the outskirts of town, and once I'd signed all the paperwork and turned over my key to the Taurus, I went outside and eagerly climbed into his two-door BMW. It was the first time I'd been in his car, and the leather seat felt like a fitted glove as I sank down onto it.

As he drove we chatted, talking through a plan to go out to dinner again on Saturday evening. When we reached the parking garage, we found Marta's Toyota on the top floor, a prepaid all-day receipt on her dash, just as she had said we would.

Sean and I would be parting there, and as I turned back around to thank him for his help, he took my face in his hands and planted a kiss right on my mouth. I was surprised at first, but then I allowed myself to go with it, refusing to let thoughts of James enter my mind.

When we finally pulled apart, Sean grinned.

"Sorry about that," he teased softly. "But I just knew you were going to say 'How can I ever thank you,' so I figured I'd go ahead and give you your answer."

Feeling just a tad unsteady on my feet, I got into the car and started it up before rolling down the window and giving him a reply.

"Shows how much you know," I said, shaking my head in mock scorn. "I was going to give you a fruitcake."

He threw back his head and laughed.

All the way to the cottage, even as my heart felt heavy with guilt, a smile lingered on my lips.

When I arrived, Zed called me into the dining room. "I joined a Swiss genealogical site," he said. "And found some info on the property. According to a response I got, it's in the Emmental."

I peered over his shoulder. There was a posting written in German.

"Which is . . ." he clicked open a Wickipedia

screen, "located in the Canton of Bern."

"Cool." I leaned forward and skimmed the article. It was the second largest canton in Switzerland. The city of Bern, not surprisingly, was the capital, along with being the capital of the entire country. It was located in west-central Switzerland and included the Bernese Oberland, a portion of the Alps that consisted of the Jungfrau, among other peaks. The Emmental was a hilly landscape mostly devoted to farming, particularly dairy farming.

It sounded a lot like Lancaster County, minus the nearby Alps.

"Amielbach is outside the town of Langnau." He clicked open another window. The outlying area was forty-nine percent agriculture, again mainly dairy farming, and forty-two percent forested. The village was the "sunniest" in Switzerland and had only nine thousand inhabitants.

"And," Zed said, opening a fourth window, "I had a response about an Abraham Sommers, who lived in the Emmental area from the mid- to late-1800s." An email in German popped open. "But I haven't verified it's the man you're looking for," he said. "Not yet."

I thanked him for his work and then asked if I could use the computer for a minute. I logged onto the registry first. There were still no responses. Next I checked my email. I had a message from James, asking how things were going and saying he had a weekend retreat with the kids from the group home where he was doing his internship. He said he'd call me Sunday night. He didn't mention our last phone conversation.

As I stood, sliding the chair back to Zed, I asked how Ella was doing.

"Fine, I guess," Zed said. "She went out right after you left."

"What do you mean?"

He focused back on the computer as he spoke. "Someone came and got her . . ."

"Who?"

He shrugged. "Someone who needs a new muffler."

"Someone in a car?" I hoped it was a car and wasn't who I feared it was.

"Nope. Sounded more like a motorcycle."

I called Ella's phone but she didn't answer. I walked down to the bridge, listening for the telltale sound of Ezra's motorcycle, but I heard nothing except for the hoot of an owl. The sky was clear and the stars bright with no city lights to compete with, but the icy chill of the night made me shiver. Just the thought of Ella in her thin dress on the back of Ezra's bike speeding along the highway had me vaguely nauseated.

As I headed back to the cottage, I heard the distant roar of the motorcycle coming from the other direction. I made my way through the darkness as carefully and quickly as I could back toward the cottage, but it sounded like the roar had beaten me there. The sound paused and then, after a few moments, started up again. A lone headlight was coming toward me. I waved my hands for Ezra to stop, but he merely ducked his head as he buzzed by. I watched his taillight swim a little as he bounced onto the bridge. He wore his leather jacket and helmet, but another helmet was secured on the metal loop at the back of the empty seat.

When I got to the house, Ella was in the shower.

"A hot shower," Zed said. "She was really cold."

"I'll bet," I said.

"Her birthday is Saturday." Zed spoke with eyes glued to the screen.

"So she said."

"She'll be sixteen," he added, as if that explained everything. He sat up straight and his eyes popped wide. "Incoming message."

I peered over his shoulder, but this email was in German too.

Zed spoke slowly as he read. "Abraham Sommers had a daughter Elsbeth. And a property called Amielbach." Zed paused. I already knew all that. "He was a councilman in the Emmental." That I didn't know.

Zed continued. "His daughter left in—sometime in the mid 1870s—for America and ended up settling in Indiana."

I'd guessed at that, but it was nice to have it confirmed.

"Elsbeth retained the property and passed it down through her family, but it was sold twenty-four years ago and turned into a hotel."

I would have been two years old at that point.

I pulled a dining room chair next to Zed and sat down. It was too bad the beautiful house wasn't in the family anymore, but I could still visit it someday.

"And," Zed looked at me furtively and then back at the screen, "an American woman moved to Amielbach right after it sold. She lives in a little house on the property."

I took a deep breath. "What's her name?"

"No name given."

Zed kept reading silently.

"What does it say about her?"

"Just that she's not your average American and she's very private and he doesn't feel that he should give out any personal information."

"Wait a minute. Not your average American how? In what sense?"

"I don't know. That's how he put it."

I tensed. "Who is this man?"

Zed reread the email. "Hey, my German isn't perfect, but I think he owns the hotel. He's a history buff. That's why he's on the list where I posted."

"Email him back and ask him for more information about the woman. Tell him . . ." Tell him what? That I wondered if the woman might be my birth mother? What were the chances of that? "Ask him if the woman's name is Giselle."

It couldn't hurt to try.

Ella avoided me for the rest of the evening. Finally, I confronted her in her room. "I was worried about you."

"Why?" She wore a white nightgown under a terry cloth robe and sat on her bed with a textbook in front of her. Her hair hung long and wavy half-way down her back. The light caught the dark auburn sheen when she turned her head.

"Let's see . . . I didn't know where you were, whom you were with, or when you were coming back."

"I was fine." She looked up at me demurely and tucked a strand of hair behind her ear. "Besides, I already told you that Ezra and I are good friends."

"What would your mom say?"

Ella shrugged. "I turn sixteen on Saturday."

"But you're Mennonite, remember. Not Amish. We don't do *rumschpringe*s." Oops. Freudian slip—I'd meant to say "you," not "we."

"But Mom has Amish roots, you know. She's always said I'll have more freedom when I'm sixteen."

"I doubt if she ever intended that freedom to include riding on the back of Ezra's motorcycle."

"Well, she's not here, is she?" Now Ella's tone was a little bit sassy.

"Next time, if I'm still in charge, call me. Or send me a text."

She closed her textbook with a thud. "That's just it," she said. "We don't need you to be in charge. We're totally capable of taking care of ourselves."

I stepped back.

She stood. "Besides, Mom will be out soon. That's what Ezra said."

Maybe Will or Alice or someone was raising the bail.

"And you can go back to delivering babies and not feel like you need to watch my every move."

"Ella—"

"I have homework to do."

I told her goodnight and left the room, marveling at yet another mood swing in a short time. It had only been ten years since I was sixteen. Why did I have no idea how to deal with her?

The house creaked and groaned throughout the night. Around three the wind picked up and must have blown clouds in, because soon it was raining. In my restlessness I kept dreaming of a roaring motorcycle racing by Amielbach. Over and over I woke with a start.

In the morning, Ella was quiet and sullen. I checked the adoption registry site and found no messages. There was nothing concerning my adoption search in my email box, either. I turned the computer over to Zed. The man from Switzerland hadn't emailed him back. Strike three and it was only seven thirty.

After Zed and Ella left for school, the couple from Marta's church dropped off their car for me to use. It was a green Datsun B210 and was, I felt sure, older than I. I thanked them warmly and hoped it would run. After they left, I took it for a test drive down the highway and then across the covered bridge. The seat was vinyl and uncomfortable, but it seemed to have been well cared for, although it was pretty noisy. The gas tank was full and a sticker in the corner of the windshield indicated that the oil had been changed the day before.

When I returned to the cottage, I pulled my phone from my pocket. I'd missed a call and had a voice mail from Marta. "Bail's been posted. Can you come and get me?"

"Who paid your bail?" It was one question I couldn't contain as I drove Marta back to the cottage.

In true Marta form, not only did she not answer, but she didn't even acknowledge my question.

"I mean, did a group of Amish raise the money?" My face grew warm. "Like Will and Alice? Did your church contribute?" Maybe the couple who loaned me the car were closet millionaires.

"There was no group contribution," Marta said. "And, no, I asked our pastor not to use church money or money from anyone in our district on me. There are more worthy causes."

I turned and headed south. "What's the big deal in telling me who it was?"

"Some things are private," she said.

I shrugged. "I'm not going to tell anyone. I'm just curious."

She didn't answer me. Her cape was fastened at the very top and her bonnet was perfectly in place over her immaculately combed hair. There was nothing about her that looked as if she'd spent a night in jail.

After a while she sighed. "I don't want this told to anyone, not even my children." She glanced at me and I nodded.

She looked straight ahead again and said, "Klara paid the bail."

TWENTY-ONE

I gasped. *Klara?* I couldn't imagine.

"Every cent of it," Marta added.

"That's great." My voice was flat. I couldn't fathom the Klara I'd met paying anyone's bail. "But why?"

Marta didn't answer, and this time I didn't press her.

Once we reached the cottage, we fell back into our regular routines. I did the prenatal appointments and Marta handled the scheduling and the books. During a break between clients, I headed into the cottage for my sweatshirt. The office was colder than usual, even though I'd turned on the heater. I was surprised to hear Marta, who sat at the dining room table talking on her cell phone, taking on a new client. When she was off the phone, I asked her if that was a good idea.

"Why?" She placed her hand over her cell.

"What if . . . you know, you're . . ."

"Convicted?"

"Yes."

"Well, then, I'll figure out what to do if that time comes."

In the early afternoon, I headed out on a home prenatal visit. I hadn't seen the woman yet. Her name was Susan Eicher, and she was twenty-seven and six months pregnant with her fourth baby. It was her second prenatal appointment. I was learning that Amish women typically waited until they were several months pregnant before seeking medical attention.

I finally found the house above Paradise, one of many Amish villages around here that I'd noticed had a memorable name. I drove up a steep hill, through a wooded area, and then came to a modest dwelling. As I walked toward the front door, it was obvious that the place needed some upkeep. Paint was peeling on the siding, and the concrete of the walkway was cracked and crumbling here and there. The steps to the porch were nearly bare of paint, and they creaked as I climbed them. I knocked and then knocked again. Finally the door swung open and a little girl, five at the most, peeked up at me.

I told her who I was and that I'd come to see her mother. But then I realized she might not understand English and said, "Your *mamm*?"

She nodded and motioned to me with her index finger. I followed. Three baskets of laundry were on the worn hardwood floor in the living room. I was getting used to the simply furnished and decorated homes of the Plain people I served—no wall-to-wall carpeting, no portraits on the walls, no overstuffed chairs or couches, but this home was especially sparse, with just a couch in the living room and a table and four straight-back chairs in the adjoining dining room.

I could hear a child crying down the hall.

"Mueter!" the little girl called. I assumed she was saying "mother."

"I'll be right there," the mother answered in English.

The little girl pointed to the couch and I sat. The crying continued, and when Susan appeared she carried a little boy, who appeared to be about a year and a half, clinging to her neck. A second boy, maybe a year older, had his arms wrapped around her leg, forcing her to walk with a jerk. Both of the children wore pajamas. The woman's cap covered most of her light brown hair, and there were dark circles under her big blue eyes.

I stood and introduced myself. Susan sat down on the other end of the couch and pulled the second boy up onto her lap too, bumping him against her belly. The little girl scurried up beside him.

"The children have been sick." Susan's voice was soft, and I could barely hear her. "With the flu."

The youngest boy pushed his brother, and Susan took his hand and pulled him to the other side of her, wedging him into the corner of the couch.

"Sorry about the mess." She nodded at the baskets of laundry. They were mostly filled with sheets and towels. She looked me in the eye and then quickly averted her gaze.

"How long have they been ill?"

"All week." She sighed. "First my daughter. She's better now." She patted the little girl's head. "Now the boys."

"What are their symptoms?"

"Vomiting. Diarrhea." She smiled, just a little. "Crankiness and crying."

As if on cue, the younger boy began to fuss again. I glanced into the kitchen. Dirty dishes filled the sink.

"What is your name?" I asked the little girl.

The mother spoke in what I thought was Pennsylvania Dutch, and then the girl looked at me and whispered, "Louise."

A few minutes later, Louise and I tackled the dishes while Susan put the boys down for a nap. I washed and Louise dried and then pointed to where the dishes went that she couldn't reach.

During the prenatal exam, Susan said that she and her family had recently moved to Lancaster County from Indiana. Her husband was working in his uncle's buggy-making business. The uncle owned the house they were living in, but it was quite a ways away from his shop. I asked if her husband's aunt was available to help her, and she said no, the aunt had died a year ago. I asked what other support she had. "The women in our district." Her eyes dimmed.

"What is it?" I asked.

Tears filled her eyes. "It's nothing."

I patted her hand.

"I miss my mother. I don't have sisters, but I have cousins back home. Things are so different here for me—even the language."

I had one of those "aha" moments. Susan and Louise weren't speaking Pennsylvania Dutch. They were speaking the Swiss Amish dialect Mr. Miller had told me about when he translated the letter from Abraham Sommers.

I asked Susan about Indiana, and her eyes lit up as she spoke. She had grown up in a big brick house in Adams County on a dairy farm. She and her husband were from the same district, and they knew by the time they were fifteen they wanted to marry. And they had, at nineteen.

I asked why they had moved, and she said her husband had grown restless with living in the same place his entire life and wanted to see more of the country. They had come out to visit his aunt and uncle on their wedding trip, and last year his uncle had written, saying he was looking for someone to pass the buggy business on to as he didn't have any children.

"It seemed like a good idea at the time . . ." she said, her voice trailing off.

"Does your husband like it here?"

"He likes his work," she replied, and then she began talking about the buggies in Indiana. They were topless and the seats didn't have backs. "I like the buggies here much better," she said. "And," she pointed to her kitchen, "that the stove runs on propane, and we have indoor plumbing. Back home we had a woodstove and an outside pump and privy." She was nearly animated as she spoke. She laughed a little and then said, "Those I don't miss, but I do miss the yodeling back home, straight from the Alps."

I smiled. That was a sight to imagine, an Amish yodeler. I thought of my ancestor, Elsbeth Sommers, who had left Switzerland in the 1800s and ended up in Indiana. For all I knew, there had been plenty of Amish yodelers back then. I asked how far she had lived from Goshen, Indiana, where the Mennonite school, Goshen College, was.

"Oh, that's a long ways—on the other side of Fort Wayne. More than two hours by car." She went on to tell me that she had a Mennonite friend who went to college there, but she had never visited the area.

After the exam I told Susan I wanted to stay a few minutes and fold her laundry.

"No, I can do that."

I shook my head. "You need to get a nap too while your boys are still asleep. And have Louise lie down with you. All of you need to build up your strength."

She started to protest but then simply said, "Thank you." I would talk to Marta about Susan's needs. She couldn't take care of herself and sick children and a house all by herself. She needed help.

Twenty minutes later I left the house, wondering if Giselle had kept me and joined the Amish church, or if *Mammi* had chosen to raise me would I be living the life Susan was? Except I would have cousins, aunts, and a grandmother nearby. I thought of Peggy and her oldest daughter. I had no reason to believe I wouldn't have been accepted by the Amish community around me, nor that Giselle wouldn't have found a husband, meaning I would have eventually had a father. I couldn't fathom what had happened to change my destiny.

I didn't have any more appointments for the day and decided to do some more sightseeing. As the sun broke through the gray clouds to the west, I drove north and stopped at the Bird-in-Hand bakery and picked up a loaf of homemade bread and a box of sugar cookies, thinking of Zed and his afternoon snack. As I left I didn't turn toward

Strasburg and then Marta's, but instead went west toward the city of Lancaster. I drove aimlessly through residential streets, gawking at the houses and yards. Finally I turned south. It wasn't long until I knew where I was headed.

I scanned the pasture as I turned down the lane. Cows grazed lazily in the field, picking up their heads at the sound of my borrowed car. The field beyond them was plowed and ready to be seeded. I wondered what Alexander would plant.

I didn't see anyone. I parked in front of the house by a pine tree and then I stepped to the side of the yard. A new scarecrow wearing a man's shirt, pants, and straw hat was up in the planted garden, most likely to keep the birds from pecking up the just-planted seeds. I stared at the door to *Mammi's daadi haus*, wondering if Klara kept it locked all the time, and then past it toward the creek.

I heard a rustling around the corner of the house. "Hello?" someone called.

I stepped forward. Ada was walking toward me with a hoe in her hand and the sleeves of her dress pushed up to her elbows. A line of clothes danced in the breeze behind her, and the afternoon sun cast their moving shadows on the lawn. Beyond that was a garden. A few more rows had been tilled, and it appeared that Ada was working on finishing the planting.

"Oh, it's you." She smiled, her body relaxed and easy. The loose ties of her bonnet fell against her chest. I stared at her, trying to take in each feature. "Have you lost your way again?" she asked.

I shook my head, my heart racing. "No. I was hoping to see you—and *Mammi*, if she's awake."

"You know my grandmother?"

"No." I paused. "Well, sort of."

"She's not here. My parents took her to the doctor."

I imagined them lifting, pushing, and pulling the old woman into their carriage.

"Does she go to the doctor very often?"

Ada nodded. "Some."

"What's wrong with her?"

"She had a stroke a few years ago."

That made sense. I didn't notice any evidence when I saw her the other night, but I only saw her profile. Or it could be that there wasn't any physical evidence.

"*Mamm* said you're working as a midwife here for a short time."

I crossed my arms, surprised that Klara had offered her that much information.

"Did she say who I'm working with?"

"No."

"Marta. I'm working with Marta and staying with her and her kids."

"Oh." Ada stepped toward me. She seemed so open. "How are they? I haven't seen them in . . ." Her voice trailed off. "It's been *forever*." She smiled. "At least I think that's how Ella would phrase it."

"I'm their cousin," I blurted out.

Her face lit up. "On their father's side?"

I shook my head. "On Marta's side. I was given up for adoption."

"Then . . . you're my cousin too."

"It appears that way."

"I thought we looked alike." She stepped closer, touching her chin as she did.

I shivered. "Do you have a mirror inside?"

"Of course."

She led the way into the house, propping the hoe up against the back porch and kicking off her shoes, and then into a bathroom just off the kitchen. We stood side by side. Me in my purple sweatshirt and jeans, her in her blue dress and black apron. I swept my hair up off my shoulders, holding it behind my head. She took off her bonnet.

We had the same tilt to our nose, the same blond hair, and the same chin. Her eyes, brown like mine, were wider, and my eyelashes thicker. Her face was thinner and much paler, and I was a half head taller. She undid her bun and shook out her hair. I let go of mine and it fell to my shoulders again.

"Oh, my," she said, reaching for my hand. "I guess we are cousins."

I nodded, but I was pretty sure we were more than that. I was pretty sure Alexander was my father after all.

Which would make Ada my half sister.

TWENTY-TWO

I didn't say anything to Ada about my suspicion that her father might be mine as well. Her life seemed far too sheltered for her to learn something like that from me. "Yep, cousins it is," I said, smiling at her in the mirror.

Funny thing was, even though I was trying so hard, my face looked sad while hers was full of joy.

"Another cousin! Closer to my age." She turned toward me, put her hands on my shoulders, and jumped up and down. I didn't remember anyone ever showing me they were that happy to know who I was. I'm sure Mama and Dad were, way back when I was a baby, and they might have jumped up and down on the inside, but I was pretty sure no one had ever acted about me the way Ada was now. "First cousins? Right? You think we're that close?" She stopped jumping but one hand stayed on my shoulder.

"Yep," I answered, repeating quietly, "that close." I braced myself for her to ask who my birth mother was.

"Wait until I tell *Mamm* and *Daed*. I don't think they realized it when you stopped by the other day." She started pinning her hair back into place. "They've been so worried about other things . . ."

I found a ponytail fastener in my pocket and

wound it around my hair, pulling it through for a half loop and landing it high on the back of my head, even though I'd had it down before.

"So you're from Oregon, right? Why are you working with Aunt Marta?"

I made a face as I wondered how much Ada knew. It didn't sound like much. Probably not even that Marta had been arrested, much less that Klara had paid her bail. "Marta just . . . needed an assistant for a while. Her partner retired." It wasn't a lie. Not exactly.

"And how did you end up in Oregon?" Ada secured her cap and led the way out of the bathroom, her steps quick and purposeful.

I followed. "That's where my parents—my adoptive parents—lived."

She spun back toward me in the kitchen. "And they were okay with you coming out here?"

"Well, they would have been, I'm sure, but they have both passed on. My mother when I was eight, and my father just recently."

"Oh, Lexie." Ada surprised me with a half hug. "I'm so sorry." Her hand felt warm against my back, and she smelled fresh, like line-dried clothes and the spiciness of spring.

Emotion overcame me and I struggled not to cry.

"I don't know what I would do if I lost my father." She pulled away and looked me in the eye. "What a lot for you to handle on your own."

I nodded, trying to anticipate what I would

say if she asked about my birth parents, but the question didn't seem to be on her mind.

She gestured toward the yard. "I need to get back to work. Come with me."

I nodded again and followed her to the back porch, where she quickly slipped her shoes back on. She wasn't as passive as she'd seemed the other night. She actually seemed quite capable. She grabbed the hoe and marched toward the garden.

"We did most of the planting last week but didn't have time to finish. I'm working on the beans." She stepped onto the soft soil, sinking down a little. "Do you like to garden?"

I said yes, but that wasn't really the truth. Obviously she did, and for some reason I wanted something more in common with her than our looks. The morning had been cold, but now the sun was shining brightly. I pushed up the sleeves of my sweatshirt as I spoke, and in no time I was telling her about the hazelnut orchard, the pruning with Dad, and the burning of the branches in the winter.

There was something about her, maybe the way she held her head as she listened, even though she was hoeing, that made me keep talking in a way I hadn't talked to anyone for months. I rattled on about my parents' farm in Oregon, the town of Aurora, the people at church, and my work at the hospital. All the while she nodded and listened, but when I mentioned I was a nurse, she stopped hoeing.

"Oh, I notice the nurses the most when I'm at the hospital. I can see why you went into that."

I realized I'd been dominating the conversation like a bore. "How are you feeling? Will Gundy said that you've been ill."

"Will said that?" Her eyes lit up and she leaned against the hoe. "He was in the eighth grade when I started school. He was so nice to me. He was nice to everyone." She smiled. "How are his girls?"

"People seem to be a little worried about Christy, but the twins seem good." I smiled at the thought of them.

Ada looked beyond me for a moment. I turned my head. A buggy traveled along in the distance on the road and then passed behind the trees that lined the field. "Is that your parents?" I asked.

She shook her head. "But they should be home soon."

I didn't have much more time. "Tell me about you. About your health. What you—" I was going to say "want out of life," but then I realized that was a foolish thing to ask a young Amish woman. I hoped she wanted what was her only option—a husband and children.

"I'm doing okay," she said. "I had to have a transfusion last week, so I'm better now." She seemed to be uncomfortable talking about herself.

I took off my sweatshirt, tied it around my waist, and reached for the hoe, asking if I could take a turn. She handed it to me and I took over, angling the hoe so the corner scraped a row an inch deep, ready for the seeds, as my tennis shoes sank into the loamy soil. "How often do you have to have transfusions?"

"Oh, it depends. Sometimes not for a year or two. Sometimes every couple of months." She glanced off into the distance toward the road again as another buggy became visible for a moment and then passed on by. "I was supposed to teach school last year . . ." She pointed in the direction of the schoolhouse that was, if I remembered right, about two miles away. "But then I had a bad spell starting last August. I'm just starting to get my strength back."

"Will you teach this coming fall?" I finished the row as I talked.

"I hope so," she said. "If the board will allow it. Between my health and my age, they may not want me to."

"Your age?"

She shrugged. "At twenty-four I should have joined the church by now. Some of the board members have questioned my commitment to the faith."

I was curious as to why she hadn't joined the church, but before I could figure out a polite way to ask, she continued.

"Christy Gundy is a student at the school—she's in the sixth grade. In a few more years Rachael Kemp will go there and then the Gundy twins." She smiled.

I hadn't been jealous of Ada until that moment —but in that instant I started to see what she had that I didn't, and it wasn't Klara and Alexander. It was a belonging to something bigger. Something permanent. Something beyond her parents and her family. She belonged to people who knew her as a baby and would do anything to help her. And they weren't all old, not like I had back home. They were young people and old people and in between people and probably more people than could easily be counted. Someday, when she married, hundreds would attend. If I ever married, there wouldn't be any more than had been at Dad's funeral.

I became aware of Ada speaking again. "I really want to teach," she said. "More than anything."

"Why haven't you joined the church yet?"

She shook her head. "I was going to when I was twenty. But then I got really sick and they finally figured out what was wrong with me. So that postponed everything." She sighed and then lowered her voice. "And I'd really like to travel." When she resumed speaking her voice was even softer. "Sometimes I think I'd like to get more schooling too."

I nodded my head and bit my tongue, but what I was thinking was, *You go, girl!*

She was kicking the dirt from her black Reeboks onto the grass. I wondered what the chances of her being able to teach—or travel—were.

"I should leave," I said.

She nodded.

"But can I come back sometime?"

"Anytime . . ."

"Ada," I said softly. "I don't know if you noticed the other night, but your mother doesn't want me around."

"Oh, I think she will. Once she knows who you are."

I shook my head.

"I'll talk to her."

"Okay." I wrinkled my nose. I didn't want to put her in a bad position but . . . "In the meantime, until things get straightened out, could I come see *Mammi* sometime when your mom's not here?"

Ada had her eyes on the road again. Either she was worried about her parents coming home and finding me or else she was looking for someone else. She met my gaze. "*Mamm* quilts on Wednesday mornings at nine. You can come then."

"I will see you then," I said, handing her the hoe. "Thank you."

She hugged me with one arm, the other still on the hoe, and looked me in the eye. "Come sooner if you can."

I nodded but knew I wouldn't. As I drove up the lane, a buggy turned down it. Of course I expected Klara and Alexander with *Mammi* tucked into the backseat, but it wasn't them. It was Will Gundy, alone. I pulled over as far as I could onto the edge of the field. He waved as he passed me. He was grinning, and he looked more like his brother Ezra than I'd remembered.

I stepped into Marta's office to file Susan Eicher's chart and found my aunt scrubbing the walls, even though I was pretty sure she'd sanitized the place, top to bottom, just the week before.

I explained that Susan needed more support. "No problem," Marta said. "I'll get a message to her bishop. His wife will organize some meals and help around the house."

I inhaled, impressed at how simple that had been. Then I told her I'd come from Ada's. "I'm really curious about Alexander."

Marta wrung out the sponge. "We already had that discussion."

"Then why do Ada and I look so much alike?"

"You tell me. You've studied genetics more than I have."

Genetics. Marta was short and squat. Klara was tall. So was *Mammi*, or so I'd been told all those years. Zed and I, cousins with no shared genetics, looked more alike than Ella and I did, who were blood relatives. But there was something more with Ada. Something closer, I was sure. She had to be my half sister.

I sat down at Marta's desk. I'd try another subject. "So, were you surprised Klara paid your bail?"

She shook her head. "It's what *Mamm*, if she

were able, would have done." She started scrubbing again, moving her arms up and down, both hands on the sponge. Maybe the motion opened up the synapses in her brain to her speaking ability. "Klara and I were close when we were little." She sighed. "We were close when we lived in Indiana, especially after our father died. She was like a surrogate mother because *Mamm* had to work so hard. Then, when we moved here, it was Klara who looked out for me . . ."

She said they had a dairy farm in Indiana, but their father wasn't much of a businessman and mismanaged his profits. "He was a mean man. My memories are of him yelling at or whipping Giselle. She couldn't do anything to please him."

I shivered, trying not to picture it.

"Anyway, our father was killed when the hitch on the wagon broke and his horses dragged him to death." The family lost the farm after that, and *Mammi* decided they should move to Lancaster County, to live with her much older brother who was a widower. He needed someone to look after him; they needed a home to live in. The arrangement worked well for few years—until he died.

"So, you can see, we had to take care of each other," Marta said. "Klara was a good big sister to me."

"And what about Giselle?"

Marta stopped scrubbing for a moment and then started again, with more vigor. "At one time," she said, "Klara and Giselle were the best of friends."

I let that sink in for a moment and then asked where she thought Klara got the money for Marta's bail.

"I have no idea," she answered. "It's not my business."

My guess was that it was from the sale of Amielbach, but maybe Klara and Alexander had saved that much over the years.

"Did the house that Klara lives in belong to your uncle?"

"It belonged to his deceased wife's family," she answered. "*Mamm* rented it for a few years and then bought it."

That would explain why she sold the property in Switzerland. But surely it was worth far more than a farm in Lancaster County.

Marta dropped the sponge into the bucket. "I need to go check on Zed's homework and start dinner," she said. "I hope I've given you enough information to satisfy your curiosity." With that she picked up the bucket and hurried through the door.

I shook my head. I had a feeling she had given me the information on purpose. Nothing Marta did was by accident.

The night in jail seemed to have been a wake-up call to Marta. She was much more attentive to her children, hovering over Zed's homework and grilling Ella about her plans for the weekend. She heated the casserole Alice dropped by the day before and made a salad from a bag of vegetables from a church family. I wondered if, as she worked, she thought what life might be like for her children if she was found guilty and sentenced.

It wasn't until after dinner that Marta finally went upstairs and I had a chance to ask Zed if he'd had another email from the man in Switzerland. He hadn't. I decided to go to the coffee shop and check my email and the adoption registry. As I drove, I had the urge to call James and tell him about Ada, but he was away at the group home retreat. When I pulled into the parking lot and turned off the car, I sent Sean a text, asking what he was up to.

He immediately replied. *Getting off work in half an hour. Want to meet at the hospital?*

We figured out the details through a couple more texts, and then I logged onto my computer while still sitting in my borrowed Datsun, not bothering to go inside the coffee shop at all. There was still nothing on the adoption registry. I closed my laptop, discouraged.

A half hour later, on the dot, Sean walked out to the hospital parking lot, and I rolled down the window of my car.

"I hope this isn't too forward," he said, bending down as he talked, "but want to come out to my house? I have a slow cooker full of pulled pork and was going to make a sandwich."

I didn't bother to tell him I'd already had dinner. "Sounds fine," I said. "I'll follow you."

He headed northeast out of town, a direction I hadn't been yet. On the outskirts of the city, he turned off the main road. I realized he could be taking me anywhere and then smiled. My intuition was pretty good. Sean Benson wasn't a serial killer posing as a doctor. He pulled into a driveway and I followed, easing alongside a row of thick, neatly pruned shrubs that divided his property from the house next door. I parked behind him, climbed from the car, and paused to take a quick look around. His yard was immaculate, illuminated by ground lights. The grass was thick and edged, the flower beds filled with tulips. The house itself wasn't huge, but it was by no means small.

He smiled and led the way up a brick path to the front door. "I bought this place two years ago." He turned his key in the lock and pushed the door open. "But it looks like I'm going to have to sell it now."

"You got the job?" I practically stumbled over the stoop into an entryway as I spoke.

He caught my elbow, laughing. "I got the job—at least that's what the HR person on the phone told me today. I haven't seen the contract yet." He took my coat and turned toward the closet. The space was illuminated by dim overhead light.

"When do you start?"

"June first."

I'd be more than settled in Philadelphia by then.

In fact, at that point I'd only have three months left until I would be heading back to Oregon. But Baltimore was only a couple of hours from Philly. I imagined coordinating our days off and meeting in New York. Maybe even Boston. Maybe he would take me up to meet his folks . . .

He flicked on a switch as we stepped into a large living room. Taupe leather furniture—a sectional and easy chair—sat atop a white rug that graced a hardwood floor. The ceilings were high and boxed and an open staircase led to the second floor.

"What a great house," I said.

"Thanks. The kitchen's this way."

I followed him through a formal dining room with a modern high table and six chairs and then through a swinging door into the kitchen. It had totally been updated with granite counter tops and stainless steel appliances.

"Did it come this way?" I stood in the middle of the kitchen, turning slowly.

Sean shook his head. "I hired a decorator. She did a great job, huh?"

I nodded. He gave his attention to a black slow cooker in the corner on the other side of the double stove. The pork smelled delicious.

I glanced around the kitchen again. There was no clutter. And there hadn't been in the living room or dining room either. There were no stacks of books. No papers. No magazines. No projects.

Plus he could cook.

"Want a tour before we eat?"

I nodded, feeling as if I couldn't speak, wondering just how much money Sean Benson made a year.

Off the kitchen was his office. He explained that it had been a sleeping porch but he'd had it enclosed. The room was as big as my living room and dining room combined, and housed a sprawling desk with computer, a wall of bookcases, and an entertainment cabinet. He didn't open it but I guessed there was a big-screen TV and stereo system inside.

He flicked a switch, opened a sliding door, and stepped onto a patio. I followed. The backyard was illuminated too and covered with rose bushes. They weren't blooming yet—some were hardly leafed out—but I could imagine the beauty of the blossoms and the scent in the late spring and summer.

"My mother thought roses a waste of time," Sean said. "When I was little, I vowed to have a garden of them when I was grown."

"Did you put all of this in?" I asked, impressed.

"I hired someone to do the work."

Of course he did. It would have taken months and months otherwise.

"I'll take a few with me," he said. "But I'll most likely get an apartment or a condo in Baltimore. C'est la vie." He smiled but there was sorrow in his eyes.

"When will you put your place on the market?" I asked, thinking about Dad's property back home.

"Today." He stepped back into his office.

"That soon?" I laughed. There was nothing passive about Dr. Benson.

"They're putting up the sign tomorrow."

He showed me the downstairs bath and a small guestroom down the hall and then we ended up back in the kitchen. He didn't say anything about not showing me the upstairs and I didn't ask. I imagined a huge master suite with a Jacuzzi tub, like something I'd see on HGTV.

He had coleslaw and chips to go with the sandwiches, and in no time we were sitting in a little nook off the kitchen, eating as Sean talked about the ins and outs of restoring an old house. I thought, although the new job sounded really cool, that it was a shame he had to sell his first home and said so.

He shrugged. "I knew I wouldn't be here long."

"Still," I said. "It has to be hard." I could so easily imagine living in this house. It was clean and comfortable and seemed easy to manage. Everything I wanted in a home. In a life, to be honest.

"Oh, well," he said. "There's no reason to get too attached to things. I won't live in Baltimore long either. I'm not planning on putting roots down until I know where I want to settle for good."

I admired his confidence—a lot.

"How about you?" he said. "After Philadelphia, where do you want to go?"

Even though I knew I planned to go back to Oregon, I said, "I'm not sure."

"How about med school? At Johns Hopkins." His eyes were lively. "I could write you a recommendation."

"Med school? Why would I—" my phone beeped and I glanced at the screen—"do that?" It was Marta. I had a client in labor.

"Because you would make a great OB doc."

"How do you know?" I texted Marta back as I spoke, saying I was on my way.

"I can tell," he said.

"Well, right now I have a baby to deliver. Sorry to eat and run." I stood.

"See, working in a hospital would be easier. You'd be scheduled to work or you would be off —you wouldn't be at the mercy of nature."

"I'm rather fond of nature," I joked, following him into the dining room. We were silent through the dining room and living room.

"Hey," he said, retrieving my coat in the entryway and then holding it for me to slip into. "Text me when you're safely done, okay? Even if it's the middle of the night. I'll worry otherwise."

Touched I reached for his hand and squeezed it. For a moment I wanted him to kiss me, but then I waffled and stepped back quickly. "Sorry to rush off."

"Thanks for coming," he said, opening the door. "Let's try it again. I'll fix a real meal. And perhaps you'll be able to stay for the whole thing." He smiled, but I could tell he was tired. I nodded and hurried to my car. The light rain had turned cold.

TWENTY-THREE

The labor turned out to be false, and I was back at Marta's and in my little bed by two a.m., updating Sean with a quick text. The next morning Marta told me that the one appointment I had that day had been canceled, so I decided finally to go to Harrisburg to see what I could find as far as a copy of my birth certificate. It was a Friday and my best chance at making some more progress on that end.

I now had two weeks until I needed to report to work in Philadelphia. I was tempted to call and say I needed another month. That way I would leave Lancaster County at the same time Sean did. My mind started racing as I packed my computer and grabbed my purse.

Once I was in the car, I tapped in the address to the vital records department in Harrisburg in my GPS and was on my way, heading northwest and then zipping through the city of Lancaster and back out into farmland, up Highway 23 through Mount Joy and Elizabethtown, Middletown and Steelton. Finally, I was making my way through the out-skirts of Harrisburg, a bustling city built along the Susquehanna River. The capitol grounds were well laid out, and as I circled around, looking for the Health and Welfare Building on Forster Street, I eyed the capitol dome, which looked like something out of Rome when it came into view. Eventually I found a parking place, and in no time I was inside the vital records department on the first floor and stating why I was there to the receptionist.

"So it's an adoption search," she said, peering at me over her reading glasses. She looked as if she had only a minute or two left until she retired.

"A birth mother search," I replied. I didn't need to search to know I was adopted.

"We don't handle the birth certificates in those cases," she said. "They're sealed."

"I know." I leaned against her desk. "But I know the name of my birth mother. I just want a copy of the original birth certificate."

"You'll have to go to the county where you were born for that," she said. "Although they won't give it to you either, most likely."

"The county?" All the advice I'd read online had said to go the state vital records department in person. "What about the letter I sent, asking that I be notified if my birth mother tries to find information about me?"

"It's filed here." Her phone rang and she put up one finger. In no time she transferred the call.

"Is there a vital records department in Montgomery County?" I asked as she hung up.

"Go to the courthouse in Norristown. But, like I said, they'll most likely tell you they can't help you either."

It was only a piece of paper, and a copy at that, but

it meant so much to me. It meant I existed from the beginning. That there was a reason for my sadness and my grief. That I didn't just start to live once I was slipped into Mama's arms. It meant there was proof that the truth was being kept from me.

"Should I call first?" I asked.

She peered at me over the rim of her glasses again and then, quietly, said, "If you just show up, you might catch someone off guard. If you call, you're going to give them time to think about it. Maybe someone who's not in-the-know will help you."

She told me it was about a hundred miles, so I figured it would take me an hour and a half, unless there was traffic.

She glanced around the lobby and then said, "My kids are adopted. Two boys. One had no desire to find his birth family, but the second one did. I helped him search and search, but we never found a thing. Anyway," she took off her glasses, "good luck."

For a second I had the urge to share my story with her, but then the phone rang again. I mouthed a sincere "Thank you," and turned toward the heavy glass doors.

In no time I was on the Turnpike and heading east, wondering why in the world Giselle had given birth to me in Montgomery County. Had she made arrangements with Mama and Dad already and decided to go closer to Philadelphia to have the baby, closer to where I would be given away soon after? Or, if Alexander was my birth father, perhaps *Mammi* wanted Giselle to be far away from Klara when it was time for me to be born. Maybe Klara didn't even know Alexander *was* my father—although it was hard to imagine Klara not being in the know of anything. There was the fact that *Mammi* took me to the airport to relinquish me to Mama and Dad. She would have hired a driver. Maybe Giselle waited in the car while *Mammi* and I went on inside.

A semi whizzed past me and I realized I was going too slow, driving as if I were still in Lancaster County. I sped up. The morning grayness had burned off and the sun shone brightly. I drove past patches of forest, rolling hills, farms, and subdivisions. A tractor with an enclosed cab pulled a wide seeder through a plowed field. Next to it was an orchard. A melancholy feeling overtook me as I thought of my own orchard, and I wondered if maybe I should try to sell the house and keep the orchard, although I didn't know how would I continue to manage it through the years, especially if I didn't end up staying in Oregon.

Sean's offer was tempting. I wasn't too old to go to medical school, and with my work experience it wouldn't be nearly as difficult as if I were starting from scratch. In the long run I'd certainly make more money, though I'd also have more student loans to pay off. But I could do obstetrical surgery instead of assisting. I could supervise physician's assistants and nurse-midwives. I sighed. I had no idea what I should do.

The miles zoomed by, and soon I reached Valley Forge, thinking again of George Washington and the history that surrounded me as I exited the Turnpike there.

Continuing on toward Norristown, the county seat, I soon crossed a bridge over the Schuylkill River. Below, two men maneuvered a small boat across the water toward a small island. In another minute I was in Norristown, following the signs to the county courthouse. The downtown area featured some gorgeous old architecture, though many of the buildings seemed to be in various states of disrepair. It all felt very multicultural, with a Mexican market on one corner and a Caribbean grocery on another. After circling the block twice, I finally found a parking spot in front of a bail bondsman shop. Walking along the busy sidewalk toward the courthouse, I thought of my teenage fantasy of elegant, wealthy grandparents living here in this chic, genteel suburb.

Though Norristown seemed to have an energetic and friendly sort of vibe, I doubted anyone would call it either "chic" or "genteel."

The receptionist told me to come back at one thirty because the records department was closed for lunch. I decided to stop by Montgomery Hospital, which was listed on my birth certificate. I found it on my GPS, and in less than five minutes I pulled into the parking garage. The hospital was good sized, although not as big as Lancaster General or Emanuel back home. I spoke with the receptionist and told her I wanted to inquire about my records. She sent me down the administrative hall, past Human Resources, to the Health Information Department. When I told the receptionist I'd been a patient there as an infant and wanted my records, she said she would need to send someone down to the archive in the basement to search because those records hadn't been digitized. She handed me a release form, which I quickly filled out and handed back to her. She scanned it and then looked up at me.

"You were born here?"

I nodded.

"Then your records will be with your mother's. She'll need to sign the release."

"I'm not in contact with her."

The woman's face twisted, and then she asked, "Were you adopted?"

"Does it matter?" I was trying as hard as I could to sound naive.

She nodded. "Of course it matters."

"But I have the name of my mother. Why shouldn't I be able to look at the record of my birth?"

"Because the request has to come from the patient."

I decided to take a softer approach. "I don't know that she's not dead." I didn't have any reason to believe that she was deceased, but as no one had confirmed she was alive, I couldn't be sure.

"The answer is still no." She was starting to look a little angry.

"Please," I said, suddenly feeling as if the woman viewed me as a disgruntled adoptee.

"Absolutely not," she answered. "When you find your birth mother, bring her in, and once I have her signature, in person, then I'll release the information."

"What if she's infirm or out of the area?" I knew I was being difficult, but I couldn't help it.

"Then she can call, and with a notarized signature I can send her the records and then she can give them to you."

I'd read on adoption lists about the rudeness of those charged with keeping secrets safe from adoptees, but I'd never experienced it in person.

"But they're my records too."

"Take it up with the state legislature." She stared me down.

I backed out of the room, losing my grip on the knob as I stepped into the hall. The door banged, and I was on my way, feeling like a felon.

Back at the courthouse, I got the same runaround. The man in vital records first told me to call Harrisburg. I said that the office in Harrisburg had told me to come to Norristown. When I explained that I was adopted, he said that was another story and went on to tell me I could hire a lawyer and submit a petition for non-identifying information.

I told him I'd already done that, without a lawyer, but that I wanted a copy of my birth certificate. "It will be quite simple," I said. "I have my birth date, original name, and birth mother's name."

He shook his head. "Simple, maybe, but it's against the law."

"But it's *my* information!" I was surprised at my frustration, even though I'd known all along the chances of me getting what I wanted were slim.

"Look," he said, "I'm sympathetic. I get quite a few adoptees through here. But you're going to have to wait and see if your birth family responds to your petition and hope it's for more than non-identifying information. Or maybe, because you have your birth mother's name, she'll release the birth certificate. That's your best bet." He pushed up the sleeves of his white dress shirt, which were already rolled.

"Just because I have her name doesn't mean I can find her."

"Your chances are a lot better with the name," he said.

The door to the office swung open, and a middle-aged couple stepped into the office.

I thanked the man, and as I left the woman said they needed a copy of their son's death certificate. I stopped a minute in the hall and took a deep breath, wondering what that couple's story was, aware of the precariousness of life. Children and parents could be lost in more ways than one.

It was two o'clock by the time I left the court-house, and three o'clock by the time I'd driven around downtown Norristown a little more and then stopped for a sandwich at a deli. By the time I got back on the Turnpike, the Friday afternoon traffic was bumper to bumper. Because I was so close to Philadelphia, I contemplated turning around and exploring. But the traffic was at a near stop going into the city too, and surprisingly I had no desire to turn around. I felt like a homing pigeon, eager to fly home. I decided to continue west, back to Lancaster. For the first time I contemplated not taking the traveling nurse job at all.

The slow traffic gave me lots of time to think about why Giselle would have given birth to me in Norristown rather than Lancaster, but I couldn't come up with one good, solid reason. To keep my birth a secret? To be closer to the Philadelphia airport, where I would be surrendered to my parents soon after?

Whatever the reason, *Mammi* would know why. And probably Klara too. Both would also know, I felt sure, where Giselle was now. That was what I needed to focus on—finding my mother. Not chasing around Pennsylvania after paperwork I didn't have permission to access. I would visit Ada next Wednesday while Klara was at her quilting group. Maybe *Mammi* would remember more about the past than she reportedly knew about the present.

• • •

The next afternoon I had prenatal appointments in Marta's office, and by the time I ventured back to the cottage, Marta had a roast in the oven, which had been dropped off the day before by a family from her church. A cake was cooling on racks on the counter, and Marta was stirring frosting in a metal mixing bowl. "We'll eat at six sharp," she said.

"Who else is coming?"

She didn't look up from the bowl. "Just us."

I'd bought Ella a blank book and a fancy pen for her birthday, not knowing what else to get her. Clothes, jewelry, cosmetics, lotions, music—anything you would buy a normal teenage girl—would all be unacceptable, I was sure.

Dinner was quiet with just the four of us. Ella glanced at her cell phone several times. After Marta had placed the all-vanilla cake on the table with absolutely no decoration, she looked at Ella and said how thankful she was to have her as her daughter. Then Zed cleared his throat and said, "And I'm thankful to have you as my sister . . ." His voice trailed off.

Marta looked at me.

I clasped my hands together on the tabletop. "Well, I'm thrilled to have gotten to know you. And I am blessed to have you as my cousin."

Ella nodded at me, her capped head bobbing a little.

Marta cut and served the cake, and we ate in silence, except for me saying how delicious it was. As Ella finished the last bite of hers, she glanced at her phone again.

"Are you going out?" Marta asked.

The girl nodded.

"With?"

Ella blushed as she stood and picked up her plate. "Ezra."

Marta pursed her lips together.

"Thank you for the dinner and the cake," she said. "May I be excused?"

"What about her gifts?" I asked.

"We don't do gifts," Zed said, a hint of disappointment in his voice.

"Oh." I glanced at mine, sitting on the edge of the sideboard. I'd put it in her room for her to open after she returned.

A few minutes later I cleared the table as Marta started the dishes. If she heard the sound of Ezra's motorcycle, she didn't acknowledge it. A second later, Ella stood in the living room wearing jeans, a sweater, and boots. Her hair was down loose on her shoulders. She motioned to me. "Can you take a picture of us?" she asked quietly.

I wasn't happy about it, but I nodded and headed upstairs for my camera. Ella wasn't in the living room when I came back down, so I opened the front door. She was sitting on the back of Ezra's bike, one arm around his middle and the other holding a helmet. The sun had set and the evening was growing chilly. I snapped the photo, using my flash, capturing Ella's vibrant smile. Ezra looked a bit like a slacker with his goofy grin. I took another photo and then Ezra revved the motor. I wanted to say something stupid, like "Don't do anything I wouldn't do," but instead I said, "Be careful."

Ella was putting on her helmet, and I didn't think she heard me. She waved, though, as they took off down the highway, a wave that sent a current of loneliness through me as I watched them go.

I pulled my cell out of the pocket of my sweatshirt and checked the screen. Nothing. Sean was at work. James was on the retreat.

Turning around, I looked up at the cottage before mounting the steps. Marta stood in the window, watching me. My face grew warm as I slipped my camera into my other pocket and went inside.

That night, long after I fell asleep, my phone beeped. Because I'd been thinking of Sean earlier, I was sure it must be him, saying he'd just gotten off work. It wasn't. The text was from Ella's phone, but not from her. *This is Ezra. Ella's drunk. I need your help.*

TWENTY-FOUR

I held the phone to my ear, peering into the darkness. The other hand was on the steering wheel, and my lights were on high beam, but still I couldn't see the road Ezra was telling me to turn on.

"It's right past the shed, the white one."

I wanted to scream. How many white sheds were there in Lancaster County?

I could hear Ella crying in the background.

"Past the trees," Ezra said. They were on the northeast side of town, past Sean's house, along a canal. Or at least that was the landmark Ezra had given me. He couldn't believe I'd never heard of it before. It sounded as though they were at a regular old kegger, the kind I'd avoided, but James had thrived on, during high school.

I saw a grouping of trees and then a shed. I made a sharp right turn onto a dirt road, nearly dropping the phone. "Found it," I said.

"Okay, we're about a half mile down the road."

I wouldn't have had a hard time finding the group from a helicopter. The field was lit up like a sporting event by the headlights of cars circled around. Music was blaring, and a group of kids were dancing in the middle. Closer, a couple of boys were throwing a football back and forth. To my left a group of girls—two wearing dresses, aprons, and caps, and the rest dressed in jeans—were crowded around the open door of a pickup, all with cans of beer in their hands. I parked my borrowed car where no one could block me in and called Ella's phone again. After a few rings, Ezra picked up. In a moment I spotted him, the phone to his ear, his hand on Ella's back, his motorcycle parked nearby. She was bent over. I made my way toward them, stepping around piles of trash and clumps of weeds and brush.

"I told her to stop drinking hours ago."

I gave him a mean look. He never should have brought her out here.

"I didn't want to put her on my bike. I was afraid she'd fall off." He took a deep breath. "And I didn't really trust anyone here to see her home."

"Good thinking," I said to him, my heart softening a little. "Ella," I said her name softly. "We need to get you back to your house."

"Don't tell Mom." She reeked. Of course Marta needed to know, but there was no reason to tell Ella that now.

"I'm parked over here."

As the three of us made our way toward my car, several of the girls I'd seen earlier called out Ezra's name. "Come on," one of them said. "We're not drunk like your little friend. You can still have some fun tonight." Several of them giggled.

Ezra didn't respond but kept his arm tightly around Ella's shoulder. When we reached my car, he opened the door and helped Ella inside. "I'll follow behind you," he said.

"No," I said, annoyed. "Wait until you're okay to drive."

"I only had one beer," he said. "Hours ago."

I tilted my head. "Well, you can't come in the house."

He nodded. "I just want to make sure you get her safely home."

As I left the field and bumped back onto the main road, Ella muttered that she was sorry. "I don't know what happened." Her words were slurred.

I didn't answer. In a minute a single headlight was behind me as we jolted up the rutted road. By the time I reached the highway, Ella was saying she didn't feel well. I pulled over to the side of the road and Ezra stopped behind me.

As Ella staggered to the bushes with his help, I debated taking her into the ER. I had no idea if Marta had medical insurance. Probably not, but alcohol poisoning was nothing to mess with. It was a good thing she was throwing up, but she still might need her stomach pumped.

I looked off to the houses to my left. One of them was Sean's. He'd worked late tonight. He was still at the hospital at eleven when he'd last texted me. I pulled out my phone and flipped it open to my keyboard. *Are you home? Awake?*

He answered immediately. *Yes & Yes. What's up?*

I explained the situation.

Bring her by, he wrote back. *An OB doc and nurse-midwife should be able to figure this out, right?*

Thx. Her Amish boyfriend's coming too. I winced at my words.

For the first time since I'd met Ezra, he seemed hesitant as he and I, practically holding our noses, dragged Ella up to Sean's porch. He had the door wide open before we arrived and guided us down the hall to the bathroom. He looked awfully alert for having worked twenty hours straight. "I've actually had more experience with this than I should admit," he said. "Undergrad school. But like any good doctor, I decided not to just rely on personal experience, so I googled it. How much do you think she had to drink?" he asked Ezra.

"I've seen a lot worse," he said. "It wasn't that much, not really. But it hit her fast and hard."

We got her to the bathroom, and she sat down on the toilet lid.

Sean took a look at her eyes and asked her if she'd rather go to the hospital. She shook her head adamantly and then began to cry. "I'm sorry," she said again.

"Why don't I get her cleaned up?" I said. "Do you have an old pair of sweatpants she could borrow? And a T-shirt. Then we can decide."

Helping a drunk undress was never fun, but taking care of Ella was much more bearable than my previous experience when I volunteered at a detox center for community service hours in college. Regardless, I loved her. The emotion didn't totally surprise me, but pulling her socks off her sweaty feet at one in the morning as I held my breath confirmed my feelings of endearment for her. I had never felt the part of the big sister—as much as I had longed to—but tonight I did.

As I helped Ella into the warm tub, there was a knock on the door and I opened it a crack. Sean passed through a small stack of clothes without speaking: a pair of sweats, a T-shirt, and sweatshirt, all neatly folded, all smelling freshly laundered with a hint of his cologne. I thanked him and then held them to my nose for just a moment.

By the time Ella was out of the bath, her long hair combed out, she was feeling better, though completely embarrassed. "I can't face them," she said. "Can't we just run to your car and go home?"

I shook my head.

"Ezra must think I'm awful."

I found a box of small garbage bags under the sink. "He's the one who took you to the party." I dumped her smelly clothes into the bag and knotted the top.

Her voice trailed off. "But it was my idea . . ."

I opened the door to the scent of coffee and Ezra sitting on the floor of the hall, his back against the wall. "How is she?" he asked me.

"Stupid," Ella answered before I could, following me into the hall.

Ezra scrambled to his feet.

"I'm sorry," Ella whispered, leaning her head against his chest.

I kept walking down the hall toward the kitchen, their quiet voices behind me.

Sean sat at the nook table, his hands wrapped around a cup. He stood and stepped toward the counter, pouring me a cup. "How is she?"

"Mortified."

He smiled. "I remember nights like that."

"But you were homeschooled," I teased.

He shrugged. "Well, I was pretty wild by college, and then my younger siblings figured things out a whole lot younger." He hushed as Ella and Ezra came into the room and poured them each a cup.

We all crowded around the table and stared at each other for a moment. Finally, Ella said to me, "Are you going to tell Mom?"

"No. You are."

She groaned. Sean's blue eyes lit up over the rim of his cup. I liked that we were a team in this— and I liked it that we made a good one.

All Ella had for breakfast the next morning was coffee, and I could tell that the sunshine coming through the window hurt her eyes, but besides that it wasn't obvious she'd been drunk the night before. Marta declined going to church again, saying she didn't want to be a distraction. I found this odd but didn't say so.

As soon as we pulled onto the main highway on our way into town, Ella groaned and closed her eyes. "Never again," she whispered.

"Never again what?" Zed asked from the backseat.

Neither of us answered.

"What's going on?" Zed's face filled the rear-view mirror.

"Nothing," Ella barked, too loudly.

I smiled and caught his eye in the mirror. "Later," I said.

Esther and David weren't at church, which didn't surprise me. Between David's schoolwork and having a new baby, it was much better for the young family to take it easy than to be pushing them-selves. Afterward, Ella didn't want to stay around and chat, and I didn't want to answer questions about Marta, answers I wasn't sure of myself, so we hurried out of the foyer and headed home.

I'd told Ella that if she hadn't said anything to her mother about getting drunk by Monday morning, I would. I listened closely Sunday after-noon to their interactions, and from what I could tell, Ella hadn't uttered a word.

Sunday evening I sat on the bed in my alcove contemplating my immediate future, including how to tell Marta the next morning about Ella's drinking. But there were other things I needed to sort out too. How long would I stay in Lancaster? What had happened to my desire to live in Philly? Had all that changed with the discovery that my birth family didn't live in Montgomery County, that I had merely been born there?

My ties to Ella and Zed were growing tighter. Both had offered me their rooms, individually, when we'd arrived back home after church. I was touched, but I'd declined. For some reason I liked the alcove. You would think, considering I was an only child, that I wouldn't be able to tolerate a life without privacy, but I liked being part of a family, being in the middle, hearing everyone's coming and goings, knowing when Marta got up in the morning and when Ella went to bed at night. The alcove was an in-between place and that's where I was—in between Portland and Philly, in between Ella and Marta, in between Ada and Klara, and in between Giselle and the truth.

My cell rang. It was James. Yes, I was in between him and Sean too. I leaned against the wall. After we chatted for a moment, I told him about my trip to Harrisburg and then Norristown, and how I'd felt like a disgruntled adoptee as I searched. "It's not that I'm ungrateful toward Mama and Dad."

"I know."

I told him the rest of the story, and then he asked about Marta, Ella, and Zed. I didn't tell him about Ella's escapade the night before, but I did say that I was growing to love my cousins. Then I told him about seeing Ada last Thursday and about how alike we looked, how I was thinking again that Alexander might be my birth father.

"Wow, Lex. How does that make you feel?"

"It's really amazing how much we look alike—"

James interrupted me. "But how did you feel?"

I sat up straight on the bed, rolling my eyes for no one but myself. "How was your retreat?" I asked.

He sighed. "Good, thanks. I'm not sure I want to make troubled youths my future, but I'm learning a lot." We chatted about his schoolwork for a while longer. He told me he was working on a project for his Issues in Counseling class. "I'm doing it on adoption," he said.

"Oh, how's the orchard?" I asked, desperate to change the subject, once again. "Sophie said you'd done some work out there. Isn't the caretaker keeping up with things?"

"I like it down there, that's all."

"Even though you have so many other things going on . . ."

"Even though—Hey, there was a Realtor snooping around."

"Darci?"

"Yeah, I think so." He paused. "Yep, she gave me her card. Who told her she could—"

"I did. I talked with her before I left." I inched across the bed until my feet were on the floor.

"You're thinking about selling?"

"Maybe," I answered. Honestly, I was thinking about it more and more.

"Well, she sounded like she might have someone who is interested in looking at the place."

"Really? She hasn't called me."

"They're from California—and coming up this week."

"Oh." I stood, stepping to the window and bendng down to look out into the darkness, imagining my orchard.

"What are you going to do about Ada? And Alexander?"

I had been thinking about asking Ada to take a DNA test, but I wasn't going to tell James that. "I don't know."

"Does it make you feel—"

"Hey, I've got to go," I said.

"Lex."

"I'll call soon."

His voice sounded raw as he said goodbye.

That night I dreamed about the orchard. People were hiding behind the trees. Dad. Ada. Mama. James. Ella. I knew they were there but I couldn't see their faces. Others too, but I had no idea who they were. Just nameless figures partially attached to the brim of a hat, the hem of a dress, the tie of a cap blown out from behind a trunk. Sean was there too, leaning against a tree. I could see his face, and then he turned around and started walking off, toward Baltimore.

TWENTY-FIVE

Monday morning, after Ella left for school, her hair tucked behind her cap and her long-sleeved dress buttoned to her chin, I told Marta I needed to talk with her.

"Is this about Ella?" She stood at the kitchen sink, a dishtowel over her shoulder.

I nodded.

"And her night of drinking?"

I nodded again, my eyes wide.

"She told me last night," Marta said. "I'm going to catch up on some paperwork in the office." That was it. I asked Marta, before she dashed out the door, if she could reschedule Wednesday morning's appointments to Thursday, which was a light day. She nodded but didn't ask me why.

Ella and Marta seemed to get along fine both Monday and Tuesday. They were polite and cordial. Marta was a little bit more affectionate than normal, patting Ella's shoulder a couple of times. I saw Ella texting someone, but there was no indication whom she was in contact with. On Tuesday evening Marta took a meal to Esther and David, and Ella and Zed went with her. I declined to go. They weren't gone long, and when they returned home, Marta said that little Caroline had a cold and had been fussy. She said Esther was exhausted and Simon was out of sorts.

I kept expecting Ella to slip out of the house, kept listening for the roar of Ezra's motorcycle to interrupt the night, but neither happened.

Zed kept giving me updates, telling me he hadn't heard back from the man in Switzerland. He seemed to be as anxious about the whole thing as I was.

It took forever for Wednesday morning to arrive, but finally it did and I was out of the cottage before Zed and Ella had left for school, going by the Morning Mug first to spend some time on my laptop. There still weren't any responses to my posting. I considered joining an online support group so I could lament with other adoptees, but I decided it would be pointless right now because I didn't have much time to post or comment anyway, not to mention my Internet access at Marta's was minimal. I caught up on the news, bouncing between CNN and the BBC. I jumped over to the *Oregonian* website for the news in Oregon. It had been raining every day, which was no surprise. I imagined how green the trees and hillsides would be. The rhododendrons would be blossoming. Soon the roses in Washington Park, within walking distance of my apartment, would be budding too. I logged off with a sigh, feeling homeless, and took my coffee with me. It was eight forty-five. Klara should have left by now.

• • •

A buggy turned away from me as I neared Ada's house. Two figures were in it—I hoped both Klara and Alexander. They were running late. I pulled to the side of the road so they wouldn't see me and watched them proceed down the road, assuming if they had spotted me they would have come back to investigate.

When the buggy was out of sight, I turned down the lane. Ada was waiting for me on the front porch. She waved as I parked and stepped out to meet me. "I talked with *Mamm* and *Daed* about you. *Mamm* thinks you're 'questionable' and a little 'unstable.'" Ada smiled. "That's what she said anyway. *Daed* didn't say a thing. But *Mamm* didn't forbid you from coming here. She just told me not to believe everything you say."

I rolled my eyes. Klara was awfully clever, proposing I was a psych case.

"Do you want to see *Mammi*?" Ada asked. Clearly she wasn't taking her mother's opinions too seriously.

"Yes," I responded, closing the door to the car. "But I was hoping to look in the family Bible too."

Ada wrinkled her nose. "We don't have one."

"Ella said you did."

"Really?" Ada shrugged. "Ella would probably know. Did she say where it is?"

"On the bookcase in the living room, behind the puzzles."

A minute later I had it in my hands, leafing through the first few pages and stopping at the list of births. I skimmed down the names quickly, zeroing in on Giselle, Klara, and Marta. According to the birth date listed here, Giselle would have been nineteen when I was born.

The space for listing her spouse had been left blank, as had—contrary to what Ella had said—the space for her offspring. Looking more closely, I realized that wasn't exactly true. Something had been written in the offspring section but had since been whited-out. My frustration mounting, I shifted my attention to her sisters. Beside Klara was her husband, Alexander, and under them their daughter, Ada; beside Marta was Frederick, and under them Ella and Zed. Taking it in, the whole list looked like one big happy family—well, one big happy family and one tiny swipe of White-Out, obliterating an entire person.

Fighting back tears, I held up the page against the light from the window and was relieved to see my name there, under the correction fluid, clear as day. I told myself they could try to hide my name all they wanted, but they would never be able to hide the truth. I showed my discovery to Ada, hoping it was proof enough that I wasn't the unstable one in this bunch, not by a long shot.

Ada stepped closer. "Who is Giselle?" she asked.

"Your aunt. My birth mother."

"What happened to her?"

I closed the Bible. "I have no idea. I'm hoping *Mammi* can tell us."

Ada took the Bible from me and slipped it into place and then stacked the puzzles in front of it again.

As we opened the door to *Mammi*'s and stepped inside, she turned her attention toward us immediately. The same quilt was spread across her lap, and she wore a white gown and a cap on her head. Her faded blue eyes lit up and she smiled. "Ada," she said, her voice soft.

"*Mammi.*" Ada took two quick steps to her side. "This is Lexie," she said. "She's my cousin."

"Your cousin? How nice." *Mammi* gave me a warm smile and a nod. "Lexie, you say? Let's see, I don't think I remember anyone in the family by that name. You must be from another settlement. Who is your father, dear?"

That's what I'd like you to tell me.

"Um . . ." I faltered, shaking my head, realizing that she didn't understand, not at all. "You might remember me better by my full name," I said finally. "Alexandra."

It took a moment, but then the old woman's eyes grew wide and her mouth moved. No words came out. She reached for my hand and I extended it, transfixed by the paper-thin skin. For the first time in my life, I looked at someone else's body part— a hand—and wondered if mine would look like that some day. When she turned toward me, I could see that the left side of her face drooped a little. She squeezed my fingers and struggled to sit up more in her chair. "Alexandra?" she whispered.

A lump wedged in my throat. I couldn't speak but nodded, hoping she could see me.

"Alexandra?" This time her voice was louder.

"Yes," I managed to say.

"You came back." Her grip was surprisingly strong.

"To find you," I said. "And the rest of my birth family."

"Oh, dear." She let go of my hand and tried to push herself up further into a sitting position in the chair. "Ada?"

"I'll help." I pushed the lever for the recliner down and then stepped in front of her, put my hands under her arms, and lifted her straight. Ada went behind her to take the pillow out from under her head, and then I put the chair back into a reclining position but not as far.

"Ada," she said again. "Make us some tea, please." She was in much better shape than I had feared based on Klara's comments.

I pulled up a chair while Ada busied herself in the kitchen. There wasn't much time for small talk, but I couldn't just jump in with all of my questions. I started by saying that Mama and Dad had told me a little about her through the years, that according to them my birth grandmother was tall and kind and that she loved me. Listening to my words, *Mammi*'s eyes welled with tears, and one after another they spilled over and trickled down her cheeks. She didn't wipe them away.

"I have come here now because I have questions," I said softly, pulling a tissue from the box on the table and handing it to her.

Mammi nodded, dabbing at her wet cheeks, obviously trying to pull herself together.

"It seems Giselle is my birth mother?"

Startled, *Mammi* glanced toward the kitchen before answering.

"Yes," she whispered.

"Where does she live?"

Mammi shook her head.

"You don't want to tell me?"

She nodded.

Feeling crushed, I asked, "How about my birth father?" She didn't respond, so I added in an even softer voice, "I've been wondering if it's Alexander."

Though she didn't seem surprised by the question, she shook her head emphatically, saying no, it was definitely not Alexander.

"Who, then?"

Mammi touched her lips with her fingertips, glancing again toward the kitchen. I sat back in the chair, my eyes still on her, wondering how badly she'd been affected by the stroke. Her mind seemed clear.

"What does it matter now anyway?" she added. Before I could answer, she continued, finding her voice. "All that really matters is that you came back. I always knew you would, or at least I hoped you would. Someday." She lifted up a hand as if to touch my face.

I hesitated, knowing I had come here for words, not actions. Still, there was something about her expression, about the way she was reaching toward me, that pushed all other thoughts from my mind, at least for the moment. Swallowing hard, I leaned forward, allowing her fingertips to move lightly along my cheek. Though her touch was tentative, my heart pounded as if she were sending an electric jolt through my skin. I closed my eyes, all of the babies, mothers, and grandmothers I had ever worked with suddenly filling my mind. They were *family* to each other, connected by blood and tissue and sinew, just as this woman was connected to me. Time froze as I reveled in that knowledge.

When her feathery touch ceased, I took a deep breath and opened my eyes, feeling suddenly cut adrift. I was relieved to see that though the old woman had returned her hand to her lap, she continued to study my face, to take it in hungrily.

"Meine Enkelin," she whispered tenderly, the words striking some memory deep inside of me and causing hot tears to spring to my eyes. "So beautiful. All grown up now." Even as she smiled with her lips, her eyes filled again with tears as well.

She accepted my offer of another tissue, and though I managed to recover quickly, she was still crying when Ada stepped into the room a few moments later, rattling a pillbox in her hands.

"Looks like *Mamm* forgot to give you your medication," Ada said, giving the box another shake before coming to a stop, her smile fading when she saw her grandmother's tears. "What's the matter, *Mammi?*" she asked, bending down beside the chair.

"Just the past," the old woman said, sniffling.

"Well, that's why you take these pills. Right?"

A small sob caught in *Mammi*'s throat.

Not wanting to cry again myself, I offered to retrieve a glass of water. I stood and headed to the kitchen, taking deep breaths as I went. When my emotions were once again under control, I returned with glass in hand and told Ada to go ahead and finish making the tea, that I could handle things in here.

"Thanks," she replied, handing me the pillbox and giving her grandmother's arm a pat.

As she returned to the kitchen, I sat down, popping open the lid on the section of the pillbox that had been labeled for Wednesday mornings. Inside were five pills. I recognized a blood thinner and high blood pressure medicine. The other three were the same—all tranquilizers—and a dosage that was way too high. For a moment I considered palming two of the pills instead of giving them to her, but I decided it wasn't my place to alter her meds even if I did have her best interests in mind. I gave her the pills and then the glass of water, thinking it was better that I have a talk with Ada and explain my concerns directly. She would just need to think of a way to convey that information to Klara without getting herself in trouble for having let me in here.

I could tell from the sounds coming from the kitchen that the tea was almost ready, so I called out to Ada, telling her not to bother with a cup for me because my time was almost up.

"Oh, that's too bad," she called back. "But you're probably right."

While she was still out of the room I took *Mammi*'s hand in mine and told her I had to leave now but that I would come back again soon.

"Yes, please," she replied, her eyelids already beginning to droop from the medication.

"Until then," I whispered, giving her hand a squeeze as I stood, "I want you to think about my questions. I want answers. I need information."

Despite her encroaching drug haze, *Mammi* held on to me tightly, even after I tried to let go. Then she surprised me by grabbing my wrist with her other hand and pulling me toward her, obviously wanting me to come closer, much closer. I leaned down, expecting a kiss to my cheek. Instead, she put her lips to my ear.

"Burke Bauer," she whispered.

"What?"

"Burke Bauer," she repeated, slurring this time.

Then her hands relaxed, releasing me. By the time I pulled back far enough to see her face, I realized that her eyes were closed, her jaw slack. As Ada stepped into the room carrying the teapot and two cups on a tray, *Mammi* let out a loud snore.

"So much for the tea," Ada said, her steps faltering. "She will probably be conked out for hours."

"That's because she's overmedicated," I said, running a hand through my hair and trying to recover from the shock of the woman's words. Had that been the drugs talking? Or had she just whispered in my ear the name I had been seeking, that of my birth father?

"What do you mean?" Ada asked, setting the tray down on a nearby table.

"I mean, she's getting three times the amount of tranquilizers she should be getting," I explained, hoping that Ada wouldn't notice the array of emotions that were swirling around inside of me. "In fact, she really shouldn't be on tranquilizers at all. There are better medications for stroke victims than that." I went on to explain that besides being addictive, they weren't long lasting.

"But she cries all the time if she doesn't have it."

Taking a deep breath, I forced myself to focus on the matter at hand.

"Then she probably needs an antidepressant. The tranquilizers are just making her sleepy, not to mention affecting her balance. In my opinion, her doctor shouldn't be prescribing it at all."

"I'll tell *Mamm*," Ada said. "Perhaps I can say I read an article or overheard a conversation or something."

I reached the door and hesitated, my hand on the knob, knowing there was one more matter she and I needed to discuss, one I could only approach head-on.

"I was thinking you and I should have a DNA test," I said to Ada, glancing toward *Mammi* to make sure she was still asleep. Regardless of what the old woman had just told me, there was still a chance that Alexander was my father. If Ada and I got tested, I could find out for sure.

Ada took a step backward. "Why?"

"To see exactly how we're related. It's no big deal, just a swab of the inside of your cheek." I was pretty sure I could find someone at the hospital to do it, or if not I could buy a test.

"DNA is the genetic code, right?"

I nodded.

"What do you think we would find out?"

I shrugged. "Maybe nothing. Or maybe we'll learn exactly how we connect, why we look so much alike. Whatever it would or wouldn't tell us, it would mean a lot to me."

She wrinkled her nose. "I will think about it." Glancing toward her sleeping grandmother, Ada motioned for me to step outside. Together, we moved onto the porch, and after pulling the door shut behind her, Ada produced a cell phone from her pocket, flashing me a sheepish grin. "I can text you later, once I decide. What is your number?"

I rattled it off and then smiled, surprised but not shocked that Ada had a cell phone. After all, she hadn't joined the church yet. Though I didn't totally understand the rules regarding Amish cell phone usage, it seemed to me that they had a sort of "don't ask, don't tell" cell policy, at least with their as-yet-unbaptized youth.

She gave me her number as well, and I quickly entered it in my contacts, thrilled to be able to communicate with her without having to come out to the house to do so.

"It might take me a while, though," she said, "to make my decision."

"How long?" I couldn't contain my frustration.

She shrugged and a pixielike smile crossed her face. "I need to think on it."

My prenatal appointments ended at the same time Zed and Ella trudged up the drive, coming from the bus stop a quarter mile up the road. Ella was texting away as she walked through the door, and she kept on going straight up to her room. In a few minutes, when I stood halfway up the stairs, I could hear her talking on the phone.

Marta had left a note on the table saying that she'd gone into town. I assumed to talk to her lawyer.

I could take my laptop into town or recruit Zed into helping me again. He seemed to have better luck with online searches than I did and wasn't likely to share those searches with anyone else, one of the perks of recruiting an adolescent boy who hardly spoke.

I gave him the name Burke Bauer and said that the man probably lived in Lancaster County during the 1980s, maybe near where his Aunt Klara lived now. I was pretty sure there could be a slew of men with the same name and knew the chances of finding the right Burke Bauer were pretty low. And *Mammi* hadn't said that he was my father, but I didn't know why else she would have told me his name. Maybe, just maybe, it was true that my grandmother loved me. I clasped my right hand with my left, remembering her tender touch, and ducked out of the dining room, fighting back tears. Yes, I thought she loved me. Even still.

I collapsed onto the sofa in the living room and closed my eyes, blinking tears away. Ella's door opened and closed. She started down the stairs, but her cell rang again and she turned around. A moment later her door opened and closed again.

Zed spoke from his perch at the computer across the room. "Lexie, I have something."

I jumped to my feet. The kid was amazing.

"How about this?"

I looked over his shoulder. It was an obituary for a Burke F. Bauer II, who died at age forty-eight more than ten years ago. A prominent businessman in Lancaster County, he had run his family's nursery stock business for many years. Bauer was survived by his wife Lavonne and one son, B.F Bauer III.

I did the math. If the guy in the obituary was my father, he would have been more than thirty when I was born, which was too old to have been fooling around with a nineteen-year-old girl. The more likely culprit was his son, apparently also named Burke Bauer. I told Zed to see what he could come up with for that one, but after a good ten minutes of clicking around, Zed had managed to find only one thing, a brief newspaper article in a local paper about him winning the science fair in the spring of his senior year in high school. At least that information gave us his age relative to that date, so again I did the math but realized he would have been only eleven years old when I was born. That made him an even less likely paternity suspect than his father.

"What about the widow?" I asked. "Can you find anything at all on Lavonne Bauer? Is she still alive?"

In less than a minute, Zed came up with an address for a Lavonne Bauer near Paradise in Lancaster County. He also tried to find an address for the son, but nothing came up.

"Who are these people?" Zed asked after he printed out Lavonne's address and handed it to me.

"I'm hoping she's wrong," I replied, "but

according to *Mammi*, my biological father's name is Burke Bauer. At least that's what I think she was telling me. So either she was talking about a different Burke Bauer altogether, or back when my mother was nineteen she had an affair with a thirty-two-year-old married man who got her pregnant. That's . . . shocking." I stopped, realizing this subject material wasn't the best for a conversation with a twelve-year-old.

"An older guy with a younger babe?" Zed replied. "That's not shocking. That's not even all that unusual, at least not on TV."

I sighed.

"Seriously," Zed protested. "I mean, isn't that one of the signs of a midlife crisis?"

I looked at his earnest face and couldn't help but laugh.

"What are you watching, Zed? *Oprah*? *The View*?" If he was, it was online or at a friend's house because Marta didn't have a TV.

He blushed as he replied, "Well, come on. You know. Older man, younger woman, midlife crisis. End of story."

Though thirty-two wasn't exactly midlife, Zed had a point. Older man, younger woman, end of story. But was it *my* story? Had I really been the product of an extramarital affair? If so, I had to wonder how it could have happened, how a young Amish girl and a mature married man could have even met, much less ended up in a clandestine relationship. However it had begun, I couldn't imagine its progression either, especially regarding the pregnancy. Had Giselle been foolish, perhaps even gotten pregnant on purpose in the hope that Burke would leave his wife for her? Maybe once he learned of Giselle's pregnancy, he had rejected her, even tried to pay her off and send her on her way. Whatever the details, if I had the correct Burke Bauer, as I suspected I did, somehow I knew there was much more to the story than I would ever be able to learn from a simple Internet search.

At least this new evidence might help answer my most important question, which was why I had been given up for adoption at all. Obviously, a married man who already had a legitimate child of his own wouldn't have wanted me—or even been willing to acknowledge me. Perhaps Giselle's heartache was so great from his rejection that she decided that she hadn't wanted me either. But if that was the case, then surely one of her sisters could have taken me in, or even *Mammi* herself, and raised me. So why hadn't they? Before today I couldn't begin to fathom the answer to that question. But now I realized the truth, that this Amish family may have been turned against me before I was even born because I was conceived through an adulterous relationship. After all, my mother bore a scarlet letter, so to speak.

Perhaps, to their minds, that letter simply extended to me as well.

TWENTY-SIX

I left the cottage immediately. After sitting in my car for a few minutes, I went to a florist shop, picked up a bouquet of red roses, and then drove to the home of Lavonne Bauer. She lived just outside of Paradise, a couple of miles from Susan Eicher's house, in a modest, one-story colonial with a tidy, well-landscaped yard. I'd decided to pose as a delivery person. I just wanted an excuse to see her—I wasn't necessarily going to talk to her. But she wasn't home. On the way back to Marta's, I threw the roses, all twenty-seven dollars worth, out the window, one by one.

That evening I was shocked when Alexander showed up at Marta's cottage in a white van. I looked out the front window as he spoke to the driver and then climbed out. According to *Mammi*, this kind, gentle Amish man was not my father after all, a thought that filled me with a deep sense of loss.

It also confused me, given my name. If he weren't my father, then why had I been named Alexandra? Had it simply been a matter of wishful thinking? A way to honor a supportive brother-in-law? Surely it hadn't been mere coincidence, my mother giving me a name so similar to that of her sister's husband. There had to have been some reason for it, I thought, watching from the window as he walked to the door and knocked.

"Lexie? Who is it?" Ella asked from her perch at the dining room table.

"Your Uncle Alexander," I replied, moving toward the door and swinging it open, glad that Marta was upstairs. I only hoped she hadn't heard him knock.

As Alexander came inside and took off his hat, I realized for the first time that I looked nothing like him. Neither did Ada, for that matter. He greeted Ella and Zed shyly and then explained he had come here to speak with me. Obviously sensing that this was to be a private conversation, Ella told Zed that it was time to take care of the chickens.

"I'll help him," she said, giving me a funny look as she followed her brother out the door and pulled it shut behind them.

I gestured toward the living room, and once Alexander and I both sat down he spoke in a low voice, saying that Ada had told him about my request.

"Did she tell Klara?" I spoke as softly as I could.

"No, thank goodness." His hazel eyes pled with me. "Please don't pursue this."

"Are you my father?" I asked.

He shook his head.

"Are you Ada's father?"

He sat up straight. Now his eyes drilled me.

"Yes," he answered. "With everything I am, I am her father."

I swallowed hard. Ada and I both knew a daddy's love. Still, there was something odd about his choice of words.

"But . . . are you her biological father?" My voice wavered.

He fingered the brim of his hat nervously. "You don't have any idea the damage you are set to do," he said. "You are pushing all of us to the brink. You can't imagine how fragile the people involved are."

"Ada doesn't seem fragile at all. In fact—"

He interrupted me. "I beg you, let this go."

A door opened upstairs, and I inhaled. Alexander and I should have been the ones to go tend the chickens. "You should leave," I said.

"Who's here?" Marta was at the top of the stairs.

Alexander stood. "It's me."

"Alex." She hurried on down, and she smiled as she made eye contact with him. "What brings you out this way?"

He held his hat against his chest. "Sorry business, I'm afraid. Lexie has asked Ada to do one of those DNA tests."

"Lexie?" Marta stopped on the bottom step. "Why ever so? Isn't it enough that you know you're cousins?"

I looked from Alexander to Marta, from his hazel eyes to her blue. I pointed to my brown eyes

351

and thought of Ada. "Chances are Alexander is not Ada's father. Or else Klara isn't her mother. Or both."

"Oh, gracious," Marta said. Her tone was different than what I'd heard before. Patronizing, yes, but also a little showy. "You're speaking statistics, not real life. Of course Alexander is Ada's father."

I crossed my arms. "Does the name Burke Bauer mean anything to either of you?"

Marta and Alexander looked at each other, clearly alarmed, though they both managed to recover quickly.

"I think he used to own the Gundy place." Marta spoke with an air of nonchalance. "Where Will lives now."

Alexander nodded, his jaw tight. "Bauer was *Englisch*. I believe he passed away a while back."

"Oh, right. I'd heard that too," Marta replied, and then she returned her attention to me. "Why are you asking?"

"*Mammi* mentioned him to me." I felt flustered. Suddenly I realized my source didn't have much credibility.

"Ah," Marta said, nodding sadly as if in pity for me that I had believed the absurd musings of a senile old woman.

"Yes, well," Alexander added, clearing his throat, "you probably noticed that her mind is all over the place."

Our eyes met, and I knew there was more that

he wasn't saying. Looking away, he took a deep breath and continued.

"Anyway, Lexie, I'm not sorry you've come out to Lancaster County from Oregon. It's been a pleasure to meet you, really, and if I weren't afraid of what trouble you might cause, I think I would be pleased to get to know you. But you don't know the hornets' nest you're stirring." He turned to Marta. "I'll be on my way then."

She thanked him for coming and walked him out the door. "I'll talk with her," came Marta's faint voice as the door was closing behind her, "and convince her to drop this whole DNA thing."

No, you won't, I thought fiercely. I took the stairs two at a time and grabbed my computer and my purse, and then I flew back down the stairs. I was at the door before Marta had come in, and without saying a word, I breezed past her to my car.

"Lexie," she called after me, "come back."

I shook my head as I climbed into my car. I'd had enough.

Running away from Marta meant going to Lancaster General and sitting with Sean while he had a late dinner. As he ate I told him about my day, starting with finding my name whited-out from the family Bible and ending with Alexander and Marta trying to bully me about the DNA testing. He listened attentively to the whole tale, commenting occasionally, and then he urged me to stand strong on the matter of the DNA testing if it was important to me.

"Do you know how accurate those send-away tests are?" I asked.

"Not really, but I have a buddy here who works extensively with DNA. He could do the testing for you and probably have some answers back in no time."

"Seriously? Sean, that would be wonderful."

Grinning, he pulled his phone from the pocket of his lab coat and typed in a message. Moments later came the reply, which he read to me.

" 'No problem getting the test done, but sisters are hard to match. Need a DNA sample from the mother.'" Sean met my gaze, a look of pity on his face.

I slumped in my chair until I remembered the carved box with its two locks of hair, one that looked as if it had come from an infant, and the other that had probably come from an adult.

"Wait! Would hair work?" I asked, thinking of the lock of longer, thicker hair had surely been Giselle's.

Sean smiled as he texted his friend back. I held my breath. Sean's phone beeped again. He read it quickly and then met my gaze.

"Bingo! He's going to be out of town for a few days, but he can do it next Wednesday if you want."

"I'll get a hold of Ada." She was twenty-four.

Surely she could make her own decisions. But she was also totally dependent on her parents and seemed to be very much a daddy's girl. I took out my phone, wrote out a quick text, and hit "send."

"Thanks, Sean."

"If you get the info you want, do you think you can let all this go?" He picked up his turkey wrap.

I shrugged, feeling too fried to answer.

"Cuz this is the sort of thing that could send a person over the edge."

I wasn't sure if he meant me or him. I changed the subject to his house. He'd had four people look at it already and an offer had come in an hour before. He was going to think about it overnight, but he was pretty sure he'd accept.

"How about your place out West?" he asked.

I told him I hadn't called my Realtor. The truth was that I didn't have the emotional energy to deal with that too. I'd wait until she called me.

Next he asked about Marta's case.

"Oh no," I groaned. "Her pretrial hearing is next week. Wednesday. I promised I'd go with her."

"And miss your DNA test? Come on, Lexie, blow her off. Look at how she's treated you over and over."

I couldn't blow her off. I'd tried. There was Ella and Zed. She was their mother. Beyond that, she was my aunt. How could I explain to Sean that in spite of everything, she knew me *before*. She was part of my story. "I can't."

"Okay, then. I'll ask my buddy if next Thursday will work instead."

"And I'll ask Ada." Both of us pulled out our phones. I was pretty sure I had a couple of prenatal appointments Thursday morning, but Marta would simply have to reschedule them. That's all there was to it.

"Is Ada pretty passive?" Sean asked as we both sat and waited for our replies.

"What do you mean?"

"Will she do what anyone tells her to?"

I shook my head. The young Amish women I'd met so far were quite capable and not the type who could be pushed around. "No. In fact, she acts pretty normal." I hesitated. Maybe normal wasn't the word I was looking for. "Likeable."

He snorted.

"No one growing up the way she has can be normal." He leaned forward. "I speak from experience, remember? Being raised in such legalism—and the Amish are over-the-top compared to my experience—traps people completely. They have to break out and leave, like I did, to free themselves."

"I don't agree," I said. "Sure, I think it's weird that they only allow an eighth-grade education, and some of the rules do seem arbitrary, but I've seen plenty of Amish women who seem genuinely happy."

Sean shook his head. "Because they don't know

anything else. They're like indentured servants. Stockholm syndrome. You were lucky, Lexie. Even though it wasn't your choice, you got out."

Lucky? Really? I changed the subject to his work. I didn't want to discuss adoption or the Amish anymore. He was telling me about a C-section delivery involving triplets when my cell rang. "What timing. It's my Realtor," I said.

"Ooh, take it. Maybe it's a lucky day for both of us." He beamed.

I flipped open my phone. Darci said, just as James had indicated, that a couple from California was interested in seeing the house. I gave her Sophie's number to get the key and hung up, feeling ambivalent.

Sean knew what was going on from my side of the conversation and high-fived me. "That's great," he said. "You can pay for med school with your profit."

I must have winced.

"I'm serious. You would make a good doctor."

"I make a good midwife," I said, and then I corrected myself with, "nurse-midwife."

He nodded and then gave me his charming smile, his bright blue eyes lighting up like a tropical sky.

"Hey, I'm going to Baltimore for a weekend— late April or early May. Want to come with me?"

"Maybe." I couldn't think that far ahead, even though it was only a couple of weeks away.

"It would be great to have you come."

I would think about it. Baltimore could be an option. Not to go to med school, necessarily, but to get to know Sean better.

"When was the last time you went home?" I asked. I realized all of his talk about his family was years in the past. And he hadn't talked at all about any future visits in the works.

"It's been a couple of years."

"Really?" I couldn't imagine, especially when he had all those brothers and sisters.

He nodded. "At least two." He grinned again. "I've been busy."

I was trying to form a reply when he added, "Speaking of busy, I need to run for now."

I hung around the hospital after he went back to work, surfing their Wi-Fi by using the password Sean had given me. I googled Burke F. Bauer, Lancaster, Pennsylvania, and found the same articles Zed had.

Next I checked the adoption registry. Once again, no responses. I emailed Sophie, telling her the Realtor was going to call her about the key to the house so she could show it. I quickly explained I wasn't sure I was going to sell—I was just exploring my options. I skimmed a few blogs I regularly kept up with, and at ten thirty I logged off, slipped my laptop into its case, and checked my cell phone for the tenth time since I'd texted Ada. No response there, either.

A half hour later I was back at the cottage,

sneaking in the unlocked door and up to the security of my alcove.

The next morning Marta met me at the bottom of the stairs.

"In regard to last night—"

I put up my hand to stop her.

"I'm not interested in another lecture about letting things be, Marta. Unless you are willing to come clean and tell me everything I want to know, don't bother," I said curtly. I'd had enough of playing duck, duck, goose with her.

Her eyes grew cold as ice. She turned on her heel and marched into the kitchen.

I tried to ignore the tension between us as I went about my day, examining patients and thinking through my upcoming schedule. I had a short time until I was expected to report for work in Philadelphia, but besides the mystery of why I was born in Montgomery County, I realized no more information was there for me. My desire to work and live in Philly was now nonexistent.

Despite the ongoing conflict with Marta, I felt encouraged by my growing relationships with Zed and Ella, not to mention my patients. During the next week I checked my phone over and over, hoping for a text from Ada, and delivered three babies, numbers 259, 260, and 261, or numbers four, five, and six in Lancaster County. Two were primagravida mothers and the third was a gravida five who was two weeks late. Still, all three were textbook smooth with not even a moment of complications.

After the third birth, I came home Wednesday morning and slept for a few hours before accompanying Marta to the courthouse. The pretrial hearing was brief. The DA said he was ready to plea bargain. Marta spoke for herself, saying she was innocent and had no reason to bargain. Her attorney was clearly flustered and requested to speak to the judge. He granted her permission, and Connie Stanton shuffled up to the bench. The back of her gray skirt was wrinkled, and her hair, tucked into an untidy French roll, looked as if it might spring free at any moment.

As she spoke to the judge, I looked around the room, noting a few Amish and Mennonites in attendance, but none I knew. Feeling antsy, I pulled out my cell phone to check for messages. It had been a week, and even though the DNA test was scheduled for tomorrow, Ada still hadn't returned my text. Actually texts—I'd sent two more asking if she'd received the first, and she still hadn't responded.

The phone vibrated just as I was putting it away and I quickly jerked it back up, only to see that the message wasn't from Ada but instead from Sophie: *Got your email! You contacted a Realtor? What's going on? Call me . . .*

I would have to answer her later. Connie Stanton

stopped whispering to the judge and stepped away from the bench. He hit his gavel once and set a trial date of September 17. *September.* By then, I'd either be in Oregon for the hazelnut harvest or I would have sold the orchard. Maybe I would be in Baltimore. But there was no way I was going to be in Pennsylvania. Even Marta had to know I couldn't stick around that long.

She turned toward me, and a moment later I pushed open the solid wood doors and she followed me out to the second floor lobby and then down the stairs to the foyer. Neither of us said a word as we walked to the car. Once we were in the borrowed Datsun, Marta said she'd been thinking a lot about Esther and wondering how Caroline was doing. Given all she'd just been through, I marveled at her train of thought.

"Let's stop by," she said. "We're just a couple of blocks away."

Now that the baby was under the care of a pediatrician, ours was strictly a social visit. But once we got there, it soon turned into something more. David was home, and as he let us in, he explained that Caroline had a cold and her breathing seemed labored. They had an appointment with the doctor for that afternoon but had been trying to decide if they should head over sooner, if maybe they should even get her to the hospital.

"Go get your stethoscope," Marta whispered to me.

A few minutes later I had little Caroline lengthwise in my lap, her dark eyes fixed on mine, the diaphragm of my scope against her body. But I knew already, from the rise and fall of her chest, that she had pneumonia.

Marta knew it too. "You take them," she said to me. "I'll stay with Simon."

The ER doc confirmed that Caroline had pneumonia and ordered tests to find out if it was bacterial or viral. She was admitted to the pediatric critical care unit and in no time was in a warm isolette, wearing just a diaper, and hooked up to an IV.

I stayed with Esther and David, answering their questions. If the pneumonia was bacterial, Caroline would be given antibiotics. If it was viral, then all that could be done would be to give her fluids and oxygen, if she needed it. The nurses were attentive and gentle with both the baby and Esther and David. I tried to talk the parents into going down to the cafeteria for lunch, but they wouldn't leave their daughter's side.

I went down by myself, sending Sean a text on the way, and bought sandwiches for Esther and David. When I came back into the room, an oxygen mask was over Caroline's face. Esther was crying even as she was humming to the baby. It took me a second to recognize the tune, the chorus to "Our God Is an Awesome God."

"She is struggling more and more to get her

362

breath," David told me. "We leave her in God's hands."

"And the nurses' and doctors' hands," I added.

David gave me a harsh look. "And who do you think guides those hands, heals their patients? God. Only God."

I met his gaze.

"Lexie Jaeger," he said to me, "I wonder if you have not encountered much sorrow in your life."

I was taken aback by his question. I'd been abandoned by my birth mother. Mama had died when I was eight. My father had died just recently. "Yes," I told him. "I have encountered sorrow."

"And did it make you trust Jesus more?"

I looked away, heat creeping into my face. Could David tell it had done quite the opposite, that my sorrow had made me determined not to trust anyone but myself?

"My sorrow has made me trust Christ. My parents, my seven siblings, and my grandparents all died before my eyes. I trusted Jesus with them and they are in heaven. We will trust Him with our daughter."

I glanced at Esther. She had one hand on her baby and another one in the air. Her eyes were closed as she sang softly.

"Please pray for Caroline," David said. "Please trust God with her."

I left the hospital in a daze, David's words echoing in my mind. When I reached the car, I climbed in and simply sat for a long time, marveling at the odd sensation inside my chest, the slow melting of a heart that had been frozen solid for years.

I prayed right there. Then I texted Sophie to ask her and all of the church members to pray. I texted Marta. I texted Ella because I knew she would soon be out of school. I texted James. And Ada. I thought of all of us praying, all of us connected. All of us thinking about baby Caroline and Esther and David and little Simon at the same time. As I started up the car and drove away, I asked God not to let Caroline die . . . because I knew she could. I knew babies did.

Caroline was baby number 258; baby number three in Lancaster County. I wanted her to live. Esther and David had already lost so much in life. I didn't want them to go through the sorrow of also losing their little girl.

Marta stayed with Simon, and I went ahead and saw three late afternoon appointments and then called the traveling nurse agency, apologized, and withdrew my application. I had no idea where I would land next, but I did know that I wasn't done in Lancaster County.

Before we ate dinner I said the blessing—out loud, the way Dad had done when I was growing up—and asked for healing for baby Caroline. Ella and Zed both said "amen" with me. We were pretty somber as we ate. Marta called a little after nine to say that Esther was spending the night at the hospital, but that David had come home to be with Simon. Marta was staying over, though, so David could go back first thing in the morning or even during the night, if need be. She said Caroline was still on oxygen.

I had a text from Sophie, asking how the baby was doing and then one from James, asking the same. I still hadn't heard from Ada about the DNA test. I would have to call Sean in the morning and ask him to get a hold of his friend to cancel our appointment.

Right before bedtime Zed called me into the dining room. "I heard from the guy in Switzerland," he said, looking up from the screen. "He says he talked with the Giselle lady he knows. He said she reacted when he asked if she used to live in Pennsylvania but wouldn't give him any information."

"Sounds familiar," I said. It had to be Giselle. Avoidance was a family trait. Feeling weak, I slid down onto a chair.

"I emailed him back and asked him what last name the woman goes by. I also asked him if he would ask her for her email address." He glanced down at the screen and then back up again, squinting a little. "Maybe I can chat with her directly."

I wanted to hug him but settled for patting his back.

When I crawled into my alcove bed, I prayed

that somehow, someway Ada would be willing to get tested. Then I prayed again for Caroline. Just as I was drifting off to sleep, my phone rang. It was James.

I answered with a sleepy hello, and he asked how Caroline was. I gave him an update. He said he'd been praying. He said he was sorry he called so late. He just wanted to tell me "sweet dreams." I was too tired to ask him about classes or the orchard or anything else. After we said our farewells, I realized I felt a peace I hadn't for years, as if someone were tucking me into bed. Was it Mama I was feeling in my sleepy state? Or Dad? Maybe it was James. And then I realized it was none of them. After Mama died, when I used to talk to God nonstop, it was almost as if I could feel Him tuck me in at night—not physically but spiritually, right before I drifted off.

"I've missed You," I whispered, as I slipped into sleep.

The next morning Ada sent me a text at five thirty saying to pick her up at the end of the lane at nine twenty. I left the house with a few hairs from the locks tucked inside an envelope in my purse.

After I discreetly handed Chuck the envelope, he swabbed Ada and me and then we both hurried up to the pediatric ICU. So far that morning, Sophie and James had both texted me to ask how Caroline was, and Mrs. Glick and Mr. Miller had each left a voice mail message on my phone, asking the same. I needed an answer so I could get back to all of them.

Ada waited outside while I checked in with the nurse and then slipped through the door. I gasped at first—the isolette was empty. But then I spotted Esther in a rocking chair off to the side of the big room, holding Caroline in her arms, the tiny infant still hooked up to an IV and oxygen and bundled in a blanket.

"How is she?" I knelt down in front of Esther. She wore the same pair of sweatpants and pink T-shirt from the day before.

"Doing better," she answered. "She had a couple of rough moments during the night, though."

"You must be exhausted," I said, patting her hand.

She nodded and then went back to staring at her baby.

"You should go home and rest."

She didn't answer me.

When I went back out into the hall, Sean was talking to Ada. They looked like quite the pair, he in his lab coat and dress slacks, she wearing a burgundy dress, white apron, and cap. They seemed to be chatting up a storm, and Ada must have explained what I'd been doing.

"I didn't realize you knew the baby who came in yesterday," he said.

"I delivered her," I answered, surprised he would have heard about Caroline. I knew my voice sounded defensive, but I could imagine the talk going around the hospital about the home-birth baby. "And it's viral pneumonia caused by a respiratory infection," I said, needing him to know that the source of her illness was a common cold, not a bacterial infection from birth.

He held up both hands and grinned, his blue eyes dancing. "Whoa. No one's said otherwise."

I relaxed, a little.

His voice dropped and he leaned closer, as if he were going to tell us an important secret. "I was thinking about the praise meeting going on in the lobby last night. All sorts of people praying and singing, 'The Lord giveth and the Lord taketh away, blessed be the name of the Lord' and stuff like that. It was a little weird. I felt like I was back home."

A nervous smiled crossed my lips and I glanced at Ada. She had a blank expression on her face.

"No harm intended," Sean said quickly to Ada.

"I don't think the Amish have prayer meetings like that," I said.

Ada agreed and Sean shrugged, grinning again.

"Anyway," I said, desperate to change the subject, "Ada and I both got swabbed."

"So I heard," Sean said. "Chuck will get right on it. You'll know in a couple of days." He turned to Ada, charming as ever. "It's so nice to meet you," he said. "I hope I'll see you again soon." He started down the hall but then pivoted around.

"Hey, have you heard anything on your house?"

"Nothing yet." Darci hadn't called me and, frankly, I was too anxious to call her.

"That's too bad." He grinned. "I accepted the offer on mine."

I gave him a smile and big thumbs-up, and then he turned back around and continued to walk away.

TWENTY-SEVEN

"He seems really nice," Ada said as I drove down Queen Street, heading out of town.

I agreed, though I was still a little taken aback by his comments about the people praying for Caroline. But the truth was, until recently I might have said the same.

"Did he give you this bag?" she asked, holding up my purse. "It's a Coach, right?"

I was dumbfounded. "Really? You know what a Coach is?"

"*Ya,*" she answered. "You'd be surprised at what Amish women know about." She put it down on the console between us. "It's nice," she said. "The purse. So is Sean." Her voice held a hint of teasing. "Are you two courting?"

I smiled. The word was so old fashioned. So innocent. "No. And we're not dating, either. I guess you could say we're just friends." Of course I was lying. I was contemplating moving to Baltimore, for goodness' sake.

"How about you?" I asked. "Is anyone courting you?"

Ada blushed. "No," she answered. "And I'm not dating anyone, either." She gave me a sly smile and then burst out laughing. I had to laugh with her as I thought of Will Gundy stopping by to visit her while her parents were gone. Maybe we were both lying. Then again, his wife had only been dead three months. Perhaps his interest in Ada was strictly neighborly.

Once the laughter stopped, she asked me about Marta and the case against her. After I told her everything I knew, Ada said she wondered if Lydia's death had anything to do with her poor health.

"Pardon?" No one had said anything about Lydia being in poor health.

"*Ya,*" Ada said. "She used to have spells. She was an eighth grader, and I had just started at school. I was sickly myself, so I noticed that sort of thing."

"What was the matter with her?"

"I don't know exactly, but she would get tired and have to sit, although she never drew attention to herself. Then, when she was older and out of school, there was a period of time where she didn't get out much at all, not even to church. The rumor was she was very ill."

As I came to a stop at the light in Willow Street, Ada gazed out the window at the strip mall. "I wondered if having the twins was too much for her, even though she had them in the hospital.

And then she got pregnant again so soon."

No one had said anything about Lydia going to the hospital to have the twins. Surely she hadn't had a C-section. If she had, Marta would have insisted she have the next baby in the hospital too, although there were midwives who did deliver a vaginal birth at home after a C-section.

"What does Marta say?" Ada asked.

"Not much. Just that she didn't do anything wrong."

Ada sighed. "That's what Will says too."

The light turned green and I accelerated. "Do you see him much?" I blushed as soon as I spoke. After all, the man's wife had died only a few months before.

"You saw him that one day, *ya*?" Now it was Ada's turn to blush.

I nodded.

"He was driving by and thought he would stop by to visit *Daed*. He didn't know my parents were gone."

I turned off the main highway onto the country road that led to Klara's farm.

"He just talked about his girls. How they're doing." Her gaze drifted out the window. "He said next time he'll bring them by. I'd like that," she said, her voice soft. "I'd like that a lot."

Given Ella's interest in Ezra, it looked as though both my cousins—or whatever Ada was—were falling for a Gundy brother.

I thought through that family tree again. Alice gave birth to Nancy, who married Benjamin and gave birth to four kids: Will, Hannah, John, and Ezra.

Will married Lydia, who gave birth to three kids: Christy, Mel, and Mat.

Hannah married Jonas, gave birth to Rachael, and was expecting another baby soon.

John married Sally, who was currently expecting their first child.

Ezra. Well, and then there was Ezra—wild, charming, motorcycle-riding Ezra. I didn't know whether to smile or cry. Would Ella someday be around the big dining room table feasting and laughing with the Gundys too, alongside him? Or maybe Ada, alongside Will?

Again, I felt a twinge of jealousy.

Marta showed up at the cottage that afternoon, explaining that a woman from her church had dropped her off. I was alarmed, afraid Caroline had taken a turn for the worse, but Marta assured me that the church had rallied and another woman was staying the night and caring for Simon the next morning. She said Caroline was getting better, and they hoped she would be discharged the next afternoon.

My relief must have been obvious because she patted my shoulder. It was the most affectionate she'd been with me.

That evening as Marta and I did the dishes, I

brought up the subject of Lydia and her general health.

"She was fine," Marta said. "Her blood pressure ran a little high but not dangerously so."

"She had plenty of energy?" I asked as I dried a plate.

"I wouldn't say plenty, but she had enough to do what she needed to do."

I asked if she'd had a C-section with the twins. "No."

I bit my lower lip as I dried another plate and then said, quickly, "Do you still have her chart or was it taken by the DA?"

"The DA's office made a copy and took that. I still have the original."

"Mind if I take a look at it?"

Marta turned her head toward me. "Why ever so?"

"I'm curious, that's all."

She shook her head. "There's nothing in her chart. My lawyer hired an expert to go over it, and it offers no more information to the case."

I put the plate in the cupboard, bumping it against the stack. She hadn't told me yes, but she hadn't told me no, either.

Marta pulled the plug to the sink. "I'm tired." She yawned, covering her mouth with her forearm. "Poor Simon was up half the night crying for Esther. David and I took turns with him, but we weren't who he wanted."

I didn't dare go out to the office while Marta was still up. It would be too obvious. Then I remembered that I had appointments in the morning. I decided I could wait to look at Lydia's chart then.

Sometime during the night I had a text from James asking how Caroline was again. I saw it in the morning and texted him back. *Better. Thx for praying.*

My first appointment was at nine, but I was in the office by eight thirty and pulling the *Gundy, Lydia* file from the cabinet. In midwifery a mother's chart, besides keeping all the information on hand for the midwife, is the legal document of care. It safeguards both the caregiver and the mother. From what I'd seen, Marta's records were clear, concise, and accurate.

I worked my way backward through Lydia's chart, starting with the death of the baby. *4:32 a.m. stillborn baby boy delivered by C-section at Lancaster General . . . 4:10 a.m. mother DOA at Lancaster General . . . mother on life support, taken by ambulance to Lancaster General . . . EMTs arrive at patient's home . . . CPR administered for 15 minutes . . . patient stops breathing, eyes roll back . . . 3:05 a.m. called 911 against patient's wishes . . . baby's heart tones at 95 . . . patient instructed that transfer to hospital is necessary; patient declines . . . patient's blood pressure 160/110 . . .* Marta should have called 911 once Lydia's blood pressure spiked, but it might have only been another minute, just long enough to check the fetal tones, which were dangerously low. At that point, in a hospital, the mother would have been whisked down the hall for a C-section.

I kept reading. *2:45 a.m. urge to push . . . 10 cm dilated . . .* Labor had started at ten thirty p.m. the day before, January 29. At the appointment the week before, Lydia's blood pressure had been 120/90, not too bad for a woman nine months pregnant. The cervix was thinned and dilated to two. The baby's head was in a good position. There were no indications, at that point, that Lydia's and the baby's lives were in danger. I kept flipping back through the chart. At one appointment Lydia's blood pressure was 140/110, and Marta had instructed her to see her doctor. At another her pulse was elevated, 120.

I flipped to the birth of the twins. They had been delivered by a doctor at the hospital and not by Marta, but the chart from the birth had been copied from hospital records and included here anyway. According to the notes, Lydia's blood pressure was fine through the ten-hour labor and also through the delivery. It seemed like a best-case scenario situation for the birth of twins.

Christy's birth was nine years before the twins', and there was no explanation for the gap. No record of miscarriages, stillbirths, or lost babies. Labor had been longer, fifteen hours, but not bad. There was no indication of high blood pressure, although Lydia's pulse had run high at a few appointments. Gravid 2 was marked at the top, which meant Christy was her second pregnancy.

Her *second* pregnancy?

I thought about that and finally decided that maybe she'd had a miscarriage before. Because Amish women often didn't seek medical attention until well into their second trimester, a lot of miscarriages were likely missed. It could be that Lydia had had an unconfirmed one. I flipped to the next page.

Primigravida was marked, indicating her first pregnancy. Continuing backward through the file, I read Marta's notes about that birth, a healthy baby boy, though no date was listed. In fact, I realized, none of the entries related to this first birth had dates next to them. Odd. It wasn't like Marta to be so sloppy. At least, from what I could tell, the birth and pregnancy were uneventful. Turning the pages, I finally came to the very first entry in the file, when Lydia was five months pregnant with her first child.

Smoothing the pages back into place, a wave of grief washed over me. Will had lost his wife and not one but two sons. I closed the chart as my first patient of the day opened the door. But instead of the person I was expecting, I saw Hannah, Will's sister.

I quickly turned Lydia's chart over on the desk, hiding her name.

"Do you have a minute?" she asked.

I glanced at the clock. I had five. I nodded.

"Will was headed to the feed store, so I hitched a ride. I've been having nightmares. I know it's because of Lydia, but I keep dreaming this baby dies. And that Rachael dies. And that Jonas dies." I hadn't met her husband yet. "I'm hardly sleeping, and I wake exhausted from my dreams." It wasn't unusual for women to think they were dreaming excessively. In reality they were waking excessively and remembering their dreams. Although I was sure the content of a pregnant woman's dreams did tend to be bizarre, likely due to fluctuations in hormones.

I talked with her about exercise and showed her a few breathing techniques. Then I gave her a bottle of valerian tincture and told her to mix it with water or juice. "And talk about how you're feeling with someone."

She tilted her head as she took the bottle and looked confused.

"Or write it down. But you can't keep it bottled up inside, Hannah. This has been a huge loss for all of you."

"She had a premonition." She sighed and shook her head. "I'm not saying I've had a premonition. I'm just saying I'm having nightmares." She stepped toward the door. "But Lydia was afraid something bad was going to happen."

I'd heard of that before, but usually there was nothing to it. "Hannah." I wasn't sure how to phrase my question. "Did Lydia have any miscarriages or stillbirths?"

She shook her head.

"Did she lose any other babies?"

"No." She appeared absolutely sincere. "Why?"

"Oh, I've just been trying to figure out what happened that night." I smiled and stepped toward the door after her. "I'll see you Monday." She'd just started her ninth month and so would have appointments on a weekly basis from now on.

"See you then. And thank you," she replied.

Before closing the door behind her, I looked out, noticed Will waiting in the buggy, and gave him a wave. He waved back, a smile on his face, completely unaware that I had been in here snooping through his late wife's medical records. Heat burning my cheeks, I hurried back into the office to refile Lydia's chart.

I did pray for Hannah, and I also prayed I'd have a chance to talk with Will in person, alone, when I was at the Gundy and Kemp farm. Three days later I headed over there, surprised to find that just driving down the lane made my heart race. I knew Will had bought this farm from Burke Bauer, the man who *Mammi* claimed was my biological father. If that was true, then that meant this had once been my father's home, my family's land. Trying to wrap my head around that, I made my way past the greenhouses and parked beside the smaller residence. As I climbed out and grabbed my bag from the trunk, the back door to the big house opened and Will stepped onto the porch.

"Hello," I called out.

He shaded his eyes against the morning sun and then smiled once he recognized me.

"Hannah has an appointment," I said.

"*Ya.* She's over here." He started down the stairs. "She's having a difficult time, thinking about Lydia and all."

I nodded.

"Oh, that's right. You already know. I took her by your place Friday." He pulled his straw hat over his red hair. "Seems everyone is having a hard time."

"How is Christy?"

"Quiet." He was standing opposite of me on the walkway now.

"Is she depressed?"

"Maybe. But mostly she just seems worn out. Like it's an effort for her to walk across the room, let alone do her chores."

"Is she going to school?" I put my medical bag on the concrete at my feet.

"Some."

"Have you taken her to the doctor?"

He shook his head. "No, but I was thinking I should."

"That's a good idea. Make sure you explain how Lydia died. Tell them that a cause hasn't been determined, even though an autopsy was done."

He bent down and picked up my bag, but before he turned back to the house, I asked if he would mind answering a few questions about Lydia.

He sighed. "Sure."

"Did she go to the doctor about her high blood pressure after Marta told her she should?"

He shook his head. "And she never told me Marta said she should." He placed both hands on the handle of the bag. "She hated doctors, hospitals, all of that. Her mother died young despite being under a doctor's care. Then Lydia had a bad experience herself before we got married." He paused. "We had to force her to go to the hospital when she was ready to have the twins. But when Marta told her she needed to go to the hospital during labor this last time, she refused. By the time Marta called the ambulance, it was too late."

"I'm really sorry."

"*Ya.* I know. So am I." His brown eyes were kind. "And I'm really sorry for the mess Marta is in because of this."

I took a deep breath. "Can I ask you one more question?"

He nodded.

"Can you tell me about Lydia's first baby?"

"Christy?"

"No." I hesitated. "The one before."

"Who told you about him? Marta?" His voice was confused.

"No, I was doing some filing and ran across

some old notations in her office." I didn't want to admit that I'd intentionally read through Lydia's chart. Because I was part of the practice, I hadn't exactly broken the law, but that still didn't justify what I had done. If Will wanted to, he could file a grievance against me. But because he was Amish, I knew he wouldn't, and I was taking advantage of that.

He glanced off toward the greenhouses and then back at me, his head tipped downward. "Ask Marta about it if you want to," he said. "But just know this. I had no part in that first baby."

My conversation with Will weighed heavily on me as I examined Hannah. When I was finished, I noted in her chart that she was fifty percent effaced, two centimeters dilated, and the baby was in a breech position. I showed her exercises to do to turn the baby and told her that if it didn't, she would need to deliver at the hospital.

"Marta does breech home births," she said, pushing herself up to a sitting position and then clumsily swinging her bare feet to the floor.

"I know, but I don't," I said, looking her straight in the eye. "Rest as much as you can. It will be best if the baby waits another week or two. And do the exercises faithfully."

Hannah said she had slept better the night before and that her mother and *grossmammi* had the girls over at her parents' house for the day.

"There's always so much activity over there, so many hands to help. It tires all of them out."

I thought of Ezra, and of Sally and John, and of Sally's sister, Ruth. The girls were lucky to have so much going on. I had an appointment with Sally the next day. I couldn't believe I'd been in Lancaster County a couple of days short of a month.

"How about Christy?"

"She went to school today. The first time this week."

I asked Hannah if she was okay being alone, and she assured me she was. Her husband and Will would be in for lunch, and her mother would bring the girls back after their naps.

I left the house thinking about Lydia. Marta told me that the home had been built by Will, his father, and his brothers after Will and Lydia had married. She must have felt like a queen, albeit a queen with a secret. It looked like the Lantzes weren't the only family in Lancaster County hiding the past.

But it seemed Marta was a common denominator in both.

The next afternoon, I finished up a delivery—baby number 262, seventh for me in Lancaster County, and the second child of a twenty-eight year old mother, living in Strasburg proper. The husband kept his carriage in the garage and the horse grazed the double lot next door. As I said goodbye, I focused on the image of the mother, two-year-old brother, and baby girl in my mind, all on the bed with the father lovingly standing watch, committing the scene to my memory. As I pulled out of the driveway though, I took a photo of the house with the open garage and horse nearby, getting a kick out of the townie Amish family.

I stopped by the old Gundy place and examined Sally on my way home. As I did, I realized that her baby and Hannah's would be just a couple of months apart, cousins much closer in age than even Rachael and the twins.

Sally was doing fine and had lots of questions for me. Ruth stayed outside. The weather was warm, and it seemed she was gardening, but I think mostly she was on the lookout for Ezra.

A few minutes later, as I headed back to Marta's, Chuck called and I flipped my phone open to speakerphone. "The tests are back," he said.

"What's the verdict?" I so wanted to be Ada's half sister, more than I'd ever wanted anything.

Chuck cleared his throat. "You think you're the Amish girl's cousin, right?"

"Well, I suspect we may be half sisters."

"Oh."

"Am I right?"

"Maybe you two should come in. We could talk in person, and the two of you can tell me about your family tree."

I grimaced. "That's what I'm trying to figure out." I slowed as I approached a school, careful to keep my eyes on the road, not the phone in my lap.

"I can talk to you this afternoon," Chuck said. "I'm here till four."

I thanked him and told him I would get back to him with a time as soon as I could. I closed the phone, an odd apprehension gripping at the pit of my stomach. Turning off the road into the parking lot of a toyshop, I dialed Ada's cell. She picked up on the third ring, her voice quiet.

I explained what was going on and asked if she could sneak up to the end of the lane and go to the hospital with me.

"I think so," she said. "I'll be there in ten minutes. I'll text you if I can't make it."

I waited for five minutes, afraid she couldn't get away, but then there she was and out of breath, even though she'd only been walking.

"Are you okay?" I asked as she climbed into the car.

She nodded, but it took her a couple of moments until she was settled enough to speak. "I'm just tired, that's all."

Before pulling out onto the road, I called Chuck to let him know we were on our way. We met at his office, all three of us crowding into the cramped room. His desk was stacked with papers, and his bookcases were overflowing with books double-shelved and wedged in haphazardly. I hoped he had been more organized with our results. He sat down in his chair and reached for a small white board, propping it on his desk.

"Okay, so you thought you were cousins, right?" I nodded. "Our mothers are sisters."

He asked each of us the names of our moms and then started a family tree, working from the bottom up.

"And your fathers are?"

"Mine is Alexander," Ada said.

Chuck drew a circle and wrote an *A* in the middle and then connected it to Klara's name.

"And I'm not sure who mine is," I said. "But the name Burke Bauer has been mentioned." I didn't want to just spring on Ada my hope that Alexander was my father. If he was, Chuck would soon tell us. If he wasn't, there was no reason to mention it at all.

He drew a circle, added a B, and connected it to Giselle's name. Then he turned his attention back to us.

"What can you tell me about prior generations?" Chuck asked. "Do you know if your family traces back to the original Amish settlers of Lancaster County?"

"Our mothers came here from Indiana about thirty-five years ago," I said. "I don't know a lot before that, but I think our maternal great-grandmother emigrated to the U.S. from Switzerland in the mid-1870s."

"Okay." Chuck looked back at the board. "What was her name?"

"Elsbeth," I answered.

"And our grandmother is Frannie," Ada said.

He added both names slowly. I couldn't help but think he was stalling.

"So what's up?" I asked as he finished.

He turned back toward us, gripping the marker tightly.

"This is a little awkward, but I'm sure it's true." He let go of the marker and it rolled across his desk, landing on the floor. He didn't seem to notice. He clicked on the mouse in front of him, opening a document on his computer. "Cousins share an eighth of the same DNA, although it's higher among families that intermarry. From analyzing the strands of hair—and by the way, the one you gave me wasn't yours." He was looking straight at me. "It's hers." He nodded toward Ada.

He started to go on, but I leaned forward in my chair and told him to wait a second. I was puzzled at how Ada's hair could have ended up in my box, considering that my parents had whisked me away to Oregon when I was still an infant and Ada hadn't even been born yet. In fact, she wouldn't come along for another two years.

"Are you sure?" I asked, thinking that the only way that the lock of hair could have been Ada's was if it had been sent to us later. I had always been under the impression that our families had had no further contact once my adoption was final, but now I realized that wasn't correct, that someone here must have been in touch with my parents and mailed a lock of Ada's hair to Oregon after she was born.

"Positive." He stared at the screen again. "Anyway, you share much more DNA than cousins."

"Half siblings, right?" I was sure my voice was as elated as I felt, even though I was trying to be sensitive to Ada.

Chuck shook his head.

I sighed.

"Full siblings," he said.

I lurched forward. "You're kidding."

Ada grabbed my hand.

"I'm not kidding. It's not a fluke you look so much alike. You're sisters."

TWENTY-EIGHT

Ada and I sat in the parking garage, the motor running, me incapable of putting the car into reverse.

"*Mamm* must be your mother too," she said.

"Klara? If so, then why would she give me up? Why list Giselle as my mother in the family Bible?"

Ada turned toward me, tucking her feet up on the seat. "You were conceived before my parents were married, right?"

"That's what the dates in the Bible spell out."

"So, *you know*." She grinned sheepishly. "They were embarrassed."

Embarrassed, perhaps, but enough to get rid of a baby? It seemed to me that just wasn't done in the Amish community. I thought of Peggy keeping her oldest daughter and then marrying someone else. I thought of the handful of Marta's patients I had seen in the last month who were several months further into their pregnancies than they were into their marriages. They weren't proud of it, of course, but they didn't seem all that ashamed of it either. Overall, I had received the impression that the Amish didn't make a big deal out of it as long as the couple confessed and repented and, in most cases, went ahead and got married.

But maybe I was different. Maybe I cried a lot and was a pain to take care of. Was that why Klara had given me up?

I shook my head. I was back in fantasyland. No one gave a baby up because she cried too much. No, I had a strong feeling the truth was the opposite of the conclusion Ada had drawn. She thought this meant *my* mother was Klara, but I felt sure it meant that *her* mother was Giselle. I tried suggesting that to her, as tactfully as possible.

"That's ridiculous. My parents were married for two years before I was even born." She just wasn't getting it.

I sighed. Did I have to spell it out to her? "What if your dad had a thing for Giselle?"

Ada shook her head. "He adores *Mamm*. He always has."

I bit my tongue to keep from saying it seemed to me that, more than anything, he was afraid of Klara. But Ada was entitled to see things as she wanted. With an effort I managed to back out of my parking place and circle down to the street. "Whatever the real truth is, someone is lying to us."

Ada nodded. "But I'm sure there's a good reason."

I didn't respond. Maybe Sean had been right all along about Amish women being brainwashed. Ada seemed to curl up into herself as I silently drove. Finally, as I turned off the main highway onto the country road, she said, "I've always felt that *Mamm* and *Daed* were keeping something from me, but I thought it was about my illness, that it was more serious than they said." She paused a moment and then kept talking. "And there's been a lot of tension between them since, actually since before you came around the first time. Marta stopped by a few weeks before you did. They argued that night."

I slowed as I drove, not wanting to reach the farm. Ada began to shiver and I turned up the heat.

"I always wanted a sister," she said. "I used to pray for one every night."

"Me too," I whispered.

She touched my fingers on the steering wheel and then her hand fell back into her lap as I turned down the lane. I wasn't going to make her walk. She wasn't strong enough. And I needed to face my fears.

"What are we going to do?" she asked.

"Confront Klara," I answered.

"No," Ada said. "I'll talk to her. She'll tell me, I promise."

As I parked the car, Alexander hurried across the field toward us and Ada opened the passenger door. "I'll call you tonight and let you know how things go," she said. She took a step away but then she started to fall, in a gentle swoon. For a moment I wasn't sure what was happening, but then her head thudded against the open car door.

"Ada!"

I was aware of Alexander running toward us as I tore around the side of the car, rolling Ada onto her side. She was unconscious. My hands flew to her carotid. She was breathing.

"Ada!" Blood oozed from the side of her head. "Ada," I said again.

She still didn't respond. I dug my cell from my pocket and called 911 as I rolled her to her back. She could have a head injury or a neck injury. And her blood count could be dangerously low. That could be why she'd fainted in the first place.

Before I hung up the phone, Alexander was on his knees beside her, wanting to carry her inside. "No," I instructed. "Get a pile of blankets. And tell Klara what happened."

"I'll stay with *Mammi*," I said as Klara crawled into the back of the ambulance.

"You should go. You know what questions to ask," Alexander replied.

I shook my head and told him to use Ada's cell phone. "Call me. I'll talk to the doctors if you need me to. I'm in her contacts under *L*."

From inside the back of the ambulance, Klara fished out Ada's cell phone from her pocket and handed it to her husband. Alexander took it from her, still looking ambivalent.

"You're her father. You need to be with her," I insisted, a lump rising in my throat.

He nodded, sliding the phone into his own pocket as one of the EMTs directed him to sit up front.

"Thank you." I wasn't sure if Alexander was talking to the EMT or me.

I watched as the ambulance pulled away and then hurried to the *daadi haus*. As I walked in, *Mammi* said, "Ada, what's going on? I heard sirens."

"It's me. Lex—Alexandra," I said, stepping in front of her.

"Alexandra? What's happened?" She was much more lucid than when I'd seen her before.

I explained that Ada had fallen and Klara and Alexander were going with her to the hospital.

Mammi began to cry and said, "Oh, dear, oh dear," over and over again.

"She'll be all right," I said, hoping I was telling the truth.

"Why were you here when Ada fell?" *Mammi* asked, dabbing at her eyes with the tissue I handed her.

I hesitated but then decided I had nothing to lose. "I took Ada to the hospital. We had a test done . . . to see how we're related."

Mammi's eyes overflowed with tears.

"There's no reason to cry," I said, patting her arm.

"I'm afraid there is."

I sat down in the chair beside her.

"Alexandra," she said. Something in her tone made me want to cry too. So much sorrow. So much regret. She looked at me with large, damp eyes.

Now I wanted to curl up on the floor and sob. Instead I smiled at her, hoping to encourage her to keep talking.

"I'm sorry," she said.

I nodded.

"It wasn't my idea. It was Klara's. Well, Giselle's, since Klara wouldn't take you too." She began to cry again.

"Mammi." I hoped my voice was gentle even though I felt anything but. What was she telling me?

"I felt guilty from the start. That's why I wanted you to have the box and the letter. I wanted you to know where you came from. I wanted you to come back some day."

"Thank you," I said. "I have the box. Where is Giselle now?"

"She wanted to go to Amielbach, but I had to sell it."

"Did she go to Switzerland anyway?"

"Yes, but I haven't heard from her for years. She may not even be there anymore."

Mammi began to moan about how much she missed her little girl, despite the fact that Giselle would be forty-five by now, no longer a little girl by anyone's definition.

Afraid that *Mammi* might need some of her medication, I got up and searched for the pillbox, which I found in the kitchen on the windowsill. There was only one tranquilizer for each day for the rest of the week, and something new as well: an antidepressant. I was pleased, as it looked as though Ada had passed on my advice. She probably hadn't been on them long enough to experience the full effect yet, but she was already more coherent. Soon the depression would begin to lift as well. I could understand that Klara wouldn't want to listen to *Mammi*'s laments all day long, but maybe in time a balance could be found between keeping the hysteria and grief at bay and being able to enjoy the world around her.

Returning to the main room, I gave her today's dose with a glass of water and sat down as she swallowed the pills.

"Tell me what my mother was like when she

was young," I said, trying to distract *Mammi* from her tears. "Was she pretty?"

Mammi sniffled, nodding.

"Prettiest girl in Lancaster County. You would think that would be a blessing, but . . ." She shook her head as her voice trailed off, and I waited silently, willing her to continue. "Once my brother died, we were having trouble making ends meet," she finally went on, "so Giselle took a job over at the nursery, in the greenhouses. She liked the work itself, but her beauty turned out to be such a distraction to the others—many men were employed there, you know—that they finally had to move her into the main office instead. I thought things would be better after that, because only women worked in there." She barked out a noise that sounded like a sob mixed with a laugh. "I forgot about the one exception. Little did I know that by moving from the greenhouse to the office, my baby had gone from the frying pan into the fire."

I sat back, apprehension rippling through my stomach, wondering where *Mammi* was going with this.

"Giselle's boss," she explained, waiting for me to catch on. "The head of the company."

"Burke Bauer," I whispered, and *Mammi* nodded.

"It is no great mystery to see how they must have . . . how it all came to be. After having been surrounded by overeager boys for so long, Giselle would have been relieved to find herself in the company of a man, of someone far more mature, especially a successful authority figure that everyone seemed to respect. Once that man admitted to Giselle that he had fallen in love with her, the fact that he just happened to be married was beside the point as far as she was concerned. I am so ashamed for my daughter, but what can I say? She was a child on *rumschpringe*, so naive, so self-oriented. So ready to sew her wild oats, regardless of the consequences."

I thought about her choice of words, wondering if that's all I had been: a consequence.

"Bauer was indeed handsome," *Mammi* said, dabbing at her eyes. "And also rich and generous and charming. But I never understood the hold he had over Giselle. He was like a drug to her."

"Do you think she really loved him?"

"Oh yes. Desperately so."

"So Giselle and Burke had an affair," I said flatly, wishing she would get to the point, wondering where Alexander fit into this story. The same man had fathered Ada and I both. But which man? Burke Bauer, as *Mammi* believed? Or Alexander, the one I was named for, the one I wanted it to be, the one who had said of Ada, *With everything I am, I am her father.*

My heart sinking, I knew now that he had been speaking figuratively. He was her father in exactly the same way that Dad was my father. With everything he was. Except his blood.

"Of course, I knew nothing of this at the time," *Mammi* continued. "No one did. They were very careful, very discreet. Later, there were rumors, of course, that Giselle was involved with someone older, someone who was married. But even her sisters did not know who it was, or even if it was true. The only one who was fully aware of their relationship was Alexander. And that was all thanks to me." *Mammi*'s eyes suddenly filled with fresh tears.

"What do you mean?"

At my question, *Mammi* seemed startled, as if she had just remembered who she was talking to or what she was saying. She put a hand to her mouth as more tears began to course down her cheeks.

"Oh, Alexandra, I have already said too much," she wailed. "Do not ask me anymore. If I had not . . . it is just that . . . really, everything was my fault, all my fault."

At that, she began to sob in earnest.

I wanted to press her to continue regardless, but she was growing more hysterical by the minute. Finally, I had no choice but to drop it, soothing her with comforting tones and rubbing her arm until she calmed down enough to fall asleep.

An hour later, my phone rang and Ada's name popped up on the screen. It was Alexander. "She's conscious," he said. "They're doing tests to see if she has a brain injury. And they've already given her a transfusion. Her count was low again."

He went on to say that Klara had left a message at the Gundys', and Alice had called back, saying she would be over shortly. She would give *Mammi* her supper and spend the night; I was free to go. I asked if he wanted me to come to the hospital and he declined, saying it was kind of me to offer but they were fine. I could only imagine how much Klara didn't want me there.

I felt icy cold with loneliness as I watched *Mammi* sleep. I had a sister, but would I be able to have a relationship with her? I had pieces of my past, but would I ever have the whole story?

Alice was all business when she arrived. "When did Frannie eat last?" she asked.

"Lunch, I assume," I said. It was past seven. "I upset her," I said, lowering my voice. "I was asking her some questions about the—family."

Alice didn't respond as she took a jar of soup out of her basket. "Would you like some?" she asked as she stepped into the kitchen.

I declined, saying I needed to go. I'd heard the Amish were gossipy, but I certainly hadn't witnessed that. What I wouldn't give for a good dish on the Lantz family.

As I pulled out onto the highway, hungry, tired, and mad, all my frustration was headed in one direction, the only avenue open to me right now: Marta.

TWENTY-NINE

"Eat something," Marta said. "Let me make you a sandwich."

I stood in the middle of her kitchen, taking up half the tiny room, my hands on my hips, feeling like a teenager again. I could hardly believe I'd been here a month and was still begging Marta for answers.

"No, just tell me what you know." I felt like a broken record.

She wasn't matching my emotions, not at all. "I've told you what I know." She sighed. "I was twelve when you were born. No one confided in me. I don't know what *Mammi* told you today, but you *know* she's had a stroke and is on medication. I wouldn't say she's a trustworthy source."

"Whom were we born to?"

"I'm pretty sure you already figured that out."

I glared at her until she answered anyway.

"Giselle. Right? Isn't that what you discovered?"

"And who is our father?"

"I already told you. It isn't my place to say." Marta took her cap off her head and rubbed the back of her neck.

"Okay, then, tell me about Lydia's first baby."

Her eyes were no longer kind. "That's really not your business, is it?"

"Does it have anything to do with Lydia's death?"

"Of course not." Marta turned her back to me, stuffing her cap into her pocket, and then washing her hands at the sink. "Now," she said, her voice even again. "Tell me again what happened to Ada."

It was Ella, standing in the doorway, who got me out of the house before I exploded. She grabbed her coat and motioned to me. Like a fool, I thought she had some information.

"Sorry," she said, as we walked beneath the dark, cloud-covered sky toward the bridge. "I just thought you looked the way I feel when I need to get away from Mom."

I fumed some more—and then shivered. A cold front was moving in. It was mid-April but felt like February. The weather in Pennsylvania was so fickle, I wondered if spring would ever arrive.

"Maybe you should call Sean," Ella said. "He might have some advice for you."

I hadn't told him yet that Ada and I were full sisters. I hadn't told Ella either.

"So, are you pretty serious about him?"

I thought of Ada asking me the same thing. "I don't know," I answered.

"He sure has a nice house."

"He just sold it. He's moving to Baltimore."

"Bummer," Ella said, sounding like a patronizing parent.

"He asked me to go with him."

"And live with him?" She sounded shocked.

"No," I quickly said. "I would work there. Or go back to school to become a doctor."

Ella sighed. "You'd have the perfect life. Just think of the house you two could buy. When you got married, you would have something big enough for lots of kids."

Except that I was already in my mid-twenties, so by the time I was done with my residency I'd be pretty old. I always imagined having babies before my mid-thirties.

"Have you been serious with someone before?" Ella asked.

I told her about James. I was still talking when we reached the bridge, telling her how he played cribbage with an old guy in his neighborhood on Saturday mornings at the park and how he'd drive down to Aurora and go to church with Dad on Sundays. I told her how he hummed "Row, Row, Row Your Boat" when he parallel parked his old car and how he'd never let me pay for anything, even though he didn't have much money. I didn't tell her that Ezra's charm reminded me of James when he was in high school, before he grew up.

"Why did you guys stop going out?" she asked, stopping in the middle of the bridge.

"Because I came here."

She laughed. "That sounds like a stupid reason." She turned toward me. "Except that you met Sean . . ." Her voice trailed off.

"So," I said, pretty sure I knew what she really

wanted to talk about. "How's Ezra?"

She grinned. "Good. Really good."

"Ella, you're sixteen and he's Amish."

"He says he'll leave."

Obviously he hadn't joined the church yet so he wouldn't be shunned, but he wouldn't be embraced, either. It was hard for me to imagine Ezra living outside the circle of his family.

When we returned to the cottage, Marta was nowhere in sight. I was pretty sure she was out in her office but I was too tired to care. I made myself a sandwich and trudged up the stairs to my alcove.

I awoke that night to Marta shaking my shoulder. "Hannah's in labor," she said. "Jonas just called."

"She's breech," I muttered. "She needs to go to the hospital."

"She's sure the baby turned."

I'd heard that before.

"She's three weeks early."

"Two," Marta corrected.

I sighed. Sometimes due dates were debatable, and even more so with the Amish.

"Ella is going to go with you," she said. I began to be aware of the light on in the bathroom.

"I'll be fine."

"It's snowing," Marta said. "Take my car. The tires are better. Ella can help you with the chains if needed."

"Chains." My feet hit the cold floor and I

stumbled to the little window. Amazingly, there was a snowdrift piling up below.

As it turned out, we didn't put on the chains, but we should have. When we were still two miles from Hannah's house, I slid into a ditch.

While I was flipping through my contacts to call my 800 number for roadside assistance, Ella pulled out her phone and began texting Ezra, explaining to me as she did that he was at Will's right now, covering plants, and should be able to get here quickly. After a moment, her phone dinged. "Yep. He says he's on his way."

I groaned, picturing the kid racing to our rescue on his motorcycle.

"Tell him to send Will."

"Will's coming too," she said, already typing a reply.

I put my phone away, thinking of poor Hannah in labor and how fortunate for all that she had a couple of big, strong brothers—and that one of those brothers carried a cell phone.

Fortunately, though I'm sure Ezra would have preferred rescuing his sweetheart via motorcycle, the two men soon arrived in a sleigh, their horse prancing about in the frosty air. We all crowded in for the ride back. Will was calm and collected, and as we rode along I seized the opportunity to ask some questions about Hannah—how she was feeling, how often her contractions were coming, how much pain she was in. I could tell my questions were making him uncomfortable, so once I felt I had enough basic information, I dropped the matter. After that, all was quiet except for the slushy clip-clop of the horses moving us through the snow.

"Hey, did you guys hear Ada's in the hospital?" Ella volunteered. "She might even have a brain injury."

I started to speak, but Will beat me to it.

"Not to worry. Her tests came out all right. No brain injury, only a small cut. Four stitches to the head, but Alexander says they don't even show because they are hidden by her *kapp*."

Even as I was relieved to hear such good news, I felt a twinge of jealousy that Will had found out all of this before I did. She was, after all, my sister.

When we reached the farm, Hannah's husband, Jonas, met us at the door of their house, which I hadn't been in before. Hannah was in the back bedroom, and it was cold as ice. In an adjacent room, little Rachael was asleep in a crib, covered with blankets.

I instructed Ezra to build up the fire and told Ella to close all the doors in the house except for the back bedroom. If it didn't heat up soon, I would move Hannah into the kitchen. She was warm from labor and had no idea how cold it actually was.

She was right, the baby had flipped, but it was still a difficult labor with intense back pain. Hannah was quiet and withdrawn, pulling away from her husband. Finally I got on the bed beside her. "Hannah, are you afraid?" I whispered.

She nodded.

"May I pray for you?"

She nodded again.

I put my arm around her shoulder and prayed silently, the way I'd seen Marta pray all those weeks ago, asking God to take away Hannah's fear and give her the strength to have the baby. I whispered, "Amen" when I was done.

A couple of minutes later Hannah closed her eyes and growled as a contraction overtook her. After a few more contractions, I checked her. She was ready to push. An hour later, at 5:17, a little girl slipped into the world, perfect in every way. *Baby number 263; number eight in Lancaster County.* Hannah fell into her husband's arms and sobbed as I suctioned the baby. I then wrapped her in the warm blankets Ella had brought in and tucked the baby in the bed beside Hannah, covering them both with more warm blankets. A few minutes later Rachael called out from her room in Pennsylvania Dutch. Maybe she'd heard us, or maybe it was her usual waking time. Jonas went and got her. He returned with the girl and she fell onto the bed beside her mother, hugging her and then kissing her little sister's head.

In all the other deliveries I'd done over the years, I searched the faces of the babies . . . the mothers . . . the fathers . . . the grandmothers. This was the first time I searched the face of the older sister. I found myself looking at her over and over, staring when I could. Her face was lit up and full of joy. She was elated. I'd never seen such happiness.

"What do you think?" I knelt beside the bed, level with her.

"She is *wunderbar*," Rachael said. "I love her already."

I stood and slipped away, not wanting to explain my tears, my loss, not even to myself. After a while Rachael climbed off the bed and went down the hall. I heard her laughter, mingled in with Ella's and Ezra's. I heard Will's voice and then the door close. Ella returned with Rachael, holding the little girl's hand, asking Hannah what she wanted to eat and then telling me that Will and Ezra had gone after the car. The snow was already melting.

By eight o'clock, Ella and Rachael were both asleep on the living room couch and the house was warm. Hannah's mom had arrived and taken charge of the kitchen. Nancy hugged me when I entered, thanking me for taking such good care of Hannah, and inviting me to have a cup of tea and breakfast.

"I hear you're Marta's niece."

I nodded.

"Which makes your mother Giselle?"

"Yes," I said, wanting to add, *at least I think so,* but I didn't. "Did you know Giselle?"

"Oh, yes," Nancy said. "We were all very close. The Lantz sisters used to visit us a lot. My mother and Frannie were good friends. They were both young widows. It's a shame how everything turned out. I still see Klara and Marta, but it's not the same."

I wrapped my hands around my mug of tea, hoping she'd continue.

"Klara and Giselle were as close as any two sisters could be, and both were so protective of Marta." Nancy went on to say that later, during all of their *rumschpringe*s, Klara couldn't get it out of her head that Alexander was interested in Giselle, even though it was obvious he was smitten by Klara. It looked as if I'd finally found my Amish gossip. She sighed. "Poor Alexander," she said. "I don't think he's ever recovered from Klara not trusting him."

"Do you know what happened to Giselle?"

"No." Nancy looked straight at me. "I really don't know." She stood and put another piece of wood in the fire. "But I've always wondered."

After I checked on Hannah one more time and woke Ella, I asked Nancy where Will was. I wanted to thank him for pulling Marta's car out of the ditch.

"He took Christy to the doctor," she said. "Hired a driver. They left just after I arrived."

I must have looked pleased.

"He's taking her to a specialist. The first doctor thinks something is wrong with her heart."

Marta had canceled my appointments for the day, so I slept soundly until I heard a man's voice downstairs and sleepily thought it was Zed's, meaning it was late afternoon and he had arrived home from school. It wasn't until I reached the bottom stair that I realized the voice was way too deep to be Zed's—it was Will, sitting on the sofa with a girl who looked to be ten or eleven, leaning against him with her eyes closed.

"This is Christy," Will said, his voice low. "I'm afraid she's all tuckered out."

Her hair was strawberry blond and she had a pinched expression on her face, even in her sleep. I stared at her for a moment, wondering if she looked like Lydia.

Marta turned a little, her head popping out of the wingback chair, and Will cleared his throat. "I just saw Ada in the hospital. She said to tell you hello."

I searched his face, wondering if she'd told him we were sisters. From his look I didn't think she had.

"She thinks she'll go home tomorrow," he said.

Marta turned toward me again. "But that's not why Will is here. He tells me you've been sleuthing."

It took a minute, but then I realized she was probably talking about Lydia's file, the one I had read through even though I shouldn't have. So be it. I had done it for Marta's own best interests.

I ignored her as I sat on the hearth with the warm stove behind me, facing Will. "Your mother said you were taking Christy to a specialist today."

"I was just telling Marta," he said, glancing

down at a piece of paper in his hand. "He said Christy's been having a cardiac arrhythmia, caused by spasms," he added. "And he's put her on medication." He nodded toward me. "Thanks to you."

I leaned forward, my own heart racing, although not irregularly. If this were really true, it would change everything for Marta.

"I told him about Lydia, like you said," Will continued. "He told me there's some evidence the condition is hereditary. He said Lydia might have had a series of spasms during labor that cut off her oxygen—and the baby's."

I turned toward Marta. "It wouldn't have showed up in the autopsy."

"Why not?" she asked.

"Because the spasm would have relaxed once she died. There wouldn't have been any evidence. It's not like cardiac arrest. There wouldn't have been any scarring." I stood and faced my aunt. "You need to call your lawyer."

Marta moved like molasses. Will said they needed to go because they had a driver waiting. We all said goodbye. I thanked him profusely for coming by. As soon as Marta shut the door behind them, I said, firmly, "Call your lawyer, Marta. *Now*."

"You think this is significant?" Her eyes clouded over.

"Yes!" Over the past month, there had been many times I had wanted to give Marta a shake, but never as badly as right now. I was still trying to find the right words to spur Marta into action when Zed clomped up the outside steps and burst inside. His mother was still just standing there, frozen, so I told him the good news and together we finally got her to move. I think she had become so resigned to the situation that she simply didn't know how to respond now that it had been turned on its ear.

Together, she and I called the lawyer and explained everything we'd just learned. The woman sounded pleased but said we'd need Christy's medical records and an affidavit from an ob-gyn indicating that the condition could have caused Lydia's death during labor.

"No problem," I told her, certain that Will would give permission for the release of the files. I handed the phone back to Marta, pulled out my cell, and sent Sean a text saying I needed to talk with him ASAP. Waiting to hear back from him, I listened to Marta's end of her conversation, thrilled to know that she might be exonerated. I wasn't sure if the DA would pursue charging her with practicing without a license, even though the state didn't grant them, but at least it looked as if she wouldn't end up in prison.

I drove out to check on Hannah and Alice Elizabeth, the name she and Jonas, with Rachael's help, had decided on. All was well with them. Hannah was happy, a state I hadn't seen her in since I met her. Rachael was still overjoyed and followed me around like a puppy.

After that I took the long way home, slowing as I passed Klara's. A van was out front, and I assumed they had hired a driver to bring Ada home. For a moment I considered stopping, but then I decided to keep going. As I drove I called Sean, putting him on speakerphone once he answered. I explained to him what was going on, and we talked through the details of what might have happened the night Lydia died, if she did have an arrhythmia.

"It's very plausible," he said. "I had a patient last year with arrhythmia. Of course it was diagnosed, so we knew she was high risk. She ended up with a C-section." He offered to put me in touch with a buddy of his, a specialist who would probably be happy to sign an affidavit on the subject.

"This means you can finally get out of there, right?" he added.

I wasn't sure. "I don't have all my answers yet."

"Lex," he said. It was the first time he'd shortened my name, and it caught me off guard. "You're never going to get all of your answers. It's time for a new start. Think positively. You'll love Baltimore, I promise. We'll have a blast."

I kept busy over the next few days with pre- and postnatal visits, including one to Paradise to see Susan Eicher, who was doing much better. Her kids were healthy and the ladies from her district had been helping her with housework and her garden. As I left Paradise, I passed right by Lavonne Bauer's house but couldn't work up the nerve to stop.

Instead I drove into town to Esther and David's to check on little Caroline. Simon was the happy little boy I remembered from before he became a big brother, and Esther and David, although they still looked exhausted, seemed much more relaxed than they had for a while.

There were several boxes by the bookcase. "We go to Ethiopia in two weeks," David said. "Right after graduation."

I held the baby, settling into the rocker with her, and after a while she closed her eyes. Simon patted her head and then ran off. I closed my eyes too, for just a moment.

My next concern was Ada. I texted her several times but didn't hear back from her. I'd done some research on hereditary spherocytosis. I knew I didn't have it, but there was the possibility that I was a carrier. My children, depending on who their father was, could inherit the disease. Normal red blood cells lived for four months, but the cells of a person with HS only lasted three to six weeks. The spleen of a person with it was also frequently enlarged and was sometimes removed—not the case with Ada, as far as I knew. It wasn't uncommon for the disease to go undiagnosed for years and for the patient to suffer fatigue without knowing what it was from. It sounded as if that was what happened here.

At least the disease wasn't life threatening. Folic acid and ascorbic acid, which I assumed Ada took, helped. Transfusions were given when needed. Ada could live a mostly normal life, minus too much exertion and contact sports. Another interesting fact was that it was more common in those of northern European descent. That certainly fit Ada—and me, whatever the particulars of our story were.

I contemplated driving over to see Ada on Tuesday, five days after she'd been discharged, but I didn't feel comfortable with that. Maybe she didn't want to see me. I could handle being rejected by Klara, but I couldn't bear being rejected by Ada too.

It turned out that Marta's lawyer was much more efficient than I expected because Thursday morning she called, saying another pretrial hearing was scheduled for the next day.

Marta seemed to assume I would go with her. Connie Stanton met us outside the second-floor courtroom, looking as disheveled as ever.

"I have more good news," she said, brushing a strand of hair from her face. "I had a long talk with the DA." Her eyes sparkled. "He may still charge you with practicing without a license, but it looks as though he's probably not going to challenge our request for dismissal. The man's leaving to take a corporate job soon, so it's a good time for this to come up. I had the impression that he'd like to close up as many cases as he can before his time here is up."

We followed Connie through the double doors and down the aisle. I stopped at the first row and slid onto the wooden bench while Marta and her lawyer continued on to the table on the right. The DA sat at the table to the left. Because the hearing had only been posted the day before, word hadn't gotten out and no supporters were present. The four of us rose at the bailiff's command and the judge entered. A moment later we all sat again. The bailiff stated the reason for the hearing and Connie stepped forward to present the new evidence. The judge held up his hand, stopping her. "I've already reviewed the documents you submitted, Ms. Stanton." The judge turned his attention to the DA and asked if he'd had a chance to consider the new information.

"Yes, your honor," the man answered.

"And how do you respond to Ms. Stanton's request that Lancaster County drop the charges of negligent homicide against Mrs. Bayer?"

The DA dropped his head a moment, referring to the legal pad in front of him. Finally he looked up. "Due to the new evidence, I accept the request."

I put the palms of my hands together in a silent clap. Ella and Zed wouldn't be losing their mother.

"Counsel members, do we have any other issues to address?"

Connie Stanton replied with a firm, "No, your honor."

I held my breath as the DA consulted his legal pad again, hoping the man was more concerned about his upcoming career change than some old midwife. If he was, Marta might be able to practice again soon, very soon. I would no longer be needed. But I didn't have my answers. I still didn't know the truth. And I, undeniably, felt a connection of kinship with my biological relatives, although some more than others. I was going to miss Ella and Zed and, honestly, Marta too, as annoying as she was.

The DA raised his head. "No, sir," he finally said. "There's nothing more that needs addressing."

The palms of my hands came together again as I exhaled.

"You are cleared of all charges, Mrs. Bayer," the judge said. "The legal forms will be mailed to you within two weeks."

Maybe Marta was in shock or maybe she expected it all along, but as we walked out the door she barely talked to Connie. And she didn't say a word to me until I pulled out of the parking lot onto the street.

Then she whispered, "Thank you." Her voice hinted that she was close to tears. "You can go now and get on with your life. Leave all of us behind."

Now I was close to tears. Was that what she wanted? For me to simply disappear and leave her and her family alone? How could I explain to her I didn't want to depart without my story, the one I'd already asked her for so many times? Not yet. Not until I had the whole truth.

She exhaled and then said, "I can't wait to get back to work."

"The afternoon appointments are all yours."

"Since my first birth, I knew this is what I wanted to do," she said.

I told her it was the same for me and gave a brief description of that first experience assisting Sophie. Then I asked how old she was at her first delivery.

"Fourteen," she answered.

"Who was it?"

"The mother? Or baby?"

Before I could say anything, she said, "Ada was the baby." Before the words sank in, she added, "And Giselle the mother."

I took a ragged breath.

"And, Lexie, you're mistaken. You didn't see your first birth when you were sixteen. You were only two. You assisted me."

THIRTY

"Assisted you? In Ada's birth?"

Truly, I didn't understand what she was saying. When I was two, I was living on the other side of the country. How could I possibly have been here when my baby sister was being born? I said as much to Marta now, but she didn't reply at first. Instead, she just watched me as I thought it through. Finally, the truth hit me like a slam of ice water against my chest, knocking me breathless.

"I wasn't given away as an infant," I whispered. "I lived here longer than that."

Marta nodded. "You lived here until you were two and a half. Then you went away."

I was dumbfounded. This knowledge generated a flood of new questions, which I began throwing out to Marta now. She shook her head, pursed her lips, and looked out the side window, refusing to answer a single one. Wanting to throttle her, to scream, to pound my fists, instead I gripped the steering wheel and kept my eyes on the road, not responding to Marta or speaking all the way back to the cottage.

As we turned into the driveway, I could feel my anger slowly melting into something else entirely, a deep and overwhelming grief. By the time I parked the car, tears were coursing down my cheeks. Once inside, upstairs in the alcove, I buried myself under the covers and sobbed, not caring who heard me or what they might be thinking.

The lie in Marta's words pierced my very soul: *Then you went away.* How wrong she was. I hadn't merely gone away. I had been *sent* away. Banished. Ripped from the only home and family I had ever known, not as a relatively unknowing infant but as a little girl. A little two-year-old girl. The more I thought about it, the more I cried.

At one point, Sean called and asked if I wanted to go to Baltimore with him the next day, but I squeaked out a quick, "No, thank you," and gave no other explanation. He sounded annoyed as he said goodbye.

Finally, I dozed a little, but then I was woken by my Realtor, who called to say she'd had an offer on the house and orchard. I took a deep breath and asked how long I had to make a decision. "Customarily a day," she answered.

"I need three." She acquiesced but sounded annoyed too. I began to sob again as I closed my cell phone.

An hour later James called. I could barely speak, I was crying so hard. I babbled out what Marta had told me. "I wasn't adopted until I was two. Why didn't Mama and Dad ever tell me?" I felt so betrayed. All along I'd imagined myself as a newborn in their arms. Not a toddler. No wonder they had kept my name.

Instead of being the size of Elizabeth Alice, I'd been the size of Melanie and Matty. I'd been with Giselle until then. I must have felt as if *Mammi* had given me away—or as if Mama and Dad had kidnapped me. I fell into another round of sobs.

"I'm coming out," James said.

"No. You can't. You have school." I took a deep breath. I didn't want him ruining his education because of me. "I'm all right. Just talk to me. Tell me what you've been learning."

"Well," he spoke slowly. "I've been praying about things a lot, and I know what I need to do." He laughed a little. "I don't know what *you* should do. And I don't know what *we* should do. I just know what *I* need to do."

I heard the clicking of a keyboard in the background. No doubt he was writing a paper as we talked. That was something James could actually do. "What do you need to do?" I asked.

"Pray every day. And trust God."

That brought on a fresh round of tears, and then I told him how, when Caroline was so sick, I felt God tuck me in at night, how I felt Him close after so many years of not. But now He felt far away again.

"Know He's close," James said. "Right beside you. And He has been all this time." The clicking stopped. "I'll pray He tucks you in again tonight."

I didn't feel God's presence that night, nor the next day when the tears kept coming. James must have told Sophie what was going on, though, because I had a text from her asking how I was. I sent a message back, asking why she'd never told me I was two when I was adopted. *It wasn't my place,* she texted back.

As I read her words, I wanted to throw the phone across the room. I wanted to scream at her, to say she was hiding behind the same lame excuse Marta had used. Fingers flying, I typed, *YOU WERE MY FRIEND. HOW ELSE CAN I TAKE YOUR SILENCE EXCEPT AS THE ULTIMATE BETRAYAL?*

After a long pause, her next text finally came: *I'm sorry. I talked to your father about it once, thinking you should know. He didn't see that it would do you any good.*

Unwilling to accept her apology, I simply put down my phone and did not reply.

After a while my phone rang. It was Mrs. Glick. I let it go into voice mail and listened as soon as she was finished leaving the message. "Lexie, dear, we're all so worried about you. Please come home," her frail voice said.

All of them knew I was two when I was adopted. And Mama and Dad had lied all those years about my grandmother and mother loving me. If they had loved me, they would have kept me. Now, instead of a gentle handoff of an oblivious infant at the Philadelphia airport, I imagined *Mammi* shoving me into my parents' arms, me a screaming two-year-old, and then rushing away. And Klara dusting her hands as she turned her back. And Giselle . . . I stopped. I didn't even know what to imagine when it came to Giselle.

My phone beeped again. It was Sean. Everyone was weighing in today on my life except for James.

Sean's text read: *On the train to Baltimore. The little girl in front of me is Asian. Probably Chinese, with a white family. Adopted, obviously. Made me think of you. She'll probably never have the option of finding out her story. What if that were your case? Could you be happy? If so, then why not just let it go now, instead of driving yourself crazy?*

I dropped my phone onto my pillow. He didn't get it. I'd found people who knew my story. Even if the truth ended up being uglier than I had expected, they had no right to withhold it from me. For that matter, I wished that little girl on the train could have her story too. It wasn't likely she'd ever get it, but she deserved it nonetheless. Just as I deserved mine.

Oh, why had I told James not to come? Suddenly, more than anything in the whole world, I just wanted him to be here with me, wrapped safely in his loving arms. The fact that he hadn't even bothered to call since we talked last night upset me more than I could have possibly imagined. I felt adrift, abandoned, floating alone in an icy sea.

I heard steps on the stairs and then Zed's voice. "Lexie?"

My young cousin had been a huge help to me, but at the moment the sound of his voice made me cringe. I didn't want an update on Burke Bauer or his wife Lavonne or the odd American woman living in Switzerland. Not now.

"There's someone outside," he said, his voice tentative. "He wants to see you."

Oh, great. A patient's husband, no doubt. Just what I needed. "Tell him to call your mom. Explain that she's taken over the practice again."

"It's not anyone from around here," he said, appearing at the end of my bed.

I swept my fingers under both eyes and reached for a tissue. "What does he want?"

Zed shrugged, eyeing me strangely.

"I don't know. I've never seen him before. But he knew who I was. In fact, he seemed familiar with our whole family."

I sat up, the skin on my arms prickling. "What do you mean?"

"He said he was here to see you, but he also asked for Mom, and he said he wants to round up everyone over at *Mammi*'s so we can get down to the heart of the matter, whatever that means. Do you want me to call Mom?"

I was off the bed instantly, tossing Zed my phone and then taking the stairs two at a time.

"James!" I called out as I rushed through the front door.

He stood at the bottom of the stairs, smiling tentatively. Until I knocked him down.

Flat on his back, trying to raise his head with me on top of him, he gasped, "And I thought you might be mad." He laughed and then pointed toward the front door of the cottage

I turned to look. Zed stood on the small porch, my open phone in front of his face.

"You'd better get off me," James whispered, his green eyes dancing. "I think we're being filmed."

Zed used my phone to call his mom, and then rode with us to *Mammi*'s. I drove while James chatted away, asking Zed about himself. After a few minutes James turned his head toward the backseat and then glanced at me. "Boy," he said. "You two look related."

Zed and I both smiled.

"What?" James asked.

"I'm adopted too," Zed explained.

"Oh, well. Guess there's lots of blond hair and brown eyes in the family either way."

I asked James what his plan was, admitting how shocked I was at his arrival. It wasn't like me to agree to drive off somewhere without knowing exactly why.

"I have no idea if it will work or not, but it's worth a try," he said.

"What? What's worth a try?" I turned off the main highway.

"Just a little session."

"Like group therapy? Or family therapy, rather?" Inwardly, I groaned, thinking how very James-like of him to approach the situation this way.

"More like an intervention."

This time my groan was audible. He grew silent, and when I glanced at him, I could see that he was both surprised and hurt by my reaction.

"Look," he said, holding up both hands, "I know you find much of what you consider my 'psychobabble' tiresome, Lexie, but this is different. This is for your sake. To find your story and settle all of this once and for all. That is what you really want, isn't it?"

I turned down the lane, startled by the sternness in his voice and suddenly humbled by the truth of his words. He was right. Someone had to take charge and get everyone together and finally talk-ing. More importantly, he knew that such a difficult and significant encounter would be unwise without an outside party present, one who had been trained in psychology.

To my mind, that person would also need to be someone who was intuitive and kind and safe. Someone truly special. I glanced again at James, knowing he was all of the above. Silently, for the first time ever, I thanked God that this man was exactly the way he was—psychobabble and all.

"You're right. I'm sorry," I said simply, hoping that later I could more fully convey my gratitude.

The cows in the field ambled toward the white fence. Alexander stepped out of the barn and took off his hat. Marta had already arrived, and she and Ella were just climbing from their car as I pulled to a stop beside them. As we climbed out, Ella took a good look at James and then flashed me a broad smile.

Heart pounding, I ignored her, watching as James moved around the car to introduce himself to Marta. After exchanging names and handshakes, he motioned her aside, and much to my surprise she went willingly. Standing about ten feet away, the two of them spoke quietly together, their voices nearly inaudible. Seizing the opportunity, Ella moved in on me.

"Is that really James?" she whispered excitedly. "You didn't say he was so *hot*. He's even hotter than Sean! Are all the guys in Oregon that cute?"

I rolled my eyes, wishing she would be quiet so I could listen.

"Girls," Zed moaned under his breath, shaking his head at both of us.

Marta and James seemed to conclude their brief but private conversation, and then she turned toward me.

"Lexie, take James to meet *Mammi*. I'll send Ada out and then try to talk to Klara. Ella and Zed, you go with Lexie and James."

Without waiting for a reply, Marta turned and moved briskly toward the house. After I introduced James to Ella, the four of us headed up the walk in the same direction, though we weren't moving nearly as fast. Alexander met up with us before we reached the turnoff to the *daadi haus*.

"Lexie," he said, and then he nodded to Zed and Ella.

I introduced James to Alexander, who said hello and then looked away, kicking at the ground with his rounded-toe work boot. Each time I saw him, his shyness caught me by surprise.

"Marta went in the house to talk to Klara," I explained.

Alexander glanced up at me. "I'd best go in there too, then."

He started toward the back door and we followed, veering off toward the *daadi haus* at the split in the walkway.

As it turned out, Ada was already there, sitting near *Mammi*, who was lying back in her recliner chair, eyes closed, resting. Ada stood as we came inside, a smile overtaking her face. Her color looked much better as she stepped toward us, hugging each one and then graciously welcoming James in a hushed voice.

"Ada, who is it?" *Mammi* asked, opening her eyes and trying to sit up.

"It's family," Ada replied, giving me a wink.

We approached *Mammi*'s chair so that I could introduce James, but before I even spoke, the door swung open and Klara came rushing into the room.

"Out!" she cried. "Everybody out!"

"Klara . . ." Alexander was right behind her, followed by Marta.

Klara had a dishtowel over her shoulder and a wooden spoon in her hand. Her face was red, and a strand of sandy hair had come loose from her cap.

"Out! *Now!*" she snarled.

Ada stepped in front of me, protesting, as *Mammi* struggled to sit up in her chair. I spoke as well, as did the others, our voices all clamoring to be heard.

"Klara!" *Mammi*'s voice rang out, sharper and louder than all the rest, cutting through the din.

Silenced, we all turned toward the older woman, who had managed to get the recliner to the down position and was sitting tall, her cap askew and her white hair poking out from underneath it. "Please stop. This has gone on too long."

"You need to let things be," Klara replied, standing with her feet apart, hands gripping both ends of the wooden spoon. Though her eyes were on her mother, I knew she was speaking to everyone in the room.

"We just want the truth," Ada said gently, stepping forward.

Klara looked around at each of us, terror and betrayal shining clearly in her eyes.

"I won't be a part of this," she hissed. "Alexander, Ada. Come." Klara stepped around Marta and moved toward the open doorway.

I watched, heart in my throat, as Alexander remained exactly where he was, looking down at his boots, his hat in his hands, fingers kneading furiously at the brim. I turned to look at Ada, and satisfaction surged in my chest as I realized she had chosen to remain stubbornly in place as well.

Clearly noting the lack of movement behind her, Klara glanced over her shoulder when she reached the door, her face twisted into a scowl. There, she faltered in surprise that neither husband nor daughter were following orders.

"Klara, I am not Alexandra's biological father," Alexander blurted out suddenly.

Klara spun around to face her husband, her cheeks flushing an even brighter red, though whether from anger or embarrassment, I wasn't sure.

"Same old song," Klara barked. "I don't care how many times—"

"It's different now," he interrupted. "There's actual proof. Medical proof."

Klara jerked her head back, clearly shocked. She took a deep breath and held it, suddenly looking at me for confirmation. Technically, Alexander was overstating things a bit, so I tried to qualify his words by being more precise.

"I had my DNA tested. Until Alexander also is tested, we won't know if he is my father or not. But what we do know for sure, so far at least, is that Ada and I are siblings. Full siblings. She's my sister."

Klara's face went white, her mouth opening and closing like a fish, but no words came out. Before she could find her voice, Ada spoke.

"I was tested as well. The doctor said the DNA proves it. Without question, Lexie and I are sisters."

Our words had a strange effect on Klara. She exhaled slowly, her face growing pale, her jaw slack. She looked from her daughter to her husband to her sister, the spoon slipping from her hands and landing with a soft plop on the braided rug. No one moved to pick it up. Finally, she turned again toward Alexander.

He met her shocked gaze with confidence, his

shoulders squared. As they stared at each other, it was as if he stood taller than I had ever seen him. The slumping was gone, the averted eyes were no longer trained toward the floor. Even his fingers had stilled along the brim of the hat.

"I have told you this all along, Klara," he said, his voice even and deep. "You chose not to believe me, but Giselle and I were never involved, never intimate. There was no way Lexie could have been mine."

Klara tried to reply but nothing came out. Clearing her throat, she tried again, rasping, "But Giselle named the child Alexandra. Why would she have used that name unless the babe was yours?"

Mammi sat forward as if to speak, but Klara cut her off.

"I wasn't stupid," Klara continued, her voice growing stronger as she railed at her husband. "I saw how you looked at Giselle, the way she flirted with you. I caught the two of you whispering together more than once. She wouldn't tell anyone who the baby's father was, yet she named it after you. What other conclusion could I have drawn? Did you both think I was an idiot?"

Again, *Mammi* tried to speak, but she had become so worked up that all she could do was sputter and cough instead. As Ada and Ella jumped to her aid, James addressed the whole lot of us.

"Why don't we all calm down, have a seat, and do this the right way?" he asked in a voice so soothing that everyone seemed compelled to do exactly as he suggested. Even Klara obeyed, watching warily as Zed and Alexander rounded up three straight-back chairs from the rest of the small house and brought them to the living room. Once *Mammi* had recovered from her coughing fit, we all sat, with Klara, Marta, and Alexander taking the chairs, James and I on the couch with Ada next to me, and Ella and Zed seated on the floor. After we were settled, we looked to James to learn what would come next, and again I was deeply grateful for his presence.

"I think before we go any further, we should just pause for a moment and take all of this to the Lord in prayer," he said, his voice still soothing and warm. We bowed our heads, and though I expected him to pray aloud, instead he remained silent beside me as was the Amish custom. Though my brain was too frazzled to pray myself, by the time he said a gentle "amen" a minute or so later, the quiet and focus had served to calm me significantly. It seemed to have done the same for everyone.

"Okay," James said. "As a first step, let me just say that I think it's time for Lexie and Ada to learn the truth. The whole truth. That's why I wanted all of us to assemble here."

"But they don't—" Klara began.

"They already have pieces of the truth," he continued, cutting her off, "which has been making things difficult for everyone. Trust me when I say that bringing all of this out into the open will be a relief, both to the people trying to put their stories together and to those who have been keeping secrets."

Silenced, Klara pressed her lips together. Everyone else was quiet.

"So, Lexie," James said, turning toward me. "Why don't you tell us exactly what it is you want to know?"

I took a deep breath, let it out slowly, and then spoke.

"Who my birth parents really are. And Ada's. Why I was given up—and Ada wasn't. What Burke Bauer has to do with all of this. If Alexander is my father and, if not, why I was named after him. Why I was born in Montgomery County instead of here. Why my parents told me that my birth family loved me when obviously they—" I looked up at the faces surrounding me and corrected myself. "When obviously *you* didn't." I stopped abruptly and then added, "I guess that's everything."

"But we did love you," Marta whispered. "I did."

I met her eyes, ready to contradict her, but something in her expression made me realize that she was telling the truth.

"More importantly, Giselle loved you," she continued, standing. "She loved you more than she ever loved anyone."

"So why did she give me away? Why did you let her?"

Marta faltered, looking toward Klara. I looked at Klara as well, but she was staring intently at the floor now, arms crossed stubbornly over her chest. As my question hung in the air, unanswered, Marta slowly sat back down.

"Let me guess: It's not your place." I couldn't help it, my voice dripped with sarcasm.

"All right. Let's not get ahead of ourselves," James told us. "Ada, now it's your turn. What would you like to know?"

Ada grabbed my hand, and I could feel her tremble. Giving her a brave smile, I nodded, urging her with my eyes to go ahead and say what she was thinking.

"I do not . . . I have fewer questions than Lexie, of course. I just want to know who my birth mother and father were. Are." Looking at me, she added, "And I want to know why I was denied my sister. For my whole life. Who had the right to take her away from me, and why?"

She squeezed my hand, not letting go.

"Very good," James said, giving Ada an encouraging smile before again addressing the group. "Well, then why don't we start with the most basic question? Who was Ada and Lexie's biological mother?"

Mammi and Marta both whispered her name at the same moment: "Giselle."

Ada gasped and gripped my hand more tightly, her head turning toward Klara, the woman she had always considered her only *mamm*.

Klara wouldn't meet her daughter's eyes, but she spoke in a near mumble.

431

"I couldn't have any children of my own. When Giselle got pregnant the second time, I agreed to take the child, on one condition."

"And what was that condition?" James asked gently, but Klara merely shook her head and would not answer. After a beat, he spoke again. "Okay, we'll come back to that. At least we know that Giselle was the mother. So, moving along for now, who was Ada and Lexie's biological father?"

Ada and I both looked at Alexander hopefully, but he looked back at Ada and shook his head, pausing to brush a tear from his cheek with thick, rough-skinned fingers.

"In my heart, I always was and always will be your father, Ada," he said, the pain of this moment clearly written on his face.

"You're exactly right," James said, "but right now, we're asking about the *biological* father," James reminded him. "Are you their biological father?"

Sadly, Alexander shook his head no.

"Who, then?" I demanded, looking to James, wondering if we would have to do something more drastic to get to the truth.

"Burke Bauer," *Mammi* said simply. "I already told you, Alexandra. Your father was Burke Bauer. What I didn't say was that Burke was Ada's father too."

I let go of my sister's hand so I could massage

my temples. I had a terrible headache, but I needed to stay focused.

"Why don't you give us some details?" James suggested, making eye contact with *Mammi*.

In response, my grandmother launched into the same story she had laid out for me before, explainng how the beautiful Giselle had obtained a job at the nursery and fallen into a very secret, very discreet affair with her wealthy, older, and married boss. When she got to the part about Bauer's hold over Giselle, about how the girl couldn't seem to stay away from him because "he was like a drug to her," James interrupted, asking if Bauer had been a harsh person, if he'd had a cruel streak.

"Not that I know of," *Mammi* replied.

"Quite the opposite," Marta added. "For all his faults, Burke Bauer was a very gentle man. Almost to a fault, actually."

I stared at Marta, wondering how she would know that. She had only been a young girl at the time, just eleven years old or so when Giselle and Burke and had first become involved. Why would Marta have had any sort of interaction with Bauer at all?

"I see," James said, interrupting my thoughts. "Then their relationship is fairly understandable, though of course still inexcusable. We know that Giselle was terribly mistreated by her own father when she was young. It's not much of a stretch to see why she would be drawn to an older man later in life, especially one who seemed kind and gentle. My guess is that Bauer's love soothed the wounds inside of Giselle, wounds that had been inflicted years before by her own father."

Mammi seemed to process that, as did we all. I knew there was never, ever an excuse for infidelity, but at least James's logic helped us better understand what kept driving Giselle back to Burke Bauer's arms—even though she knew it was wrong, even though he already had a wife and child.

"Please continue with what you were saying," James prodded, and I recognized the reassuring half smile that he was giving to *Mammi*. "If Giselle and Burke were so discreet, how did you find out about their affair?"

Mammi's eyes filled with tears.

"It was all my fault," she said. "If I hadn't sent Klara over to get her that night, if Alexander hadn't gone with her and then gone inside . . ."

She began to sob quietly, and when it was clear she couldn't continue, James tried another approach.

"Alexander? If you know what she's talking about, why don't you take it from there."

Nodding, Alexander cleared his throat and then spoke.

"Klara and I were courting," he said softly, "and I was over to see her one evening. Of course, Giselle and Marta were still living here as well."

He glanced at Marta, who gave him an encouraging, sisterly nod. He continued.

"*Mammi* got word that Giselle would have to work late at the office but not to wait up, that she would be home after she was finished. I think Giselle was eighteen then, on *rumschpringe*, so Klara and I were not concerned when she hadn't shown up by the time I left. We both assumed that Giselle had left work and gone directly out with friends, perhaps to a party or two. It was a Friday night, you see, and Giselle often disappeared on the weekends." Alexander looked over at James and me, pausing to explain. "Some kids tend to . . . uh . . . exploit their time of *rumschpringe* more than others. You might say that Giselle was one of those."

Klara glanced sharply at Alexander and then returned her gaze to the floor.

"In any event," he went on, "I had gone over to the Gundy place where I was boarding because I worked for Benjamin. *Mammi* was a worrier, so when it grew very late and still Giselle had not come home, she woke Klara and asked her to take the buggy over to the nursery to see if she could find out what had happened. She came and got me to go with her. We thought *Mammi* was concerned over nothing, but she was so agitated by that point that Klara was willing to do as she asked and I was willing to help her."

At that *Mammi*'s sobs grew louder still.

"When we reached the nursery, things seemed quiet and empty. But there was a light on in the main building and a single car in the parking lot, so I thought we should take a look inside. I left Klara with the horse, saying I would be right back."

It wasn't until that moment that I realized what was coming next. Sure enough, Alexander went on to tell us that when he got up to the office, he discovered that the only ones there were Giselle and her boss, but that they had definitely *not* been working.

"They had . . . uh . . . fallen asleep in each others' arms," Alexander said, not needing to elaborate. "I tiptoed away and got myself out of there, rejoined Klara in the buggy, and drove away. Apparently, Giselle was completely unaware that I had been there at all."

"Did you tell *Mammi* what you'd seen?" I whispered.

He shook his head.

"No. I simply said that Giselle was still at the office, and that if I were *Mammi* I would not wait up. Then Klara and I tended to the horse, put away the buggy, and said goodnight. My long walk back to the Gundy place gave me plenty of time for thought and prayer."

Klara interrupted suddenly, her voice sharp as glass.

"My husband is leaving out an important detail. He chose not to tell *me* what he had seen either. That was his first big mistake."

"Klara—"

"If you had been honest with me from the start, Alexander, perhaps none of the rest of it would have happened."

He shrugged, looking to James.

"Regardless of what my wife is saying," he explained, two bright blotches of pink appearing on his cheeks as he spoke, "please understand that this is the Amish way. We do not speak openly of private matters, of sexual intimacy. Between a man and his wife as God intended, yes, there is total freedom of words there. But not to others, and not *of* others. It was not my place to speak of the intimacies of my future sister-in-law. Giselle was an adult. What she did in her more private moments back then was between her and God. The most I could do was pray for her. Which I did after that, regularly and with deep concern. She was going to be my new sister, and though she was a very troubled girl, I loved her." At Klara's scowl, he added defiantly, "I loved her very much. As a *sister*."

Turning away, Klara recrossed her arms over her chest, set her jaw tightly, and slunk further into her seat.

"If you didn't tell *Mammi* about the affair, how did she find out?" I asked, wanting to get back on track.

"Eventually, once Klara and I were married and I was living here as well, Giselle began . . . show-ing signs," Alexander replied. "That is when I knew I had no choice."

"You mean signs that she was pregnant? Morning sickness? Baggy clothes? Things like that?"

"Yes," Alexander replied. "Once I realized what was going on, I decided my best course of action was to speak to Giselle directly. So I did, telling her that I knew about her and Bauer, and that I suspected that she was with child. Much to my surprise, she responded by denying everything, claiming instead that I had designs on her, that I was—how did she put it?—playing out my own fantasies by conjuring up lies regarding her with other men." Again, this sweet fellow's cheeks colored brightly.

"The best defense is a good offense," James offered, and after a moment Alexander's eyes widened and then he began nodding vigorously, as if James had just handed him the missing piece to a lifelong puzzle.

"That is it exactly. By making such claims about me, Giselle may have been able to avoid the real issue for a while, but, unfortunately, by so doing she also planted doubts in the mind of my wife."

"And that was his second mistake," Klara added with a huff. "Not telling me then, either."

Much to my surprise, Alexander nodded.

"You are right, Klara. At that point I should have told you everything. I was wrong, but my motives were pure. Truly, I wanted to protect you."

"Protect me? From what?" she sneered.

"From the uglier things of this world. From the nature of Giselle's sin. From the knowledge that even as God seemed to have chosen not to bless you and me with a child, in His unique wisdom He had not withheld that same blessing from your unmarried sister."

Klara's mouth worked silently for a moment, again making her look like a fish. The cold truth of her husband's words seemed to shut her up, at least temporarily, and I was glad.

"After talking with the bishop about the situation at length," Alexander continued, speaking now mostly to Ada and me, "I followed his advice and spoke to *Mammi* about it. She already had her own suspicions about a pregnancy, and once she learned that Giselle had a lover, those suspicions were confirmed. I told *Mammi* everything I knew and had no more involvement after that." Glancing at Klara, he added, "Except, of course, to defend myself against Giselle's insinuations. And Klara's response to them. Over and over for the rest of my life."

After an awkward silence, James turned to *Mammi*, whose sobs had quieted at last.

"Can you tell us what happened next? Did you confront your daughter? What made her decide to give the baby up for adoption?"

Mammi looked back at him helplessly and shook her head, though whether she was unwilling or unable to speak I wasn't sure. After that, to my surprise Marta cleared her throat and picked up the story.

"I wasn't quite twelve when all of that was going on, but I can tell you how things went from my perspective."

We nodded at her.

"I remember a lot of drama, a lot of fighting. Giselle yelling at *Mammi* and slamming doors. Klara screaming at Alexander and sometimes even making him sleep in the barn. Once, I overheard a whispered conversation between Alexander and Giselle myself. Even though I knew it was none of my business, I listened anyway. I don't remember the specifics, but I do recall that I never heard anything to justify Klara's suspicions about the two of them. Mostly, I remember feeling bad for Alexander, because he was sweet and Giselle wasn't herself at all, she was so mean to him. She had a sharp side to her, one that came out when she felt cornered. She hated hearing when she'd done something wrong, even if she knew it was true. Like James said, Giselle's best defense had always been to go on the offense. And so she did. With a vengeance."

"You can say that again," Alexander mumbled.

"Anyway, around here things only got worse, not better. Personally, what I hated most was all of the gossip. It just about drove me nuts. Every-one wanted to know who the father was, but even though there were plenty of rumors, Giselle would never confirm or deny any of them, not even to her own sisters. At some point the church leaders got

440

involved. They started coming here and trying to talk some sense into her. Like *Mammi*, they wanted Giselle to confess and repent, to put an end to her reckless *rumschpringe*, and to join the church. They suggested she get married—to someone Amish, of course—and let him raise the child as his own, regardless of the actual paternity. To that end I know she had several prospects, but she wasn't interested. Instead, she dug in her heels, told everyone to leave her alone, and turned her back on God and the church."

Marta sounded bitter, but as she spoke I felt pity surging within me for the poor, pregnant Giselle. She had made some very bad decisions, yes, but I just kept remembering that at the time she had only been all of nineteen. Who at nineteen hadn't done some stupid things? All of that scrutiny must have served to only magnify the problems.

"Of course, the bigger Giselle's stomach grew," Marta continued, "the more insanely jealous Klara became." Looking at her sister, Marta added, "I was never quite sure if Klara was really angry because she suspected Alex was the father or simply because her sister had gotten pregnant even though she herself hadn't."

I glanced at Klara, surprised to see that her cheeks were wet with tears. So the woman had a soul after all. James seemed to notice the tears as well, because he held out a hand to Marta and addressed Klara instead.

"I have a question for you. Would you say that your father was a good man?"

Klara sat up, looking uncomfortable, but at least she answered.

"No. Not by anyone's definition."

"Have you known many good men in your life?"

She squinted at James, silently asking what he was getting at.

"Just go with me for a minute. Have you known many good men? And by good, I mean men who are kind, dependable, trustworthy . . ."

Klara shrugged.

"There are some in the church like that, I suppose. The bishop. A few of the deacons."

"How about at home? Are there any good men in your home?"

Klara stared at James for a long moment before understanding slowly began to creep across her face.

"Why, Alexander, of course," she whispered. "He is good, through and through. He is very, very good. To me. To everyone. He is the most *gut* man of all!" At that, much to my amazement, Klara burst into tears.

To his credit, her husband didn't even hesitate in his response. Instead, he simply slipped from his chair to his knees and took Klara in his arms, holding her tightly and patting her back as she wept.

"I think sometimes when we grow up with a parent who is deeply flawed," James explained to us as Alexander and Klara remained locked in their tearful embrace, "we learn, subconsciously at least, to expect the worst from everyone else as well. Given the kind of man her father was, no doubt at some level Klara believed that all men were bad. Even with Alexander, whom she loved, she would have had trouble accepting that his goodness was genuine, or at least that it would last. When Giselle started spewing her lies, Klara's natural suspicions were confirmed, and she was more than ready to believe them. It's sad, and it's wrong, but it's certainly understandable." After a moment, he added, "Fortunately, it doesn't have to be that way forever. We can all learn to see with new eyes if we try."

I was dumbfounded at what had just happened, and I looked at James with respect. Though this certainly wasn't the most pressing issue of the day, he had spotted an opportunity for healing and had gone with it.

Seeing with new eyes, indeed.

"So who can tell us why Lexie was born in Norristown rather than here?" James asked, taking the conversation back to the next logical question.

No one spoke, so after a moment, Ella shyly raised her hand.

"Yes, Ella?" James said.

"I wasn't there, obviously, but I bet I can guess. Lexie probably can too."

At the moment I wasn't interested in hearing

theories, but James regarded her with interest.

"With all of these people ragging on her all the time, Giselle probably just had enough one day and took off out of here." Glancing at her mother, she added, "Sometimes we all need space, to catch our breath and maybe calm down and get some perspective."

"You are partly correct," *Mammi* interjected, and I was relieved to hear her finally rejoin the discussion. "She did take off after a particularly bad argument with Klara, but Giselle did not just need some air. She was leaving for good. Like many of the *youngie* on *rumschpringe*, Giselle had purchased a car. Once she drove off in it, I thought she was long gone and I might never see her again."

"What happened to her?" I whispered, leaning forward to take in every word.

"We learned later that she headed east, but she only made it as far as Exton before she felt a contraction. Determined to press onward, she drove for another half hour before she finally had to admit to herself that she was in labor and needed to get to a hospital, so she drove herself to the nearest emergency room which happened to be in Norristown. She was determined to get through the entire labor and delivery all by herself, but as the night wore on, her resolve weakened. Finally, she called a neighbor here and asked if they could get word to us about where she was and what was happening. The moment they told me I hired a driver and had him take me straight to Norristown Hospital to be with her. I made it just in time to see you come into the world."

I expected *Mammi* to burst into tears at the very thought, but instead a broad smile broke out on her face.

"You were so perfect, Alexandra. So beautiful. At that moment, I knew it didn't matter who your father was or what Giselle had done in the past. You were here, and that was enough."

As I wondered what happened to derail that thought, *Mammi* continued, glancing at Klara before she added that there was just one problem.

"Giselle was very hurt by Klara, not just from the angry words they had exchanged but also from the fact that Klara had declined to come with me to the hospital. So she did something out of spite— something I know she eventually lived to regret."

Even before *Mammi* said it I knew. As a final stick of the knife both to Klara and her husband, my mother had decided to name me Alexandra.

My sympathies dimmed for the helpless Giselle as I thought how absolutely cruel and wrong that had been. No matter how hurt or angry she was, what had given her the right to do something as awful as that?

"Of course," *Mammi* continued, "once she and I brought little Alexandra back home, things went from bad to worse. Klara and Giselle could hardly bear the sight of each other. Poor

Alexander was angry and embarrassed, especially when church members began speculating about the reason for the child's name. Thank goodness Alexander had involved the bishop from the very beginning, telling him everything, or the church might have eventually taken action to have him excommunicated and shunned."

I looked over at Alexander, who was back in his chair now but holding on to Klara's hand. I felt terribly sorry, even complicit somehow, and I wished there was some way I could apologize on behalf of my mother.

"What kind of mom was she?" I asked, almost afraid to hear the answer.

"In spite of everything, Giselle loved you very much," *Mammi* replied, "but she had no idea how to take care of an infant, and she did not seem interested in learning. She left the hard parts to Marta and me and spent most of her time either resting or quietly playing with you."

"Sounds like she may have been suffering from postpartum depression," James interjected. I had a feeling he was right.

James and I both looked back at *Mammi*.

"Whatever was causing it," she continued, "at that time all I could do was wring my hands and pray for patience and try to prod her into action."

I nodded, trying to picture it, knowing that must have been a difficult time for everyone. No wonder they had eventually given me away. Sick, my own mother thought I was too much trouble to bother with.

"Given that Giselle is Ada's mother too," James said to *Mammi*, "I assume that at some point she and Burke Bauer rekindled their affair?"

"Worse than that," *Mammi* replied. "They ran off together."

Ada and I looked at each other in surprise.

"At first Giselle tried to stay away from him. She focused on the baby and helped around the house —when she was not resting. Mostly, she withdrew into herself. But one day, when Alexandra was about six months old, Giselle got the notion to go into town. We had sold her car, so she strapped up a horse to the buggy, took Alexandra, and left. I do not know what her intention was at that point. She said she only wanted to do some shopping, maybe visit with some friends. But I think perhaps she was lying, that what she really intended was to go straight to Burke Bauer and show him his daughter."

"She did not come back?" Ada asked breathlessly.

Mammi shook her head, blinking away fresh tears.

"That night several young men from the nursery brought back the horse and buggy, along with a letter from Giselle. It said something about how she and the baby were fine but that they were not coming home. I was not to worry because, as she had written, 'We are a family now.' Can you imagine that? This man with a trusting wife and a young son and a successful business threw it all away to go off and play house with his mistress and their love child."

"Believe it or not," Marta added softly, "one of those young men who came here was Burke Bauer's own son. He had no idea what was in the letter, of course, nor that his father had taken off with Giselle. He was just doing as Daddy had requested, delivering a horse and buggy to a local Amish family."

For some reason, the pain of that thought shone clearly in Marta's eyes. I agreed that what Bauer had done was awful, using his son as a pawn in his scheme, but I didn't understand the depth of her emotion.

"How long were they gone?" Ada asked, impatient now to hear about the circumstances of her own birth.

"More than a year, maybe thirteen, fourteen months. By the time they came back, Alexandra had really grown. She was a toddler. And Giselle was a different person. More mature. Almost repentant. Dedicated to caring for Alexandra. She never spoke much of the time she had been away, but the relationship must have run its course because eventually I realized that it was truly over. I also realized that, once again, she had managed to get herself pregnant."

"Bauer's son was just a year younger than I was, and he and I had become friends by then," Marta interjected, "so I was able to find out more of the inside scoop from his point of view. Giselle didn't want us to know any of it, but *Mammi* and I were both glad to hear that Bauer was trying to put his real family back together again. We were especially relieved when his wife finally forgave him. As for the son, he tried to give his dad a chance too, but he was quite emotionally fragile, and the wound of his father's betrayal ran deep. We *never* talked about my sister's new pregnancy. That would have just made things a thousand times worse."

I sat back, realizing that was a period of my life that I would never really know about. Given that I had been in the care of both mother and father, at least for a short time, I supposed I had been kept safe and warm. On the other hand, the sudden appearance and disappearance of my birth father from my life could only have served as the first chink in my many abandonment issues.

"So Giselle came back pregnant with me," Ada said, clearly impatient for *Mammi* to get on with the rest of the story.

"Yes. She was also depressed and overwhelmed and very afraid of being a single mother of *two* children. She and her sister eventually found a sort of peace, and by the time Giselle was in her ninth month Klara offered to take the baby and raise it as her own. If she and Alexander could not conceive a child, which was becoming more and more apparent, well, then at least it seemed God was providing another way. When the baby was born, we all knew it was the right choice."

"Lexie, I already told you that you were with me when Ada was born," Marta said. "I was the one who snipped the lock of your mother's hair and then your sister's. I tried to cut a lock of yours too, but you wouldn't let me." She smiled. "I tied the strands with black ribbon and gave them both to *Mammi*. Then Klara came and took the baby."

We all turned and looked at Klara then. She was tightly gripping her husband's hand, her face flushed and eyes still fixed firmly on the floor.

"What was the condition?" I asked suddenly, my voice sounding pinched and foreign to me. When no one replied, I added, "The condition, Klara. You said earlier that when Giselle got pregnant the second time, you agreed to take the child, on one condition."

Finally, Klara met my eyes with her own.

"I was still afraid that Alexander had fathered you," she said, the desperation clear in her voice.

"Of course you were," I retorted sharply. "But, given the timing, there was no way he could be the father of this new one. So you decided to take it and raise it as your own. What was your condition? Go ahead. We all want to hear it."

After a long moment of silence, Klara whispered, "That Giselle go away forever and take you with her."

My mind reeled.

"I begged Klara not to hold her to it," *Mammi* cried. "I told her that even if Alexander was the father—which I knew he was not—she must forgive and forget. I reminded her that we believe in delayed justice, in *demut*. I said if her suspicions were true then God would judge Giselle and Alexander someday. *God* would. Not us."

I felt myself slipping into that cold, icy place, until James reached for me, bringing me back. I thought of Ada beside me, aware that she was holding on to me too. I squeezed her hand.

Mammi again took up the story from there.

"Klara would not listen to me. The most she was willing to offer was a bit more time. She said Giselle could stay until she had her strength back, perhaps until she had lined up a job somewhere else, an alternate plan. But then she would have to take Alexandra and go."

"Only that took longer, way longer, than it should have," Marta added. "After a few months, Klara thought Giselle was just faking, but *Mammi* and I knew that she really was unwell. She spent much of her days in bed, rising only to care for you and play with you and read to you, but she didn't interact with anyone else. She grew thin, too thin. We all knew she wouldn't be leaving any time soon. She could barely take care of herself, much less a toddler."

"As time went on," *Mammi* said, "I knew I had to do something drastic. For years I had been talking about selling Amielbach, but Giselle had always convinced me not to. She was determined to travel there someday. Out of all three girls, she had always been the most adventurous, and I liked the idea of a child of mine returning to our ances- tral home. But it slowly became obvious that Giselle could not even walk down the street, much less travel to another country, so I decided to look for a buyer. I had an idea, one that would give me some leverage. As difficult as it was, I sold Amielbach and then I told Klara that if she would let you and Giselle stay with us, I would use the money to buy this place for her and Alexander. I said they could farm the land, and we could put up a smaller house on the property for Giselle and Alexandra, so they would not always be under-foot. Klara was not thrilled with my offer, but even she could see that Giselle needed help."

"You had it all worked out," I muttered, looking from *Mammi* to Klara. "So why was I given away?"

Mammi let out a sob as Ada placed a comfort-ing hand on my arm.

"I needed time to make up my mind," Klara said defensively.

"While we were waiting for her verdict," *Mammi* sobbed, "the unthinkable happened."

She seemed too overcome with emotion to continue, so Marta picked up where her mother left off.

"Giselle had grown worse by then," Marta said.

"I mean, she almost never got out of bed anymore, and she stopped speaking, even to you, Lexie. One afternoon I was outside in the garden, harvesting the last of the potatoes. You were supposed to be asleep, napping in the bed with Giselle. I was so busy with the stupid potatoes, I don't know how I knew to look up at that moment, but I did. Maybe it was God, telling me that something was wrong."

I leaned forward, listening intently.

"From where I was working," she continued, "I could see the creek, and something felt off about it, you know? The water was icy cold, but it hadn't frozen over yet, and at first I just thought that maybe I had seen a fish pop up at the surface or something. Whatever it was, I put down the hoe and went over to take a closer look. On the muddy bank were tiny footprints, and that's when I knew that while Giselle slept, you had woken up, wandered off, and ended up toddling right down to the creek's edge. I started screaming, and then I heard you cry. You were under a willow tree, clinging to a low branch. Your bare foot was wedged between two rocks, and the water was swirling up to your chin."

"I heard her screams from the house," *Mammi* moaned. "When I hurried out to the yard, Marta was splashing out of the creek, carrying you in her arms."

I shuddered, looking at my aunt and realizing that I owed her my very life. I may have saved her from jail, but she had saved me from death.

"As horrible as that was, at least the incident seemed to snap Giselle from her stupor," *Mammi* continued. "In truth, it was a real shock for all of us. After that, Giselle knew she had to leave, not just her home but her child. In the condition she was in, she was not a fit mother. That night, she packed a bag, wrote us all a note, and left. In it, she asked Klara to raise you as well."

Klara bent forward, putting her face in her hands.

"Mamm?" Ada whispered.

"But you wouldn't do it, would you?" I asked Klara, my voice sounding strangely calm. "Even with Giselle gone for good, you wouldn't take me."

Klara didn't answer, so *Mammi* spoke for her.

"No, she would not. And she did not want me to, either. In fact she forbade me to. She said she wanted Alexandra as far away from here as humanly possible. You were only two years old, but to Klara you were the enemy." *Mammi*'s face turned toward the window. "I thought of an old friend, an *Englisch* woman who had moved clear across the country, to Oregon. That seemed pretty far." *Mammi*'s eyes were back on me now. "I wrote to my friend and asked if there were any Plain communities there, if she might know of some childless couple who was good, who was loving and kind, that God could bless with a beautiful two-year-old girl. She did. Of course, we worked with a lawyer and did it all legally. And that is how you ended up with your parents, Alexandra."

And that is how you ended up with your parents. Her words ricocheted inside my head, the words I had waited a lifetime to hear.

James placed a warm hand on my arm and spoke. "I know this is difficult for you, Lex, but can't you see how God was in all of this? Just like with Joseph, He wrought good from bad."

And that is how you ended up with your parents. Because God wrought good from bad. Because He was watching over me, had been watching over me all along.

"I remember the day you left," Marta said suddenly. "*Mammi* hired a driver to go to Philadelphia, to the airport. You were two, wearing your little Amish dress, apron, and cap and holding the folded quilt *Mammi* had made for you. I stood on the balcony and watched you go."

I gasped.

Marta kept talking through tears. "You turned and blew me a kiss, as if you were leaving on a short trip. As if you would soon return."

I was that little girl again, looking back at the house, the balcony. My mother was gone. I was blowing my teenage aunt a kiss. I had no idea what was ahead of me.

I leaped to my feet, knocking against James.

"Lexie?" He was scrambling to follow me.

I stumbled through the room, nearly tripping over Zed's outstretched foot, brushing past Alexander. I fumbled for the knob and pushed through the door.

"Lexie!" James was behind me. I started to run, around the back of Klara's house. There was the creek—the icy waters of my waking nightmares. The back door was ajar and I dashed inside, tearing through the kitchen and into the dining room, around to the open staircase. Up I went, taking the steps two at a time. On the landing, I turned. There was the room with the balcony, the door open. Ada's room, I presumed. I stepped inside. A quilt, bigger than mine but the same pattern, was spread across the double bed. Dresses and caps hung on pegs along the wall. I stepped to the French doors at the balcony and pushed them open, taking the short step to the iron railing and gripping it tightly through the vines that had wound around it.

Below, a pink dogwood tree bloomed to the side of the house. The cows had crowded around the white fence and one looked up at me. I turned my head toward the stand of trees, catching the scent of pine. Beyond them, the steel blades of a windmill, that wasn't visible from the road, spun in the breeze.

I thought of how Mama and I used to sit in the shadow of our own windmill, how sometimes Dad would join us. I thought of how they gained my trust. Soothed my sorrow. Accepted me as I was, not knowing what my past had been. There was no way they could have guessed.

Tears stung my eyes.

I had the missing pieces. I had the truth. I had my story.

"Lexie?" James stood in the doorway. Behind him were Ella and then Marta. In a moment they were crowded around me, hugging me. Holding me.

THIRTY-ONE

By the time we were ready to go, I was so weary I asked James to drive.

"Sure, but you'll have to navigate," he said, taking the keys from my hand as he walked to the passenger door, unlocked it, and held it open for me. "Or maybe Zed can point the way."

Zed hesitated, gesturing toward Marta's car. "I thought I would ride back with Mom."

"No problem. Go ahead," I said tiredly. "James can just follow you guys."

Nearly collapsing onto the seat with exhaustion, I closed my eyes and leaned back against the headrest. James started up the car, and for a while we drove along in silence. I was grateful that he seemed to sense my need for a little space and quiet. I so appreciated all he had done today, but my head was spinning and my heart was too full for mere words. Would I ever be able to process everything I had learned? Would I ever be able to thank James for his part in making it happen?

The silence continued, but finally I forced my eyes open and looked around to get my bearings.

We were just another few minutes from Marta's home. I knew that despite his enormous self-control, James was desperate to talk, to probe my psyche. I reached out and put a hand on his shoulder and gave it a loving squeeze.

"Go ahead."

"Go ahead what?" he asked, glancing my way.

"Go ahead and talk. I know you're dying to ask me some deep, psychological questions."

"How do you know that?"

"Because your silence is so loud it's practically shouting."

We both laughed.

"Fine," he said. "How are you feeling?"

"Overwhelmed. Confused. Exhausted."

"Good. And?"

I looked away, a single tear sliding down my cheek before I wiped it away.

"Complete," I added. "Very, incredibly, strangely complete."

He reached out and took my hand and gave it a squeeze.

"It's no wonder. You wanted your story, Lex. Now you have it."

Nodding, I squeezed his hand even more tightly in return.

"You *do* have your story now, right?" he added. "I mean, you're not planning to go traipsing across Europe in search of Giselle or anything, are you?"

I smiled. Oddly enough, though I wouldn't rule

out a visit with my birth mother in the future, I had no burning desire to find her any time soon. I had finally gotten the truth. For now, that felt sufficient.

"What about you, James?" I asked, releasing his hand and shifting in my seat. "Now that you know the whole ugly truth about my birth family, are you sure you still want me?"

"Are you kidding?"

"It's just that now that I've heard my story, well, what can I say but it makes families in country western songs look functional. After all we learned today, I wouldn't blame you if you wanted to hit the hills running."

James shook his head sadly and reached out to again take my hand. "There is no shame in this, Lex. God ordained the days of your life, just like it says in Psalm 139. The story you so desperately wanted to hear was written by Him."

"Surely, this wasn't His will."

"He allowed you to be created in the first place."

I couldn't argue with that. For as easy as it was for some people to get pregnant, each baby was still a miracle.

"He knew your numbers," James added.

"My numbers?"

James nodded. "God ordained that you would be with your birth mother for two years, and with your mama until you were eight, and He knew that you would have your father until you were twenty-six."

Tears again threatened at the back of my eyes.

James was right. God knew my numbers. I didn't want to think about what else He knew, but that was for another day. Giselle and Burke Bauer and everyone else in the broken world we lived in had free will. If they used it in all the wrong ways, well, as *Mammi* had said, ultimately that was between them and God.

James slowed to steer around a large pothole and then sped up and kept going. "Look at you and Ada. Look at what God redeemed there."

I was quiet for a long moment, taking that in and thinking of all of the many things in this situation He had redeemed. Praying silently, I thanked God for His redemptive powers, for bringing me to Ada, for breaking the silence of my birth family. Glancing at the man beside me, my heart surged with joy and I added one last thank you.

Once I was blind but now I see.

I turned my attention forward, watching Marta's car lead the way home in front of us. As settled as I was feeling on the inside, I knew there was one more element of this puzzle that was still missing.

"I know I have my story now," I said. "But Marta has another secret. Don't ask me how I know. I just do."

"Maybe it's not exactly a secret. Maybe it's just something she wants to keep private."

"Maybe. But it still bugs me."

James flashed me a grin.

"You're impossible, you know that?"

"I know," I replied, leaning over to kiss his cheek. "But you love me anyway."

"That I do. That I surely, totally do."

Settling back in my seat, I looked at James. As he slowed the car and put on the blinker to turn into Marta's drive, the word "kindred" came to mind. My adoptive parents might have passed away, but at least now I did have kin, even if I'd had to go out and find them myself. More importantly, I had a true kindred spirit, someone who really cared about me. Someone who was connected to me by choice. His choice. And mine.

James went in the house while I stayed out in the yard and spent fifteen minutes on the phone with Sean. Awkwardly bowing out of his life, I explained that I was returning to Oregon, but I was grateful for all of his help while I was in Lancaster County. He was very gracious and we both wished the other happiness as we said goodbye.

"We could've had a blast, you know," he told me before hanging up.

Sliding the phone into my pocket, I smiled, knowing that with James I was getting more than just a blast. I was getting a lifetime with the man I truly loved, the one God intended for me.

Later, just before sunset, Marta seemed surprised when I asked her to go for a walk with me. As we headed down to the covered bridge, the sky streaked with gold and purple, I told her I thought

461

there was something more to the story.

"No, you have it all," she said, sounding earnest.

"I don't mean my part of the story. I mean the whole story. I mean there's something more you haven't told me." She was silent as we crossed to the other side of the road, so I added, "I said as much to James, but he said I should let it be, that if you want to keep something private it's probably none of my business anyway."

"James said that, huh?" Marta smiled. "He's a keeper, that one."

"I know. I plan to."

We reached the bridge and stopped in the middle. The water level had lowered significantly. A dove swooped down from above and rested on the railing, looking at us.

"I wouldn't call it a secret," she said, staring out onto the water, "but I suppose there is a final element you're not aware of. To be honest, I'm surprised you haven't figured it out on your own."

I looked at her, wondering if I had missed something.

"Remember earlier when we were talking about Burke Bauer's son, Freddy?" she asked. "The boy who helped bring us the buggy the night his father ran off with Giselle?"

I nodded. Marta looked up at the dove, which had begun to make soft cooing sounds, perhaps calling out to some far-off mate.

"What about him?"

Marta stood up straight and slipped her hands into the pocket of her apron. "Freddy was like his father in many ways. He, too, was charming, kind, and gentle. Unfortunately, he, too, was weak. But I didn't realize that back then. I just knew that I liked him, that I wanted to know him better. He carried a lot of pain from what his father had done, and because of my sister's actions, I felt responsible in some way."

"But you weren't."

"No, I wasn't. But at twelve I still thought the whole world revolved around me, even the bad parts. Crazy as it sounds, I think I felt drawn to Freddy the first time I saw him, even if he was a year younger than I was. Of course, our little friendship eventually petered out, but when we were older we ran into each other again, though by that point he was no longer a boy at all but instead had grown into a very handsome young man. We compared notes, and as it turned out, none of us except *Mammi* had ever heard from Giselle again once she left for good—not even the great Burke Bauer himself. Freddy said his parents were still together, though not very happy, and that he was pretty sure his dad had had a few more extramarital affairs over the years."

"Did you ever see Freddy again after that?"

Marta laughed.

"Why, yes. Given the history there between our two families, we began to fancy ourselves as a modern-day Romeo and Juliet. Our love would prevail, regardless of the factors that divided us. Made for a very exciting relationship, you know, so clandestine and romantic and everything."

I turned to her, my eyes wide.

"So you *dated* Freddy Bauer?"

She nodded, saying, "Way more than that, Lexie. We got married. Freddy Bauer was my husband. Ella's father."

"I can't believe it!" I cried, my hands flying to my cheeks.

"It's true."

I was speechless for a moment as I tried to grasp what she was telling me.

"But . . . that means my biological father was your father-in-law?"

"Yes."

"So you're not just my aunt, you're also my . . . my what?"

Marta smiled.

"Your half brother's wife. We're sisters-in-law, of a sort."

My jaw remained open. Truly, if I had thought our family sounded like a bad country song before, at that point I could have sung the chorus and then some!

"Wait a minute," I told her, shaking my head, trying to align what I knew with what I was learning. "Your married name isn't Bauer. It's Bayer."

Marta shrugged. "When I first got pregnant

with Ella, Freddy decided to anglicize our name, changing the Bauer to Bayer. He said it would be easier on our kids, but I always suspected he had mostly done it as a dig at his father. When it came to Burke, my husband tended to be a bit passive-aggressive."

"I can see that. So how did the two of you end up as Mennonites? Was that also some sort of dig at Dad?"

Marta shook her head. "No, it wasn't like that. When my time of *rumschpringe* ended, I was in love with Freddy and decided not to join the Amish church. He belonged to a nondenominational group, but I needed something Plainer. We finally reached a compromise and became Mennonite." She hesitated and then added, "At least I thought that's how it was at the time. But maybe you're right. Maybe Freddy used it as yet another dig at his father—turning his back on Burke's wealth to join a Plain community."

I looked away, her words ringing in my ears. His father was also *my* father. Suddenly, I wanted to meet my half brother more than anything.

"Where is he now, Marta? What happened to end your marriage?"

"Lexie!" she suddenly cried, throwing her hands out and tilting her head toward the sky. "Can you not leave a single stone unturned?" Her voice was loud but not necessarily angry. More like exasperated. Worn down.

I couldn't help but grin, thinking that lately I had become pretty good at wearing people down.

"Fine!" she said, dropping her arms to her sides and turning to face me. "Fine. You want to know? Just like his father, Freddy was a cheat. Worse than that, his affair was with an Amish girl, just like Daddy. A local Amish girl. That he got pregnant. Yes, Lexie, history had repeated itself. Can you imagine how that made me feel?"

I was stunned. After all of the pain that Burke's actions had caused his family, how could Freddy, of all people, have turned around and done the very same thing to his?

"Believe it or not, he tried to minimize it. 'No big deal'? 'It meant nothing'? Had he really forgotten how it felt to be that betrayed young man who showed up at our house all those years ago with Giselle's horse and buggy, only to learn what his father had done?" She allowed her questions to hang in the night air and then added, "Despite all that, I tried to make things work, I really did. For Ella's sake, I think I could have gotten past the infidelity, with counseling and time. But Freddy wasn't having any of it. He stuck it out for a while but eventually insisted on a divorce, saying he wanted a 'fresh start' somewhere else. Last I heard, he was living up in Canada somewhere. Probably still running around with women half his age."

So much for wanting to meet my half brother.

Instead, I felt a deep surge of pity for Marta, not to mention an even stronger bond.

"What happened to the one here, the Amish woman, and their baby?" I whispered.

Marta studied my face for a long time as all around us crickets chirped and fireflies lit up the night.

"You already know the answer to that question."

Then she turned and began walking back toward the house. After a beat, I raced to catch up with her, my mind spinning.

"I do?"

Marta glanced at me and kept walking.

"She was so young, so ashamed, so ambivalent about all that lay ahead. Finally, after much prayer, I felt the Lord leading us to raise the baby as our own. I suggested adoption."

"You and Freddy tried to adopt her baby? His baby?"

"Well, actually, that's what we told people, but in truth only *I* adopted him. Freddy didn't need to, because he was already the child's father."

I stopped walking, my mouth flying open. She was talking about Zed! The baby Marta's husband had conceived out of wedlock with an Amish woman was Zed. The boy Marta loved and cared for and had raised as her son—despite the fact that he was living proof of her husband's infidelity—was Zed.

"That's the only reason Freddy stuck around at

first and tried to make a go of our marriage, because he had a new son," Marta told me now when she saw I had been rendered speechless. "But it was no use. By the time Zed could crawl, Freddy had walked out on all three of us, gone for good."

Still stunned, I ran my hands through my hair, gathered it into my fist, and let it fall.

"What happened to the woman?"

"Crazy as it sounds, she and I became friends."

"Friends? Marta, how on earth—"

"It started during the pregnancy. Despite all that had happened between her and my husband, once she agreed to the adoption, I knew I wanted to be there when my baby was being born. I only intended to observe, but when I learned she was actually willing to let me be the midwife, of course I agreed."

"Unbelievable," I said, shaking my head, knowing that such an arrangement was surely due to their faith, to the concept of not just forgiving but also forgetting. Just as I had with James earlier, suddenly I was seeing Marta with new eyes.

"Throughout the entire pregnancy and birth, I guess you could say that she and I bonded, as odd as that sounds. Of course, once we brought Zed home, nothing mattered at all except that he was ours. Mine." Her eyes grew fierce. "He *is* mine, you know, as surely as if he had come from my own womb."

I knew. Remembering Mama, remembering

Dad. I knew. Smiling, I thought of James's words earlier, of how God could redeem a bad situation and bring from it, in the end, so much good.

"You stayed in touch with his birth mother?"

"Yes. She eventually married a wonderful Amish man, and when they were expecting their first child, she asked me to be her midwife again. I was happy to do it. In fact, I successfully delivered all of her babies. Until the last one, that is." Marta shuddered.

"What happened?"

She gave me a look, as if to say, as she had before, that I already knew. "What happened is that she was in labor with her fifth child when something went wrong. Both she and the baby died."

"Come again?" I asked, wondering if I had misunderstood.

Holding out her hands, palms upward, Marta simply looked at me, willing me to get it. Then it came to me. The person she was talking about, the one who had given birth to Zed so long ago, had been *Lydia,* the very patient Marta had lost in childbirth all these years later.

The very patient Marta been accused of killing.

I said Lydia's name aloud. Glancing around us, Marta moved closer, gripped my arm above the elbow, and lowered her voice to a whisper.

"Yes. It was Lydia. Now that you know, you can understand the astonishing position I have found myself in over these past few months. Freddy's

469

affair with her happened years ago. Water under the bridge. Forgiven. Forgotten. Truly, I had nothing but love for Lydia, nothing but gratitude for her having given me my son."

I nodded, believing her, knowing it was true.

"But once I was implicated in her death, everything changed. *I* knew my hands were clean, that the past was past, but try convincing a jury of that in a court of law. A secular jury who doesn't understand God's ways. Can you imagine? With this knowledge, a clever attorney could have twisted things around completely, maybe even raised the charges from manslaughter to first-degree murder. How hard would it have been, really, to convince a jury that I had wanted Lydia to die? If they learned of the connection between us, they would have seen it as payback for the affair she'd once had with my husband. Since the moment I first learned the DA was going to pursue this case, I have lived in terror of someone involved finding out about this other connection between us."

Marta released her hold on my arm but continued to lean close as she spoke.

"For a while, it looked like I was home free, that this other matter wasn't going to come up and complicate things after all. But then *you* showed up and started asking questions. Like a big house of cards, I knew then they were going to fall. Since my night in jail, I've even been trying to prepare myself for the electric chair."

I was so stunned it was hard to speak. "Did your lawyer say that could happen?"

Marta shook her head. "Connie doesn't know about any of this. Until now, I haven't breathed a word to a soul, except you. After the way I've treated you—and all you did for me in spite of it—I suppose I owe you that much."

I took a big step backward, resisting the urge to exclaim out loud. So that's what all of this had been about for her? That's why she had been so cruel to me? Almost as if an earthquake were reshuffling the ground under my feet, I found myself realigning with this new knowledge. It changed everything.

"I'm sure I don't have to tell you how important it is that you keep my secret," Marta added, her face solemn. "The case has been dismissed, but the DA could always reopen it if he thought he had new evidence against me."

My mind raced, uncomfortable with the weight of what I had learned. "What about Lydia's family? How could they not know about her affair with Freddy, about Zed?"

"Oh, some of them do, of course. Lydia's mother. Her grandmother. Even Will. But it would never have dawned on any of them to bring that up now. Like me, they see that as far in the past and in no way relevant to what's been going on in the present."

Her words made sense. To the Amish, it

always came down to repenting, which Lydia had obviously done. Once forgiven was indeed once forgotten. Marta had thought her big secret was safe until the moment I appeared on her doorstep and demanded to know the truth and started to ask questions about the entire family. No wonder she had been so mean to me. She'd been fighting for her very life.

Putting a hand to my mouth, I shook my head slowly, from side to side. "I am so sorry Marta. If only I had known . . ."

She held up a hand to stop me.

"Don't say you're sorry, Lexie, I'm the one who needs to apologize. And I do. I apologize for the way I've treated you this whole time. You weren't wrong in coming here, not at all. It's just that, for me, it was bad timing. Really bad timing."

I admitted to her that timing never had been my strong suit, and we shared a smile. Marta slid her hands into her pockets, her shoulders visibly relaxed. She gestured toward the house with a tilt of her head, and we both began walking again.

"For what it's worth," she said as we went, "I'm actually glad about what happened this afternoon over at *Mammi*'s, especially because Zed was there to hear it. If he ever wants to know the truth about his parentage, he'll have an easier time of it because of you. Because of what he saw today. I thank you for that."

I nodded, soothed by Marta's apology and

her thanks, both from the woman I had thought incapable of either. How very wrong I had been.

We walked together in companionable silence, my aunt and I, but as we reached the driveway to the cottage, I hesitated, still concerned about the secret she had confided in me.

"If we learned anything today," I said carefully, "it's how destructive secrets can be."

Marta nodded, her eyes narrowing as she waited to see where I was going.

"Even though your case has been dismissed, Marta, I think you need to share this information with Connie so she can tell the DA. That may not be the safest or the smartest move, but it's definitely the right one."

She exhaled slowly, lowering her head. She looked so sad that I added, "I think there's a very good chance that he'll see the situation in its entirety and let the matter go. But if you don't bring this to his attention one way or another, you're always going to know that you hid a part of the truth, and it's going to eat away at you like a cancer."

Marta blinked, sending twin tears down her ruddy cheeks. As she wiped them away, she gave a sardonic laugh. "This from the woman who made Ella tell me about her drunken episode with Ezra. I guess I should have expected the same standards to apply."

"They're not my standards, Marta. They're God's."

Again she nodded, and I could tell from her expression that she would do as I was urging. Before either of us spoke, my cell phone began vibrating in my pocket.

"Think about it," I said. "We can talk later."

She nodded, gave me a quick hug, and told me to go ahead and take the call. I pulled out my phone to see Ada's name on the screen. Marta went on inside as I answered.

Her voice was raw and I asked how she was doing. "So-so," she said. "*Mamm*, *Daed*, and I have been talking all afternoon. That's been good." She asked if I could come over the next morning. It was Sunday, but it was their week off from services. They were all asking for me to visit.

I said James and I would stop by.

Then she said, "*Mamm* wants to talk with you."

I swallowed hard, not at all sure that *I* wanted to talk to *her*. But then Klara was on the phone and I had no choice. "Lexie," she said. Her voice was soft and timid, not the way she spoke in person at all. "I wanted to say that I am sorry for how things were handled, for my part in all of it."

I could find neither voice nor words to reply. As I stood there with my mouth hanging open, she spoke again.

"I understand if this sounds like too little, too late. I will pray for your forgiveness, and perhaps in time God will grant that prayer and soften your heart."

Cheeks flushing with sudden humility, I swallowed hard and managed a small "thank you" in reply.

"I also wanted you to know I have Giselle's address. She lives in Switzerland. I'll give it to you tomorrow."

Before I could respond, Ada was back on the phone, saying goodbye and that she would see me the next day. After I hung up, I went over Klara's words in my brain. Though it would probably take some time, I would make an effort to forgive her. She was my aunt, after all, and that was the Amish way.

James rested on the sofa, and Zed was on the computer when I walked into the cottage. Marta stood behind her son. She looked alarmed as she turned toward me. "Zed has an email from Switzerland."

"Did the man talk to Giselle?" I asked, hurrying to her side with James following me from the living room.

"No. Well, probably." She pointed to the screen. The email was written in English. "Read it," she said, stepping back. James stood beside me.

Dear Zed,
Thank you for inquiring after me. It is good to have word of home and information

about my daughters. I am pleased they have met again after all these years. I am quite happy living in Switzerland and have found a measure of rest and peace. I think of my mother and sisters, and my daughters, often. I will think of my niece and nephew too, now that I know they exist.

I have no plans to travel to the United States. However if my daughters would like to contact me, or even come and see me, they are welcome to do so.

Sincerely,
Aunt Giselle

THIRTY-TWO

I took three copies of the email the next day. One for my aunt, one for my sister, and one for my grandmother. I also took the carved box, the century-plus letter, and the locks of hair. The photo of Dad and my baby quilt were safely packed inside my suitcase. James drove his rental—I'd already returned the borrowed Datsun—and I directed him to Klara's.

From the road, I could see buggies parked in

front of the house as James and I turned down the lane. There were extra horses in the field, eight or nine at least, and streamers were strung across the railing of the balcony of the house.

"It looks like a party," he said. I couldn't imagine.

He parked behind a buggy and I climbed from the car, my Coach bag over my shoulder and the other things in my hands. Marta's car was parked over to the side.

I spotted Will and his girls first in the side yard. He and Christy were batting a volleyball back and forth over a net, and the twins were twirling around his legs. Rachael came around the corner with a bratwurst in her hand.

"Lexie!" she called out and then ran toward me.

Will looked up and smiled. "Everyone is in the backyard."

"Everyone?" I asked, astonished.

James had to introduce himself to Will and the girls as I was in a daze. I floated around the corner of the house. Alice was there, sitting beside *Mammi*. Someone had moved my grandmother's recliner outside. Hannah was holding Elizabeth Alice. Esther was holding Caroline and sitting beside Marta, and Zed was playing with Simon. Ella and Ezra stood at the edge of the yard, laughing, next to a long table covered with food. John and Sally, who was well into her seventh month, sat together, and Ruth was off to the side, pretending to listen to her sister but keeping an eye on Ezra all the while.

Alexander stood beside the barbecue grill as smoke swirled out from under the lid. Beyond him was Klara, her arms wide.

"Wilkom," she said as she hugged me.

After only a moment's hesitation, I found myself hugging her in return. I had expected the process of forgiveness to take a while, but already my resentment seemed to be floating off to the sky and dissipating away, just like the nearby smoke. Surely, God was doing a mighty work in me.

For the next several hours, James and I both immersed ourselves into the gathering—devouring the food, enjoying the people, soaking in the warm afternoon sun. I relished the relationships we were forging here, and already I wondered when we might come back for a visit. At one point, I looked out across the yard at the babies and children and adults young and old, and my heart was so full I thought it might burst. Heaven had to be something like this, I thought, but with Mama and Dad and the folks from back home and even Giselle as well. Wrapping my arms around myself, I simply took it in, uttering a silent prayer of thanks to God, who had finally led me here, had finally led me home.

Thinking of home, I made a point of texting Sophie and apologizing for the angry words I had sent her the day before. Of course, I still wished she had told me all that she had known about my past, but what's done was done. In keeping silent, she had simply been respecting my father's wishes, not willfully attempting to deceive me.

After a few moments came her reply: *Thank you for this grace. Now come HOME, Lexie. We miss you!* Smiling, I wrote back *Will do, miss you too,* and put away my phone.

As the shadows began to grow long on the lawn, I managed to steal a quiet moment with Ada so that we could talk. We sat in the car, which was parked in the driveway, a rousing game of volleyball taking place off to one side of the yard. At the cottage earlier, I had carefully halved the locks of hair, turning the two into four. Though I would keep a set for myself, I gave Ada an envelope containing the other set now, along with copies of Giselle's email and of the old letter. Ada was fascinated by the wooden box, and as she ran her delicate hands over the surface, she asked me if I planned to go to Switzerland.

I shook my head. "Maybe someday. For now, I just plan to go home." James and I had tickets for the evening flight from Harrisburg to Portland, and our packed bags were already in the car. I was going back to my job, my house, my orchard. I'd called the Realtor the night before and told her I wasn't interested in selling after all.

Ada nodded, handed me back the box, and glanced at her copy of the email from Giselle, the one she had insisted I read to her last night over the phone several times.

"You seem so settled," she told me, folding up the letter and sliding it into her pocket along with the envelope that held the locks of hair. As her eyes met mine, I realized that for her the opposite was true. She seemed less settled than she had since we'd met.

"I found closure here," I told her, sounding a lot like James. "The end of a long journey to the truth."

Again she nodded, and I realized that although my journey may have ended, hers had in a sense just begun. After all, I'd spent a lifetime wanting answers, but she hadn't even known there were any questions until just a few days ago. She and her parents seemed well on their way to making peace and dealing with the past, which was important. But now I recognized something in Ada's expression that I had seen in my own mirror countless times before, a hunger for understanding, a need to connect with her true past.

"You want to go to Switzerland." I meant it to be a question but it came out more like a statement.

"Ya," she answered dreamily, a faraway look in her eyes. Then, as if remembering herself, she blushed prettily and added, "But of course I . . . It's not possible."

Glancing around at her large, extended family, I tried to find the right words to say. Though I deeply respected Ada's Amish heritage, I wanted to remind her that she had a choice, that she was free

480

in this life to do whatever she wanted, regardless of how far away it might take her.

Unable to come up with the words after all, instead I reached into the backseat and pulled out the Coach bag, which I had emptied that morning. "For you," I said, handing it to her.

Stunned, she shook her head, again looking around at her Amish surroundings. "I'm sorry, I cannot accept it. It wouldn't be fitting."

I understood her resistance, knowing that the purse was far too "fancy" for one who lived Plain.

"Maybe not around here. But I have to tell you, Ada, it makes a great travel bag. Might be the perfect accessory for a trip to Europe."

The blush in her cheeks spread to cover her whole face. "It is very beautiful." She reached out a finger and traced it along the handle. "But what about you? You have travels too, *ya*?"

I smiled.

"My big adventure is over for now," I told my sister, again holding it up for her to take. "But something tells me yours has just begun."

Later, back outside, I couldn't help but linger at *Mammi*'s chair, even though I knew our time was nearly up and James and I needed to head to the airport. I had no doubt I would see most of these people again, but *Mammi* was old and in poor health, and I couldn't help but be aware that this might be our final visit. That made our time together now bittersweet, our parting that much more difficult.

"You will write to me of your home out there in Oregon, yes?" she asked, taking both of my hands in hers as I knelt beside her. "I would love to hear from you now and then, to know you are doing well."

I nodded, biting my lip, afraid that if I tried to speak I would cry. She seemed to understand. With effort, she raised one fine, wrinkled hand and placed it against my cheek.

"That's a good girl," she said, and her words echoed in my heart, stirring wisps of memory from our long-ago last farewell.

We said our goodbyes and then it was time for the rest: David and Esther and Simon and Caroline. Alice and Nancy. Will and Christy and the twins, Mat and Mel. Jonas and Hannah and Rachael and Elizabeth Alice. Klara and Alexander and Ada— my sweet sister, Ada.

Then, at last, came Marta and Ella and Zed. Marta hugged me fiercely, and before we pulled apart she whispered in my ear, saying that she'd spoken to Connie, who had already talked with the DA, and the case was to remained closed.

"Thank you for making me tell the whole truth," she added as we pulled apart.

I simply smiled, looking from her to Klara, who had moved to stand beside Alexander and was discreetly holding his hand. A verse came to mind, one that applied to all of us: *Then you will know the truth and the truth will set you free.*

Ella and Zed insisted on walking us to our car. We bid a last farewell to the others gathered there in the backyard and then walked toward the front with the two teens just as the sun began to dip below the horizon.

"So if you guys get married, can I be a brides-maid?" Ella asked, linking her arm in mine as we walked.

I could feel my face blushing a hundred shades of red, but James simply grinned and said, "Absolutely, Ella, as long as you're willing to come to Oregon. I'm thinking maybe we'll have the ceremony in the orchard."

Both James and Ella looked at me, waiting for my assent. Nothing would thrill me more than to join hands in marriage with this man there in the heart of my father's beloved grove of hazelnut trees, in the midst of some of the Creator's most beautiful handiwork.

"Well, Lexie, what do you think?" Ella prodded me.

I looked from her to James.

"I think someone needs to ask a certain question before someone else is going to start discussing details," I said.

Zed chuckled and James laughed, but Ella merely pouted.

"I tell you what, Miss Ella," James said, noticing her scowl. "There is a certain question I'll be ask-ing someone very soon, so maybe before I do I could text it to you and you could let me know if I've worded it romantically enough."

That drew a small smile from her lips.

"Okay, but remember, it has to be *very* romantic. Don't just throw it out there like it's nothing."

"Duh, Ella," Zed chimed in, "why do you think he's not down on one knee right now? Get a clue. It has to be just right."

Now it was my turn to laugh, wondering how James and I were suddenly being bulldozed by mere munchkins.

Our time for chatting was done, and at the car we said our final goodbyes to the kids. I would miss Ella, of course, but when I hugged Zed and thanked him for all of his help, I could feel an actual, physical pang deep in my heart. He was my nephew, but I couldn't tell him. Chances were, he might never find out.

It wasn't until I was in the car and James had started it up that I realized it didn't really matter whether Zed ever learned of our special bond or not. To him, family was family, regardless of DNA. That was a truth I had always known, of course, but it didn't hurt to be reminded of it now.

"Ready to go?" James asked.

I turned and looked at him, at his handsome face, his loving eyes, his furrowed brow.

"What's wrong?"

He shrugged. "I just want to make sure you're good. It's been quite an eventful trip."

Placing one hand on his arm, I assured him I was better than I'd been in a long time, and I was leaving here in peace this time, not in pain, and that made all the difference.

Relaxing somewhat, he backed the car around and headed toward the main road. As we went down the lane I turned and looked back over the grassy, gently sloping lawn one last time. Hungrily, I took in the image, imprinting it on my mind.

As we pulled away, I thought about pulling out my camera and snapping one final picture but decided against it. I didn't need a camera to remember this home, these families, this feeling of being so absolutely surrounded in love. I didn't need to flip through an album to remember the eight babies I'd delivered in Lancaster County either, nor their mothers and fathers, brothers and sisters. I didn't need photos to recall the peacefulness of these rolling hills, the warmth and vitality of the Amish homes, the complex and fascinating people who shared my blood and my heart. All were pictures I would never, ever forget. Put together, they told my story.

The story I had found at last.

DISCUSSION QUESTIONS

1. Lexie is surprised to find that her father withheld parts of her adoption story. What was her father's motive? Do you think he was right or wrong in doing so?

2. What role does Sophie play in Lexie's life? Does Sophie reveal too little information about the past to Lexie? Or too much?

3. According to the Benchmark Adoption Survey (1997), sixty percent of Americans have a personal experience with adoption, meaning that they, a family member, or a close friend was adopted, adopted a child, or relinquished a child for adoption. Many other Americans have an indirect connection. Do you have a connection with adoption? If so, what is it? Has this story changed the way you view adoption?

4. Lexie has a long-standing fantasy about her birth family. How did her fantasy help her through the years of not knowing the truth about her past? Have you ever held onto a childhood fantasy or known someone who has? What were the benefits? What was the harm?

5. How does Lexie's Mennonite community in Oregon compare to the Amish community she encounters in Pennsylvania? What does she find attractive about the Amish? What do you find attractive about the Amish?

6. Who is Marta trying to protect by not being forthright with Lexie? Why does Marta think it's better to leave the past alone? What does Marta have to lose if the truth is discovered?

7. The Amish practice of "letting be" is at odds with the individualism central to most modern cultures. When do you think Christians should "let things be" and when do you think they should be more proactive?

8. James tells Lexie there is no shame for her in her story. Is there an area in your life that you have experienced false shame? How did you overcome it?

9. Lexie finds comfort in Psalm 139:16. Is there a particular verse that has brought you comfort? What is it and why?

10. Lexie is intrigued with both the word "kinship" and its concept. Have you found kinship in any unexpected places? What impact has it had on your life?

ABOUT THE AUTHORS

The Amish Midwife is Mindy Starns Clark's fifteenth book with Harvest House Publishers. Previous novels include the bestselling *Whispers of the Bayou*, *Shadows of Lancaster County*, *Under the Cajun Moon*, and *Secrets of Harmony Grove*, as well as the well-loved Million Dollar Mysteries.

Mindy lives with her husband, John, and two adult daughters near Valley Forge, Pennsylvania.

ෆ ෨

Leslie Gould, a former magazine editor, is the author of numerous novels, including *Beyond the Blue* and *Garden of Dreams*. *The Amish Midwife* is her first book with Harvest House.

Leslie received her master of fine arts degree from Portland State University and lives in Oregon with her husband, Peter, and their four children.

ෆ ෨

For a detailed "Family Tree Companion Guide to *The Amish Midwife*," visit Mindy's and Leslie's websites at www.mindystarnsclark.com and www.lesliegould.com.